RAT QUEENS™

VOLUME FIVE:
THE COLOSSAL MAGIC NOTHING

Shadowline®

image

FIRST PRINTING: AUGUST 2018

ISBN: 978-1-5343-0677-6

5

KURTIS J. WIEBE
story

OWEN GIENI
art, colors, covers (unless otherwise noted)

RYAN FERRIER
letters

TIM DANIEL
frame

SWEENEY BOO

JIM VALENTINO and OWEN GIENI

MINDY LEE

LEILA del DUCA

JOSEPH MICHAEL LINSNER

alternative covers

IMAGE COMICS, INC.
Robert Kirkman—Chief Operating Officer
Erik Larsen—Chief Financial Officer
Todd McFarlane—President
Marc Silvestri—Chief Executive Officer
Jim Valentino—Vice President

Eric Stephenson—Publisher/Chief Creative Officer
Corey Hart—Director of Sales
Jeff Boison—Director of Publishing Planning
& Book Trade Sales
Chris Ross—Director of Digital Sales
Jeff Stang—Director of Specialty Sales
Kat Salazar—Director of PR & Marketing
Drew Gill—Art Director
Heather Doornink—Production Director
Nicole Lapalme—Controller
IMAGECOMICS.COM

LAURA TAVISHATI
edits
MARC LOMBARDI
communications
JIM VALENTINO
publisher/book design

RAT QUEENS created by KURTIS J. WIEBE and ROC UPCHURCH

A
Shadowline®
PRODUCTION

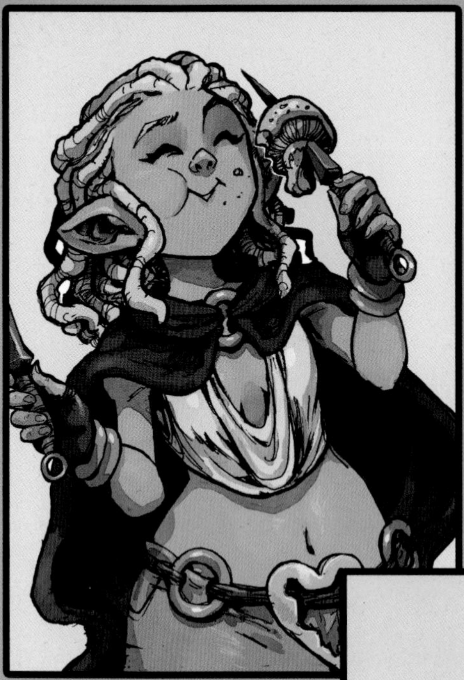
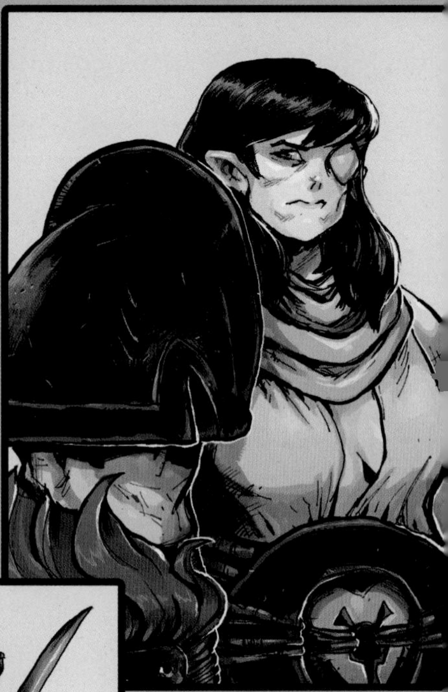
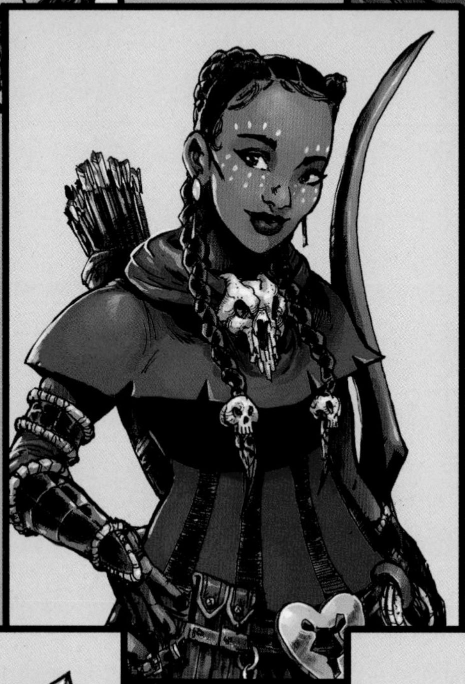
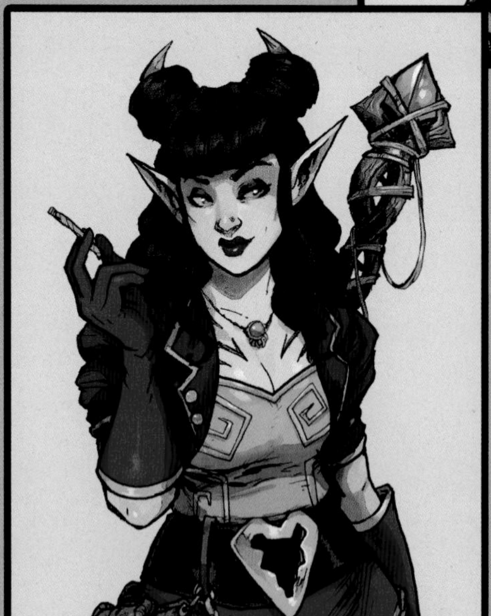
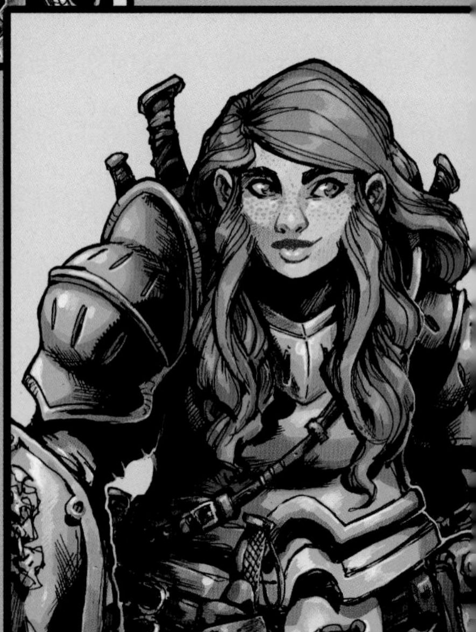

ORC DAVE SPECIAL cover by FIONA STAPLES

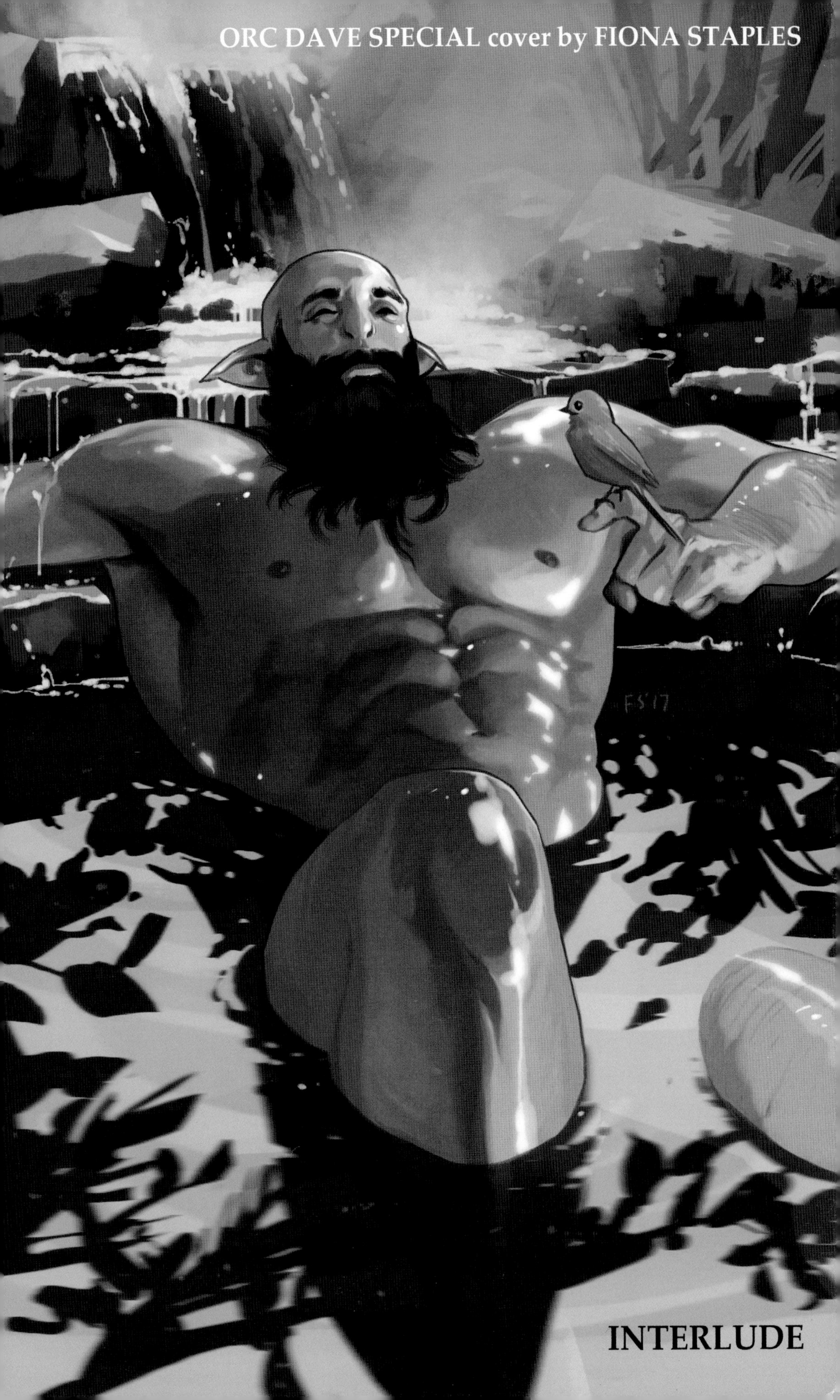
FS'17

INTERLUDE

ORC DAVE SPECIAL

KURTIS J. WIEBE
story

MAX DUNBAR
art

MICAH MYERS
lettering

TAMRA BONVILLAIN
colors

FIONA STAPLES
cover

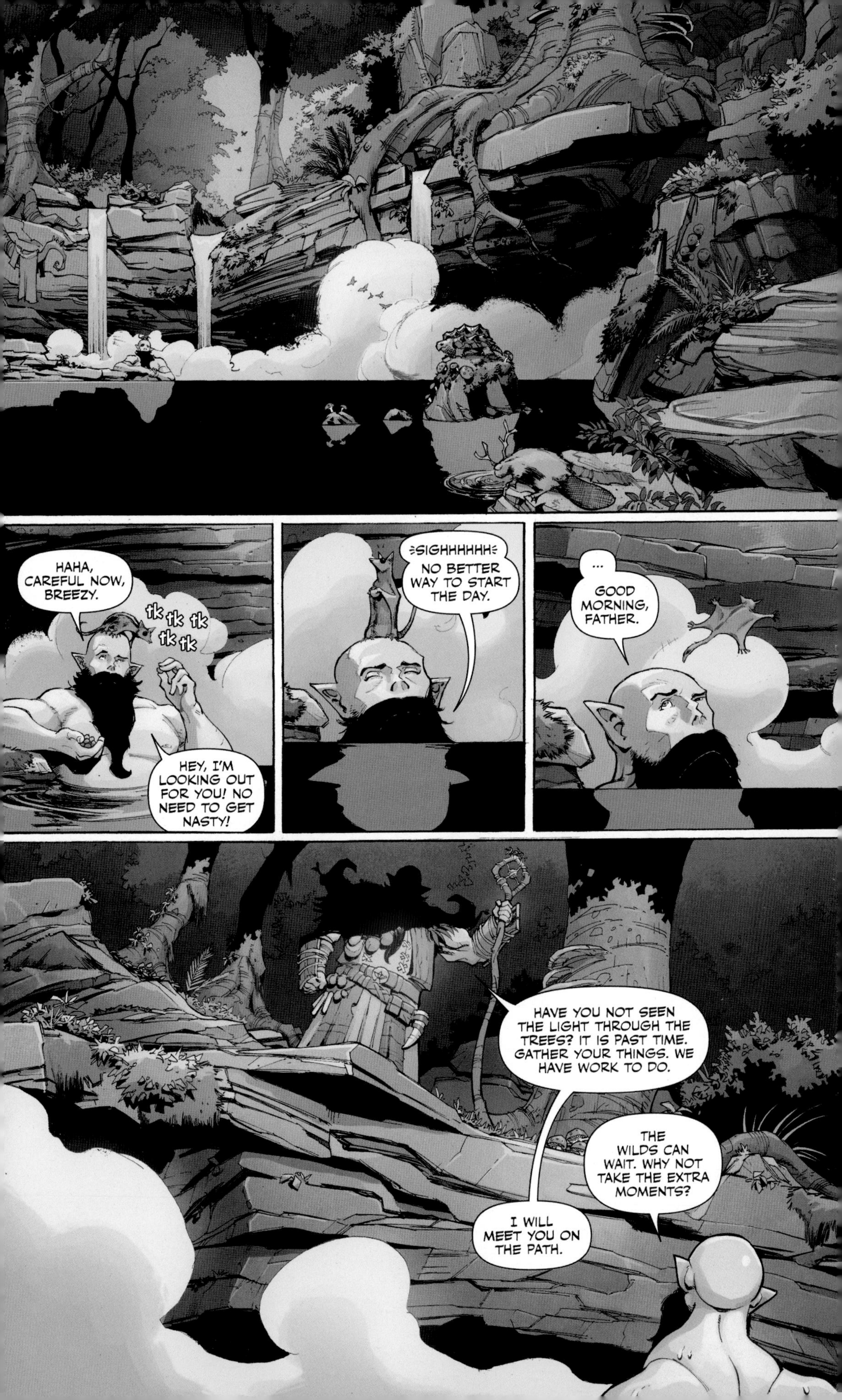
HAHA, CAREFUL NOW, BREEZY.
tk tk tk tk tk
HEY, I'M LOOKING OUT FOR YOU! NO NEED TO GET NASTY!
SIGHHHHHH
NO BETTER WAY TO START THE DAY.
...
GOOD MORNING, FATHER.
HAVE YOU NOT SEEN THE LIGHT THROUGH THE TREES? IT IS PAST TIME. GATHER YOUR THINGS. WE HAVE WORK TO DO.
THE WILDS CAN WAIT. WHY NOT TAKE THE EXTRA MOMENTS?
I WILL MEET YOU ON THE PATH.

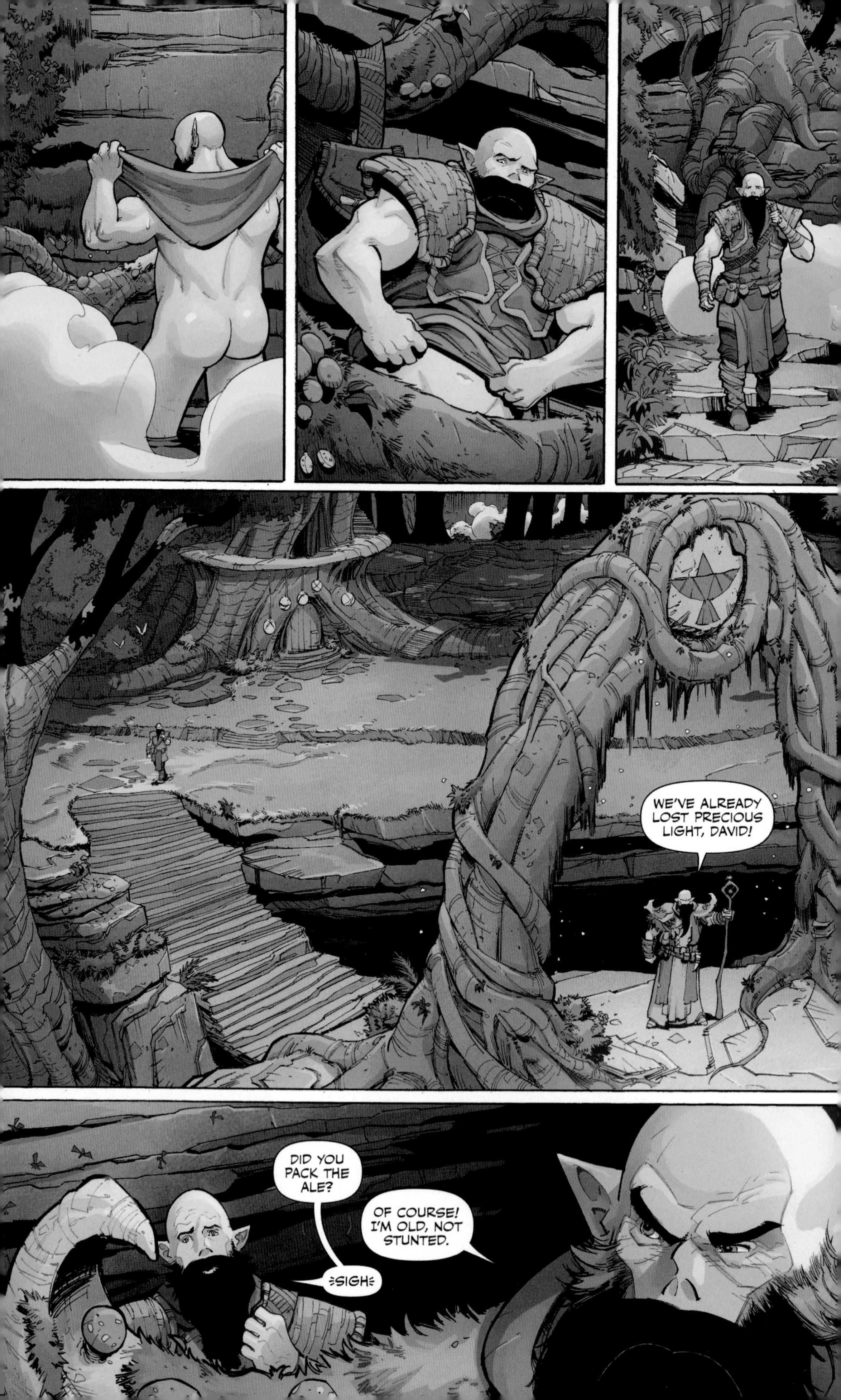
WE'VE ALREADY LOST PRECIOUS LIGHT, DAVID!
DID YOU PACK THE ALE?
OF COURSE! I'M OLD, NOT STUNTED.
SIGH

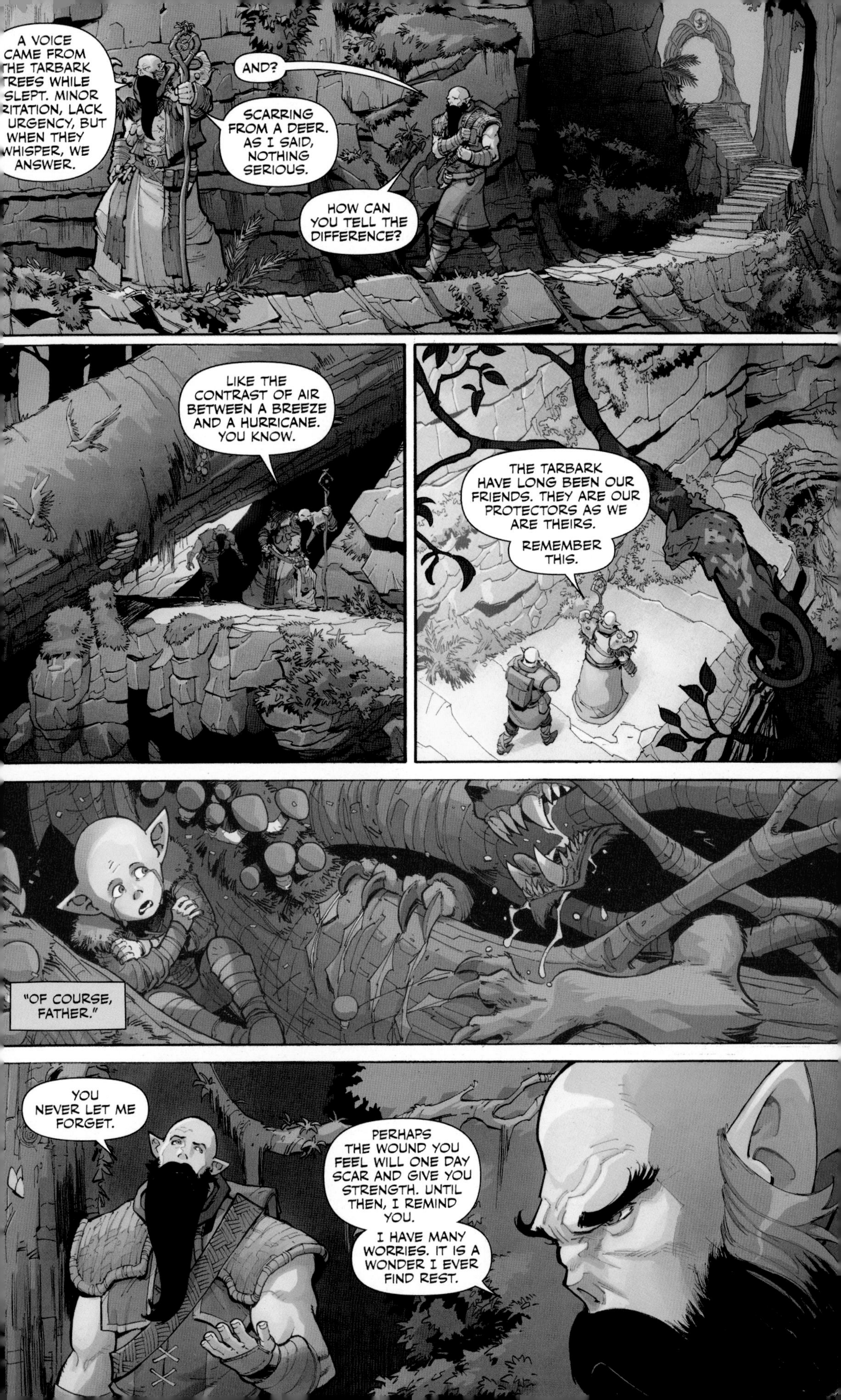
A VOICE CAME FROM THE TARBARK TREES WHILE SLEPT. MINOR RITATION, LACK URGENCY, BUT WHEN THEY WHISPER, WE ANSWER.
AND?
SCARRING FROM A DEER. AS I SAID, NOTHING SERIOUS.
HOW CAN YOU TELL THE DIFFERENCE?
LIKE THE CONTRAST OF AIR BETWEEN A BREEZE AND A HURRICANE. YOU KNOW.
THE TARBARK HAVE LONG BEEN OUR FRIENDS. THEY ARE OUR PROTECTORS AS WE ARE THEIRS.
REMEMBER THIS.
"OF COURSE, FATHER."
YOU NEVER LET ME FORGET.
PERHAPS THE WOUND YOU FEEL WILL ONE DAY SCAR AND GIVE YOU STRENGTH. UNTIL THEN, I REMIND YOU.
I HAVE MANY WORRIES. IT IS A WONDER I EVER FIND REST.

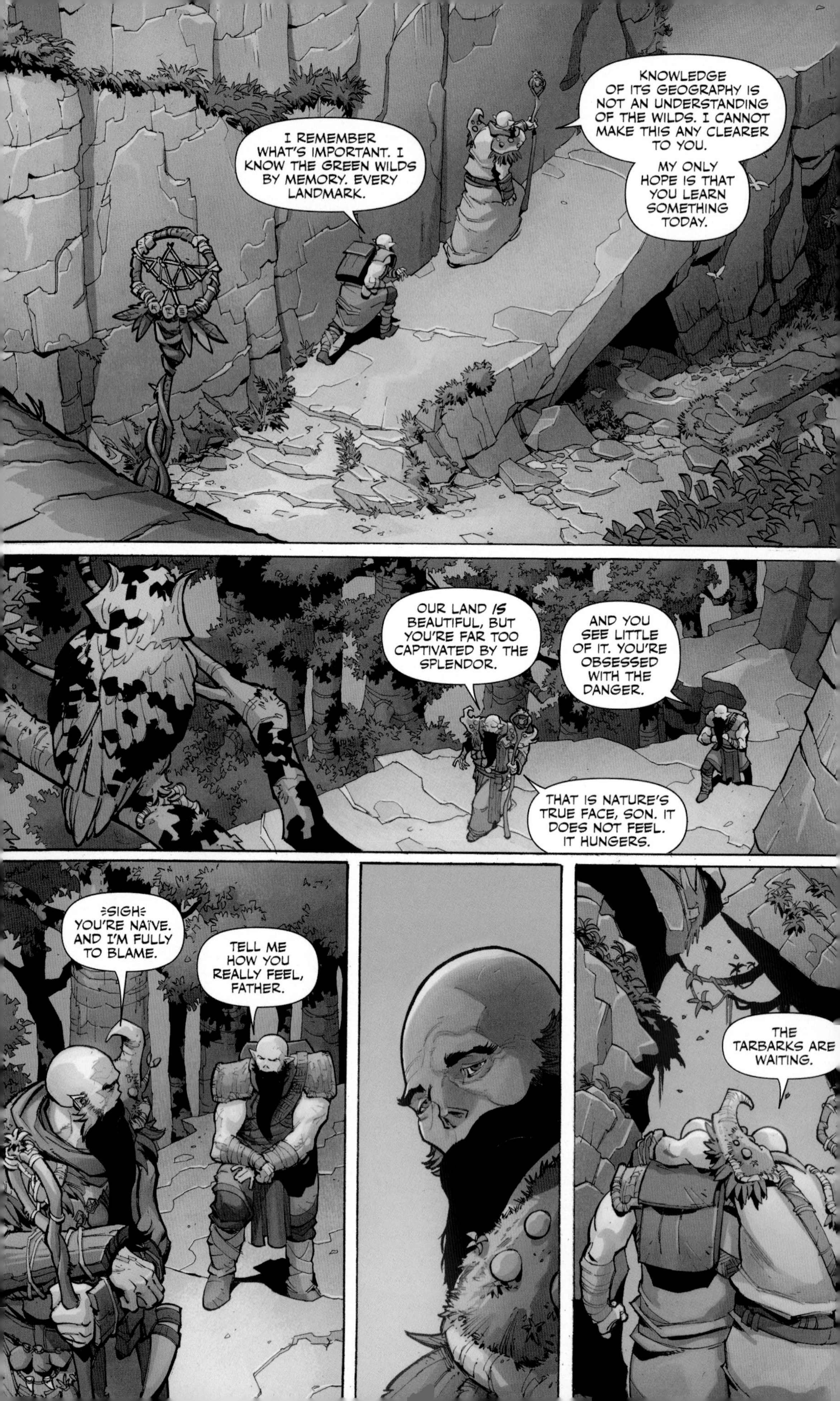
I REMEMBER WHAT'S IMPORTANT. I KNOW THE GREEN WILDS BY MEMORY. EVERY LANDMARK.
KNOWLEDGE OF ITS GEOGRAPHY IS NOT AN UNDERSTANDING OF THE WILDS. I CANNOT MAKE THIS ANY CLEARER TO YOU.
MY ONLY HOPE IS THAT YOU LEARN SOMETHING TODAY.
OUR LAND *IS* BEAUTIFUL, BUT YOU'RE FAR TOO CAPTIVATED BY THE SPLENDOR.
AND YOU SEE LITTLE OF IT. YOU'RE OBSESSED WITH THE DANGER.
THAT IS NATURE'S TRUE FACE, SON. IT DOES NOT FEEL. IT HUNGERS.
SIGH YOU'RE NAÏVE. AND I'M FULLY TO BLAME.
TELL ME HOW YOU REALLY FEEL, FATHER.
THE TARBARKS ARE WAITING.

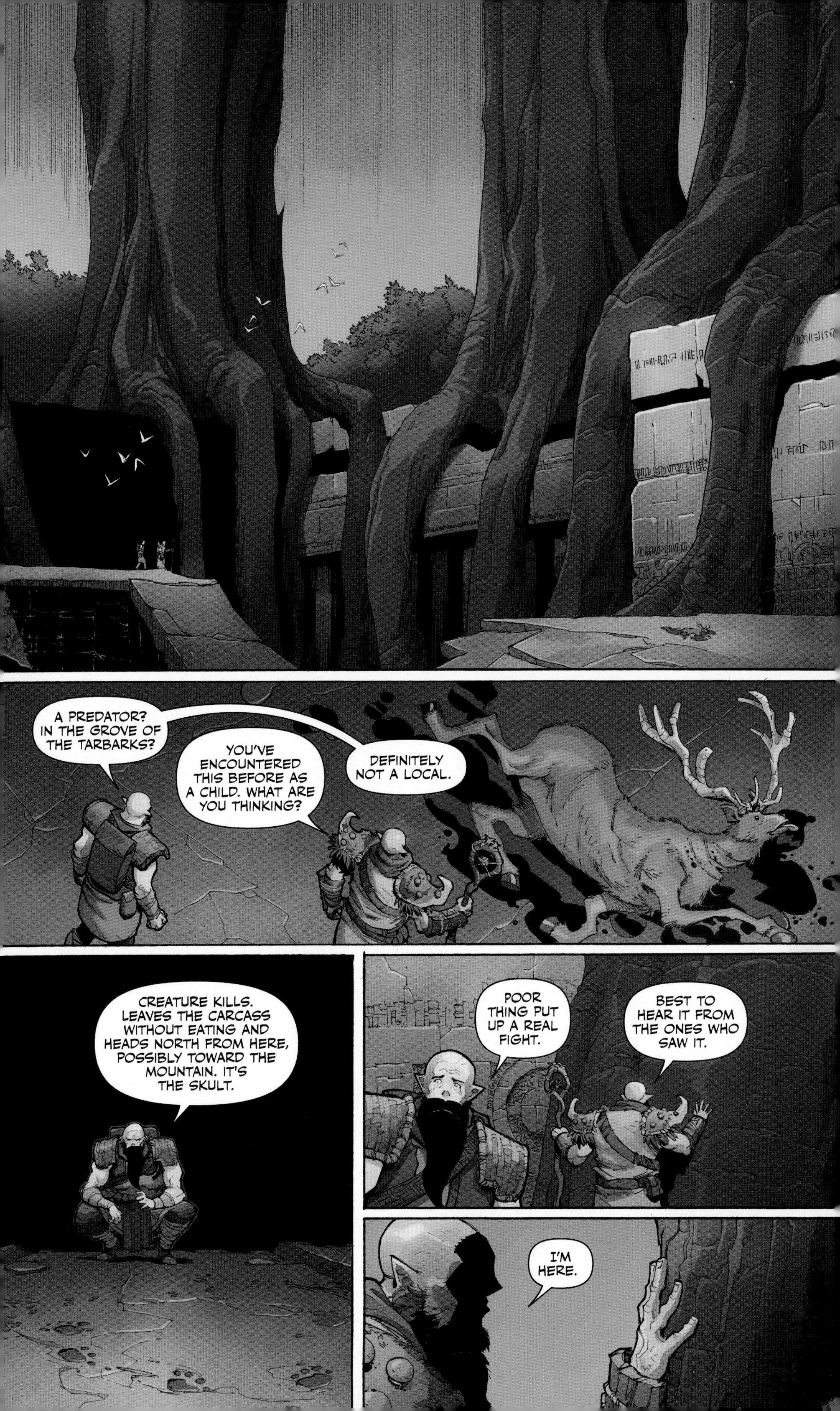
A PREDATOR? IN THE GROVE OF THE TARBARKS?
YOU'VE ENCOUNTERED THIS BEFORE AS A CHILD. WHAT ARE YOU THINKING?
DEFINITELY NOT A LOCAL.
CREATURE KILLS. LEAVES THE CARCASS WITHOUT EATING AND HEADS NORTH FROM HERE, POSSIBLY TOWARD THE MOUNTAIN. IT'S THE SKULT.
POOR THING PUT UP A REAL FIGHT.
BEST TO HEAR IT FROM THE ONES WHO SAW IT.
I'M HERE.

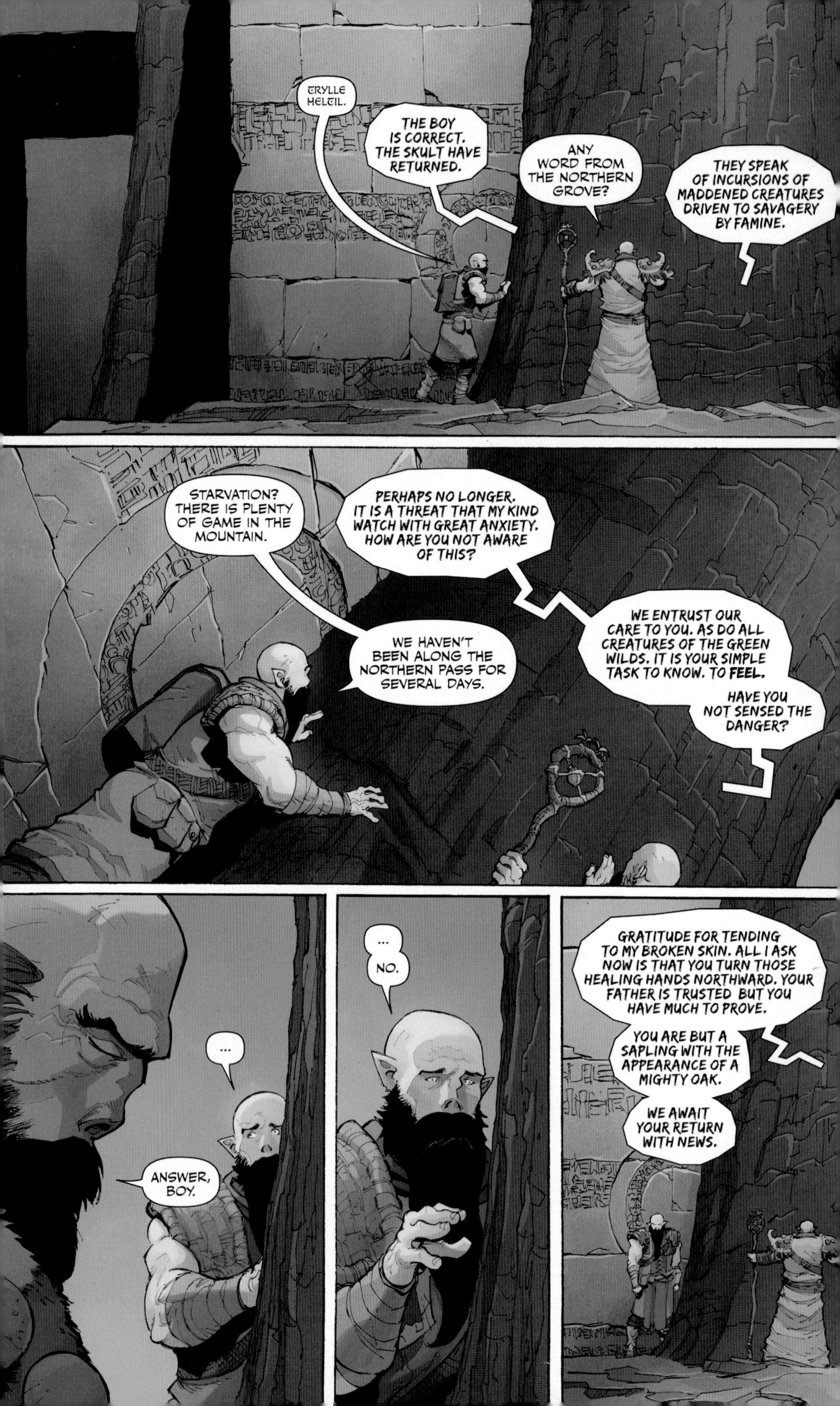
TRYLLE HELTIL.
THE BOY IS CORRECT. THE SKULT HAVE RETURNED.
ANY WORD FROM THE NORTHERN GROVE?
THEY SPEAK OF INCURSIONS OF MADDENED CREATURES DRIVEN TO SAVAGERY BY FAMINE.
STARVATION? THERE IS PLENTY OF GAME IN THE MOUNTAIN.
PERHAPS NO LONGER. IT IS A THREAT THAT MY KIND WATCH WITH GREAT ANXIETY. HOW ARE YOU NOT AWARE OF THIS?
WE HAVEN'T BEEN ALONG THE NORTHERN PASS FOR SEVERAL DAYS.
WE ENTRUST OUR CARE TO YOU. AS DO ALL CREATURES OF THE GREEN WILDS. IT IS YOUR SIMPLE TASK TO KNOW. TO FEEL.
HAVE YOU NOT SENSED THE DANGER?
...
ANSWER, BOY.
...
NO.
GRATITUDE FOR TENDING TO MY BROKEN SKIN. ALL I ASK NOW IS THAT YOU TURN THOSE HEALING HANDS NORTHWARD. YOUR FATHER IS TRUSTED BUT YOU HAVE MUCH TO PROVE.
YOU ARE BUT A SAPLING WITH THE APPEARANCE OF A MIGHTY OAK.
WE AWAIT YOUR RETURN WITH NEWS.

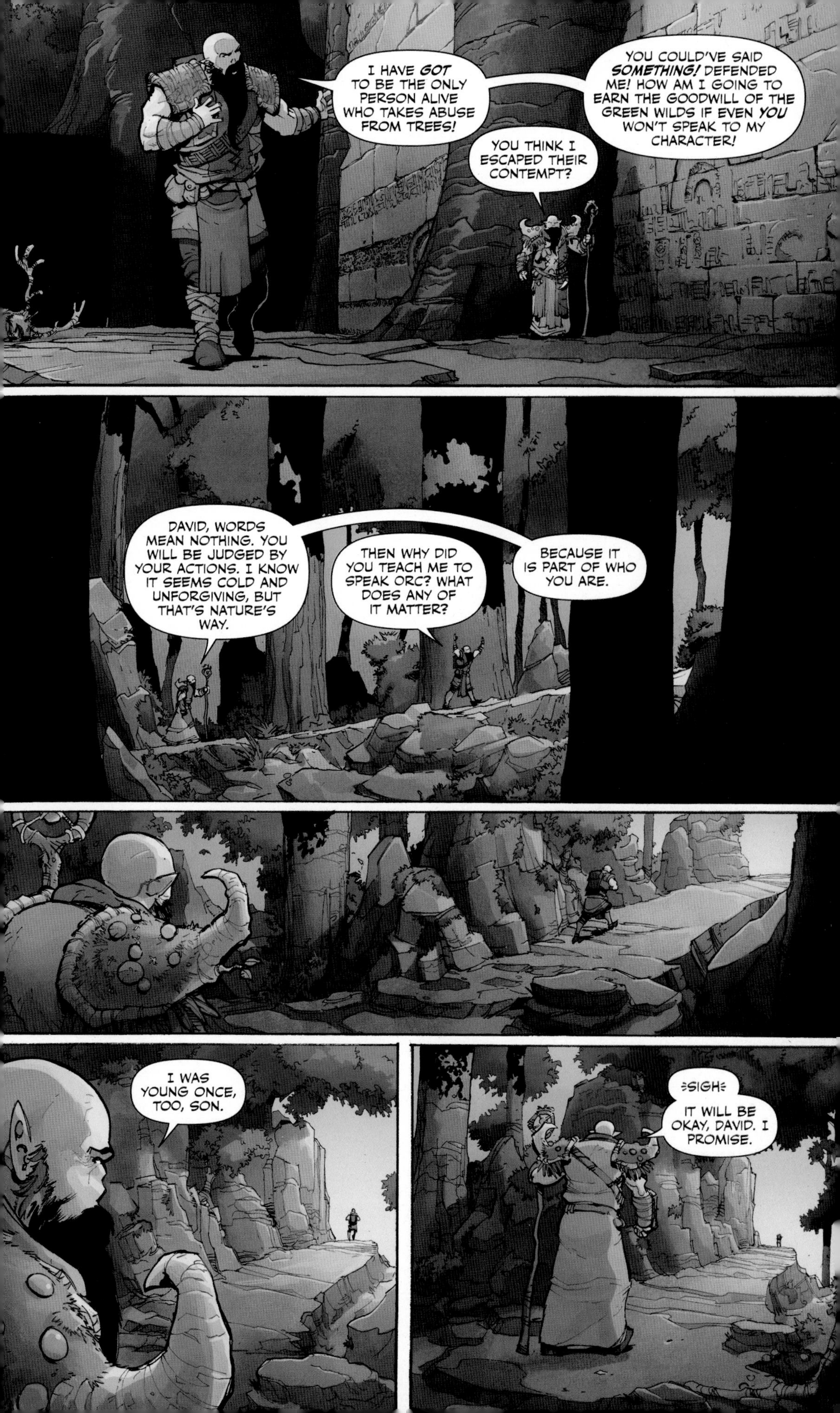
I HAVE *GOT* TO BE THE ONLY PERSON ALIVE WHO TAKES ABUSE FROM TREES!
YOU COULD'VE SAID *SOMETHING!* DEFENDED ME! HOW AM I GOING TO EARN THE GOODWILL OF THE GREEN WILDS IF EVEN *YOU* WON'T SPEAK TO MY CHARACTER!
YOU THINK I ESCAPED THEIR CONTEMPT?
DAVID, WORDS MEAN NOTHING. YOU WILL BE JUDGED BY YOUR ACTIONS. I KNOW IT SEEMS COLD AND UNFORGIVING, BUT THAT'S NATURE'S WAY.
THEN WHY DID YOU TEACH ME TO SPEAK ORC? WHAT DOES ANY OF IT MATTER?
BECAUSE IT IS PART OF WHO YOU ARE.
I WAS YOUNG ONCE, TOO, SON.
SIGH
IT WILL BE OKAY, DAVID. I PROMISE.

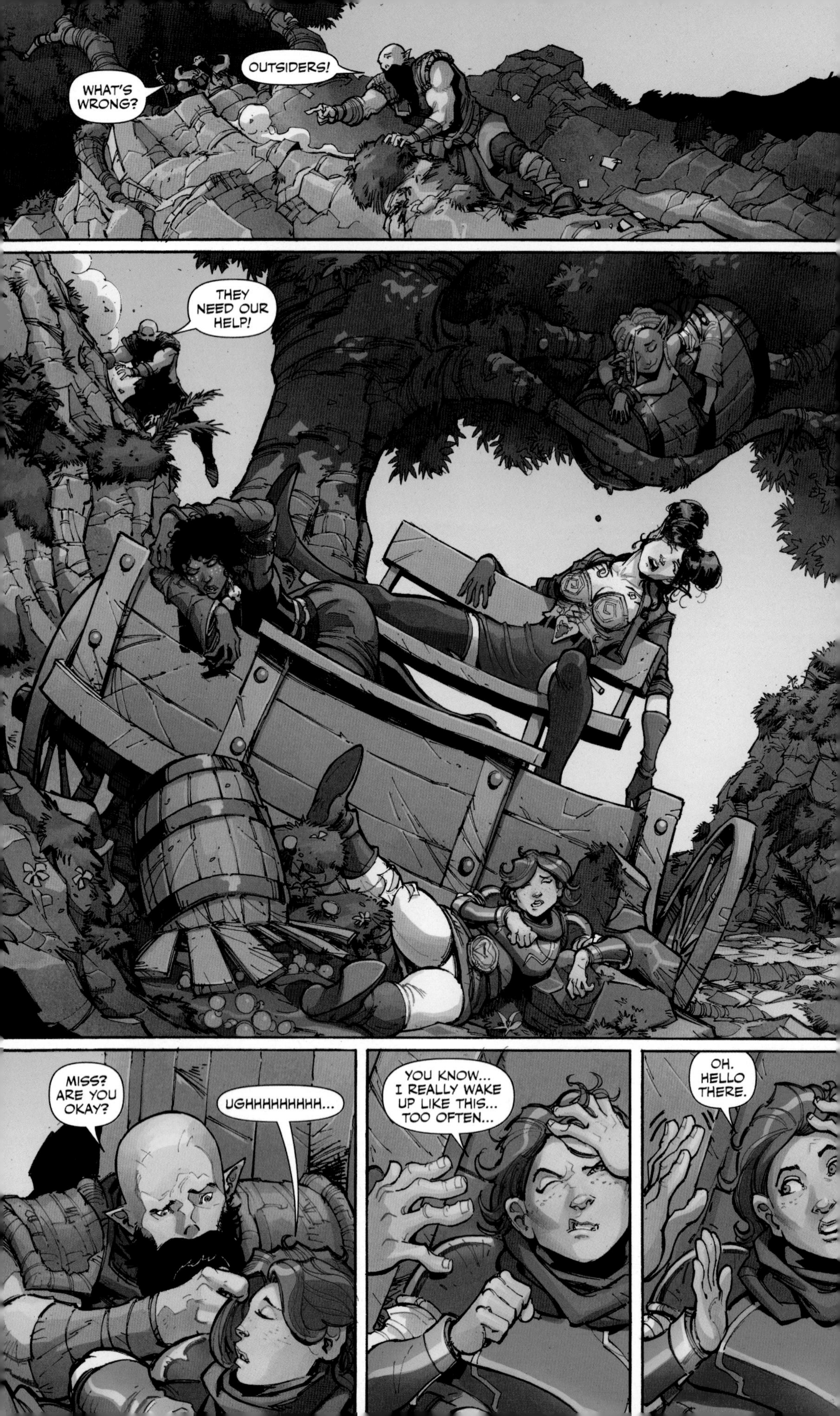
WHAT'S WRONG?
OUTSIDERS!
THEY NEED OUR HELP!
MISS? ARE YOU OKAY?
UGHHHHHHHHH...
YOU KNOW... I REALLY WAKE UP LIKE THIS... TOO OFTEN...
OH. HELLO THERE.

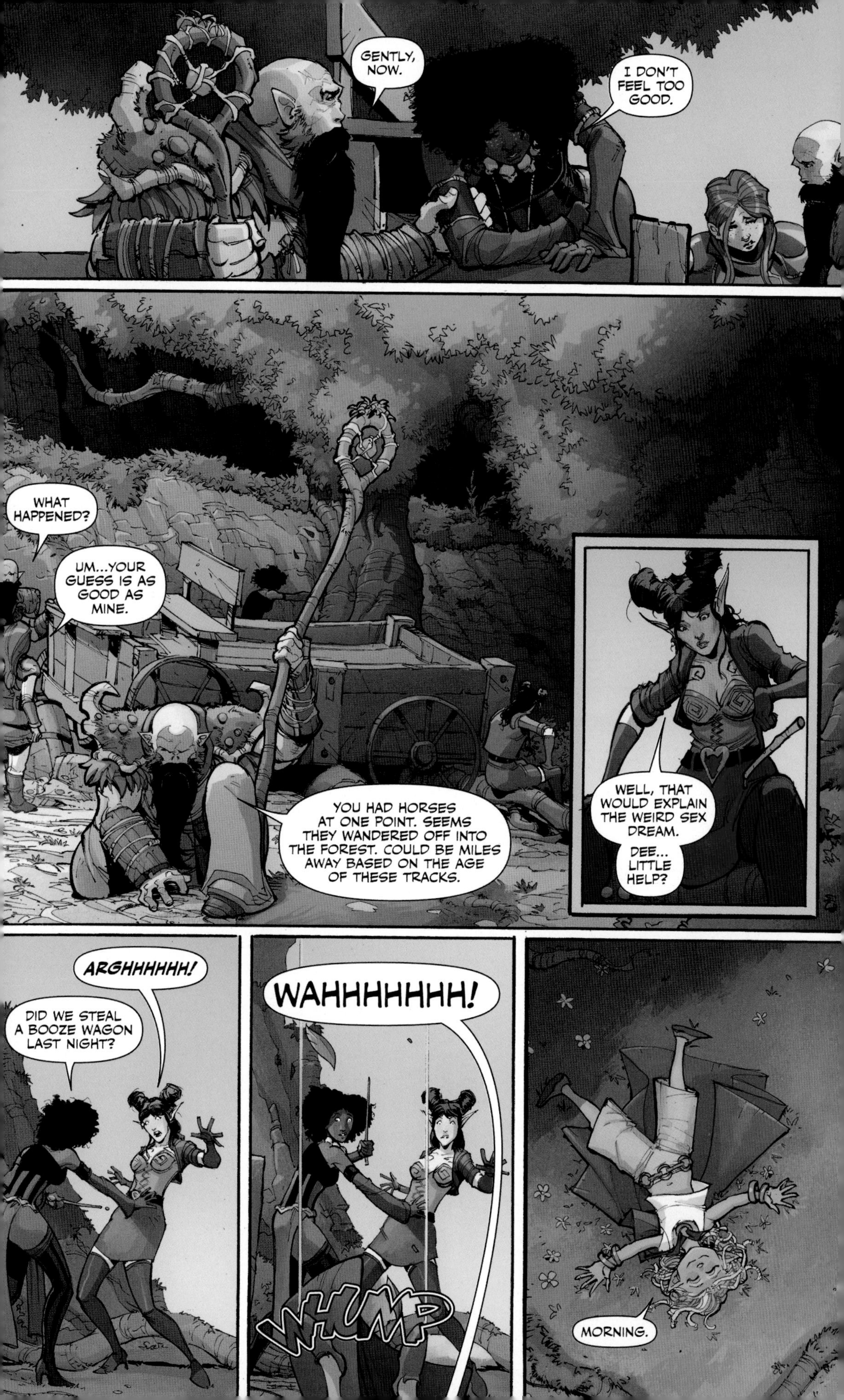
GENTLY, NOW.
I DON'T FEEL TOO GOOD.
WHAT HAPPENED?
UM...YOUR GUESS IS AS GOOD AS MINE.
YOU HAD HORSES AT ONE POINT. SEEMS THEY WANDERED OFF INTO THE FOREST. COULD BE MILES AWAY BASED ON THE AGE OF THESE TRACKS.
WELL, THAT WOULD EXPLAIN THE WEIRD SEX DREAM.
DEE... LITTLE HELP?
DID WE STEAL A BOOZE WAGON LAST NIGHT?
ARGHHHHHH!
WAHHHHHHH!
WHUMP
MORNING.

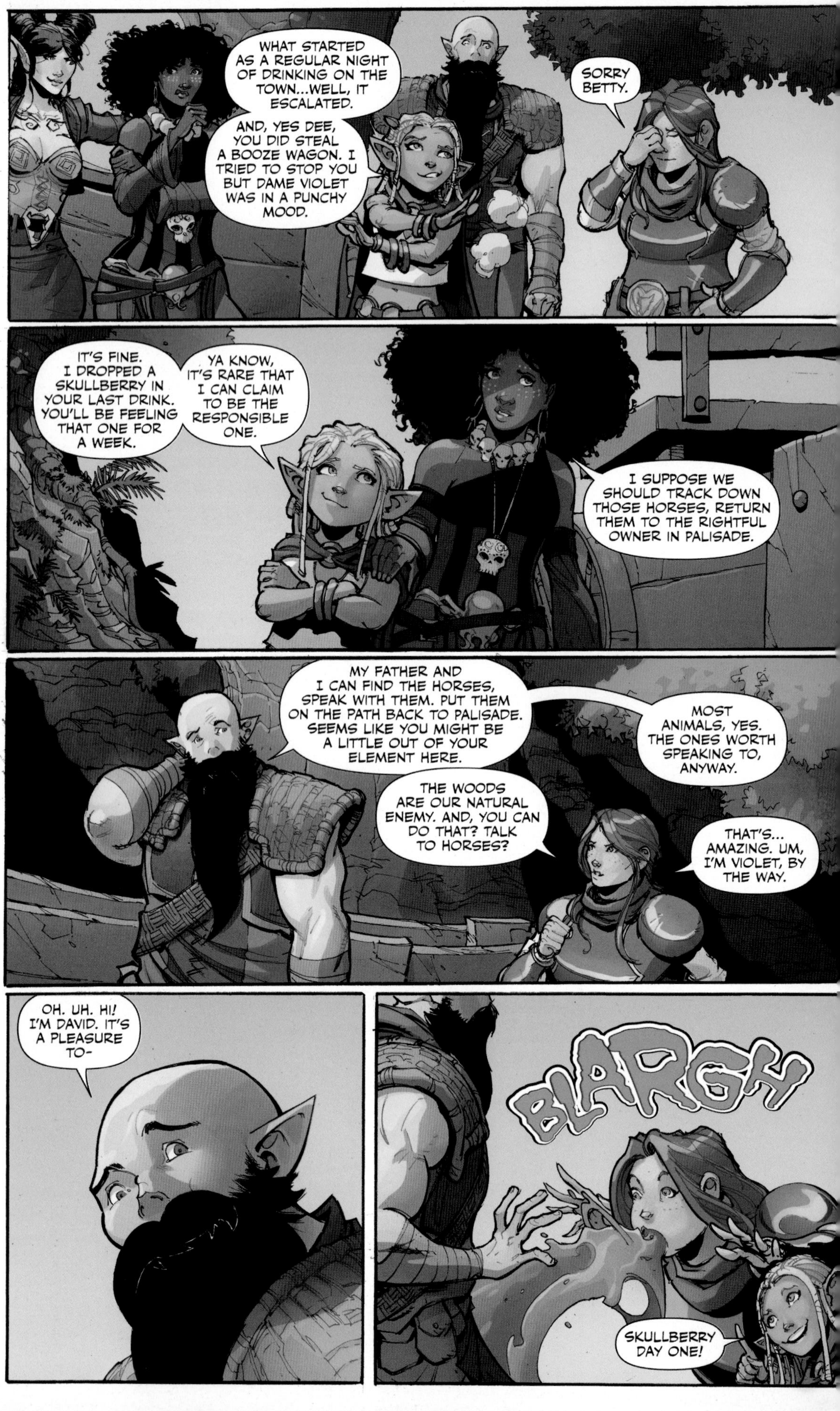

WHAT STARTED AS A REGULAR NIGHT OF DRINKING ON THE TOWN...WELL, IT ESCALATED.
AND, YES DEE, YOU DID STEAL A BOOZE WAGON. I TRIED TO STOP YOU BUT DAME VIOLET WAS IN A PUNCHY MOOD.
SORRY BETTY.
IT'S FINE. I DROPPED A SKULLBERRY IN YOUR LAST DRINK. YOU'LL BE FEELING THAT ONE FOR A WEEK.
YA KNOW, IT'S RARE THAT I CAN CLAIM TO BE THE RESPONSIBLE ONE.
I SUPPOSE WE SHOULD TRACK DOWN THOSE HORSES, RETURN THEM TO THE RIGHTFUL OWNER IN PALISADE.
MY FATHER AND I CAN FIND THE HORSES, SPEAK WITH THEM. PUT THEM ON THE PATH BACK TO PALISADE. SEEMS LIKE YOU MIGHT BE A LITTLE OUT OF YOUR ELEMENT HERE.
THE WOODS ARE OUR NATURAL ENEMY. AND, YOU CAN DO THAT? TALK TO HORSES?
MOST ANIMALS, YES. THE ONES WORTH SPEAKING TO, ANYWAY.
THAT'S... AMAZING. UM, I'M VIOLET, BY THE WAY.
OH. UH. HI! I'M DAVID. IT'S A PLEASURE TO-
BLARGH
SKULLBERRY DAY ONE!

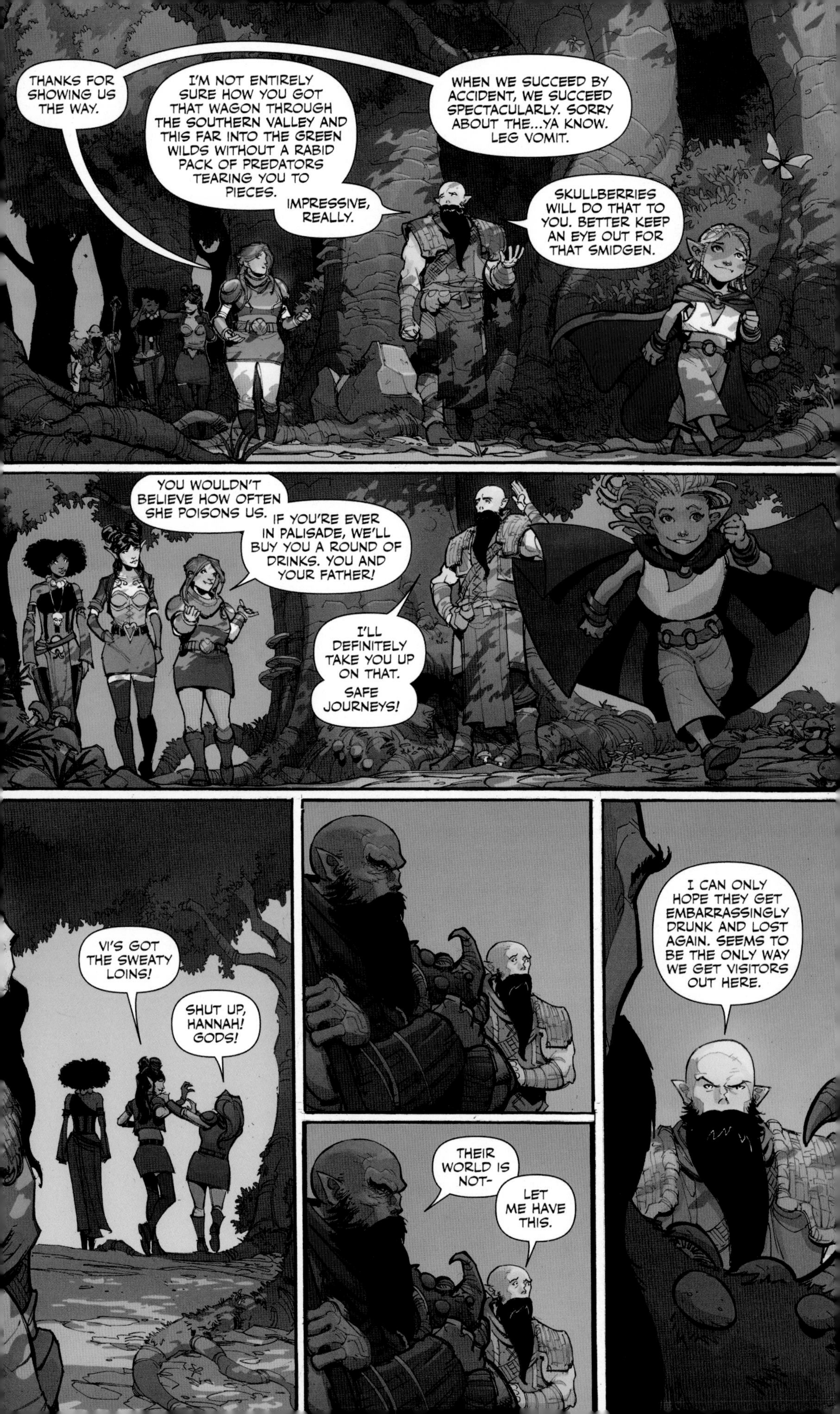
THANKS FOR SHOWING US THE WAY.
I'M NOT ENTIRELY SURE HOW YOU GOT THAT WAGON THROUGH THE SOUTHERN VALLEY AND THIS FAR INTO THE GREEN WILDS WITHOUT A RABID PACK OF PREDATORS TEARING YOU TO PIECES.
IMPRESSIVE, REALLY.
WHEN WE SUCCEED BY ACCIDENT, WE SUCCEED SPECTACULARLY. SORRY ABOUT THE...YA KNOW. LEG VOMIT.
SKULLBERRIES WILL DO THAT TO YOU. BETTER KEEP AN EYE OUT FOR THAT SMIDGEN.
YOU WOULDN'T BELIEVE HOW OFTEN SHE POISONS US.
IF YOU'RE EVER IN PALISADE, WE'LL BUY YOU A ROUND OF DRINKS. YOU AND YOUR FATHER!
I'LL DEFINITELY TAKE YOU UP ON THAT.
SAFE JOURNEYS!
VI'S GOT THE SWEATY LOINS!
SHUT UP, HANNAH! GODS!
THEIR WORLD IS NOT-
LET ME HAVE THIS.
I CAN ONLY HOPE THEY GET EMBARRASSINGLY DRUNK AND LOST AGAIN. SEEMS TO BE THE ONLY WAY WE GET VISITORS OUT HERE.

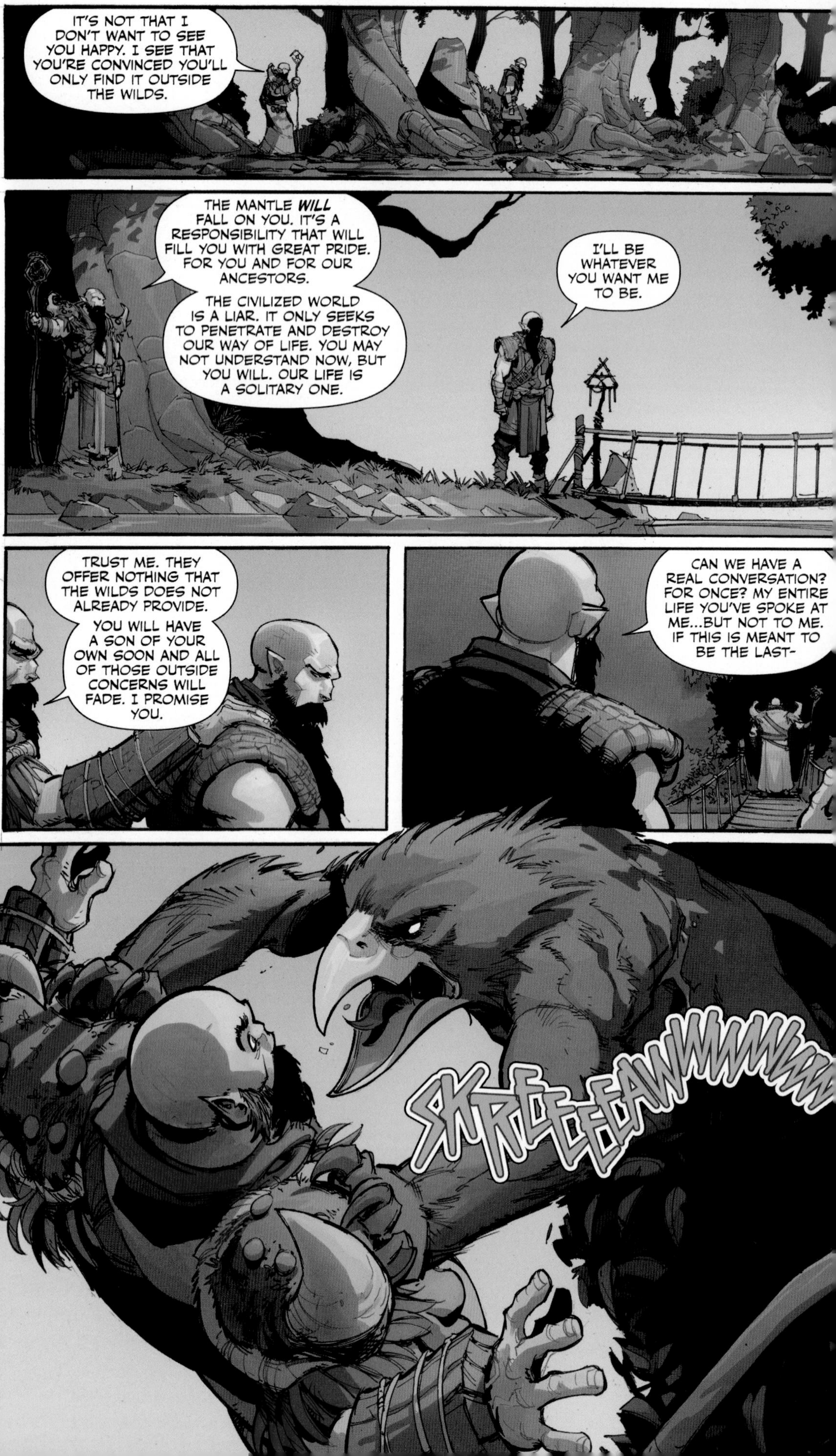
IT'S NOT THAT I DON'T WANT TO SEE YOU HAPPY. I SEE THAT YOU'RE CONVINCED YOU'LL ONLY FIND IT OUTSIDE THE WILDS.
THE MANTLE *WILL* FALL ON YOU. IT'S A RESPONSIBILITY THAT WILL FILL YOU WITH GREAT PRIDE. FOR YOU AND FOR OUR ANCESTORS.
THE CIVILIZED WORLD IS A LIAR. IT ONLY SEEKS TO PENETRATE AND DESTROY OUR WAY OF LIFE. YOU MAY NOT UNDERSTAND NOW, BUT YOU WILL. OUR LIFE IS A SOLITARY ONE.
I'LL BE WHATEVER YOU WANT ME TO BE.
TRUST ME. THEY OFFER NOTHING THAT THE WILDS DOES NOT ALREADY PROVIDE.
YOU WILL HAVE A SON OF YOUR OWN SOON AND ALL OF THOSE OUTSIDE CONCERNS WILL FADE. I PROMISE YOU.
CAN WE HAVE A REAL CONVERSATION? FOR ONCE? MY ENTIRE LIFE YOU'VE SPOKE AT ME...BUT NOT TO ME. IF THIS IS MEANT TO BE THE LAST-
SKREEEEAWWWWWW

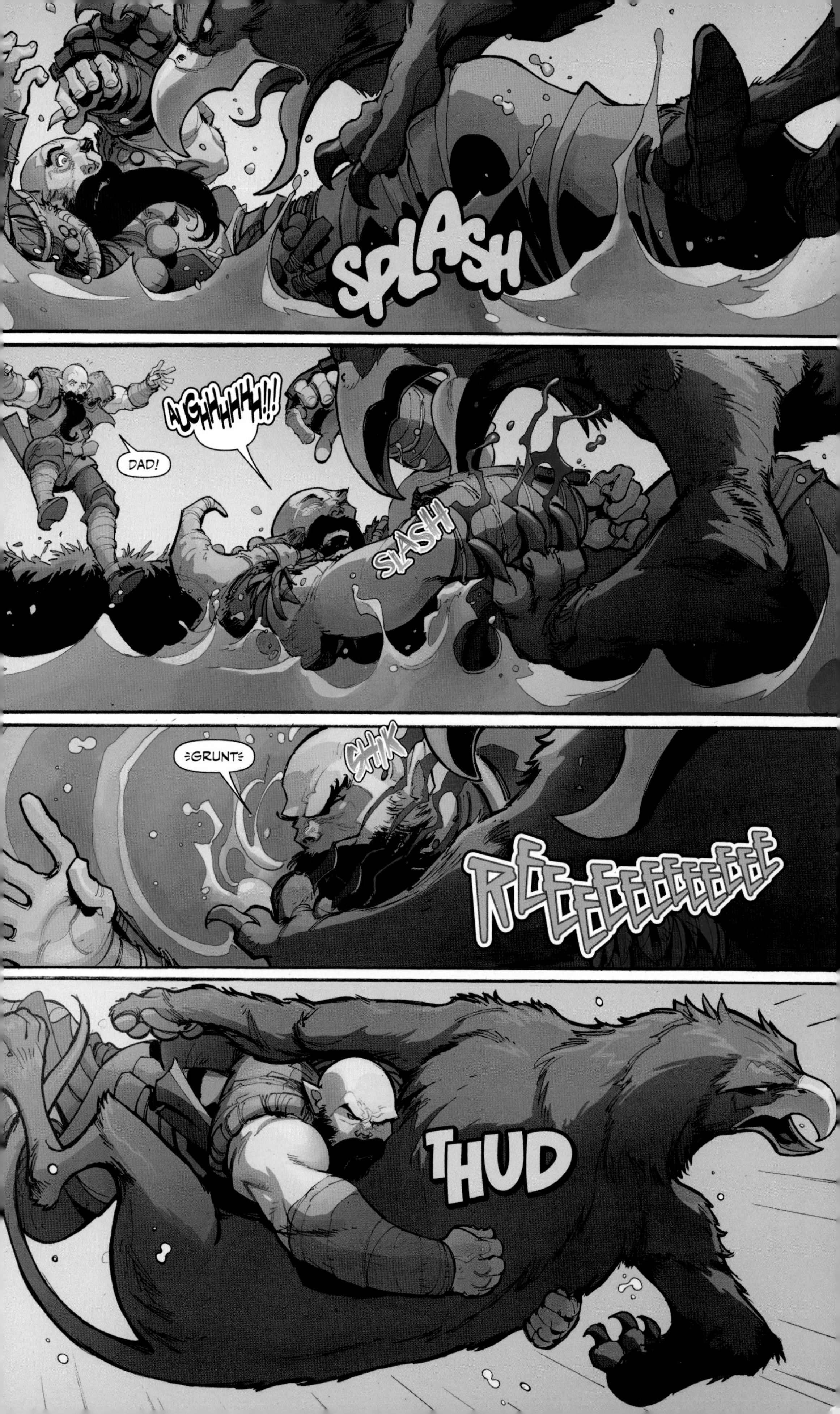
SPLASH
AUGHHHHHH!!!
DAD!
SLASH
GRUNT
SHIK
REEEEEEEEEEEE
THUD

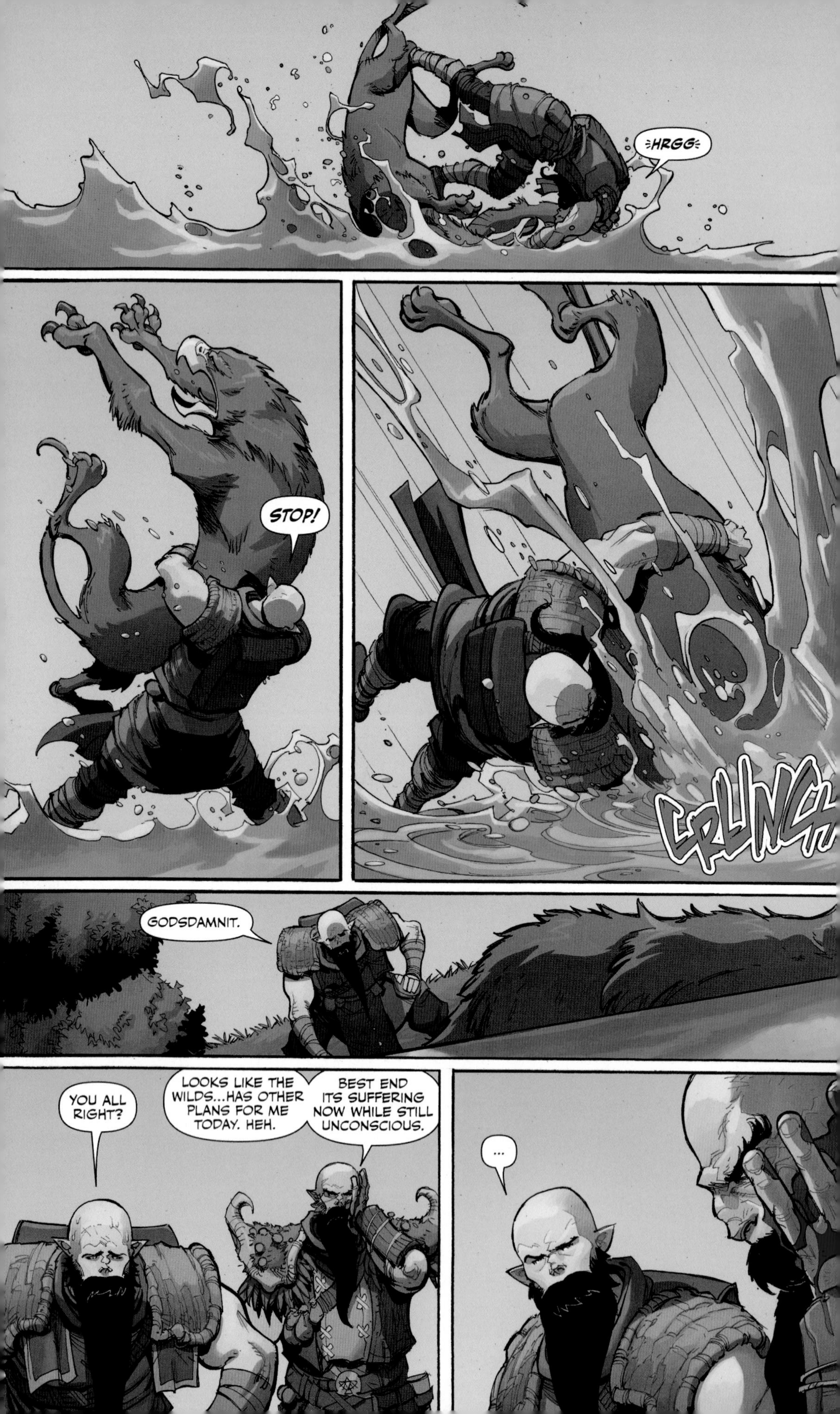

HRGG
STOP!
CRUNCH
GODSDAMNIT.
YOU ALL RIGHT?
LOOKS LIKE THE WILDS...HAS OTHER PLANS FOR ME TODAY. HEH.
BEST END ITS SUFFERING NOW WHILE STILL UNCONSCIOUS.
...

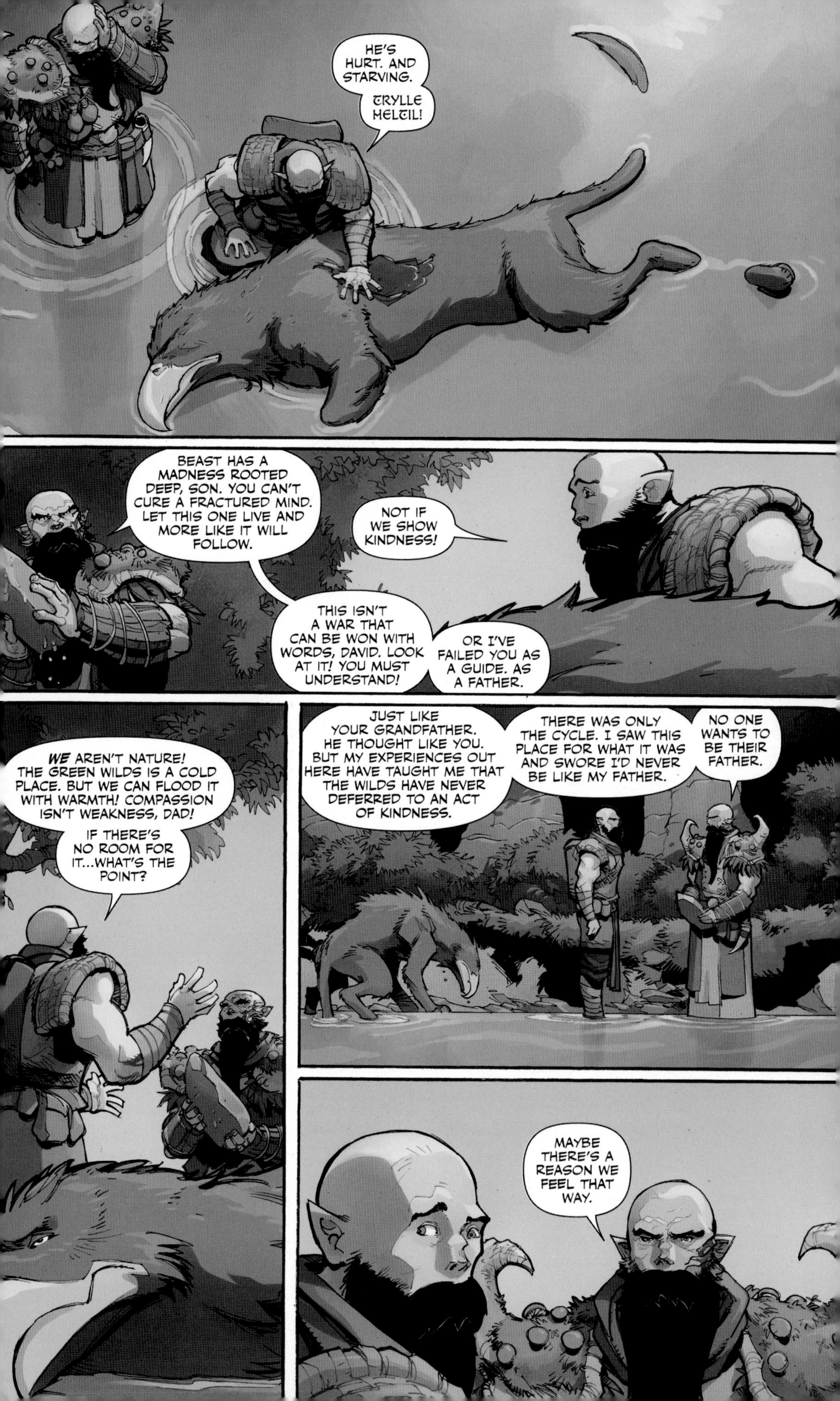
HE'S HURT. AND STARVING.
TRYLLE HELTIL!
BEAST HAS A MADNESS ROOTED DEEP, SON. YOU CAN'T CURE A FRACTURED MIND. LET THIS ONE LIVE AND MORE LIKE IT WILL FOLLOW.
NOT IF WE SHOW KINDNESS!
THIS ISN'T A WAR THAT CAN BE WON WITH WORDS, DAVID. LOOK AT IT! YOU MUST UNDERSTAND!
OR I'VE FAILED YOU AS A GUIDE. AS A FATHER.
WE AREN'T NATURE! THE GREEN WILDS IS A COLD PLACE. BUT WE CAN FLOOD IT WITH WARMTH! COMPASSION ISN'T WEAKNESS, DAD!
IF THERE'S NO ROOM FOR IT...WHAT'S THE POINT?
JUST LIKE YOUR GRANDFATHER. HE THOUGHT LIKE YOU. BUT MY EXPERIENCES OUT HERE HAVE TAUGHT ME THAT THE WILDS HAVE NEVER DEFERRED TO AN ACT OF KINDNESS.
THERE WAS ONLY THE CYCLE. I SAW THIS PLACE FOR WHAT IT WAS AND SWORE I'D NEVER BE LIKE MY FATHER.
NO ONE WANTS TO BE THEIR FATHER.
MAYBE THERE'S A REASON WE FEEL THAT WAY.

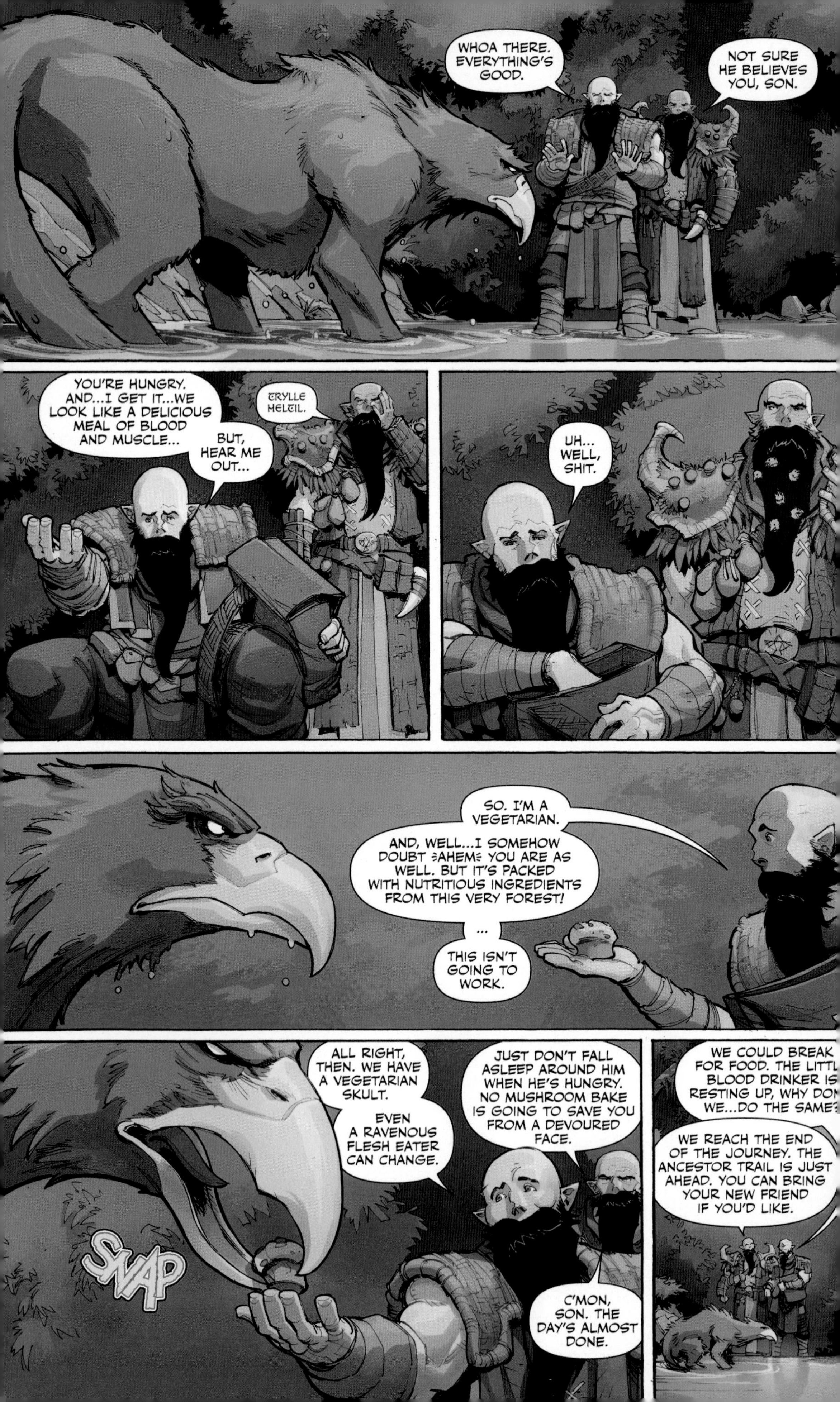
WHOA THERE. EVERYTHING'S GOOD.
NOT SURE HE BELIEVES YOU, SON.
YOU'RE HUNGRY. AND...I GET IT...WE LOOK LIKE A DELICIOUS MEAL OF BLOOD AND MUSCLE...
BUT, HEAR ME OUT...
TRYLLE HELTIL.
UH... WELL, SHIT.
SO. I'M A VEGETARIAN.
AND, WELL...I SOMEHOW DOUBT =AHEM= YOU ARE AS WELL. BUT IT'S PACKED WITH NUTRITIOUS INGREDIENTS FROM THIS VERY FOREST!
...
THIS ISN'T GOING TO WORK.
SNAP
ALL RIGHT, THEN. WE HAVE A VEGETARIAN SKULT.
EVEN A RAVENOUS FLESH EATER CAN CHANGE.
JUST DON'T FALL ASLEEP AROUND HIM WHEN HE'S HUNGRY. NO MUSHROOM BAKE IS GOING TO SAVE YOU FROM A DEVOURED FACE.
C'MON, SON. THE DAY'S ALMOST DONE.
WE COULD BREAK FOR FOOD. THE LITTL BLOOD DRINKER IS RESTING UP, WHY DON WE...DO THE SAME?
WE REACH THE END OF THE JOURNEY. THE ANCESTOR TRAIL IS JUST AHEAD. YOU CAN BRING YOUR NEW FRIEND IF YOU'D LIKE.

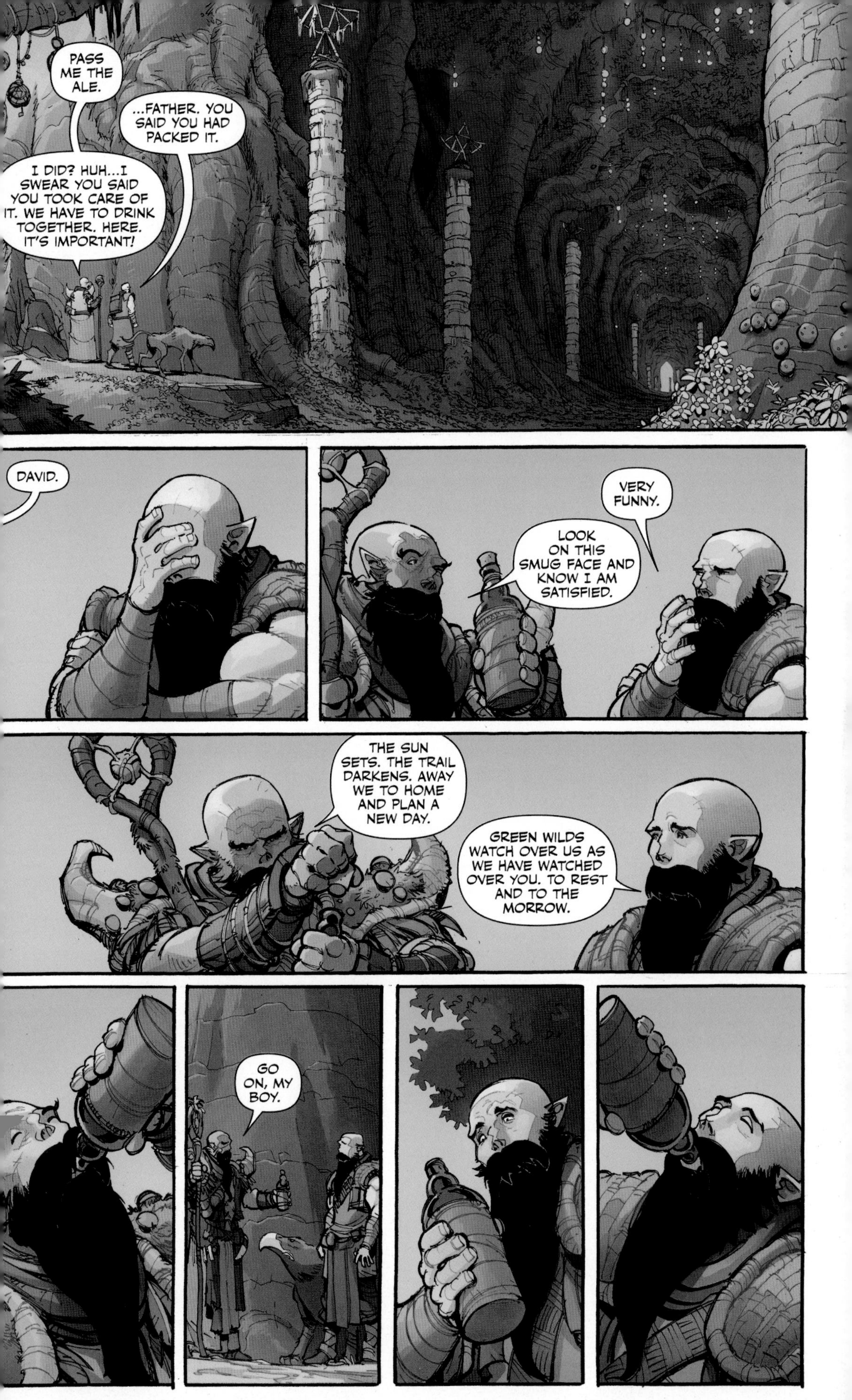
PASS ME THE ALE.
...FATHER. YOU SAID YOU HAD PACKED IT.
I DID? HUH...I SWEAR YOU SAID YOU TOOK CARE OF IT. WE HAVE TO DRINK TOGETHER. HERE. IT'S IMPORTANT!
DAVID.
LOOK ON THIS SMUG FACE AND KNOW I AM SATISFIED.
VERY FUNNY.
THE SUN SETS. THE TRAIL DARKENS. AWAY WE TO HOME AND PLAN A NEW DAY.
GREEN WILDS WATCH OVER US AS WE HAVE WATCHED OVER YOU. TO REST AND TO THE MORROW.
GO ON, MY BOY.

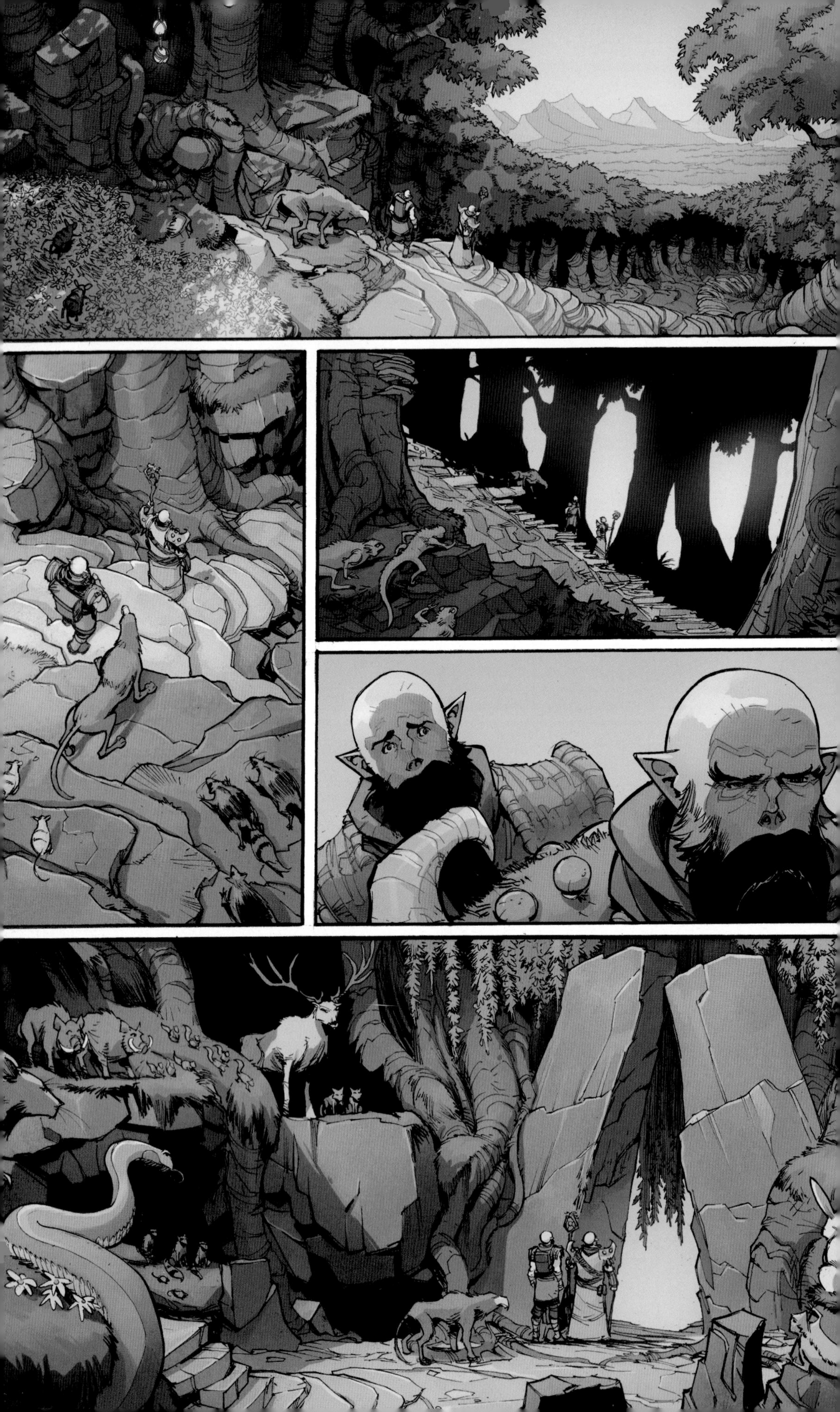

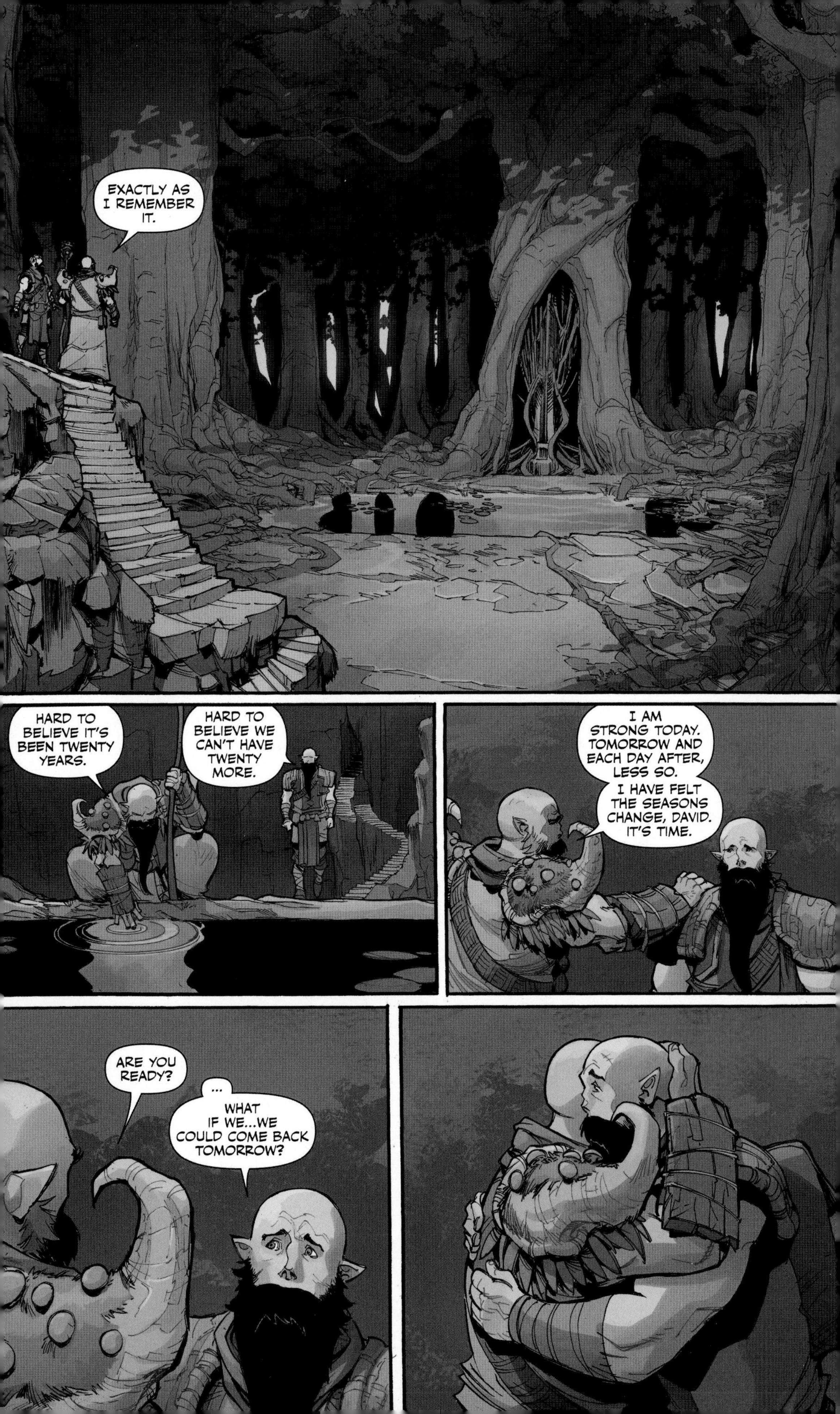
EXACTLY AS I REMEMBER IT.
HARD TO BELIEVE IT'S BEEN TWENTY YEARS.
HARD TO BELIEVE WE CAN'T HAVE TWENTY MORE.
I AM STRONG TODAY. TOMORROW AND EACH DAY AFTER, LESS SO.
I HAVE FELT THE SEASONS CHANGE, DAVID. IT'S TIME.
ARE YOU READY?
...
WHAT IF WE...WE COULD COME BACK TOMORROW?

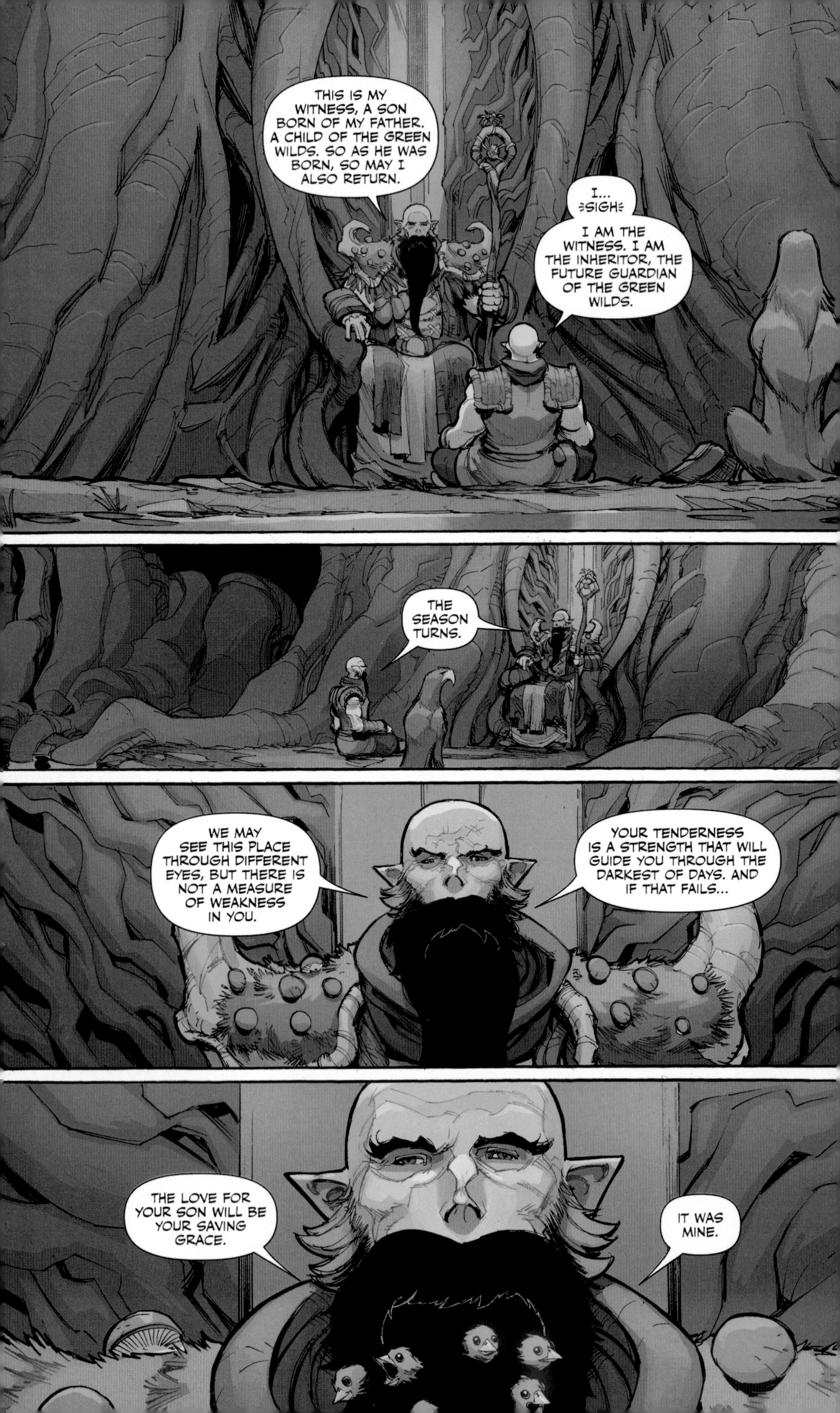
THIS IS MY WITNESS, A SON BORN OF MY FATHER. A CHILD OF THE GREEN WILDS. SO AS HE WAS BORN, SO MAY I ALSO RETURN.
I... ≈SIGH≈
I AM THE WITNESS. I AM THE INHERITOR, THE FUTURE GUARDIAN OF THE GREEN WILDS.
THE SEASON TURNS.
WE MAY SEE THIS PLACE THROUGH DIFFERENT EYES, BUT THERE IS NOT A MEASURE OF WEAKNESS IN YOU.
YOUR TENDERNESS IS A STRENGTH THAT WILL GUIDE YOU THROUGH THE DARKEST OF DAYS. AND IF THAT FAILS...
THE LOVE FOR YOUR SON WILL BE YOUR SAVING GRACE.
IT WAS MINE.

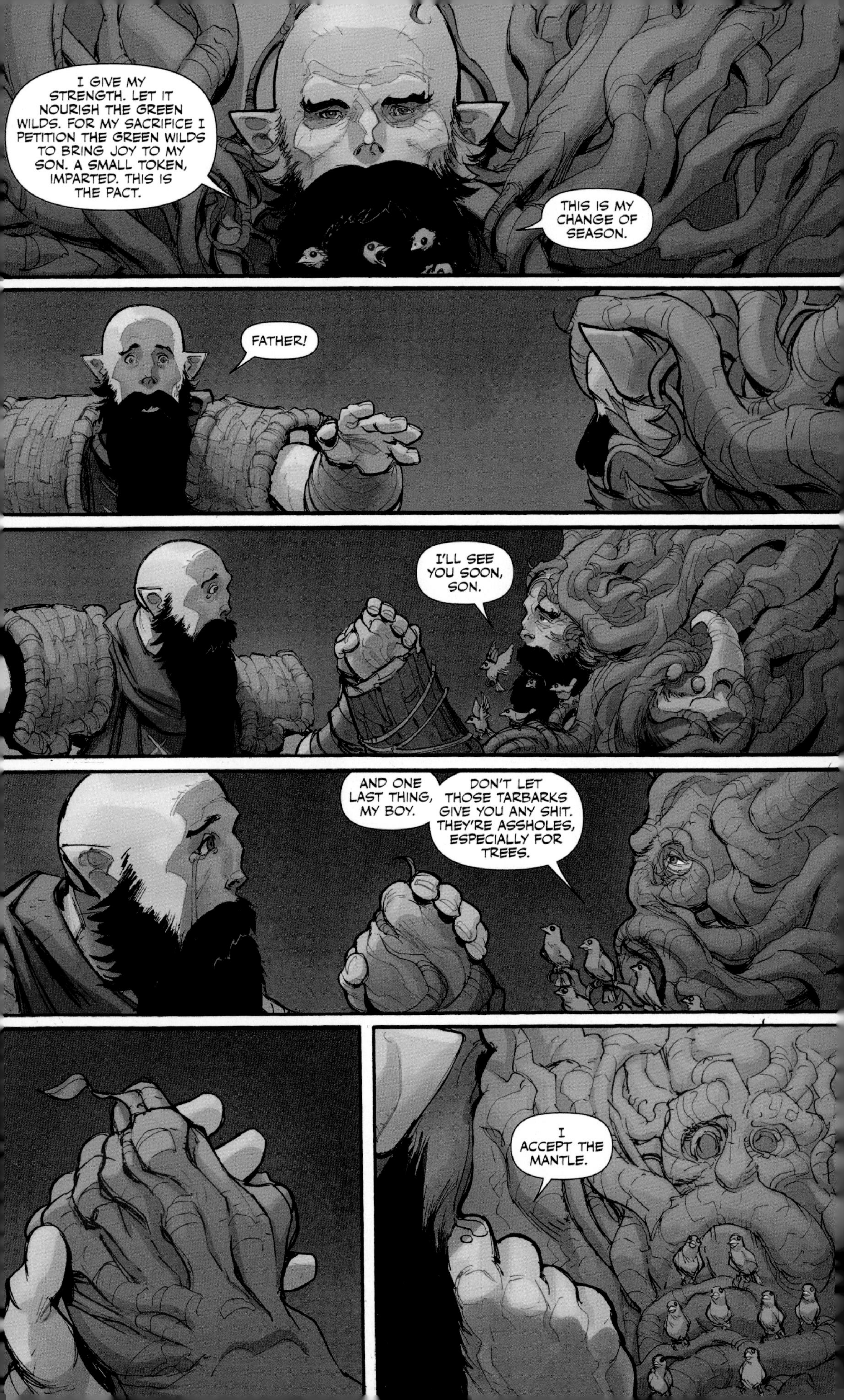
I GIVE MY STRENGTH. LET IT NOURISH THE GREEN WILDS. FOR MY SACRIFICE I PETITION THE GREEN WILDS TO BRING JOY TO MY SON. A SMALL TOKEN, IMPARTED. THIS IS THE PACT.
THIS IS MY CHANGE OF SEASON.
FATHER!
I'LL SEE YOU SOON, SON.
AND ONE LAST THING, MY BOY.
DON'T LET THOSE TARBARKS GIVE YOU ANY SHIT. THEY'RE ASSHOLES, ESPECIALLY FOR TREES.
I ACCEPT THE MANTLE.

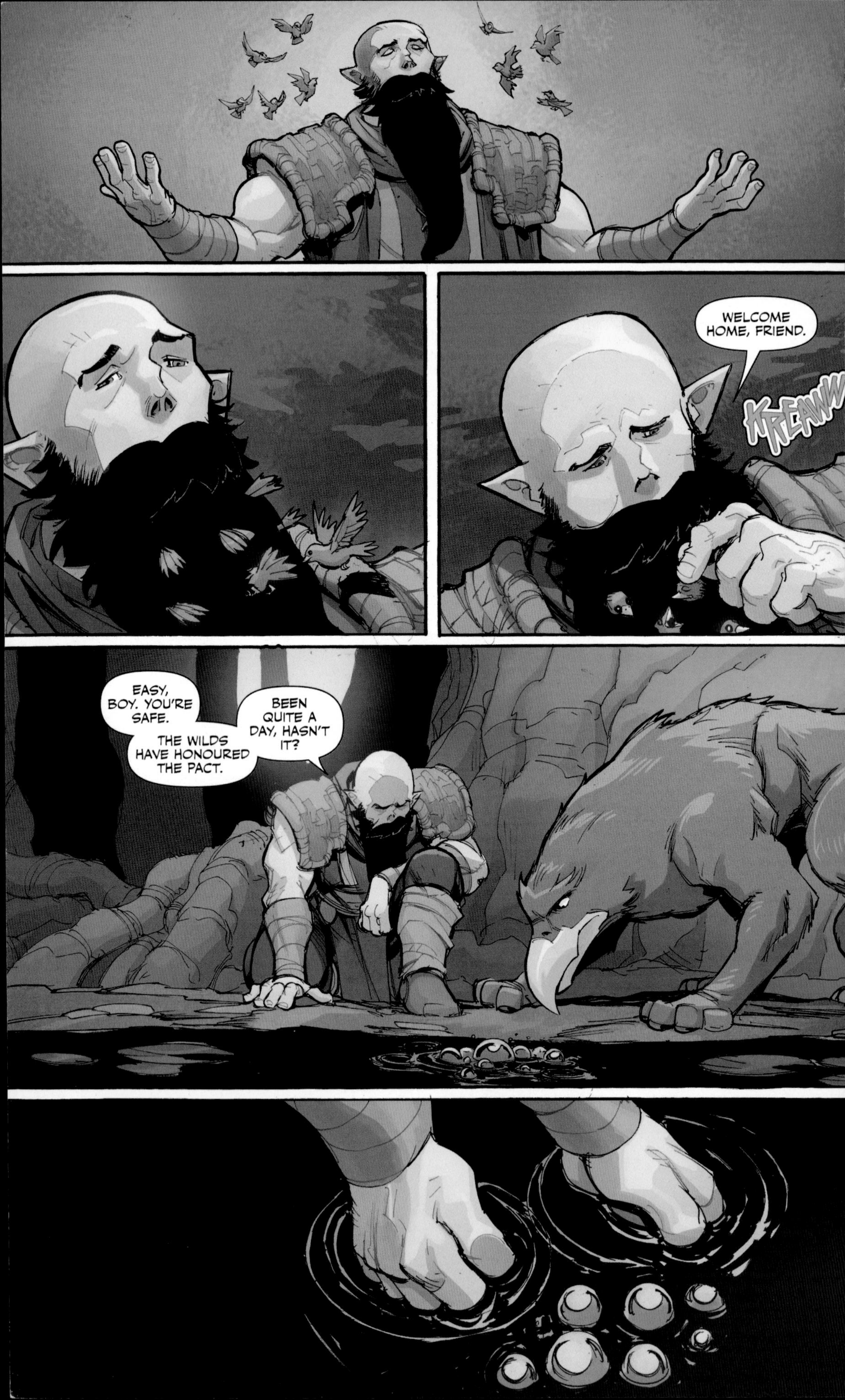

WELCOME HOME, FRIEND.
KREAWW
EASY, BOY. YOU'RE SAFE.
THE WILDS HAVE HONOURED THE PACT.
BEEN QUITE A DAY, HASN'T IT?

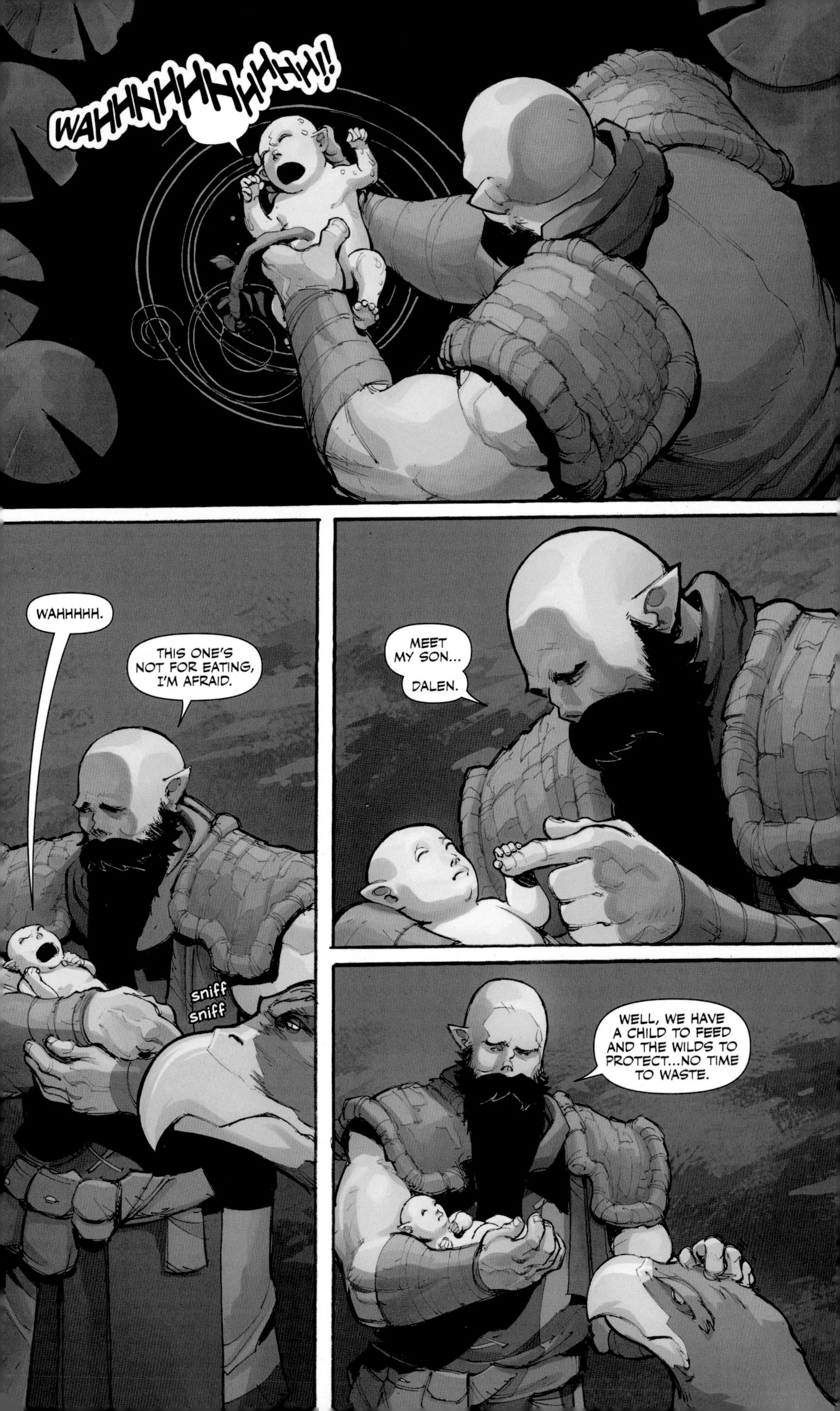
WAHHHHHHHHHH!!
WAHHHHHH.
THIS ONE'S NOT FOR EATING, I'M AFRAID.
sniff sniff
MEET MY SON... DALEN.
WELL, WE HAVE A CHILD TO FEED AND THE WILDS TO PROTECT...NO TIME TO WASTE.

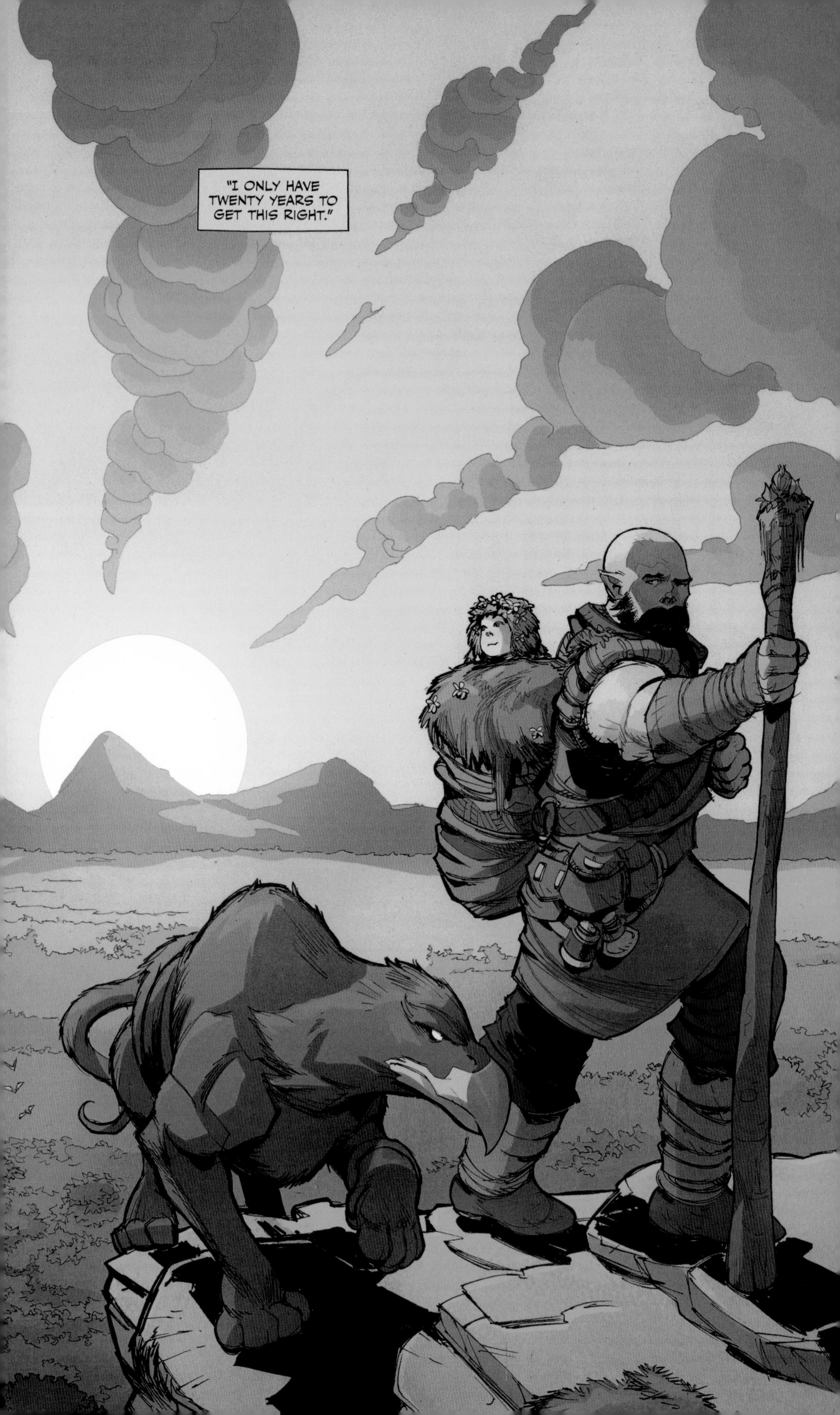
"I ONLY HAVE TWENTY YEARS TO GET THIS RIGHT."

CHAPTER SIX

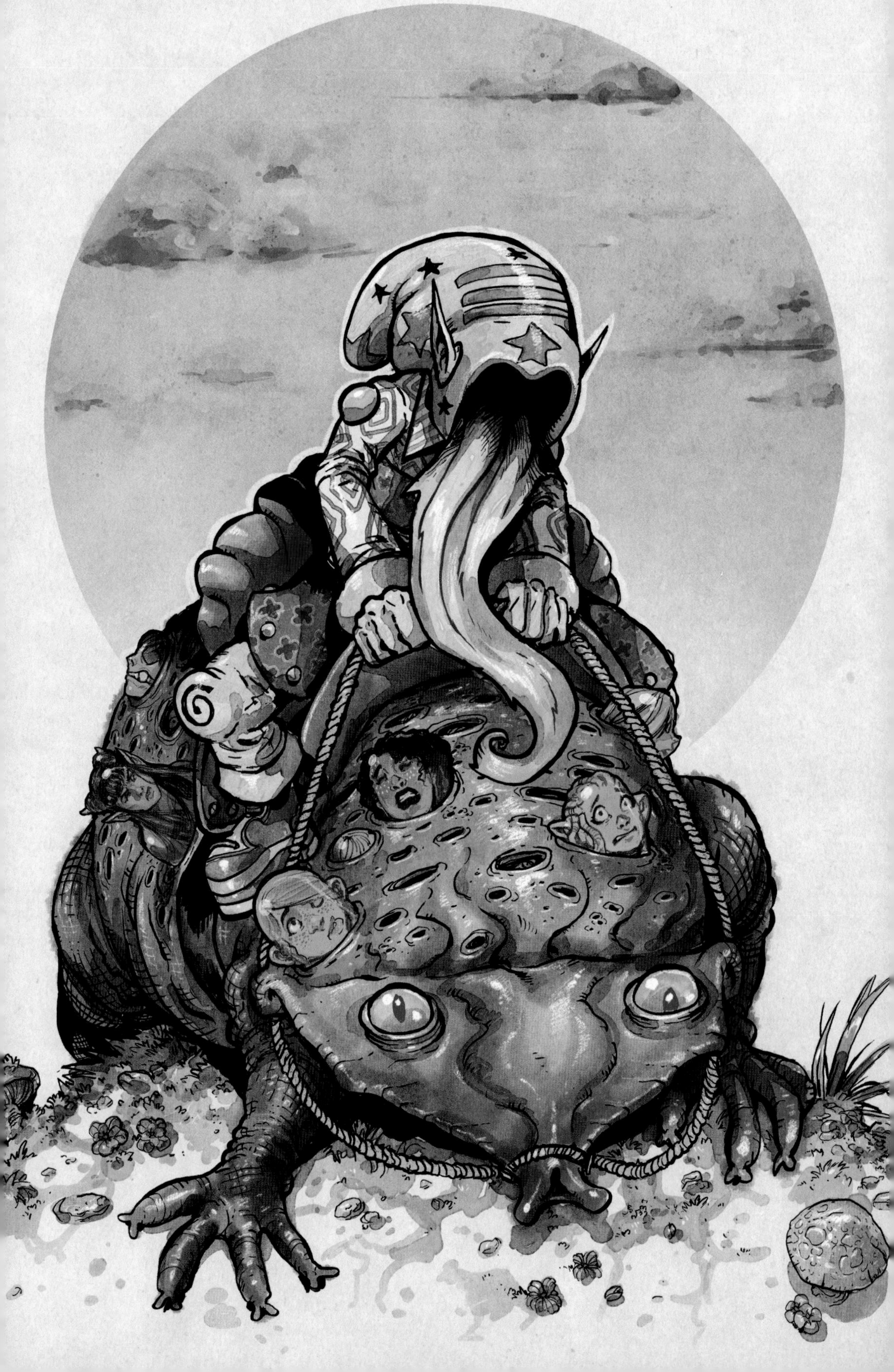

Issue 6 cover B by SWEENEY BOO

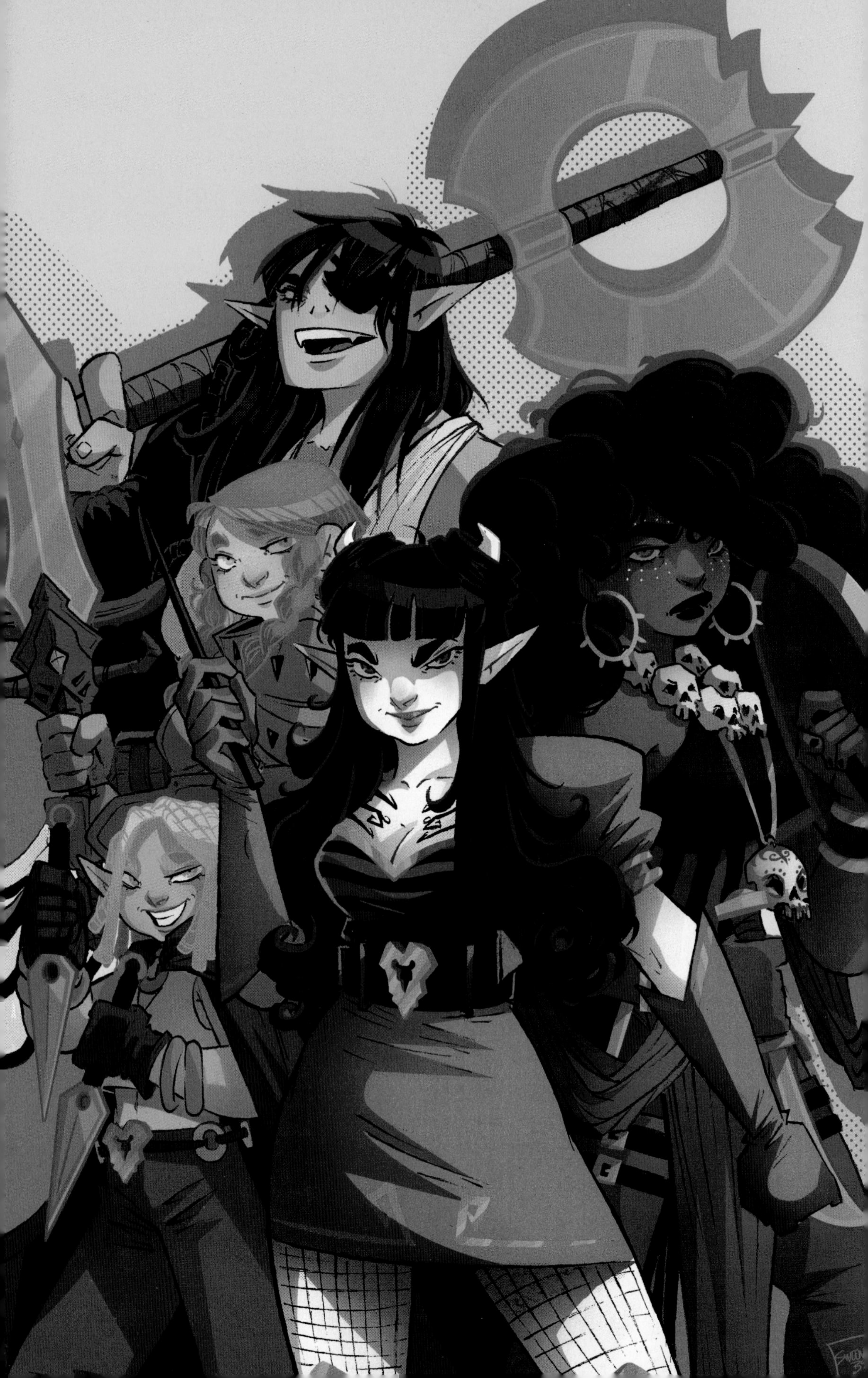

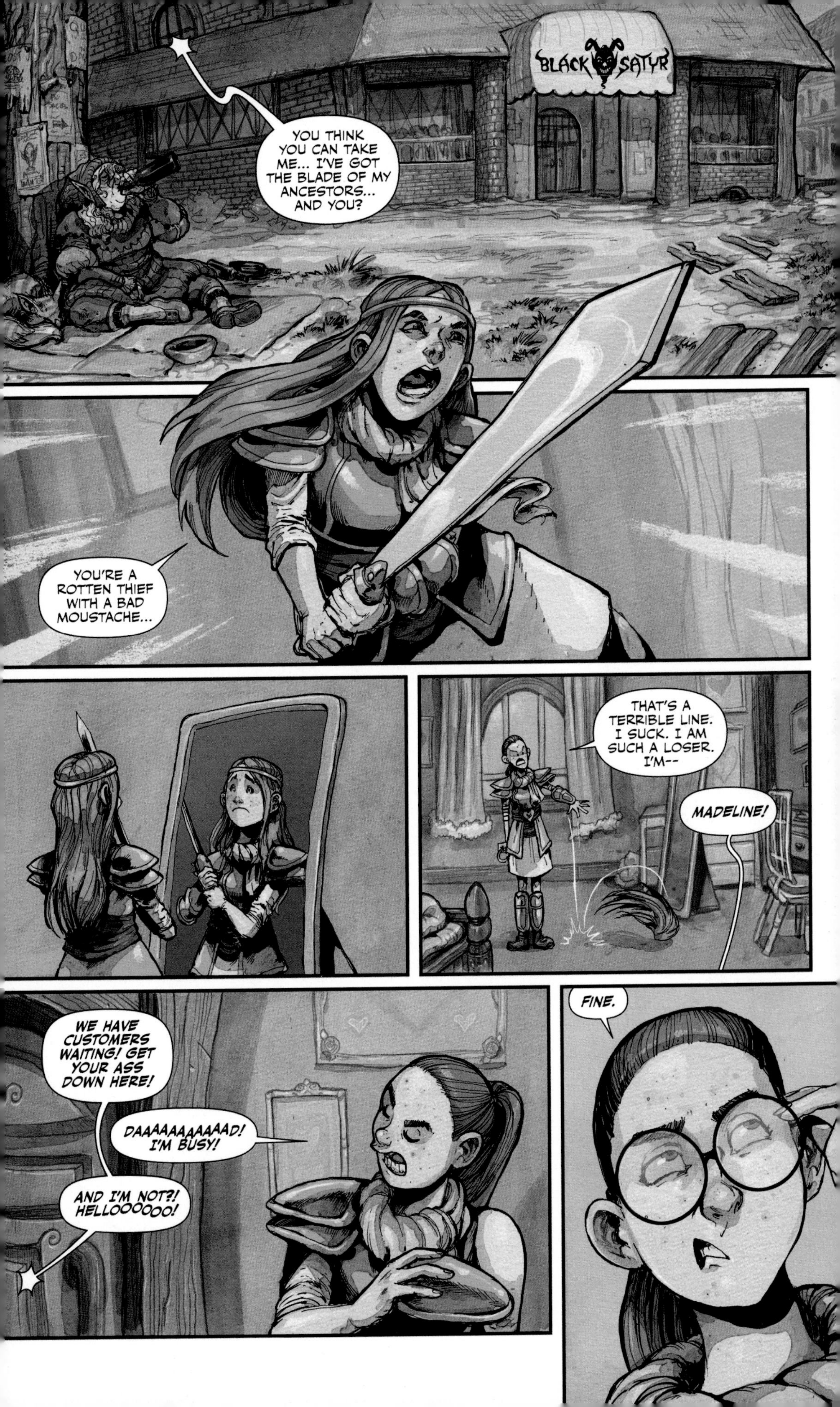
YOU THINK YOU CAN TAKE ME... I'VE GOT THE BLADE OF MY ANCESTORS... AND YOU?
BLACK SATYR
YOU'RE A ROTTEN THIEF WITH A BAD MOUSTACHE...
THAT'S A TERRIBLE LINE. I SUCK. I AM SUCH A LOSER. I'M--
MADELINE!
WE HAVE CUSTOMERS WAITING! GET YOUR ASS DOWN HERE!
DAAAAAAAAAAAD! I'M BUSY!
AND I'M NOT?! HELLOOOOOO!
FINE.

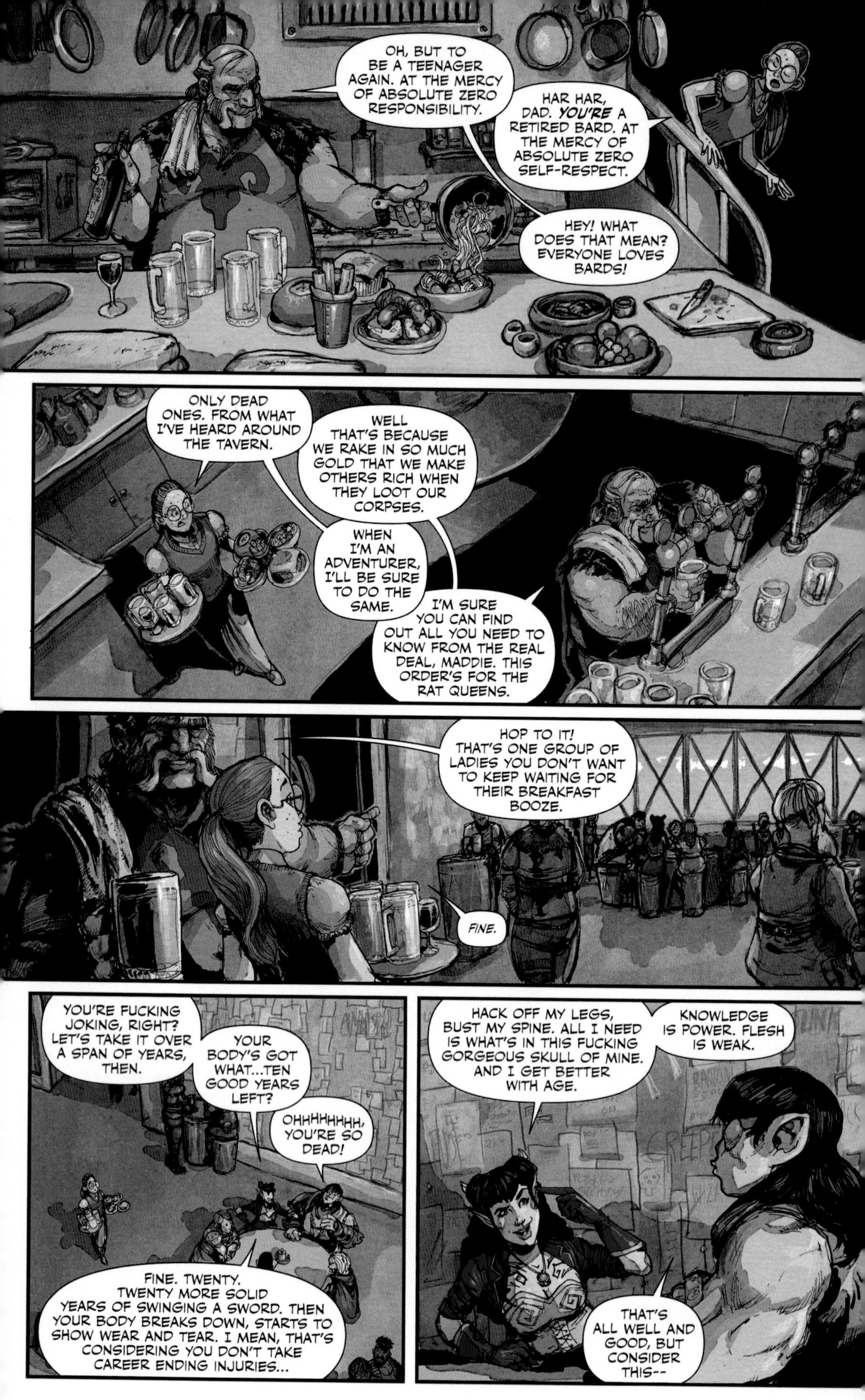
OH, BUT TO BE A TEENAGER AGAIN. AT THE MERCY OF ABSOLUTE ZERO RESPONSIBILITY.
HAR HAR, DAD. *YOU'RE* A RETIRED BARD. AT THE MERCY OF ABSOLUTE ZERO SELF-RESPECT.
HEY! WHAT DOES THAT MEAN? EVERYONE LOVES BARDS!
ONLY DEAD ONES. FROM WHAT I'VE HEARD AROUND THE TAVERN.
WELL THAT'S BECAUSE WE RAKE IN SO MUCH GOLD THAT WE MAKE OTHERS RICH WHEN THEY LOOT OUR CORPSES.
WHEN I'M AN ADVENTURER, I'LL BE SURE TO DO THE SAME.
I'M SURE YOU CAN FIND OUT ALL YOU NEED TO KNOW FROM THE REAL DEAL, MADDIE. THIS ORDER'S FOR THE RAT QUEENS.
HOP TO IT! THAT'S ONE GROUP OF LADIES YOU DON'T WANT TO KEEP WAITING FOR THEIR BREAKFAST BOOZE.
FINE.
YOU'RE FUCKING JOKING, RIGHT? LET'S TAKE IT OVER A SPAN OF YEARS, THEN.
YOUR BODY'S GOT WHAT...TEN GOOD YEARS LEFT?
OHHHHHHHH, YOU'RE SO DEAD!
FINE. TWENTY. TWENTY MORE SOLID YEARS OF SWINGING A SWORD. THEN YOUR BODY BREAKS DOWN, STARTS TO SHOW WEAR AND TEAR. I MEAN, THAT'S CONSIDERING YOU DON'T TAKE CAREER ENDING INJURIES...
HACK OFF MY LEGS, BUST MY SPINE. ALL I NEED IS WHAT'S IN THIS FUCKING GORGEOUS SKULL OF MINE. AND I GET BETTER WITH AGE.
KNOWLEDGE IS POWER. FLESH IS WEAK.
THAT'S ALL WELL AND GOOD, BUT CONSIDER THIS--

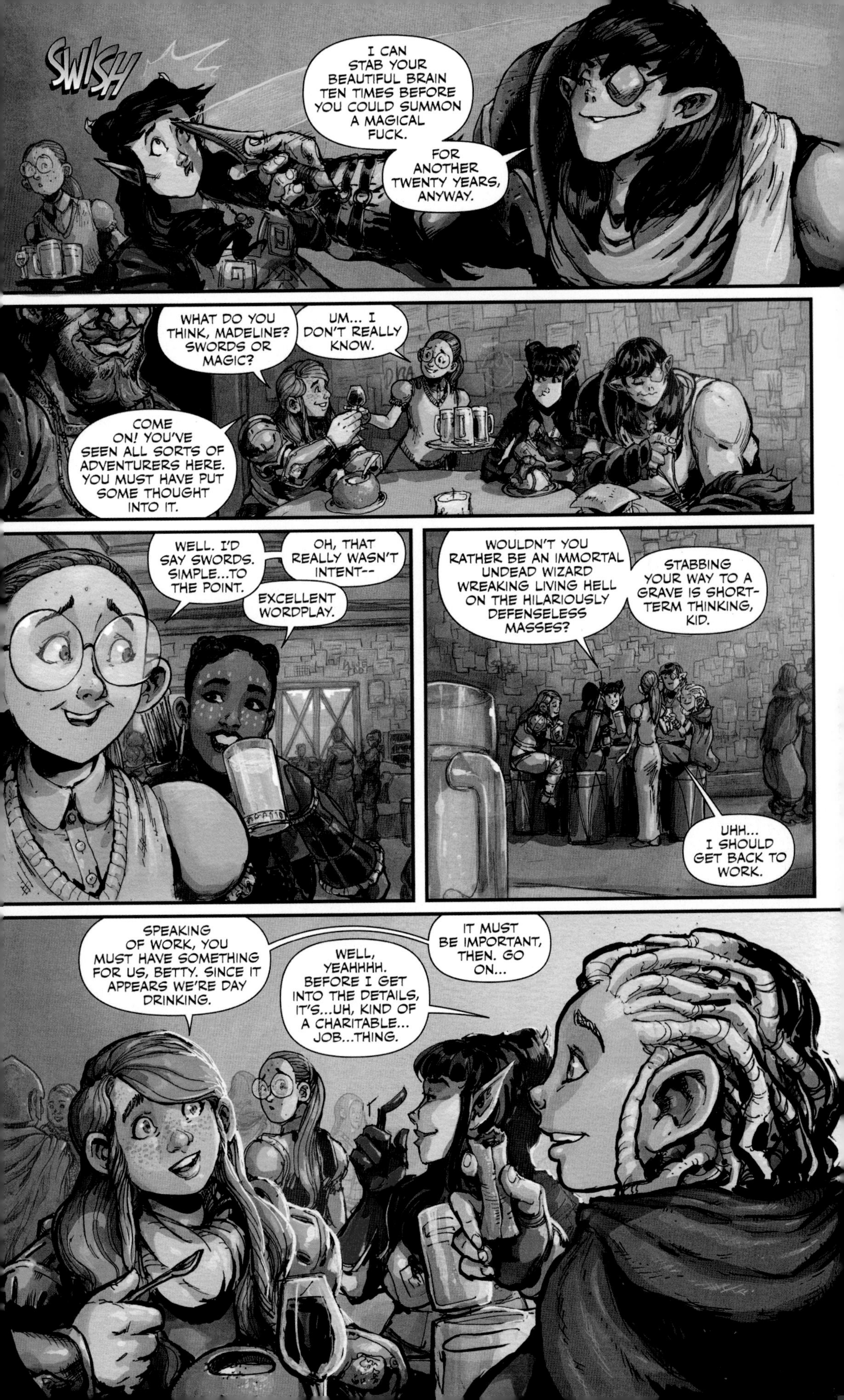
SWISH
I CAN STAB YOUR BEAUTIFUL BRAIN TEN TIMES BEFORE YOU COULD SUMMON A MAGICAL FUCK.
FOR ANOTHER TWENTY YEARS, ANYWAY.
WHAT DO YOU THINK, MADELINE? SWORDS OR MAGIC?
UM... I DON'T REALLY KNOW.
COME ON! YOU'VE SEEN ALL SORTS OF ADVENTURERS HERE. YOU MUST HAVE PUT SOME THOUGHT INTO IT.
WELL. I'D SAY SWORDS. SIMPLE...TO THE POINT.
OH, THAT REALLY WASN'T INTENT--
EXCELLENT WORDPLAY.
WOULDN'T YOU RATHER BE AN IMMORTAL UNDEAD WIZARD WREAKING LIVING HELL ON THE HILARIOUSLY DEFENSELESS MASSES?
STABBING YOUR WAY TO A GRAVE IS SHORT-TERM THINKING, KID.
UHH... I SHOULD GET BACK TO WORK.
SPEAKING OF WORK, YOU MUST HAVE SOMETHING FOR US, BETTY. SINCE IT APPEARS WE'RE DAY DRINKING.
WELL, YEAHHHH. BEFORE I GET INTO THE DETAILS, IT'S...UH, KIND OF A CHARITABLE... JOB...THING.
IT MUST BE IMPORTANT, THEN. GO ON...

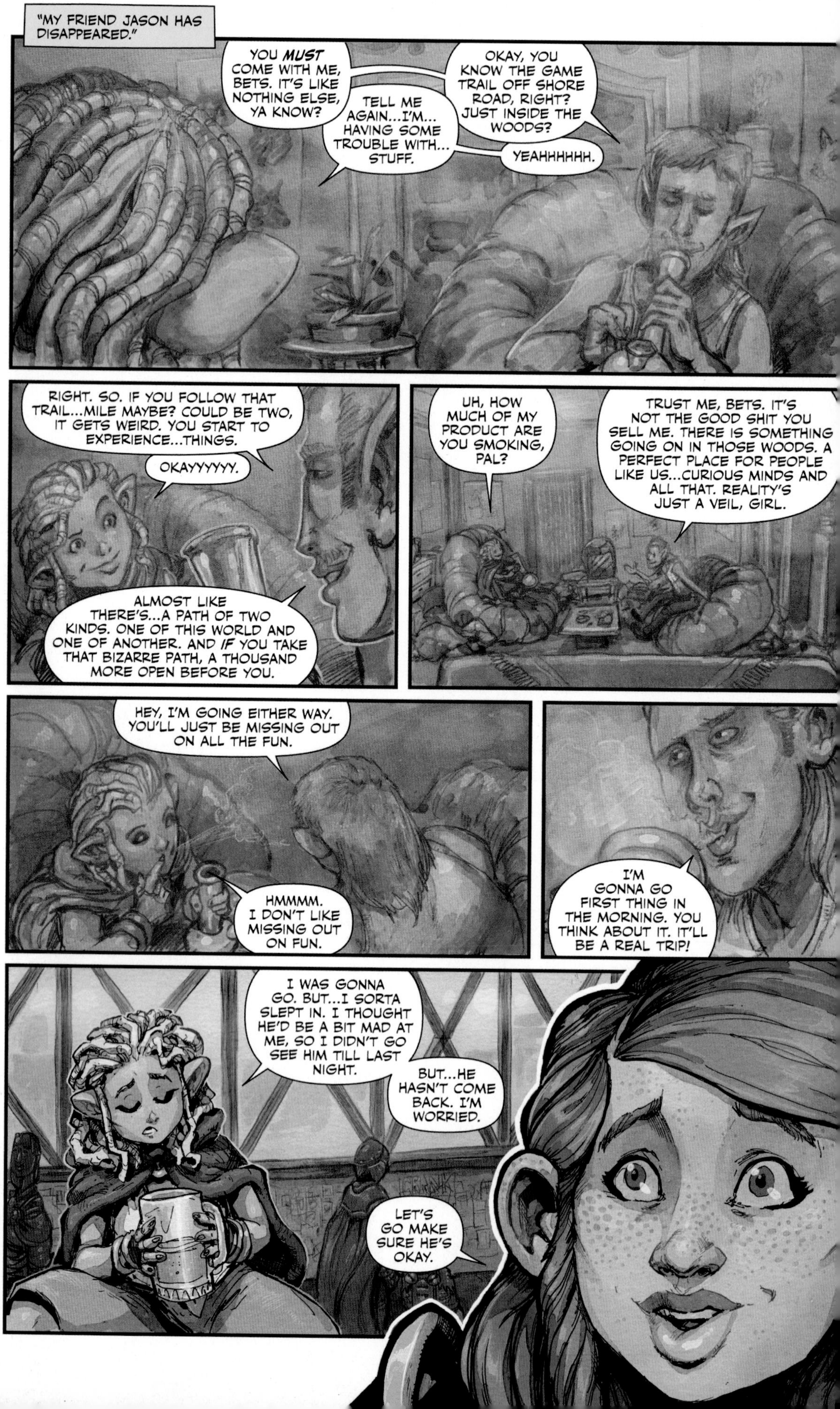
"MY FRIEND JASON HAS DISAPPEARED."
YOU *MUST* COME WITH ME, BETS. IT'S LIKE NOTHING ELSE, YA KNOW?
TELL ME AGAIN...I'M... HAVING SOME TROUBLE WITH... STUFF.
OKAY, YOU KNOW THE GAME TRAIL OFF SHORE ROAD, RIGHT? JUST INSIDE THE WOODS?
YEAHHHHHH.
RIGHT. SO. IF YOU FOLLOW THAT TRAIL...MILE MAYBE? COULD BE TWO, IT GETS WEIRD. YOU START TO EXPERIENCE...THINGS.
OKAYYYYYY.
ALMOST LIKE THERE'S...A PATH OF TWO KINDS. ONE OF THIS WORLD AND ONE OF ANOTHER. AND *IF* YOU TAKE THAT BIZARRE PATH, A THOUSAND MORE OPEN BEFORE YOU.
UH, HOW MUCH OF MY PRODUCT ARE YOU SMOKING, PAL?
TRUST ME, BETS. IT'S NOT THE GOOD SHIT YOU SELL ME. THERE IS SOMETHING GOING ON IN THOSE WOODS. A PERFECT PLACE FOR PEOPLE LIKE US...CURIOUS MINDS AND ALL THAT. REALITY'S JUST A VEIL, GIRL.
HEY, I'M GOING EITHER WAY. YOU'LL JUST BE MISSING OUT ON ALL THE FUN.
HMMMM. I DON'T LIKE MISSING OUT ON FUN.
I'M GONNA GO FIRST THING IN THE MORNING. YOU THINK ABOUT IT. IT'LL BE A REAL TRIP!
I WAS GONNA GO. BUT...I SORTA SLEPT IN. I THOUGHT HE'D BE A BIT MAD AT ME, SO I DIDN'T GO SEE HIM TILL LAST NIGHT.
BUT...HE HASN'T COME BACK. I'M WORRIED.
LET'S GO MAKE SURE HE'S OKAY.

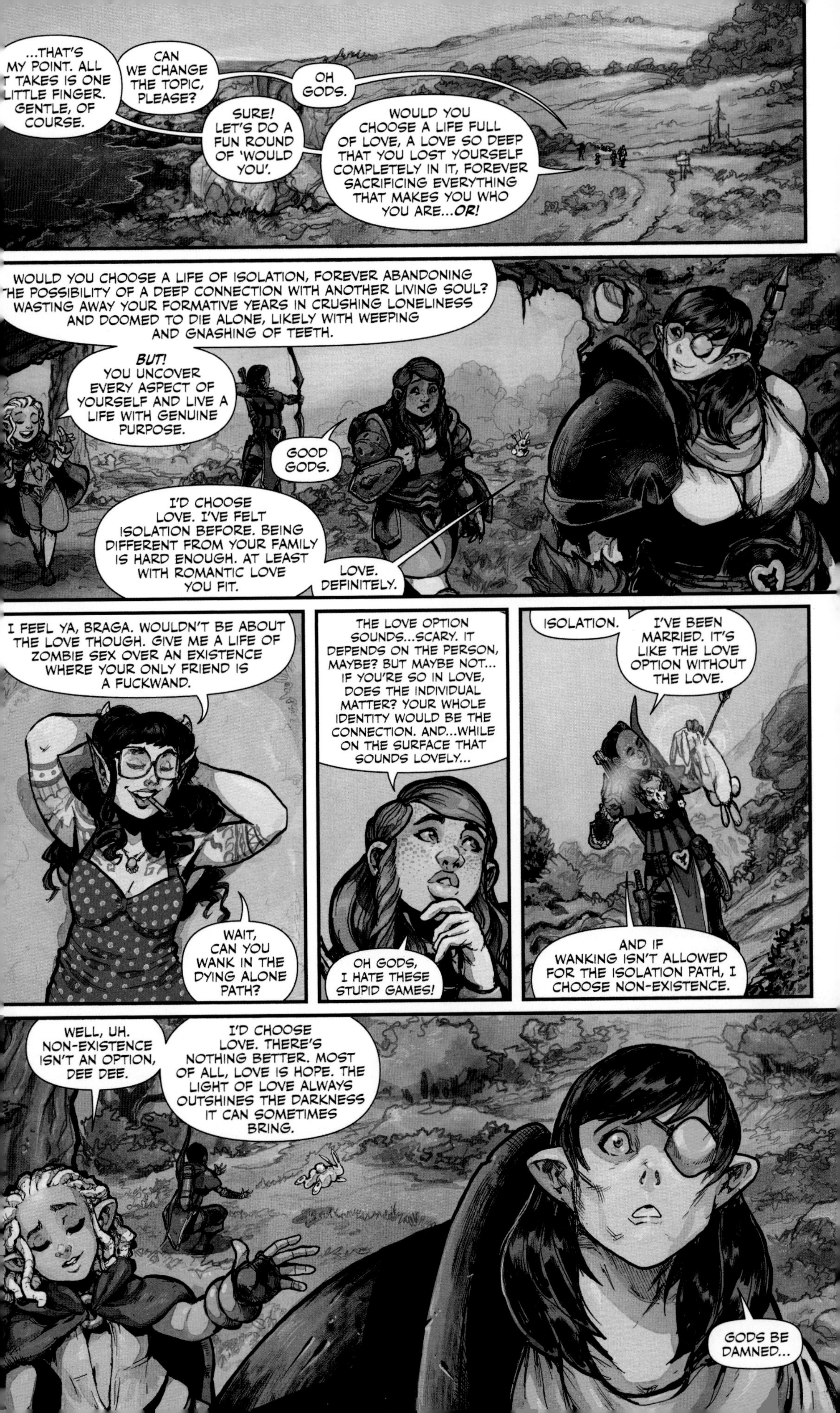
...THAT'S MY POINT. ALL IT TAKES IS ONE LITTLE FINGER. GENTLE, OF COURSE.
CAN WE CHANGE THE TOPIC, PLEASE?
OH GODS.
SURE! LET'S DO A FUN ROUND OF 'WOULD YOU'.
WOULD YOU CHOOSE A LIFE FULL OF LOVE, A LOVE SO DEEP THAT YOU LOST YOURSELF COMPLETELY IN IT, FOREVER SACRIFICING EVERYTHING THAT MAKES YOU WHO YOU ARE...*OR!*
WOULD YOU CHOOSE A LIFE OF ISOLATION, FOREVER ABANDONING THE POSSIBILITY OF A DEEP CONNECTION WITH ANOTHER LIVING SOUL? WASTING AWAY YOUR FORMATIVE YEARS IN CRUSHING LONELINESS AND DOOMED TO DIE ALONE, LIKELY WITH WEEPING AND GNASHING OF TEETH.
BUT! YOU UNCOVER EVERY ASPECT OF YOURSELF AND LIVE A LIFE WITH GENUINE PURPOSE.
GOOD GODS.
I'D CHOOSE LOVE. I'VE FELT ISOLATION BEFORE. BEING DIFFERENT FROM YOUR FAMILY IS HARD ENOUGH. AT LEAST WITH ROMANTIC LOVE YOU FIT.
LOVE. DEFINITELY.
I FEEL YA, BRAGA. WOULDN'T BE ABOUT THE LOVE THOUGH. GIVE ME A LIFE OF ZOMBIE SEX OVER AN EXISTENCE WHERE YOUR ONLY FRIEND IS A FUCKWAND.
WAIT, CAN YOU WANK IN THE DYING ALONE PATH?
THE LOVE OPTION SOUNDS...SCARY. IT DEPENDS ON THE PERSON, MAYBE? BUT MAYBE NOT... IF YOU'RE SO IN LOVE, DOES THE INDIVIDUAL MATTER? YOUR WHOLE IDENTITY WOULD BE THE CONNECTION. AND...WHILE ON THE SURFACE THAT SOUNDS LOVELY...
OH GODS, I HATE THESE STUPID GAMES!
ISOLATION.
I'VE BEEN MARRIED. IT'S LIKE THE LOVE OPTION WITHOUT THE LOVE.
AND IF WANKING ISN'T ALLOWED FOR THE ISOLATION PATH, I CHOOSE NON-EXISTENCE.
WELL, UH. NON-EXISTENCE ISN'T AN OPTION, DEE DEE.
I'D CHOOSE LOVE. THERE'S NOTHING BETTER. MOST OF ALL, LOVE IS HOPE. THE LIGHT OF LOVE ALWAYS OUTSHINES THE DARKNESS IT CAN SOMETIMES BRING.
GODS BE DAMNED...

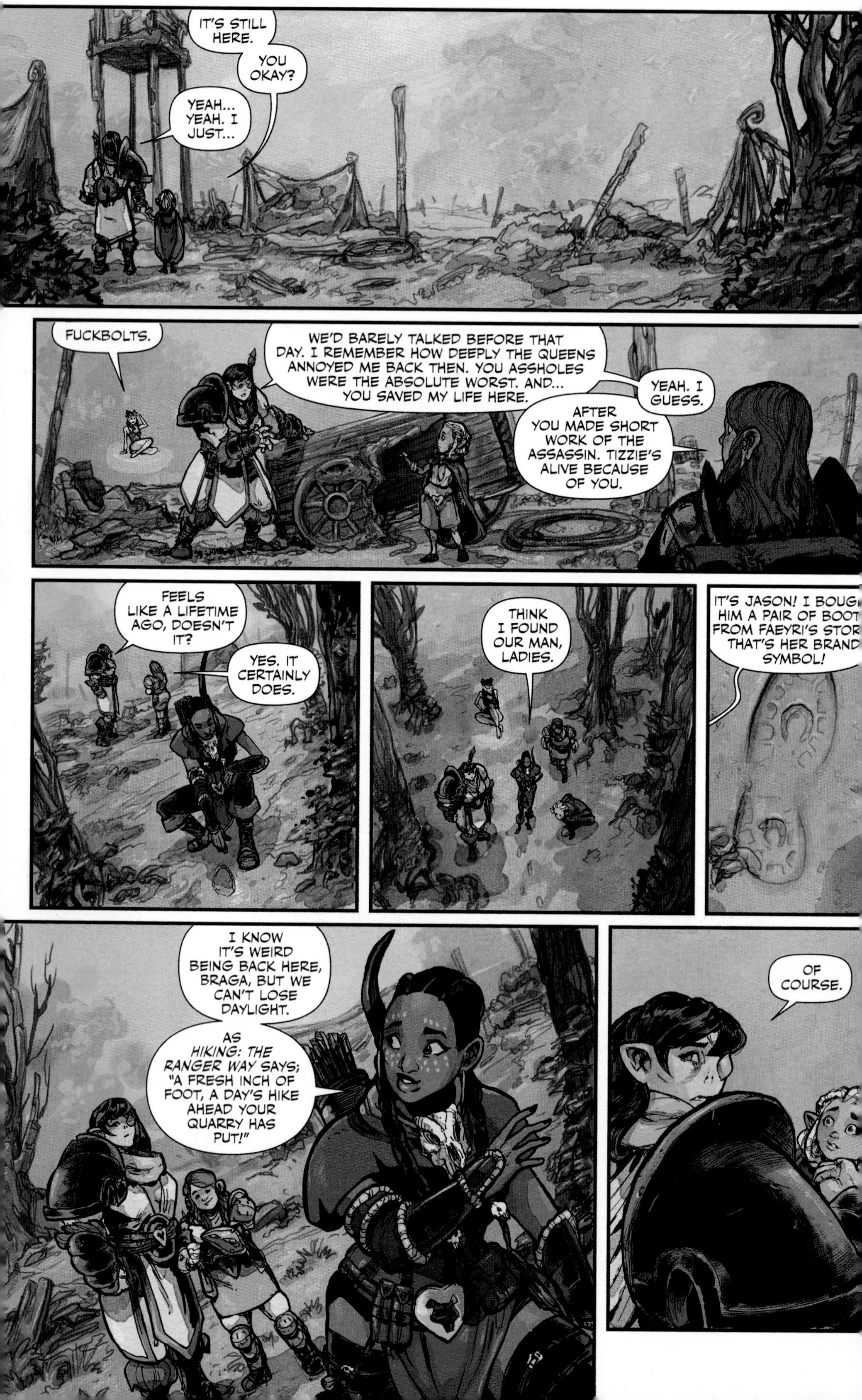
IT'S STILL HERE.
YOU OKAY?
YEAH... YEAH. I JUST...
FUCKBOLTS.
WE'D BARELY TALKED BEFORE THAT DAY. I REMEMBER HOW DEEPLY THE QUEENS ANNOYED ME BACK THEN. YOU ASSHOLES WERE THE ABSOLUTE WORST. AND... YOU SAVED MY LIFE HERE.
YEAH. I GUESS.
AFTER YOU MADE SHORT WORK OF THE ASSASSIN. TIZZIE'S ALIVE BECAUSE OF YOU.
FEELS LIKE A LIFETIME AGO, DOESN'T IT?
YES. IT CERTAINLY DOES.
THINK I FOUND OUR MAN, LADIES.
IT'S JASON! I BOUG HIM A PAIR OF BOOT FROM FAEYRI'S STOR THAT'S HER BRAND SYMBOL!
I KNOW IT'S WEIRD BEING BACK HERE, BRAGA, BUT WE CAN'T LOSE DAYLIGHT.
AS *HIKING: THE RANGER WAY* SAYS; "A FRESH INCH OF FOOT, A DAY'S HIKE AHEAD YOUR QUARRY HAS PUT!"
OF COURSE.

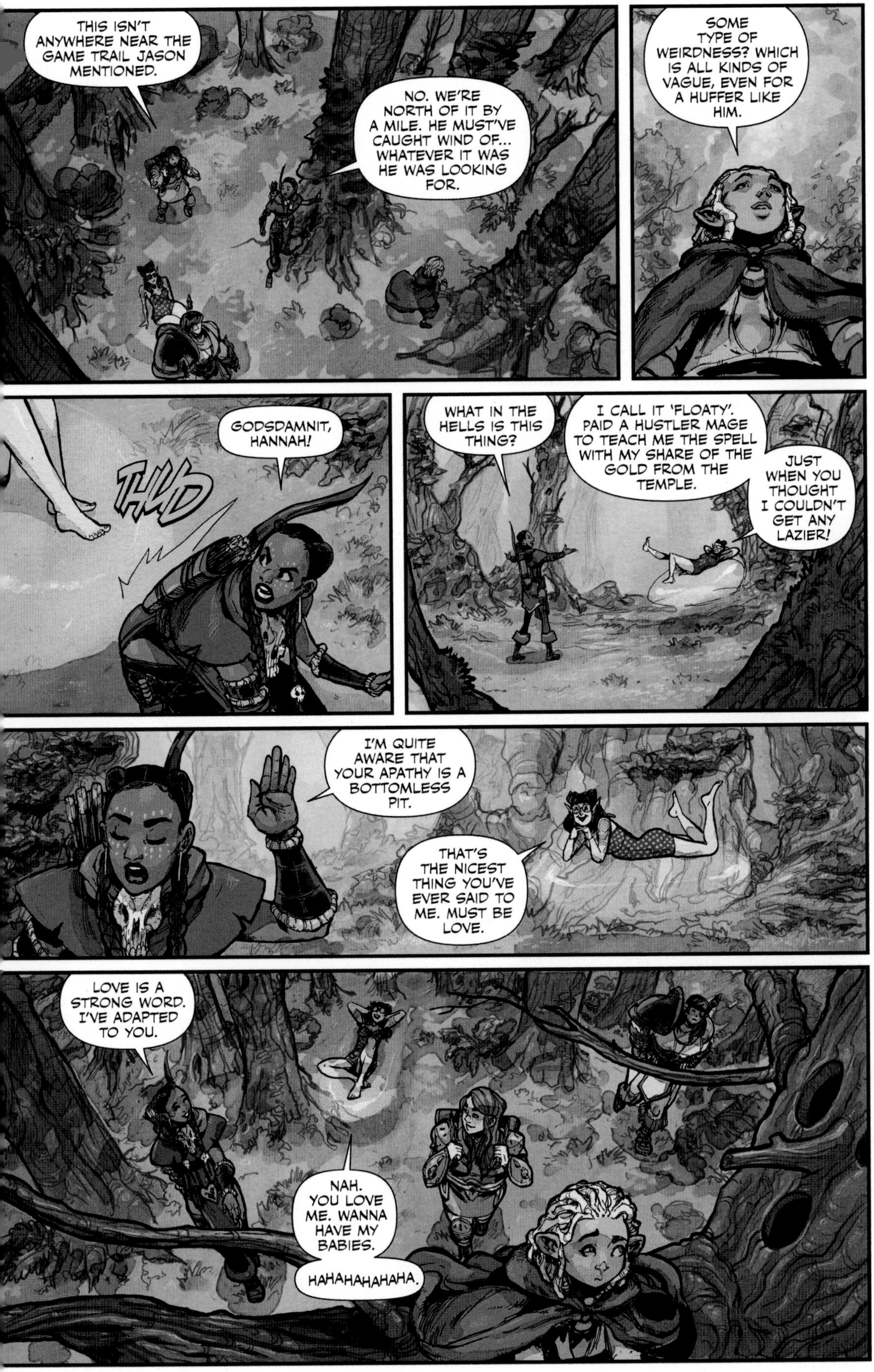
THIS ISN'T ANYWHERE NEAR THE GAME TRAIL JASON MENTIONED.
NO. WE'RE NORTH OF IT BY A MILE. HE MUST'VE CAUGHT WIND OF... WHATEVER IT WAS HE WAS LOOKING FOR.
SOME TYPE OF WEIRDNESS? WHICH IS ALL KINDS OF VAGUE, EVEN FOR A HUFFER LIKE HIM.
THUD
GODSDAMNIT, HANNAH!
WHAT IN THE HELLS IS THIS THING?
I CALL IT 'FLOATY'. PAID A HUSTLER MAGE TO TEACH ME THE SPELL WITH MY SHARE OF THE GOLD FROM THE TEMPLE.
JUST WHEN YOU THOUGHT I COULDN'T GET ANY LAZIER!
I'M QUITE AWARE THAT YOUR APATHY IS A BOTTOMLESS PIT.
THAT'S THE NICEST THING YOU'VE EVER SAID TO ME. MUST BE LOVE.
LOVE IS A STRONG WORD. I'VE ADAPTED TO YOU.
NAH. YOU LOVE ME. WANNA HAVE MY BABIES.
HAHAHAHAHAHA.

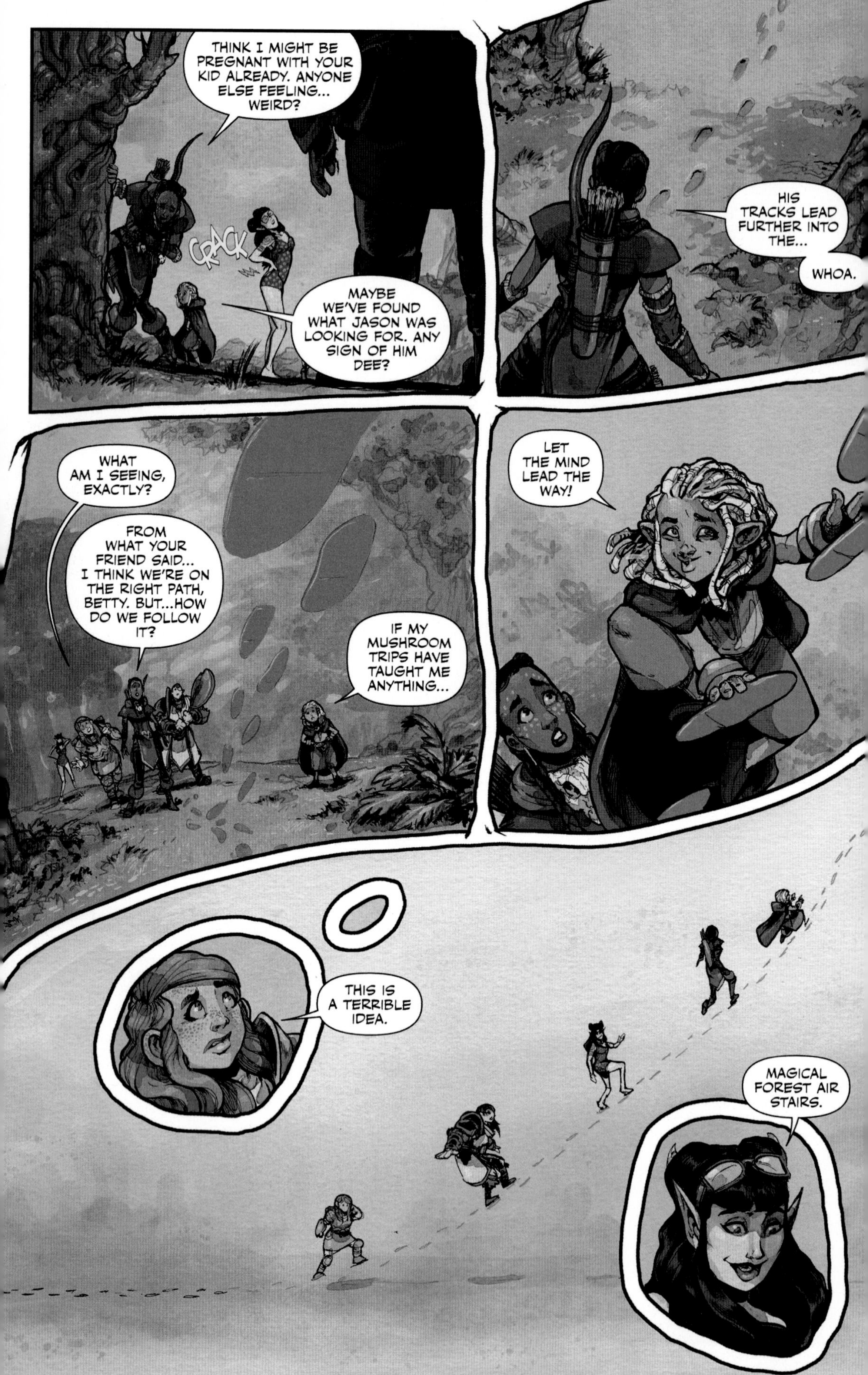
THINK I MIGHT BE PREGNANT WITH YOUR KID ALREADY. ANYONE ELSE FEELING... WEIRD?
CRACK
MAYBE WE'VE FOUND WHAT JASON WAS LOOKING FOR. ANY SIGN OF HIM DEE?
HIS TRACKS LEAD FURTHER INTO THE...
WHOA.
WHAT AM I SEEING, EXACTLY?
FROM WHAT YOUR FRIEND SAID... I THINK WE'RE ON THE RIGHT PATH, BETTY. BUT...HOW DO WE FOLLOW IT?
IF MY MUSHROOM TRIPS HAVE TAUGHT ME ANYTHING...
LET THE MIND LEAD THE WAY!
THIS IS A TERRIBLE IDEA.
MAGICAL FOREST AIR STAIRS.

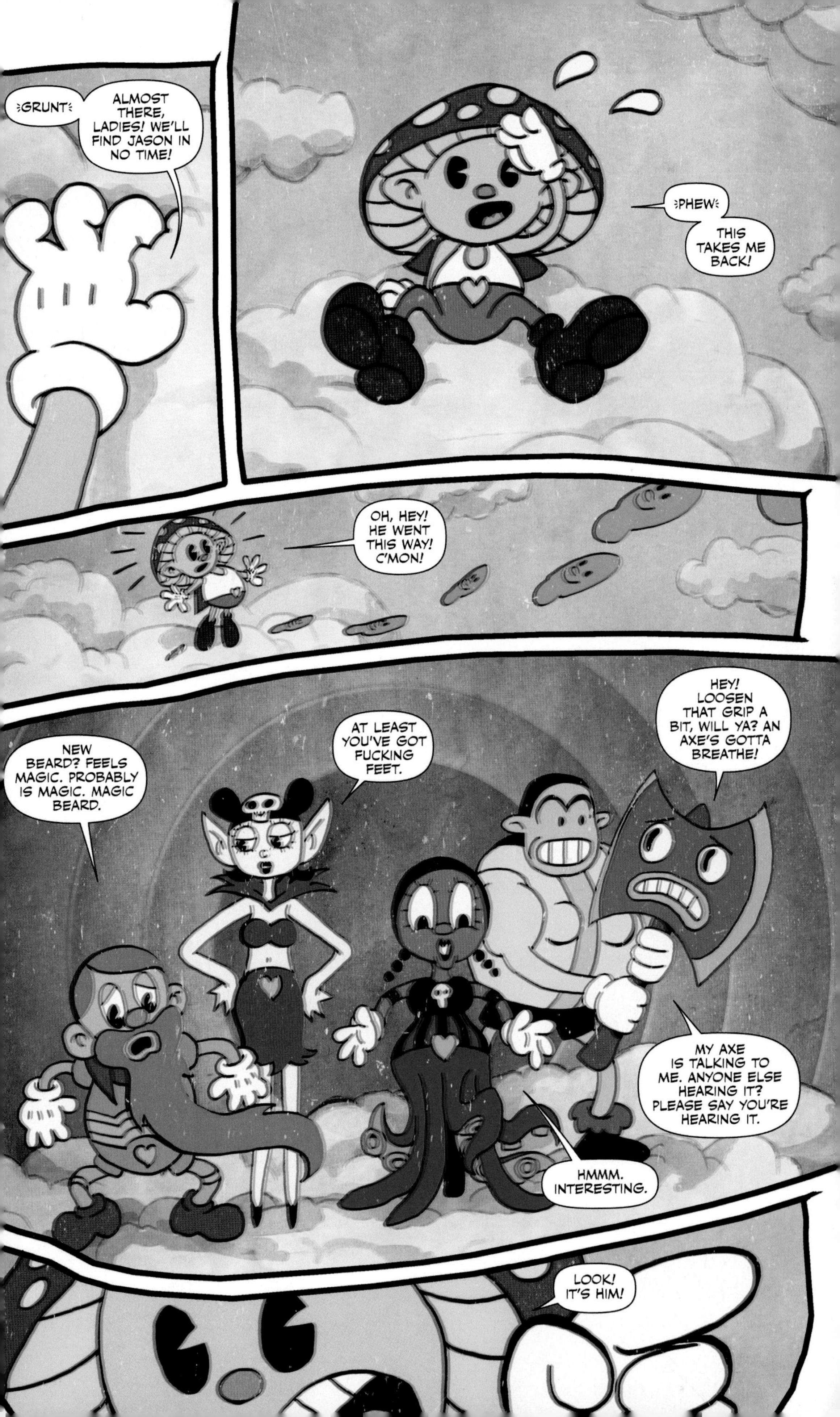
GRUNT
ALMOST THERE, LADIES! WE'LL FIND JASON IN NO TIME!
PHEW
THIS TAKES ME BACK!
OH, HEY! HE WENT THIS WAY! C'MON!
NEW BEARD? FEELS MAGIC. PROBABLY IS MAGIC. MAGIC BEARD.
AT LEAST YOU'VE GOT FUCKING FEET.
HEY! LOOSEN THAT GRIP A BIT, WILL YA? AN AXE'S GOTTA BREATHE!
MY AXE IS TALKING TO ME. ANYONE ELSE HEARING IT? PLEASE SAY YOU'RE HEARING IT.
HMMM. INTERESTING.
LOOK! IT'S HIM!

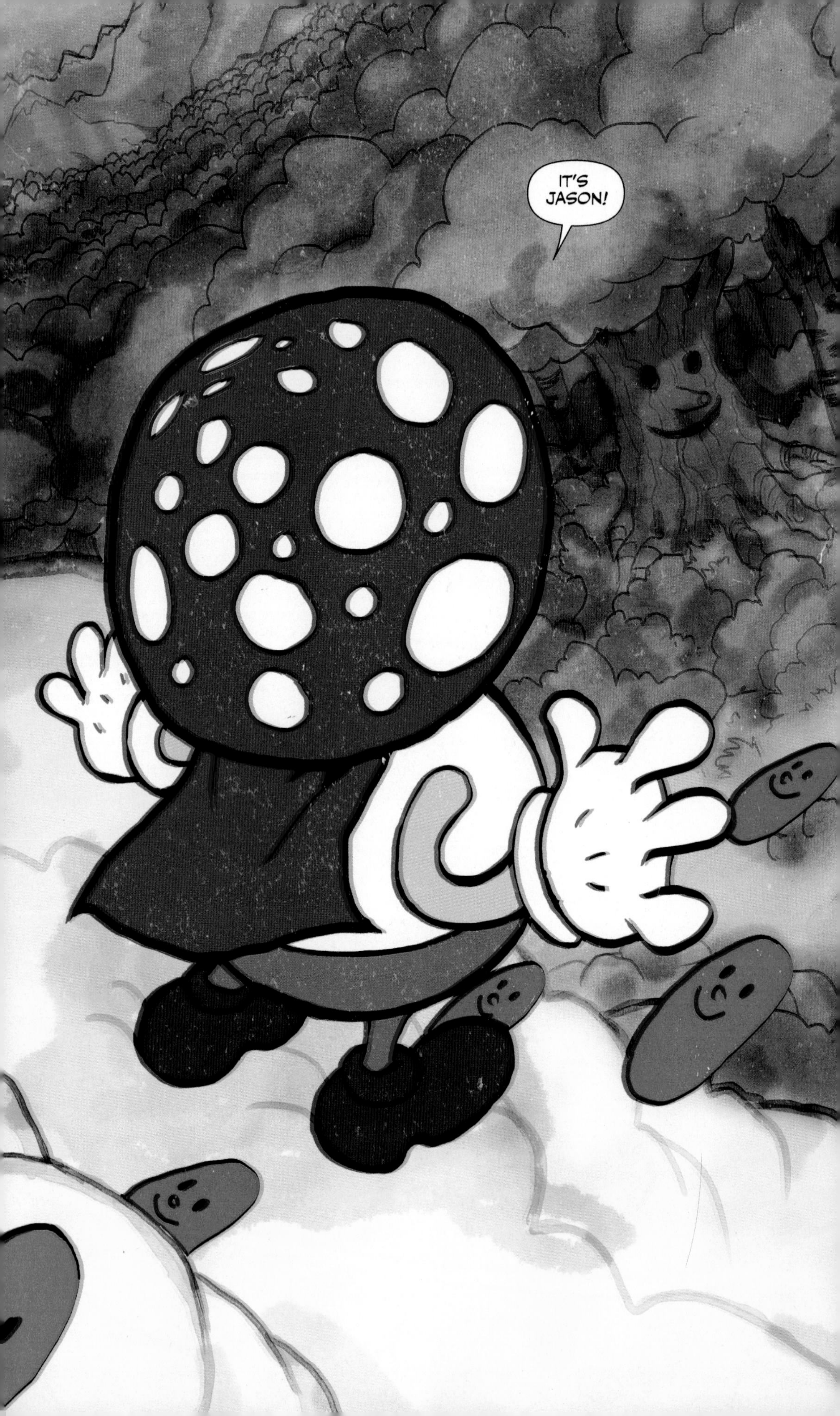
IT'S JASON!

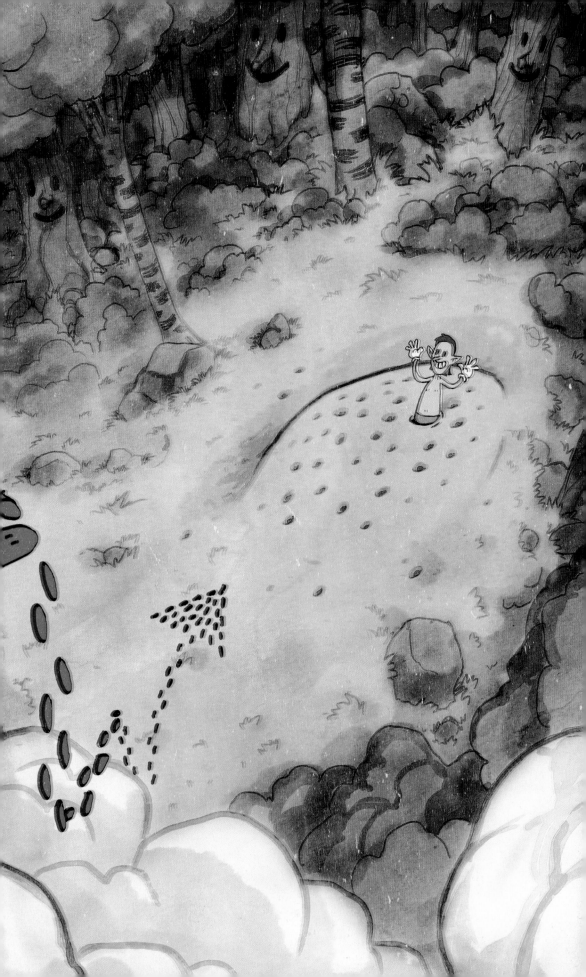

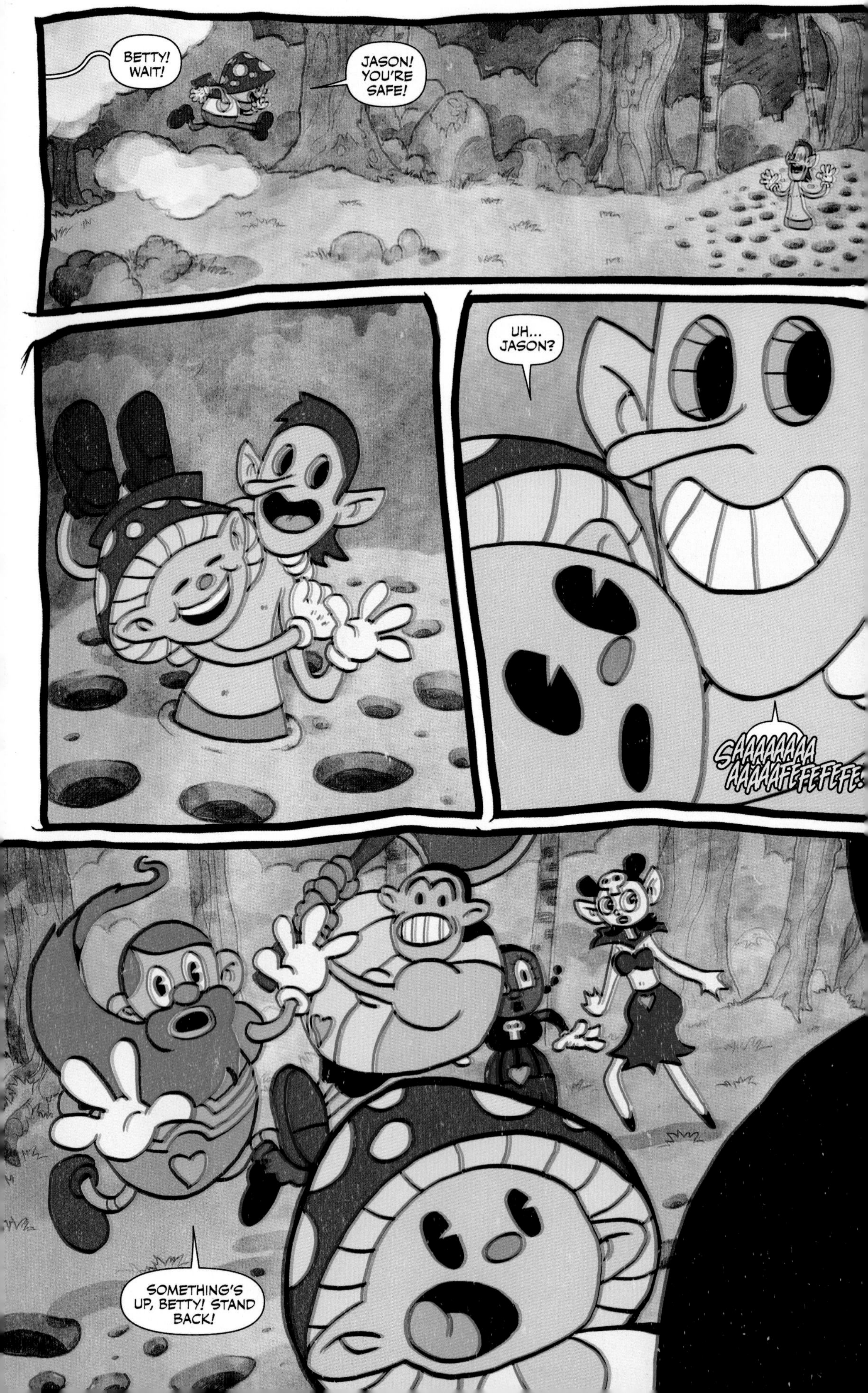
BETTY! WAIT!
JASON! YOU'RE SAFE!
UH... JASON?
SAAAAAAAA AAAAAFFFFFFFFF.
SOMETHING'S UP, BETTY! STAND BACK!

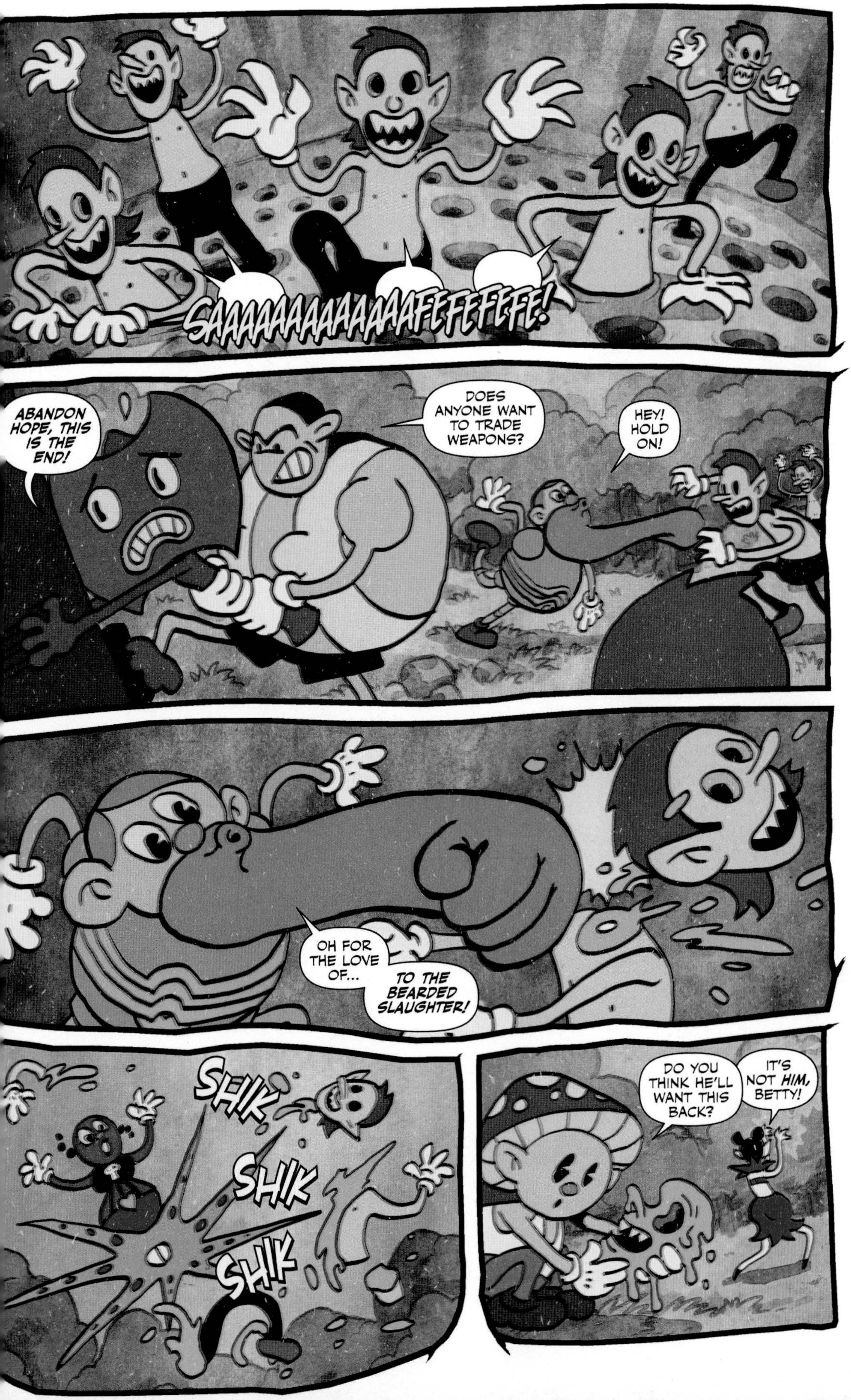
SAAAAAAAAAAAAAFEFEFEFE!
ABANDON HOPE, THIS IS THE END!
DOES ANYONE WANT TO TRADE WEAPONS?
HEY! HOLD ON!
OH FOR THE LOVE OF...
TO THE BEARDED SLAUGHTER!
SHIK
SHIK
SHIK
DO YOU THINK HE'LL WANT THIS BACK?
IT'S NOT HIM, BETTY!

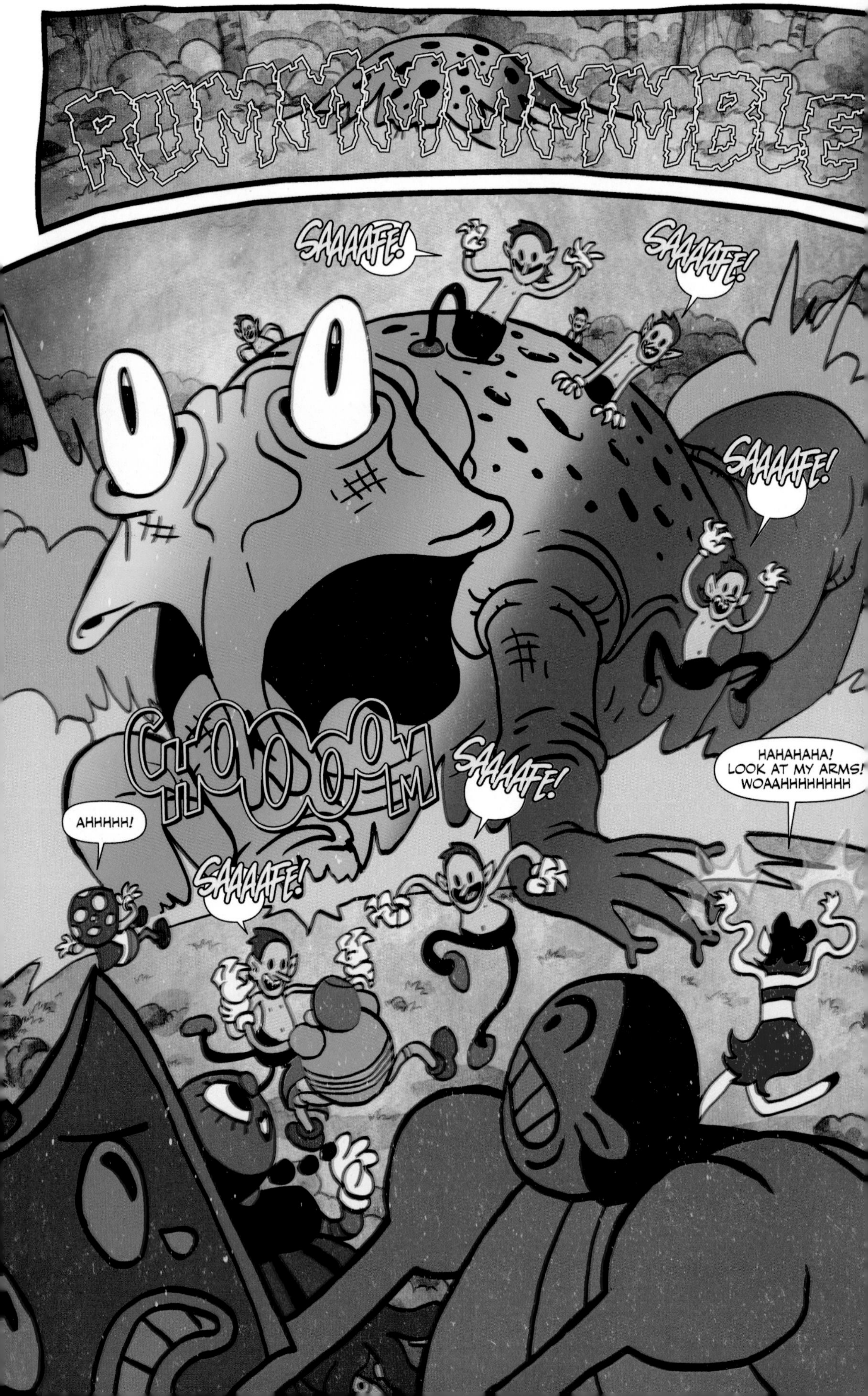
RUMMMMMMMBLE
SAAAAFE!
SAAAAFE!
SAAAAFE!
CHOOOOOM
SAAAAFE!
HAHAHAHA! LOOK AT MY ARMS! WOAAHHHHHHHH
AHHHHH!
SAAAAFE!

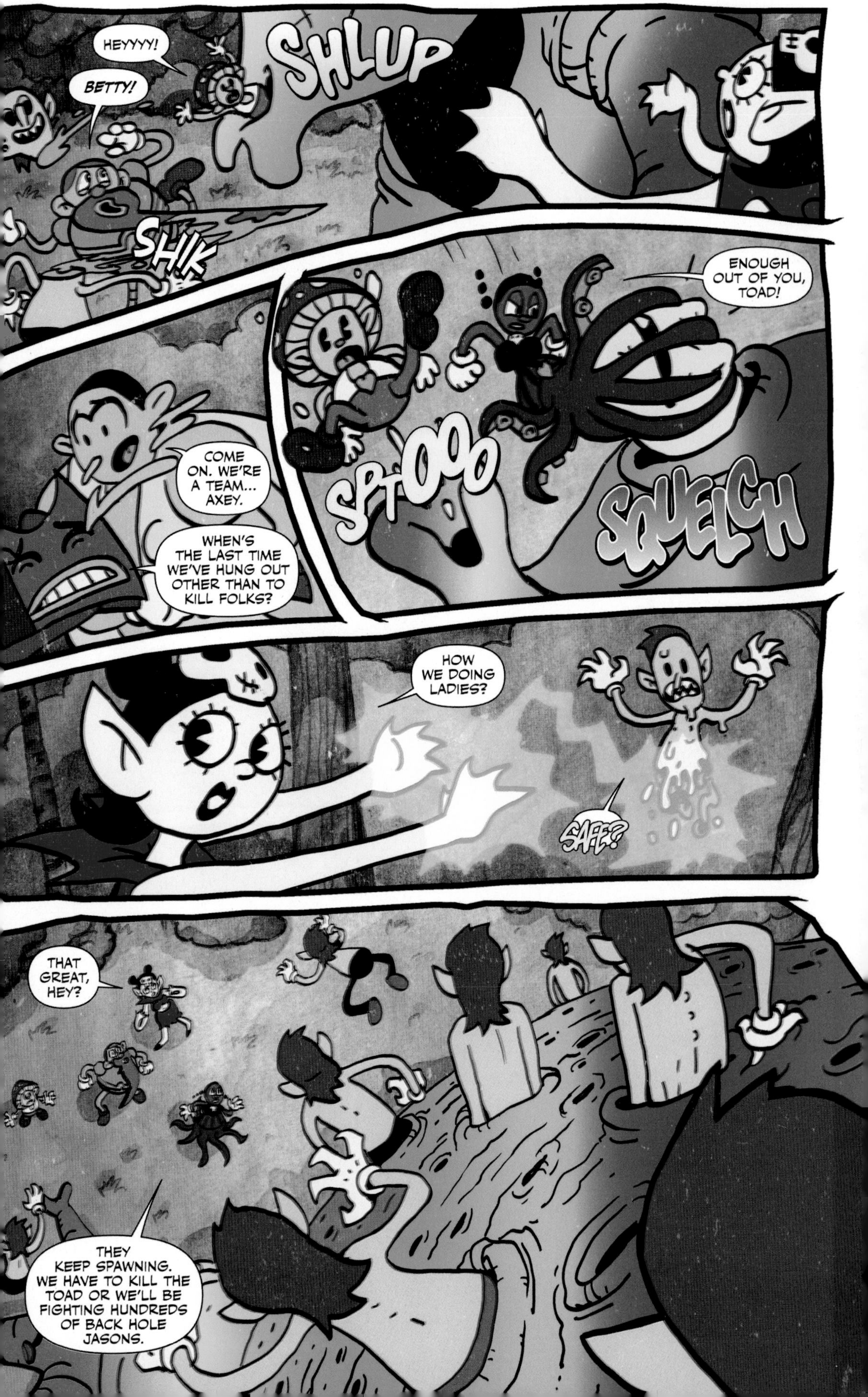
HEYYYY!
BETTY!
SHLUP
SHIK
COME ON. WE'RE A TEAM... AXEY.
WHEN'S THE LAST TIME WE'VE HUNG OUT OTHER THAN TO KILL FOLKS?
ENOUGH OUT OF YOU, TOAD!
SPTOOO
SQUELCH
HOW WE DOING LADIES?
SAFE?
THAT GREAT, HEY?
THEY KEEP SPAWNING. WE HAVE TO KILL THE TOAD OR WE'LL BE FIGHTING HUNDREDS OF BACK HOLE JASONS.

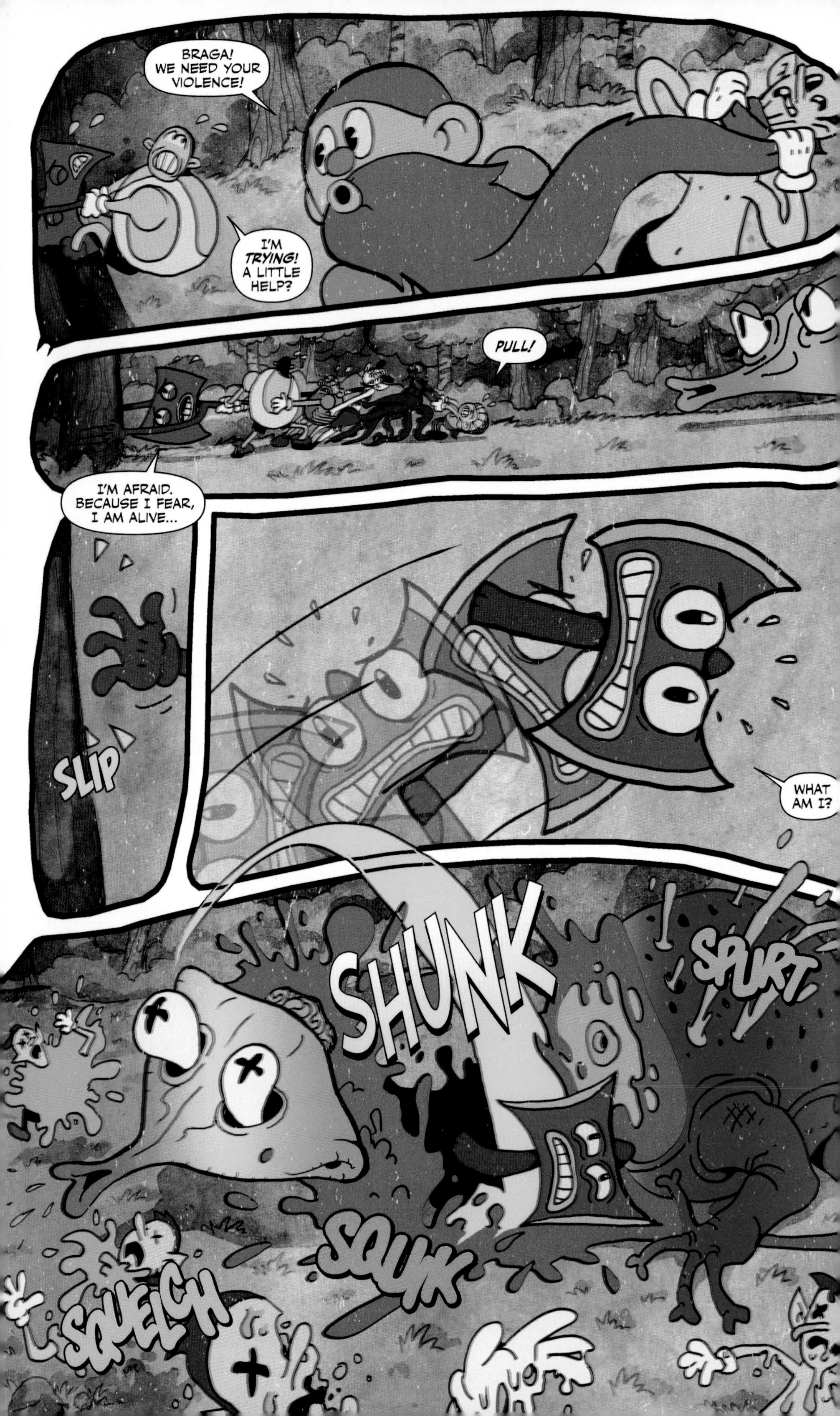
BRAGA! WE NEED YOUR VIOLENCE!
I'M *TRYING!* A LITTLE HELP?
PULL!
I'M AFRAID. BECAUSE I FEAR, I AM ALIVE...
SLIP
WHAT AM I?
SHUNK
SPURT
SQUIK
SQUELCH

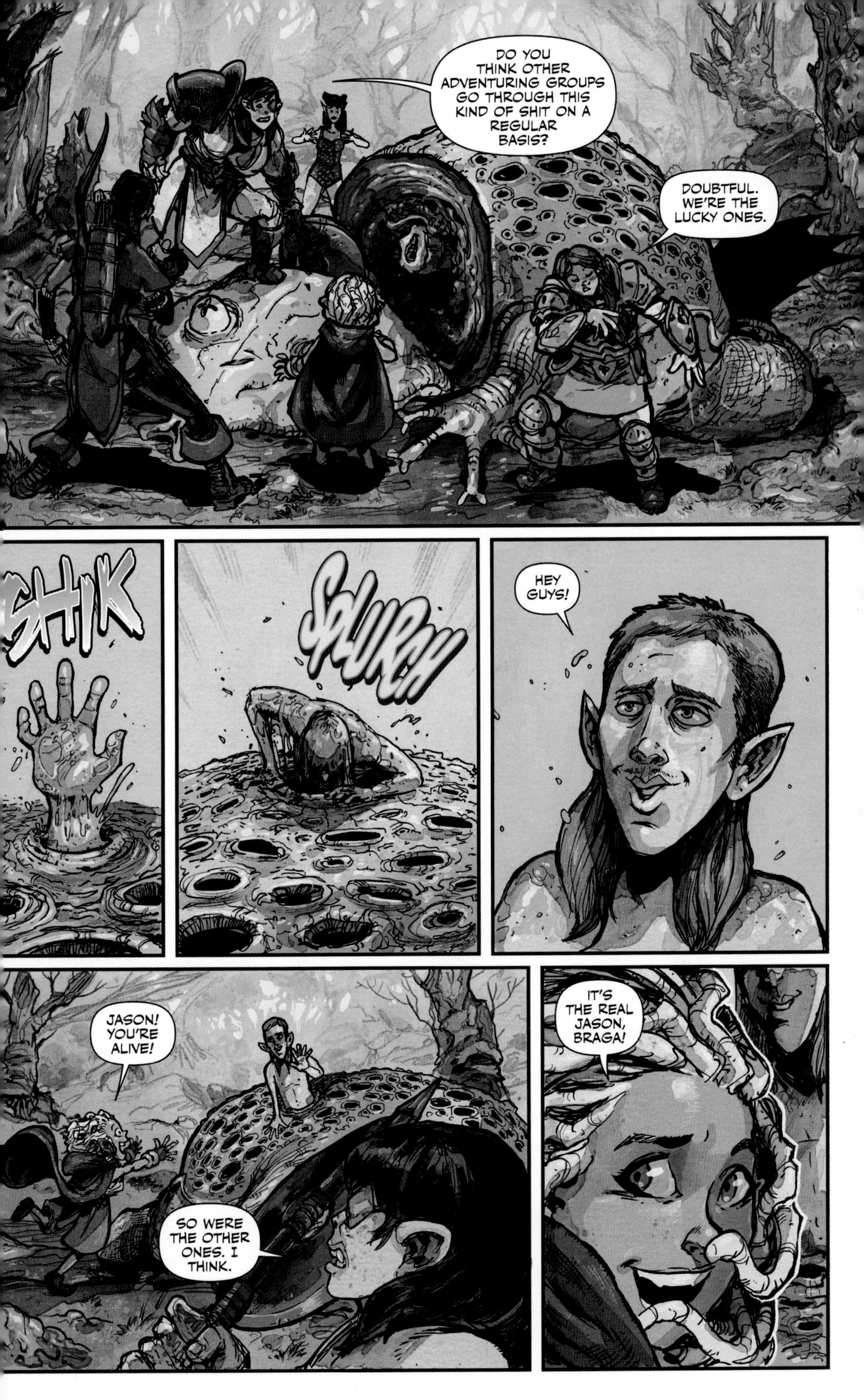

DO YOU THINK OTHER ADVENTURING GROUPS GO THROUGH THIS KIND OF SHIT ON A REGULAR BASIS?
DOUBTFUL. WE'RE THE LUCKY ONES.
SHIK
SPLURCH
HEY GUYS!
JASON! YOU'RE ALIVE!
SO WERE THE OTHER ONES. I THINK.
IT'S THE REAL JASON, BRAGA!

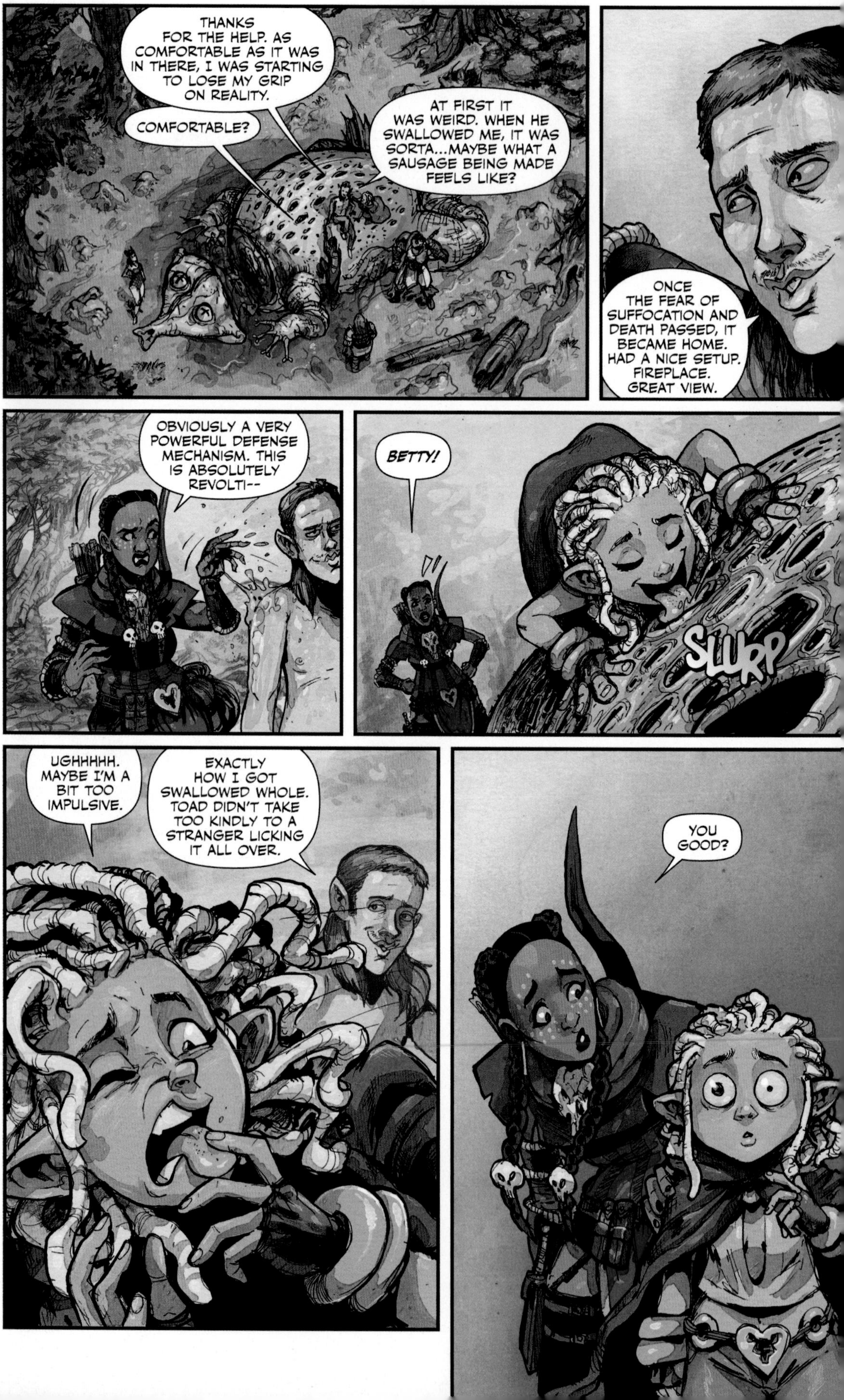

THANKS FOR THE HELP. AS COMFORTABLE AS IT WAS IN THERE, I WAS STARTING TO LOSE MY GRIP ON REALITY.
COMFORTABLE?
AT FIRST IT WAS WEIRD. WHEN HE SWALLOWED ME, IT WAS SORTA...MAYBE WHAT A SAUSAGE BEING MADE FEELS LIKE?
ONCE THE FEAR OF SUFFOCATION AND DEATH PASSED, IT BECAME HOME. HAD A NICE SETUP. FIREPLACE. GREAT VIEW.
OBVIOUSLY A VERY POWERFUL DEFENSE MECHANISM. THIS IS ABSOLUTELY REVOLTI--
BETTY!
SLURP
UGHHHHH. MAYBE I'M A BIT TOO IMPULSIVE.
EXACTLY HOW I GOT SWALLOWED WHOLE. TOAD DIDN'T TAKE TOO KINDLY TO A STRANGER LICKING IT ALL OVER.
YOU GOOD?

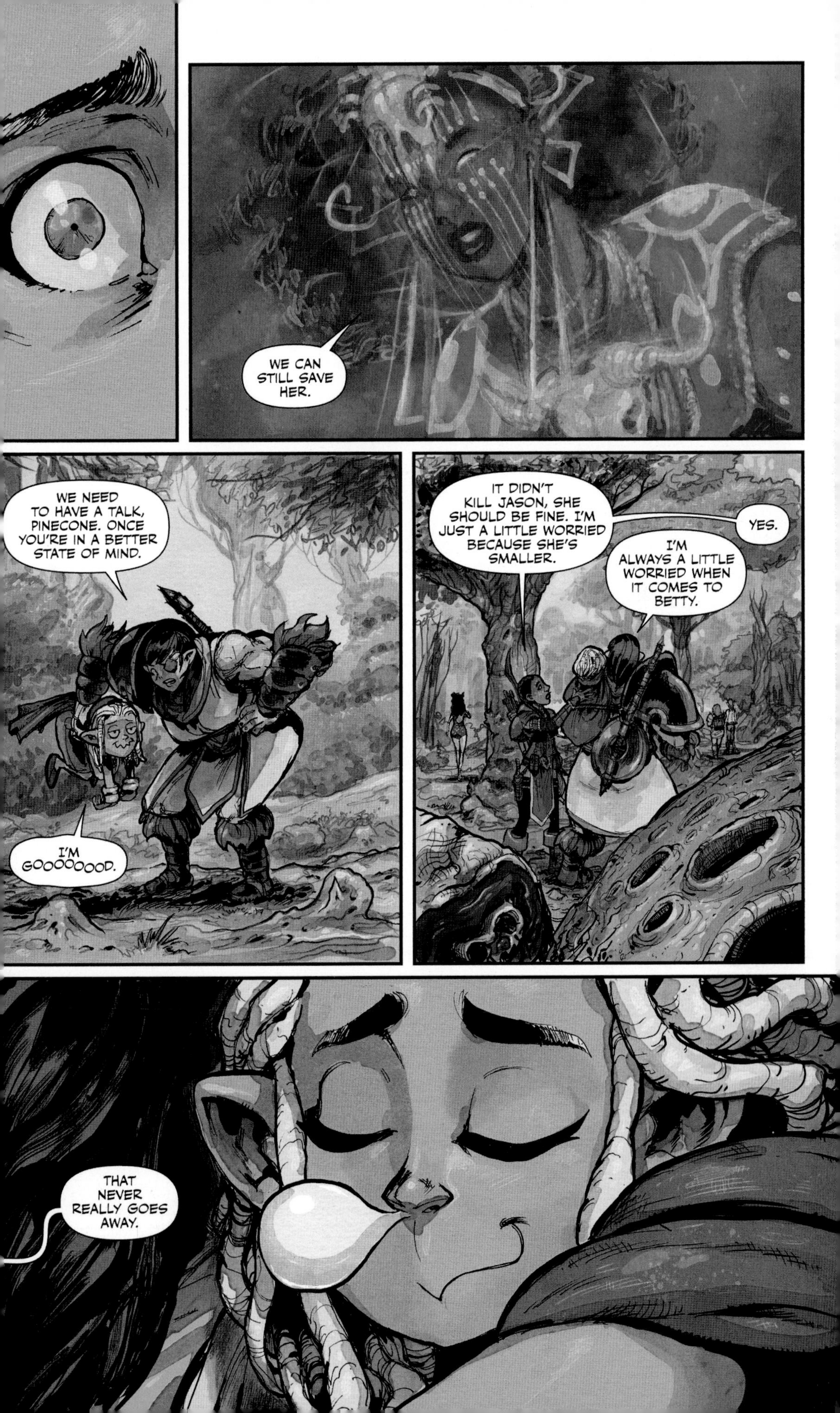
WE CAN STILL SAVE HER.
WE NEED TO HAVE A TALK, PINECONE. ONCE YOU'RE IN A BETTER STATE OF MIND.
I'M GOOOOOOOD.
IT DIDN'T KILL JASON, SHE SHOULD BE FINE. I'M JUST A LITTLE WORRIED BECAUSE SHE'S SMALLER.
YES.
I'M ALWAYS A LITTLE WORRIED WHEN IT COMES TO BETTY.
THAT NEVER REALLY GOES AWAY.

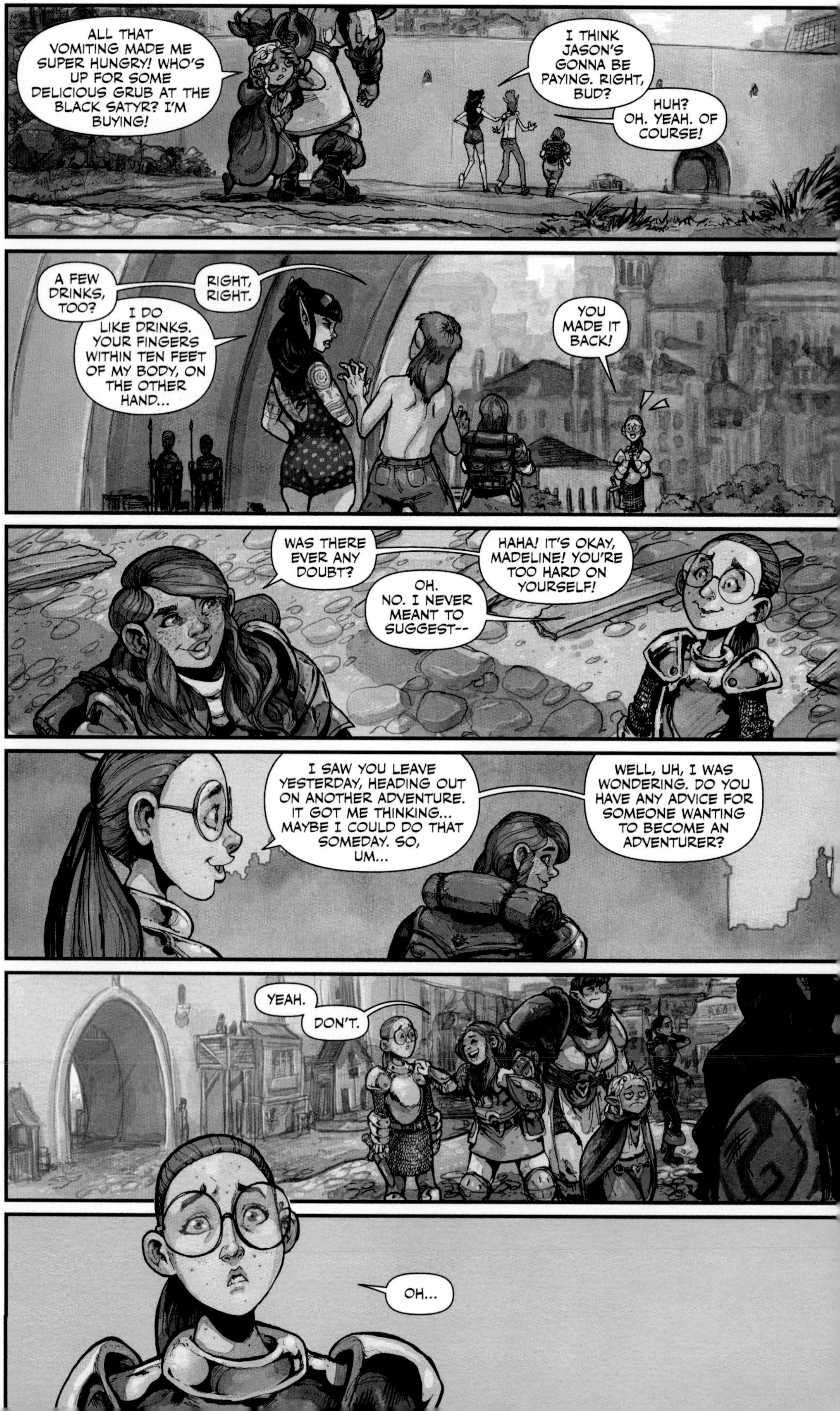

ALL THAT VOMITING MADE ME SUPER HUNGRY! WHO'S UP FOR SOME DELICIOUS GRUB AT THE BLACK SATYR? I'M BUYING!
I THINK JASON'S GONNA BE PAYING. RIGHT, BUD?
HUH? OH. YEAH. OF COURSE!
A FEW DRINKS, TOO?
RIGHT, RIGHT.
I DO LIKE DRINKS. YOUR FINGERS WITHIN TEN FEET OF MY BODY, ON THE OTHER HAND...
YOU MADE IT BACK!
WAS THERE EVER ANY DOUBT?
OH. NO. I NEVER MEANT TO SUGGEST--
HAHA! IT'S OKAY, MADELINE! YOU'RE TOO HARD ON YOURSELF!
I SAW YOU LEAVE YESTERDAY, HEADING OUT ON ANOTHER ADVENTURE. IT GOT ME THINKING... MAYBE I COULD DO THAT SOMEDAY. SO, UM...
WELL, UH, I WAS WONDERING. DO YOU HAVE ANY ADVICE FOR SOMEONE WANTING TO BECOME AN ADVENTURER?
YEAH.
DON'T.
OH...

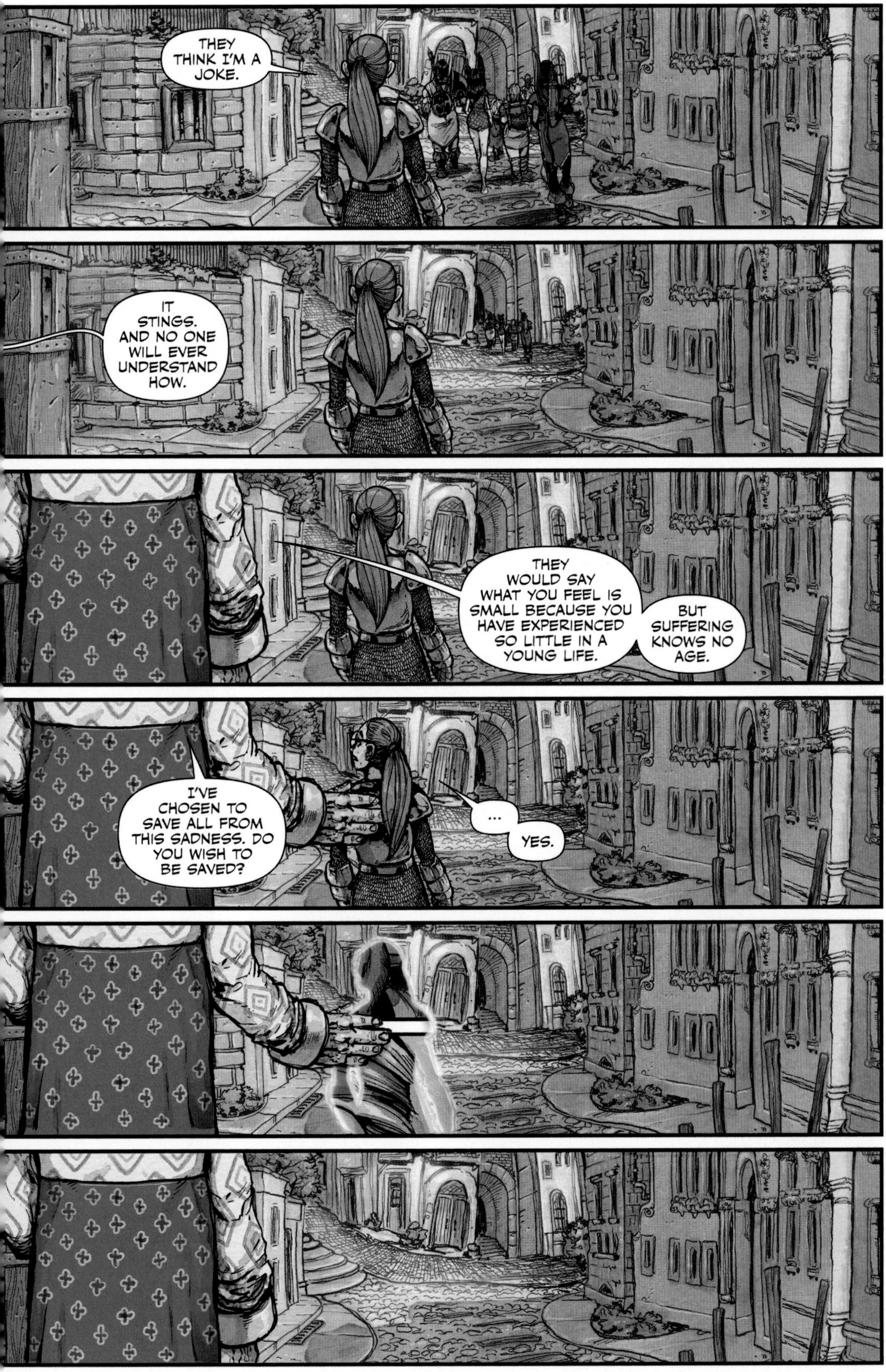
THEY THINK I'M A JOKE.
IT STINGS. AND NO ONE WILL EVER UNDERSTAND HOW.
THEY WOULD SAY WHAT YOU FEEL IS SMALL BECAUSE YOU HAVE EXPERIENCED SO LITTLE IN A YOUNG LIFE.
BUT SUFFERING KNOWS NO AGE.
I'VE CHOSEN TO SAVE ALL FROM THIS SADNESS. DO YOU WISH TO BE SAVED?
...
YES.

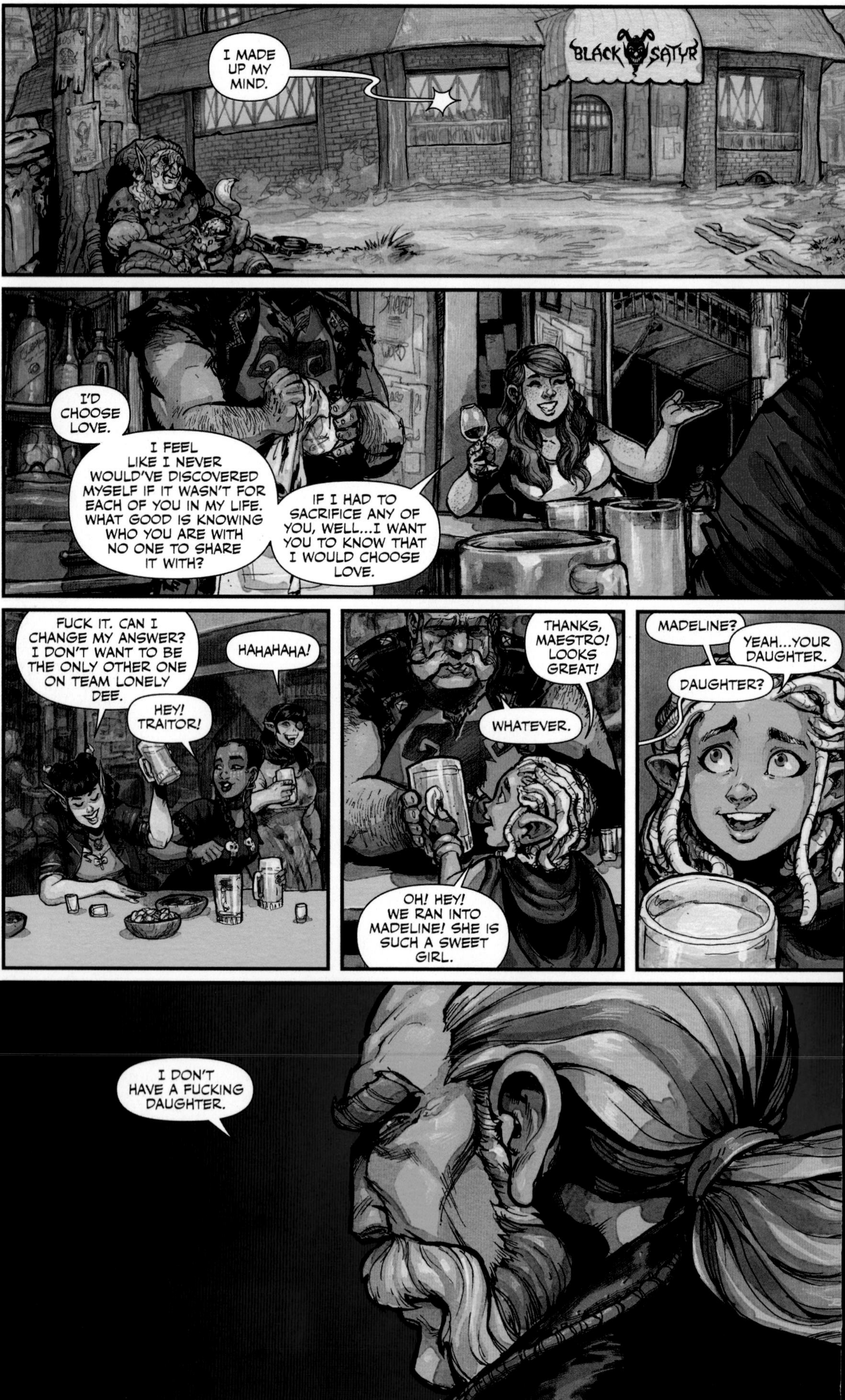
I MADE UP MY MIND.
BLACK SATYR
I'D CHOOSE LOVE.
I FEEL LIKE I NEVER WOULD'VE DISCOVERED MYSELF IF IT WASN'T FOR EACH OF YOU IN MY LIFE. WHAT GOOD IS KNOWING WHO YOU ARE WITH NO ONE TO SHARE IT WITH?
IF I HAD TO SACRIFICE ANY OF YOU, WELL...I WANT YOU TO KNOW THAT I WOULD CHOOSE LOVE.
FUCK IT. CAN I CHANGE MY ANSWER? I DON'T WANT TO BE THE ONLY OTHER ONE ON TEAM LONELY DEE.
HAHAHAHA!
HEY! TRAITOR!
THANKS, MAESTRO! LOOKS GREAT!
WHATEVER.
OH! HEY! WE RAN INTO MADELINE! SHE IS SUCH A SWEET GIRL.
MADELINE?
YEAH...YOUR DAUGHTER.
DAUGHTER?
I DON'T HAVE A FUCKING DAUGHTER.

CHAPTER SEVEN

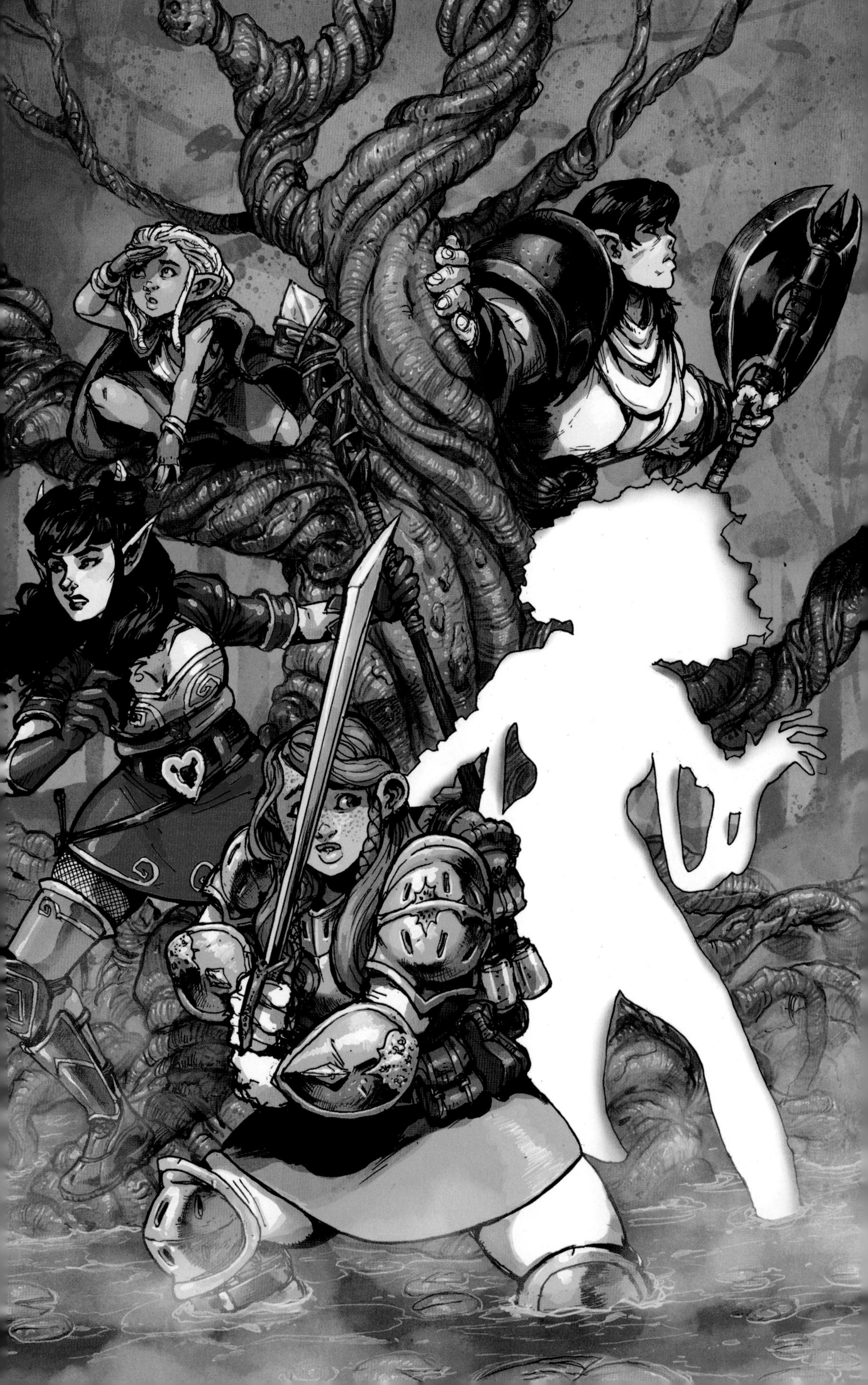

Issue 7 cover B by
JIM VALENTINO and OWEN GIENI

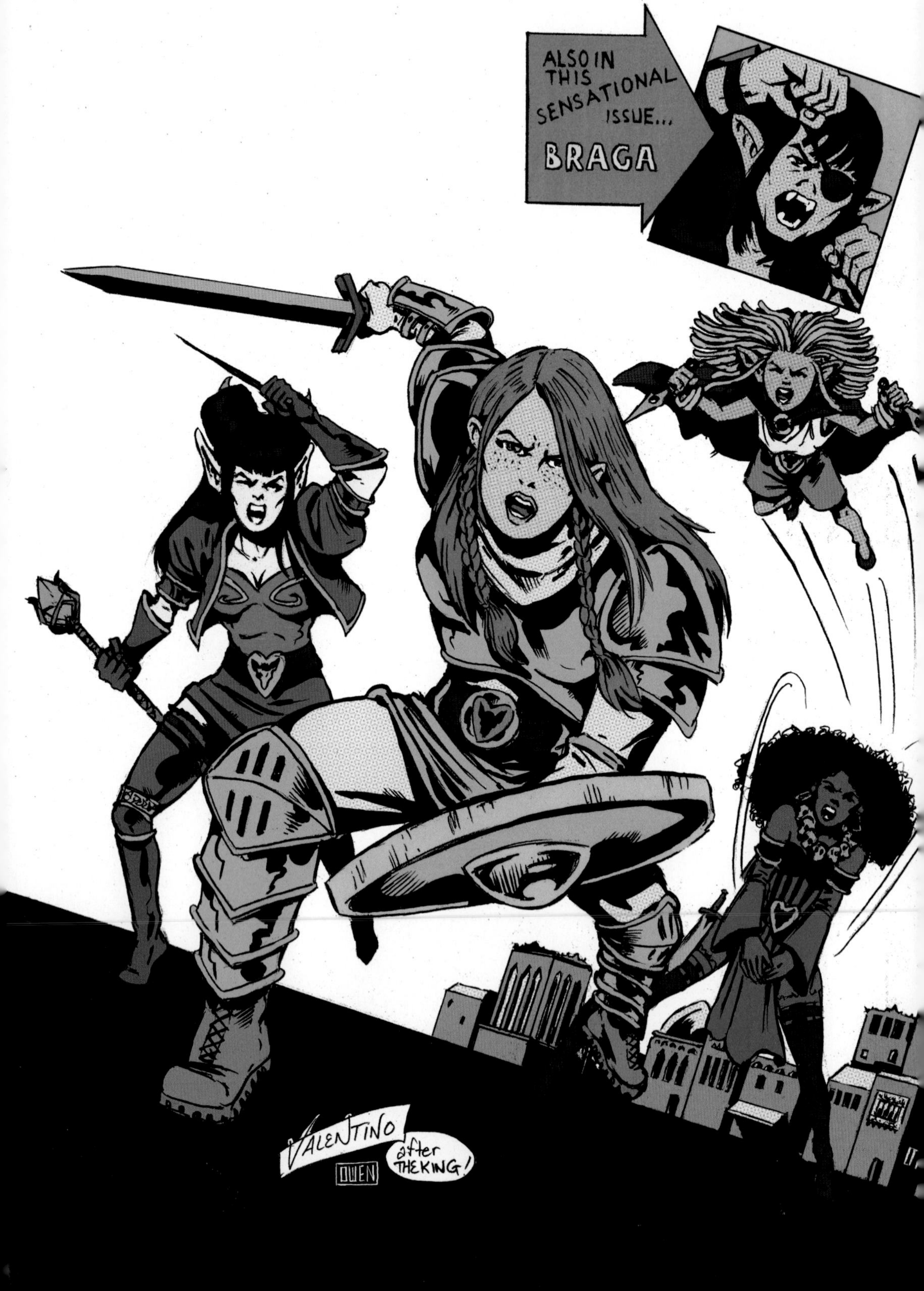
ALSO IN THIS SENSATIONAL ISSUE...
BRAGA
VALENTINO
OWEN
after THE KING!

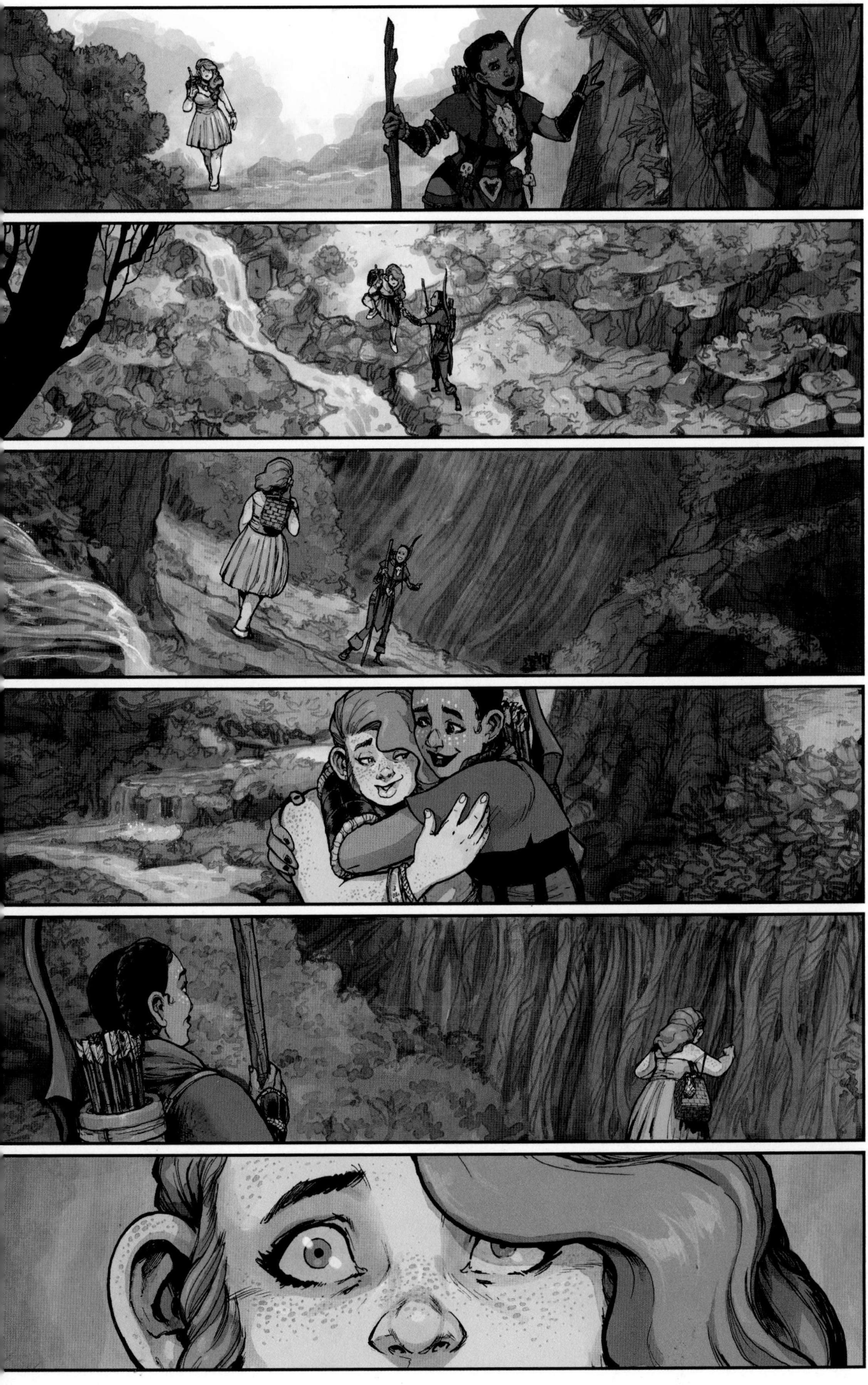

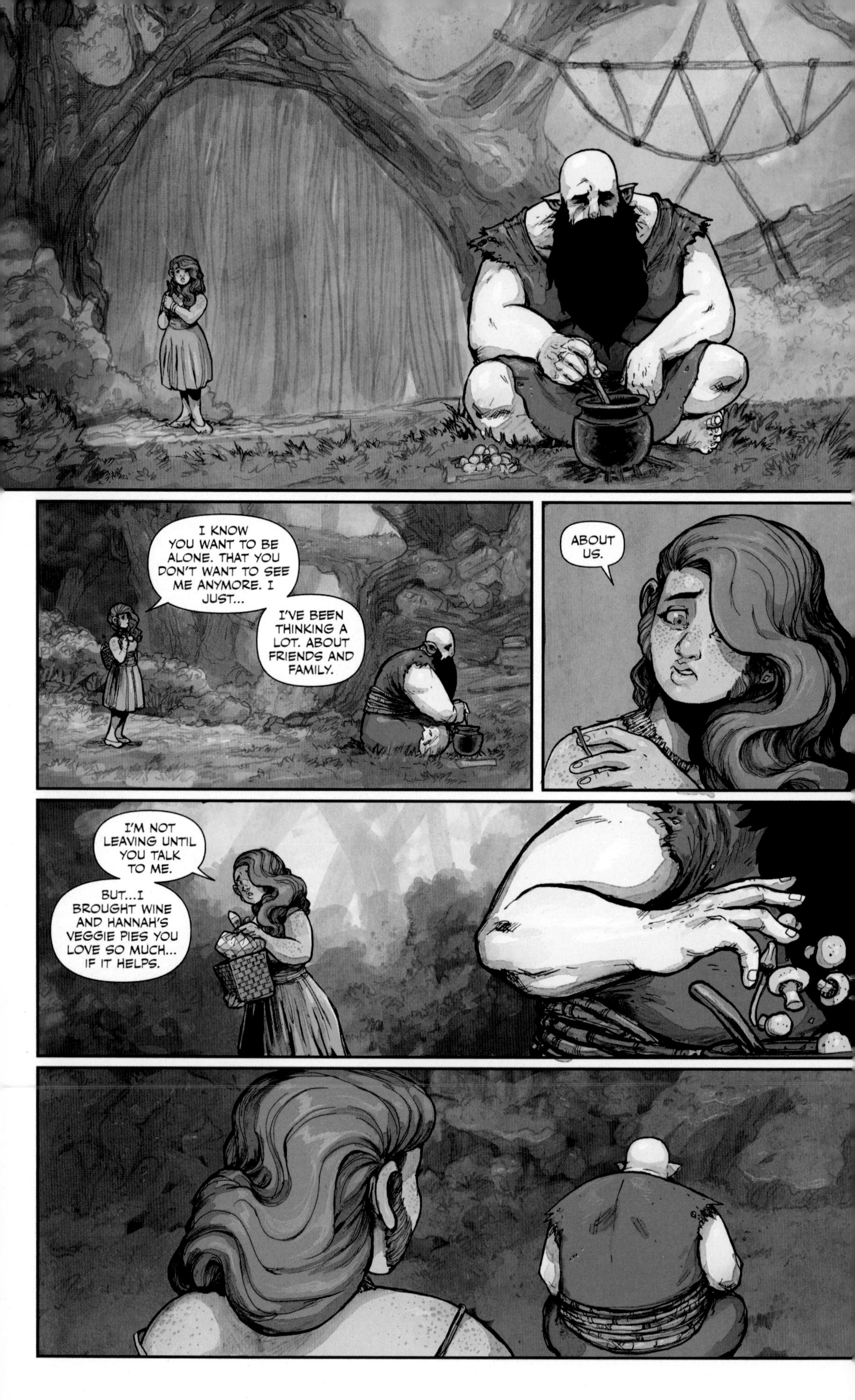
I KNOW YOU WANT TO BE ALONE. THAT YOU DON'T WANT TO SEE ME ANYMORE. I JUST...
I'VE BEEN THINKING A LOT. ABOUT FRIENDS AND FAMILY.
ABOUT US.
I'M NOT LEAVING UNTIL YOU TALK TO ME.
BUT...I BROUGHT WINE AND HANNAH'S VEGGIE PIES YOU LOVE SO MUCH... IF IT HELPS.

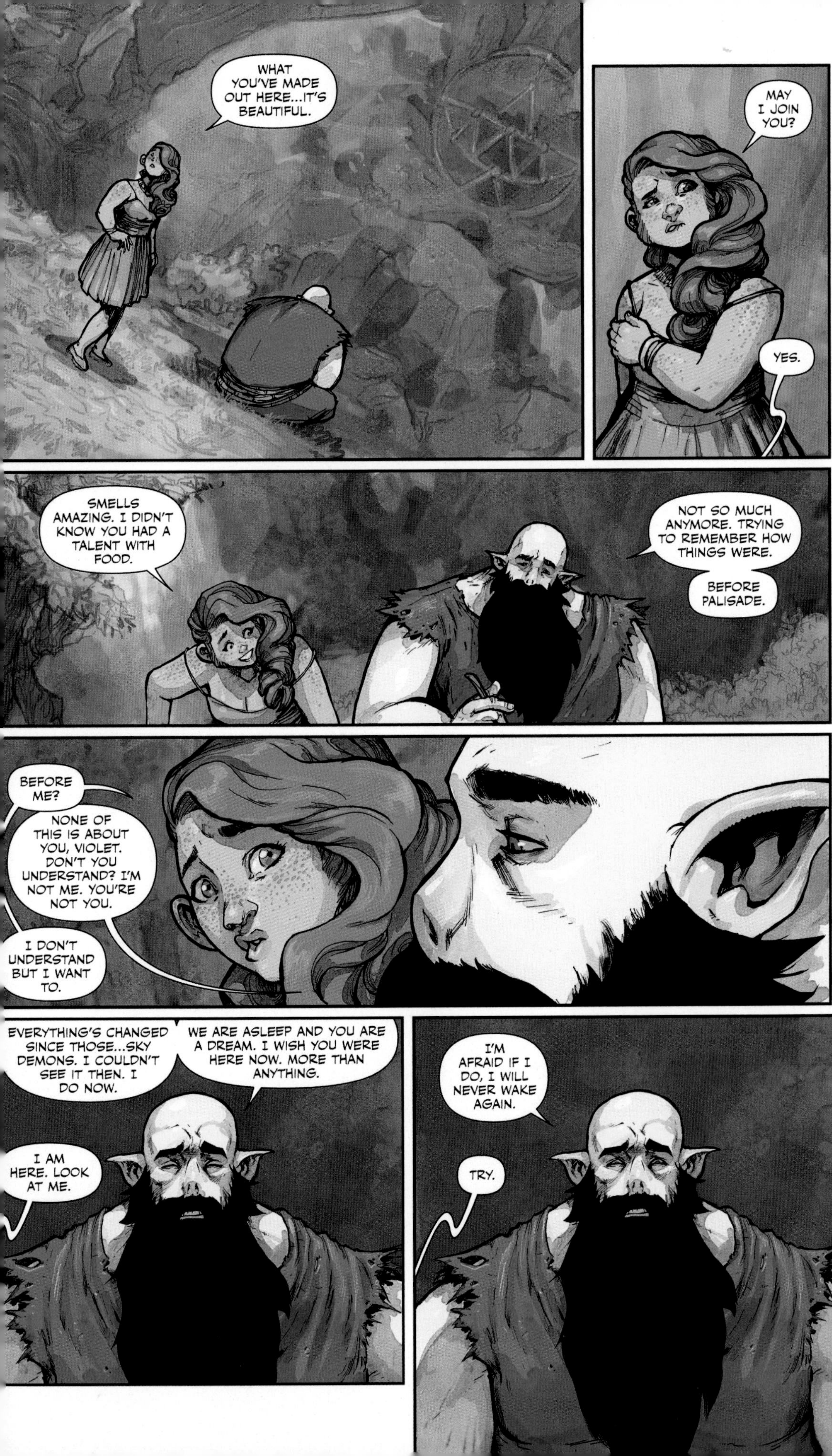
WHAT YOU'VE MADE OUT HERE...IT'S BEAUTIFUL.
MAY I JOIN YOU?
YES.
SMELLS AMAZING. I DIDN'T KNOW YOU HAD A TALENT WITH FOOD.
NOT SO MUCH ANYMORE. TRYING TO REMEMBER HOW THINGS WERE.
BEFORE PALISADE.
BEFORE ME?
NONE OF THIS IS ABOUT YOU, VIOLET. DON'T YOU UNDERSTAND? I'M NOT ME. YOU'RE NOT YOU.
I DON'T UNDERSTAND BUT I WANT TO.
EVERYTHING'S CHANGED SINCE THOSE...SKY DEMONS. I COULDN'T SEE IT THEN. I DO NOW.
WE ARE ASLEEP AND YOU ARE A DREAM. I WISH YOU WERE HERE NOW. MORE THAN ANYTHING.
I AM HERE. LOOK AT ME.
I'M AFRAID IF I DO, I WILL NEVER WAKE AGAIN.
TRY.

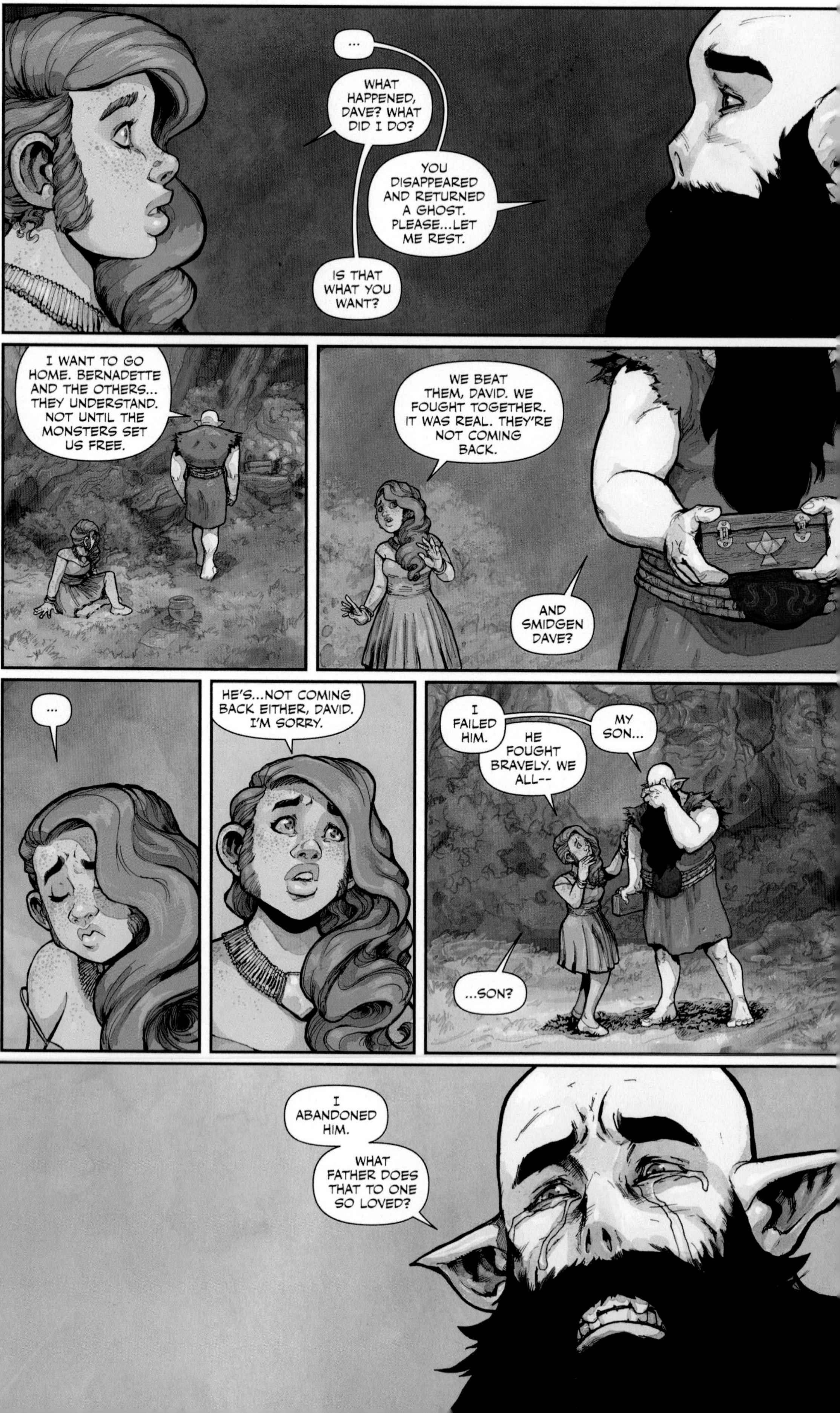
...
WHAT HAPPENED, DAVE? WHAT DID I DO?
YOU DISAPPEARED AND RETURNED A GHOST. PLEASE...LET ME REST.
IS THAT WHAT YOU WANT?
I WANT TO GO HOME. BERNADETTE AND THE OTHERS... THEY UNDERSTAND. NOT UNTIL THE MONSTERS SET US FREE.
WE BEAT THEM, DAVID. WE FOUGHT TOGETHER. IT WAS REAL. THEY'RE NOT COMING BACK.
AND SMIDGEN DAVE?
...
HE'S...NOT COMING BACK EITHER, DAVID. I'M SORRY.
I FAILED HIM.
HE FOUGHT BRAVELY. WE ALL--
MY SON...
...SON?
I ABANDONED HIM.
WHAT FATHER DOES THAT TO ONE SO LOVED?

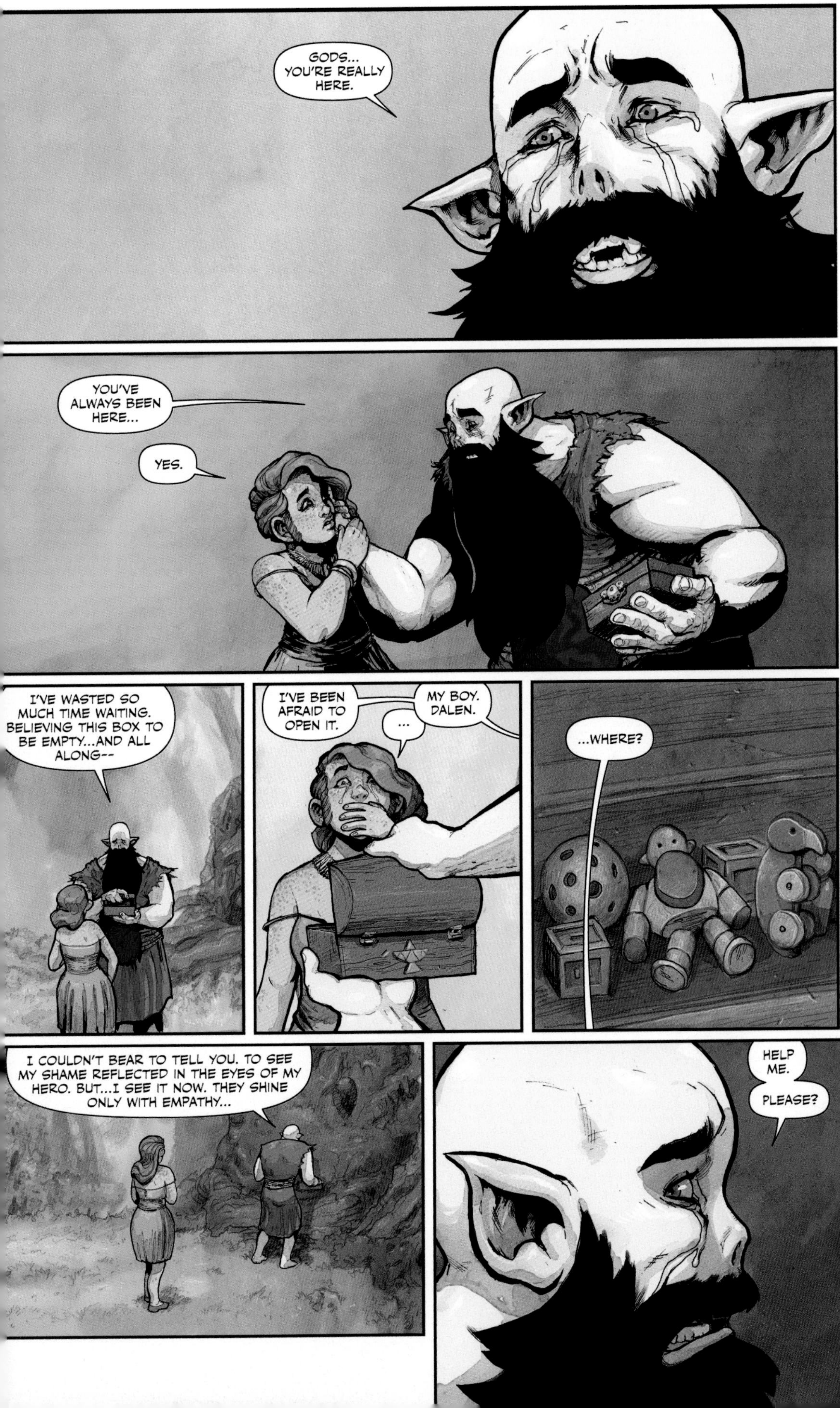
GODS... YOU'RE REALLY HERE.
YOU'VE ALWAYS BEEN HERE...
YES.
I'VE WASTED SO MUCH TIME WAITING. BELIEVING THIS BOX TO BE EMPTY...AND ALL ALONG--
I'VE BEEN AFRAID TO OPEN IT.
...
MY BOY. DALEN.
...WHERE?
I COULDN'T BEAR TO TELL YOU. TO SEE MY SHAME REFLECTED IN THE EYES OF MY HERO. BUT...I SEE IT NOW. THEY SHINE ONLY WITH EMPATHY...
HELP ME.
PLEASE?

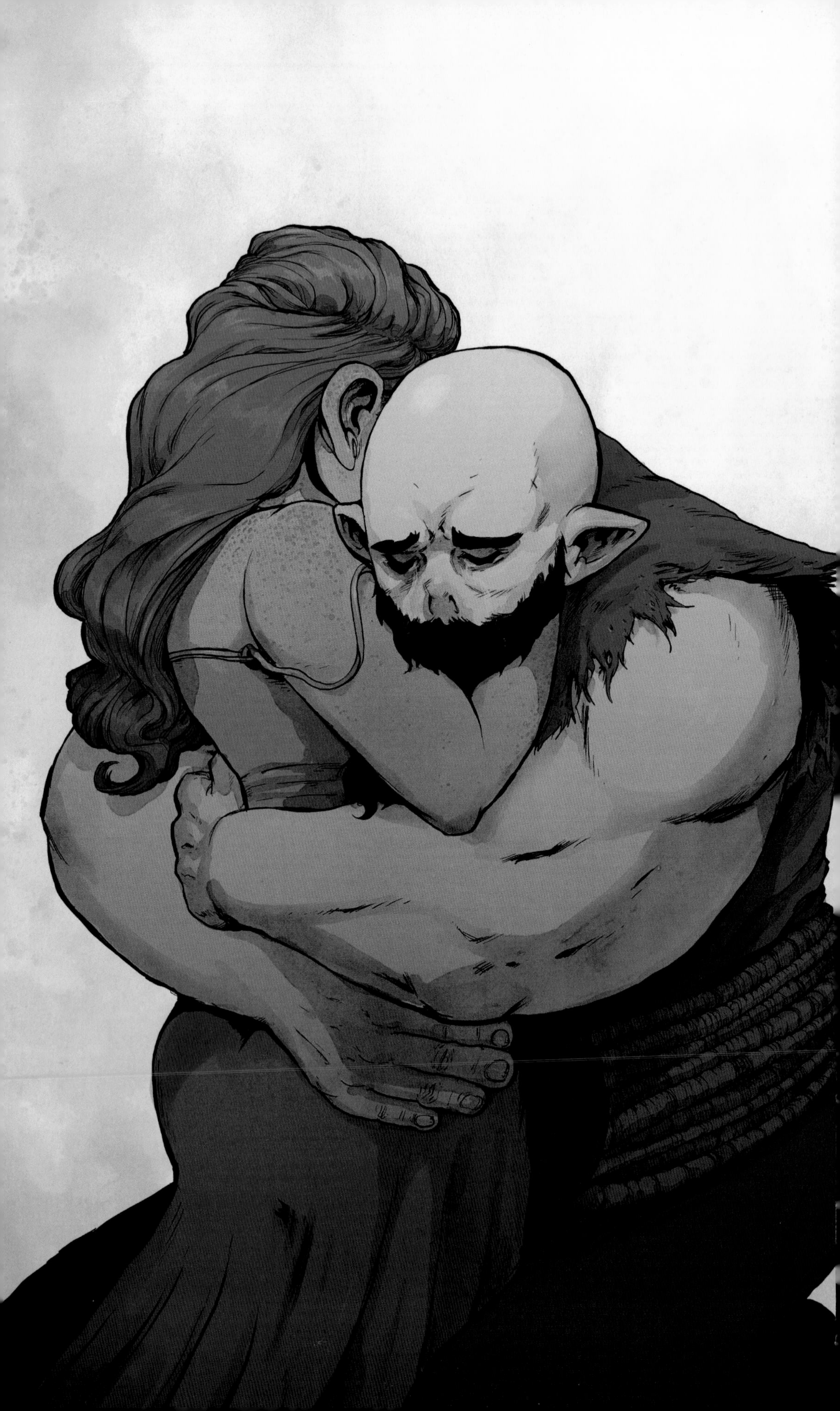

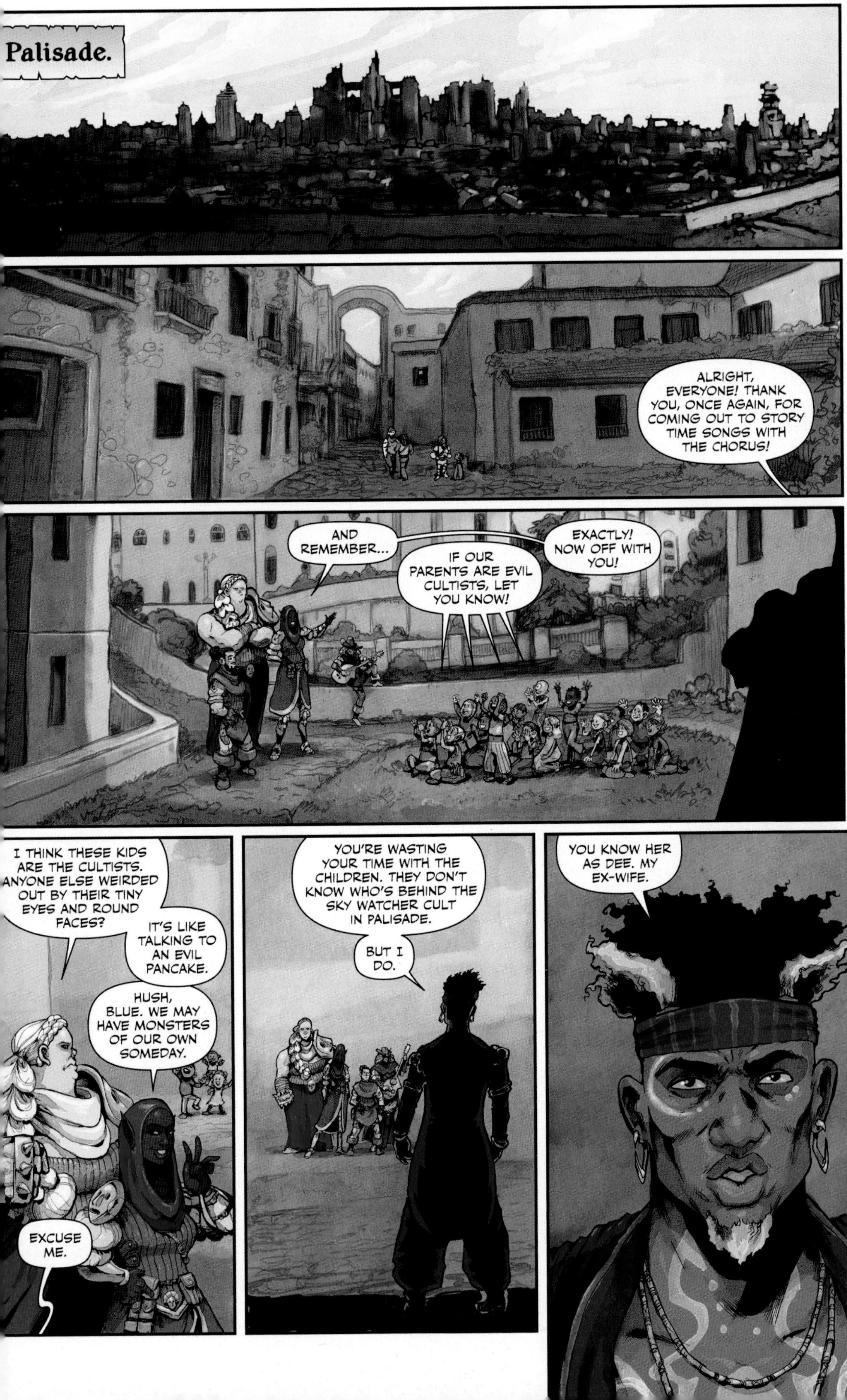
Palisade.
ALRIGHT, EVERYONE! THANK YOU, ONCE AGAIN, FOR COMING OUT TO STORY TIME SONGS WITH THE CHORUS!
AND REMEMBER...
IF OUR PARENTS ARE EVIL CULTISTS, LET YOU KNOW!
EXACTLY! NOW OFF WITH YOU!
I THINK THESE KIDS ARE THE CULTISTS. ANYONE ELSE WEIRDED OUT BY THEIR TINY EYES AND ROUND FACES?
IT'S LIKE TALKING TO AN EVIL PANCAKE.
HUSH, BLUE. WE MAY HAVE MONSTERS OF OUR OWN SOMEDAY.
EXCUSE ME.
YOU'RE WASTING YOUR TIME WITH THE CHILDREN. THEY DON'T KNOW WHO'S BEHIND THE SKY WATCHER CULT IN PALISADE.
BUT I DO.
YOU KNOW HER AS DEE. MY EX-WIFE.

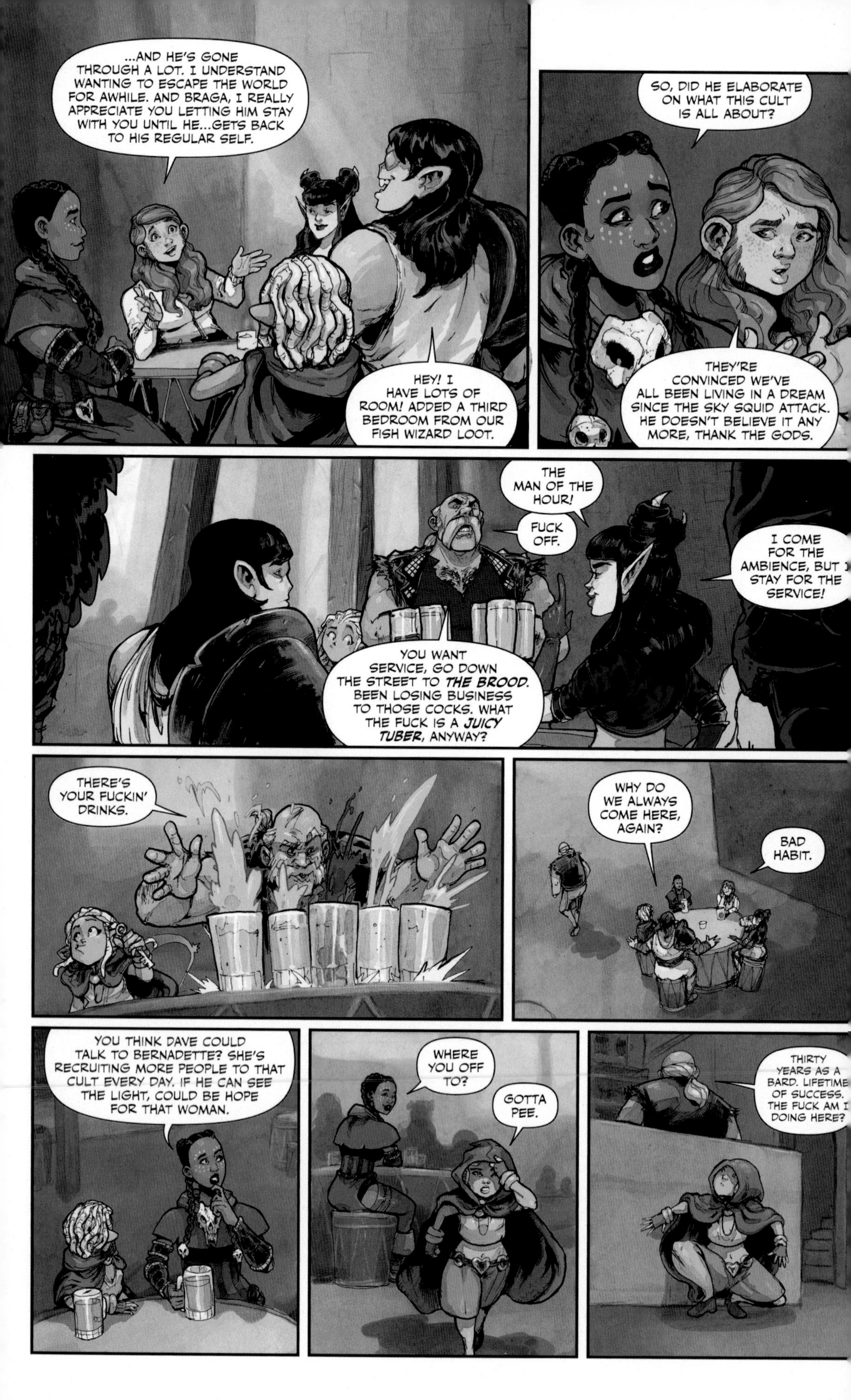
...AND HE'S GONE THROUGH A LOT. I UNDERSTAND WANTING TO ESCAPE THE WORLD FOR AWHILE. AND BRAGA, I REALLY APPRECIATE YOU LETTING HIM STAY WITH YOU UNTIL HE...GETS BACK TO HIS REGULAR SELF.
HEY! I HAVE LOTS OF ROOM! ADDED A THIRD BEDROOM FROM OUR FISH WIZARD LOOT.
SO, DID HE ELABORATE ON WHAT THIS CULT IS ALL ABOUT?
THEY'RE CONVINCED WE'VE ALL BEEN LIVING IN A DREAM SINCE THE SKY SQUID ATTACK. HE DOESN'T BELIEVE IT ANY MORE, THANK THE GODS.
THE MAN OF THE HOUR!
FUCK OFF.
I COME FOR THE AMBIENCE, BUT I STAY FOR THE SERVICE!
YOU WANT SERVICE, GO DOWN THE STREET TO THE BROOD. BEEN LOSING BUSINESS TO THOSE COCKS. WHAT THE FUCK IS A JUICY TUBER, ANYWAY?
THERE'S YOUR FUCKIN' DRINKS.
WHY DO WE ALWAYS COME HERE, AGAIN?
BAD HABIT.
YOU THINK DAVE COULD TALK TO BERNADETTE? SHE'S RECRUITING MORE PEOPLE TO THAT CULT EVERY DAY. IF HE CAN SEE THE LIGHT, COULD BE HOPE FOR THAT WOMAN.
WHERE YOU OFF TO?
GOTTA PEE.
THIRTY YEARS AS A BARD. LIFETIME OF SUCCESS. THE FUCK AM I DOING HERE?

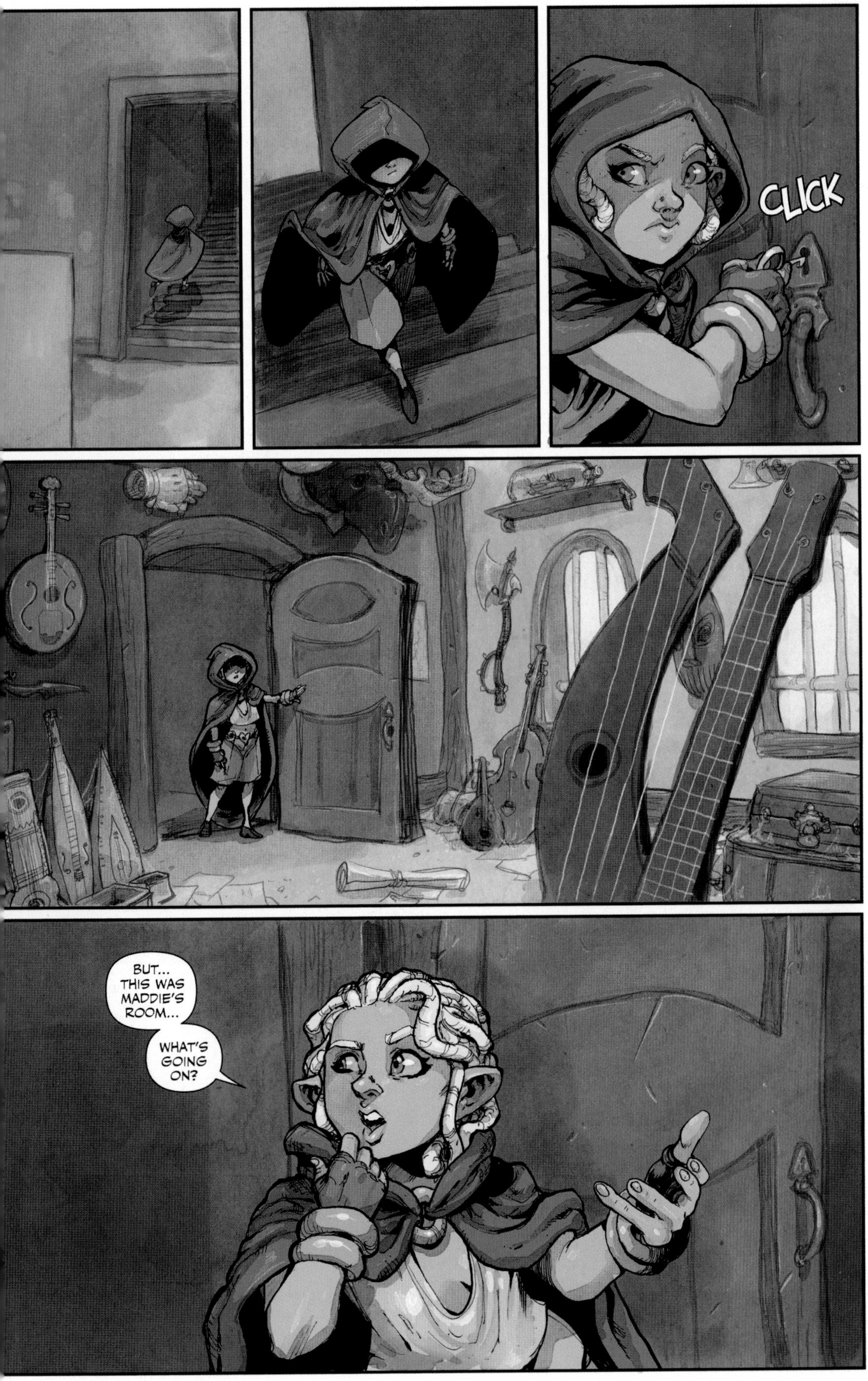
CLICK
BUT... THIS WAS MADDIE'S ROOM...
WHAT'S GOING ON?

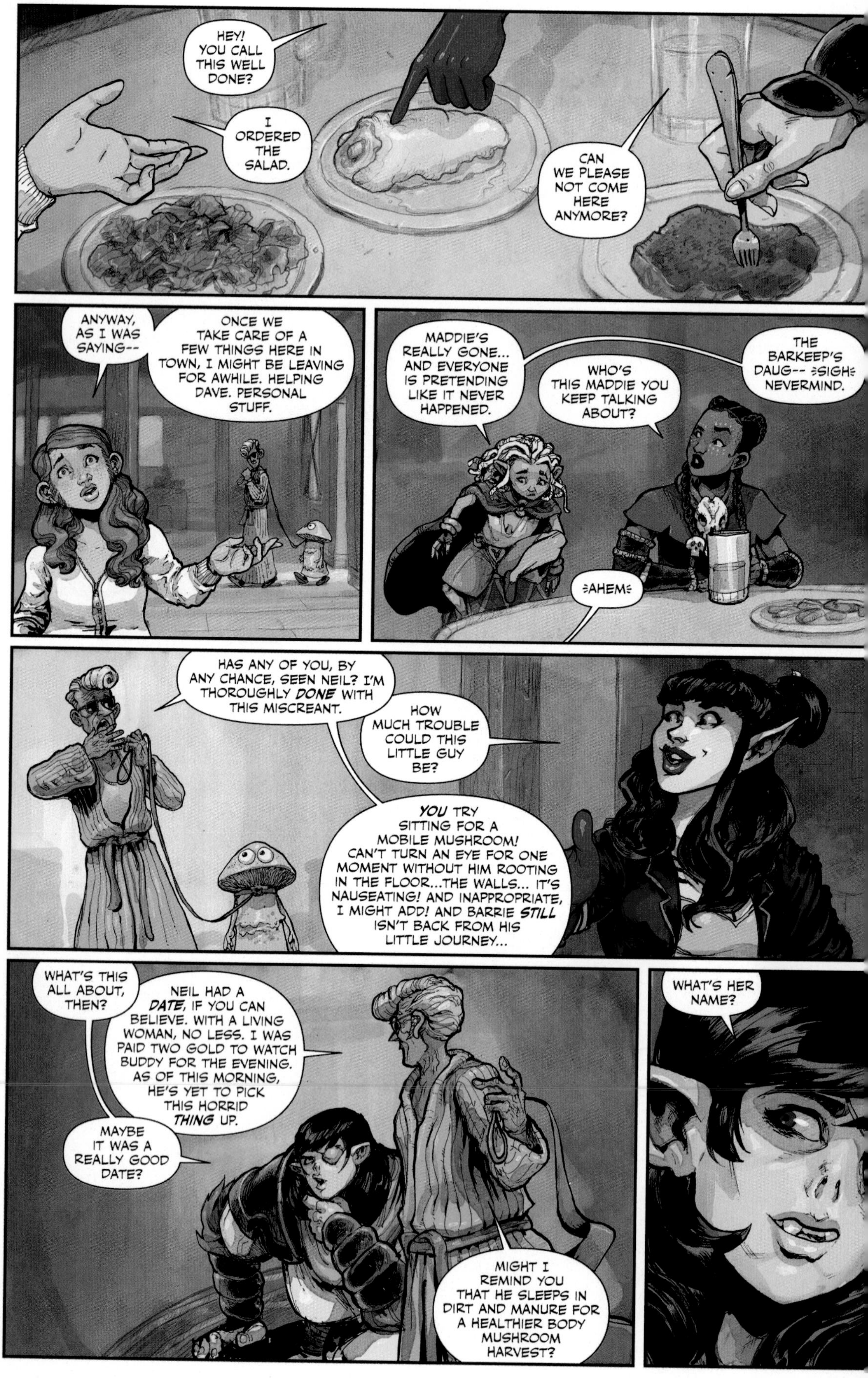
HEY! YOU CALL THIS WELL DONE?
I ORDERED THE SALAD.
CAN WE PLEASE NOT COME HERE ANYMORE?
ANYWAY, AS I WAS SAYING--
ONCE WE TAKE CARE OF A FEW THINGS HERE IN TOWN, I MIGHT BE LEAVING FOR AWHILE. HELPING DAVE. PERSONAL STUFF.
MADDIE'S REALLY GONE... AND EVERYONE IS PRETENDING LIKE IT NEVER HAPPENED.
WHO'S THIS MADDIE YOU KEEP TALKING ABOUT?
THE BARKEEP'S DAUG-- *SIGH* NEVERMIND.
AHEM
HAS ANY OF YOU, BY ANY CHANCE, SEEN NEIL? I'M THOROUGHLY *DONE* WITH THIS MISCREANT.
HOW MUCH TROUBLE COULD THIS LITTLE GUY BE?
YOU TRY SITTING FOR A MOBILE MUSHROOM! CAN'T TURN AN EYE FOR ONE MOMENT WITHOUT HIM ROOTING IN THE FLOOR...THE WALLS... IT'S NAUSEATING! AND INAPPROPRIATE, I MIGHT ADD! AND BARRIE *STILL* ISN'T BACK FROM HIS LITTLE JOURNEY...
WHAT'S THIS ALL ABOUT, THEN?
NEIL HAD A *DATE*, IF YOU CAN BELIEVE. WITH A LIVING WOMAN, NO LESS. I WAS PAID TWO GOLD TO WATCH BUDDY FOR THE EVENING. AS OF THIS MORNING, HE'S YET TO PICK THIS HORRID *THING* UP.
MAYBE IT WAS A REALLY GOOD DATE?
MIGHT I REMIND YOU THAT HE SLEEPS IN DIRT AND MANURE FOR A HEALTHIER BODY MUSHROOM HARVEST?
WHAT'S HER NAME?

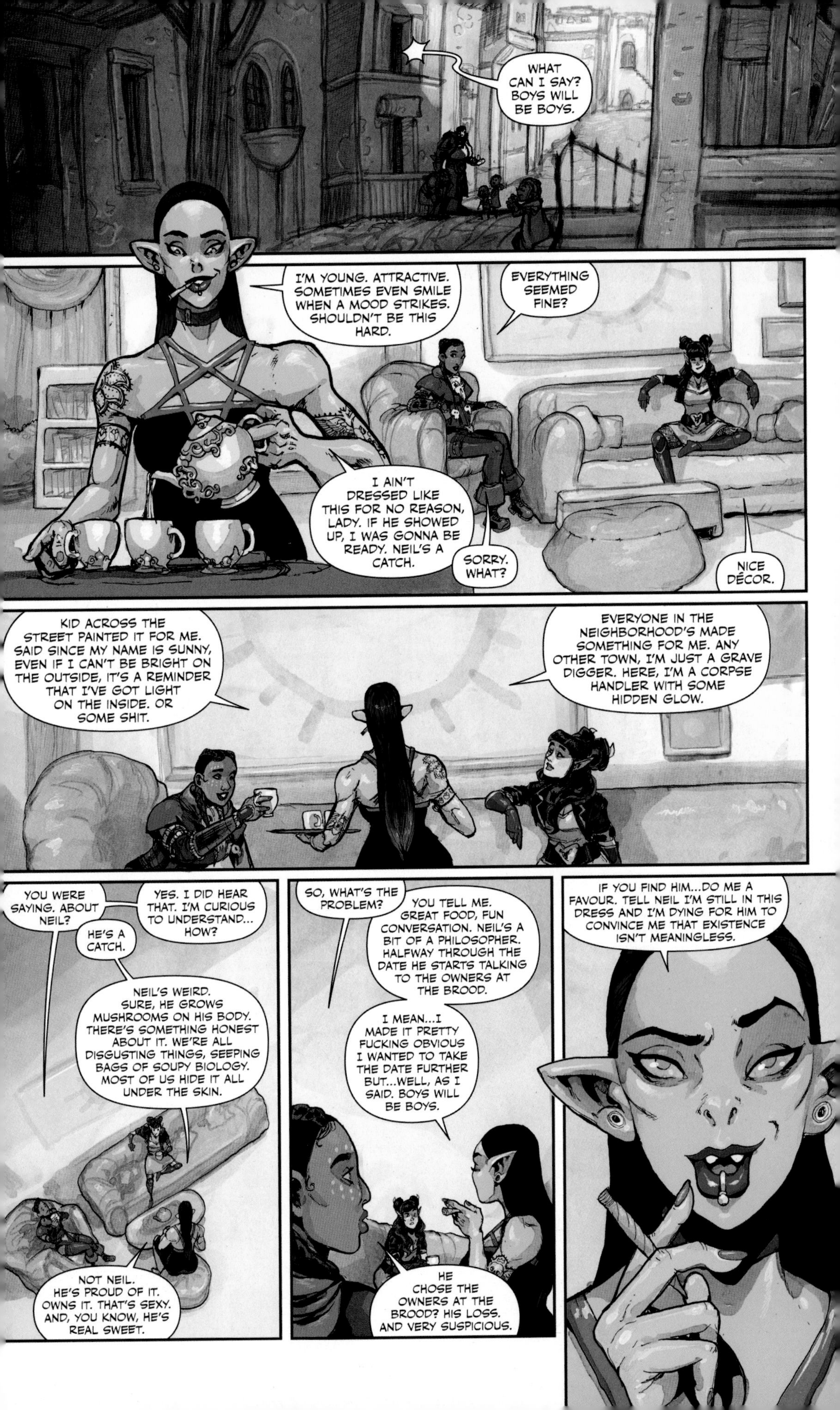

WHAT CAN I SAY? BOYS WILL BE BOYS.
I'M YOUNG. ATTRACTIVE. SOMETIMES EVEN SMILE WHEN A MOOD STRIKES. SHOULDN'T BE THIS HARD.
EVERYTHING SEEMED FINE?
I AIN'T DRESSED LIKE THIS FOR NO REASON, LADY. IF HE SHOWED UP, I WAS GONNA BE READY. NEIL'S A CATCH.
SORRY. WHAT?
NICE DÉCOR.
KID ACROSS THE STREET PAINTED IT FOR ME. SAID SINCE MY NAME IS SUNNY, EVEN IF I CAN'T BE BRIGHT ON THE OUTSIDE, IT'S A REMINDER THAT I'VE GOT LIGHT ON THE INSIDE. OR SOME SHIT.
EVERYONE IN THE NEIGHBORHOOD'S MADE SOMETHING FOR ME. ANY OTHER TOWN, I'M JUST A GRAVE DIGGER. HERE, I'M A CORPSE HANDLER WITH SOME HIDDEN GLOW.
YOU WERE SAYING. ABOUT NEIL?
YES. I DID HEAR THAT. I'M CURIOUS TO UNDERSTAND... HOW?
HE'S A CATCH.
NEIL'S WEIRD. SURE, HE GROWS MUSHROOMS ON HIS BODY. THERE'S SOMETHING HONEST ABOUT IT. WE'RE ALL DISGUSTING THINGS, SEEPING BAGS OF SOUPY BIOLOGY. MOST OF US HIDE IT ALL UNDER THE SKIN.
NOT NEIL. HE'S PROUD OF IT. OWNS IT. THAT'S SEXY. AND, YOU KNOW, HE'S REAL SWEET.
SO, WHAT'S THE PROBLEM?
YOU TELL ME. GREAT FOOD, FUN CONVERSATION. NEIL'S A BIT OF A PHILOSOPHER. HALFWAY THROUGH THE DATE HE STARTS TALKING TO THE OWNERS AT THE BROOD.
I MEAN...I MADE IT PRETTY FUCKING OBVIOUS I WANTED TO TAKE THE DATE FURTHER BUT...WELL, AS I SAID. BOYS WILL BE BOYS.
HE CHOSE THE OWNERS AT THE BROOD? HIS LOSS. AND VERY SUSPICIOUS.
IF YOU FIND HIM...DO ME A FAVOUR. TELL NEIL I'M STILL IN THIS DRESS AND I'M DYING FOR HIM TO CONVINCE ME THAT EXISTENCE ISN'T MEANINGLESS.

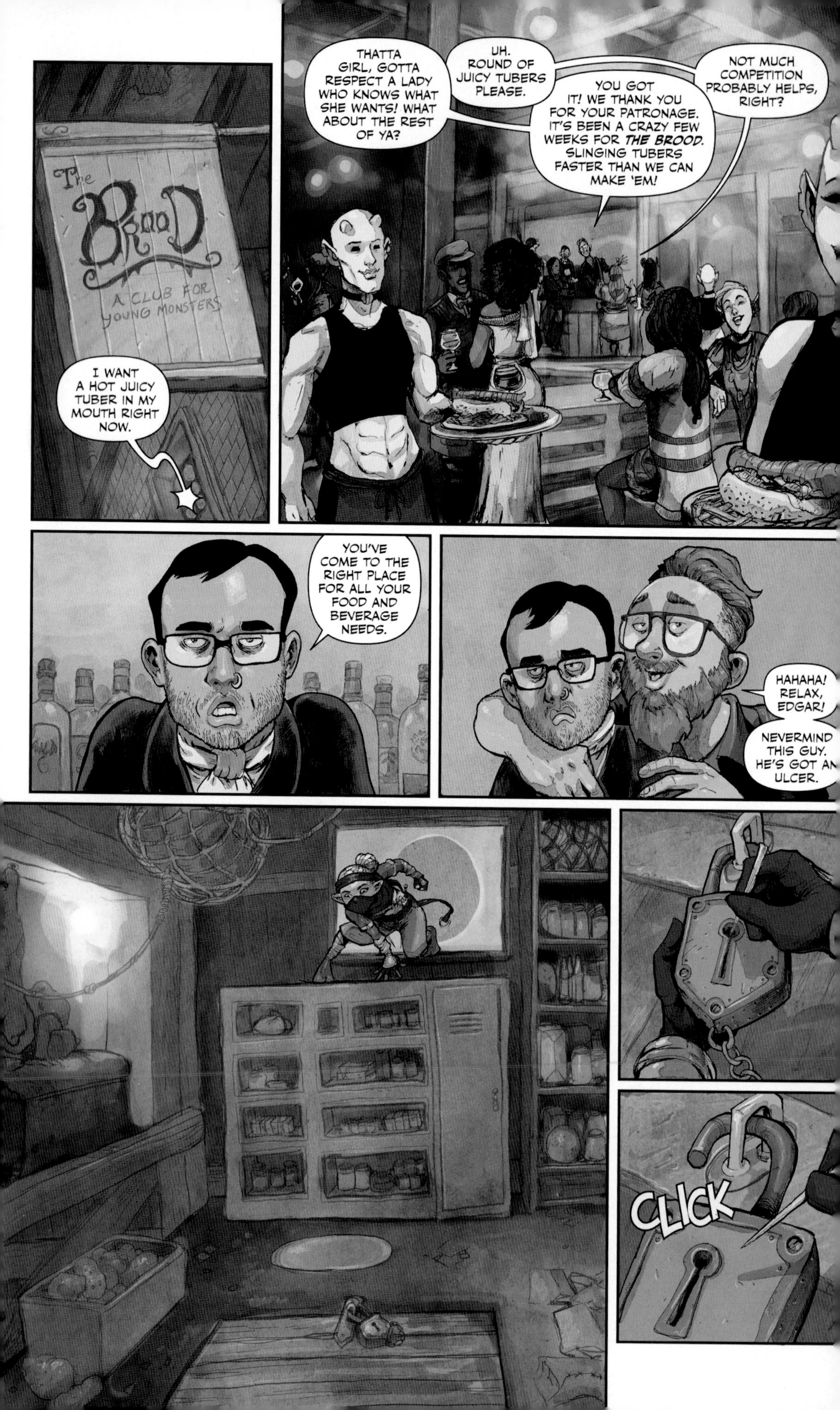
The Brood
A CLUB FOR YOUNG MONSTERS
I WANT A HOT JUICY TUBER IN MY MOUTH RIGHT NOW.
THATTA GIRL, GOTTA RESPECT A LADY WHO KNOWS WHAT SHE WANTS! WHAT ABOUT THE REST OF YA?
UH. ROUND OF JUICY TUBERS PLEASE.
YOU GOT IT! WE THANK YOU FOR YOUR PATRONAGE. IT'S BEEN A CRAZY FEW WEEKS FOR THE BROOD. SLINGING TUBERS FASTER THAN WE CAN MAKE 'EM!
NOT MUCH COMPETITION PROBABLY HELPS, RIGHT?
YOU'VE COME TO THE RIGHT PLACE FOR ALL YOUR FOOD AND BEVERAGE NEEDS.
HAHAHA! RELAX, EDGAR!
NEVERMIND THIS GUY. HE'S GOT AN ULCER.
CLICK

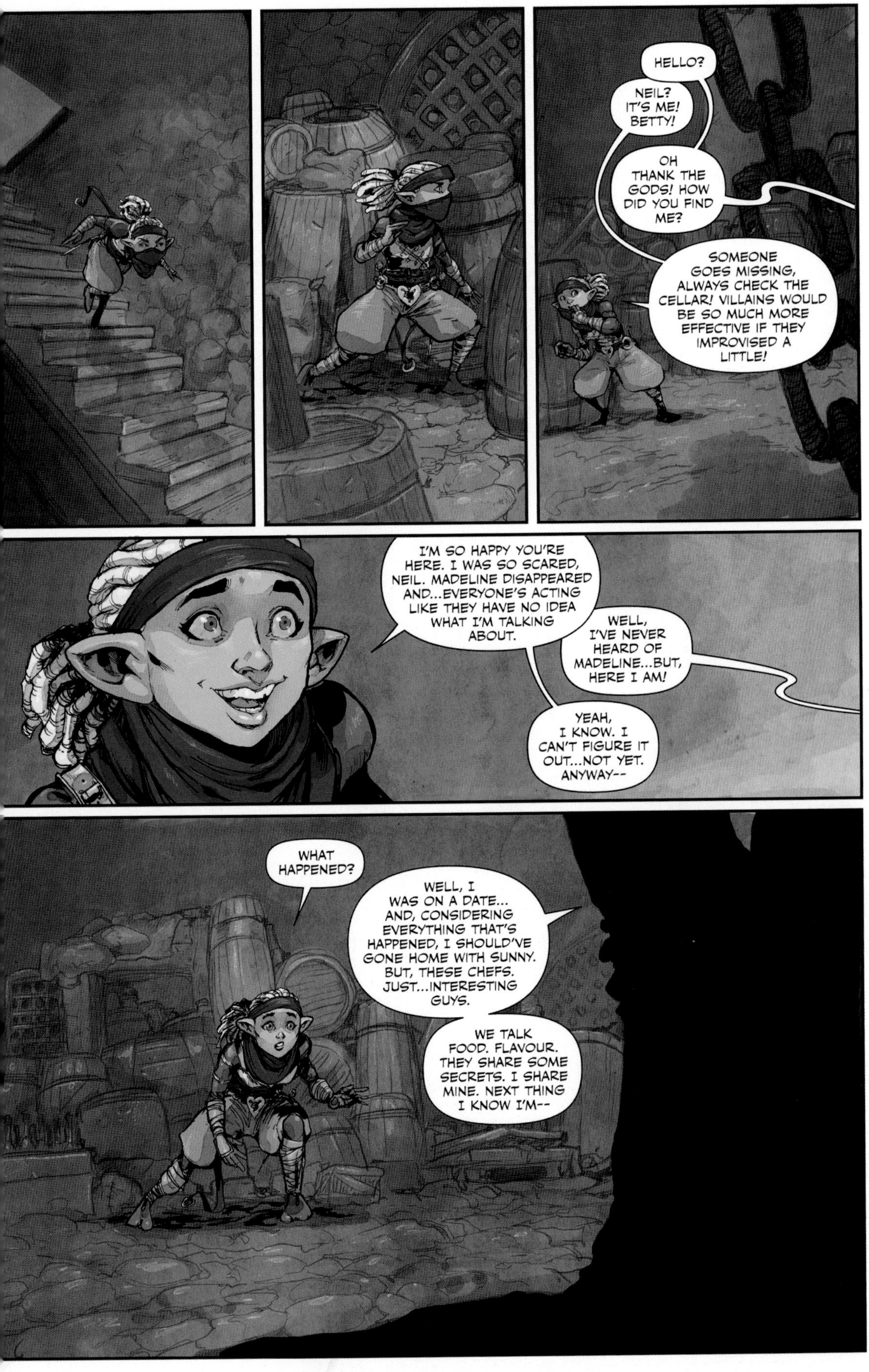
HELLO?
NEIL? IT'S ME! BETTY!
OH THANK THE GODS! HOW DID YOU FIND ME?
SOMEONE GOES MISSING, ALWAYS CHECK THE CELLAR! VILLAINS WOULD BE SO MUCH MORE EFFECTIVE IF THEY IMPROVISED A LITTLE!
I'M SO HAPPY YOU'RE HERE. I WAS SO SCARED, NEIL. MADELINE DISAPPEARED AND...EVERYONE'S ACTING LIKE THEY HAVE NO IDEA WHAT I'M TALKING ABOUT.
WELL, I'VE NEVER HEARD OF MADELINE...BUT, HERE I AM!
YEAH, I KNOW. I CAN'T FIGURE IT OUT...NOT YET. ANYWAY--
WHAT HAPPENED?
WELL, I WAS ON A DATE... AND, CONSIDERING EVERYTHING THAT'S HAPPENED, I SHOULD'VE GONE HOME WITH SUNNY. BUT, THESE CHEFS. JUST...INTERESTING GUYS.
WE TALK FOOD. FLAVOUR. THEY SHARE SOME SECRETS. I SHARE MINE. NEXT THING I KNOW I'M--

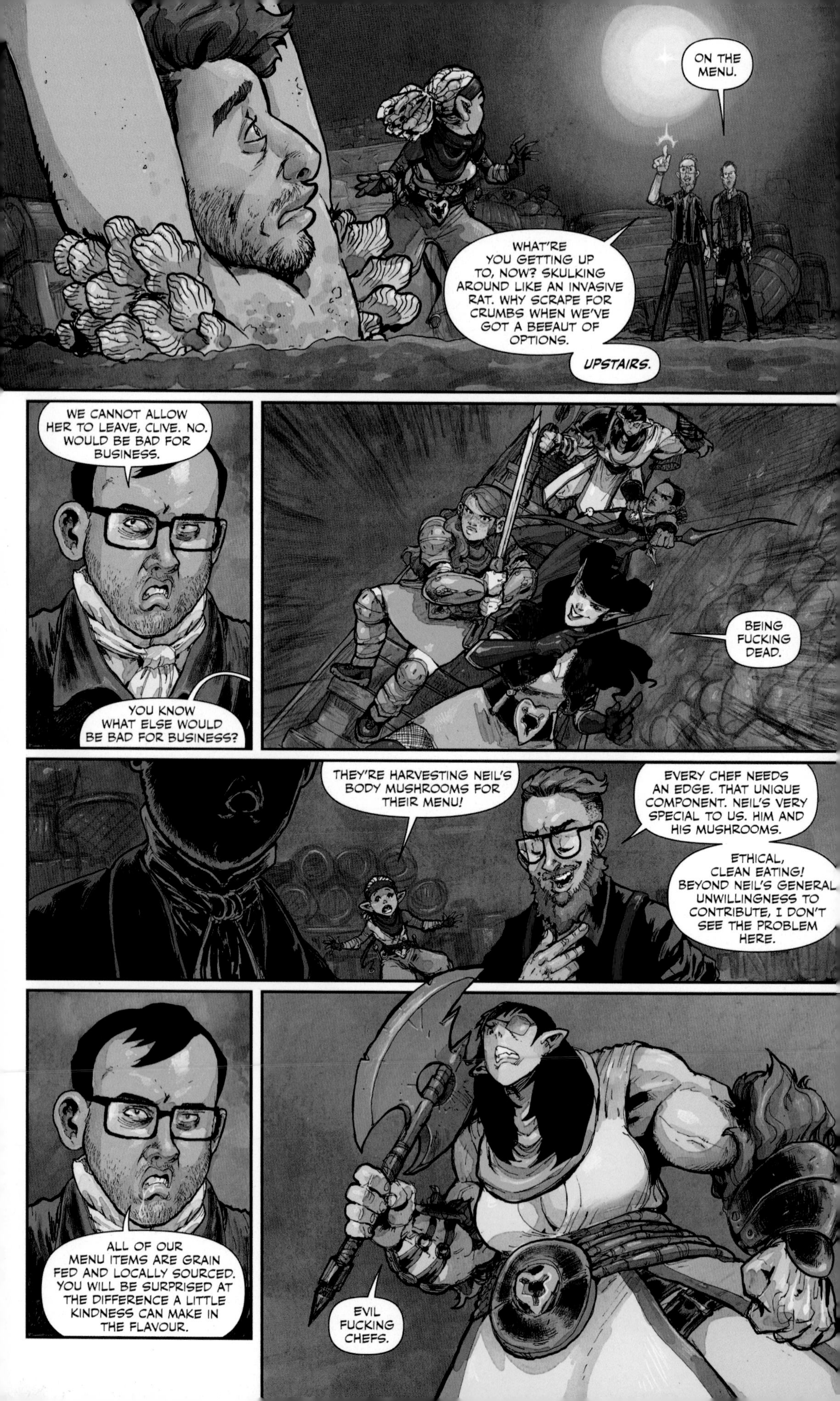
ON THE MENU.
WHAT'RE YOU GETTING UP TO, NOW? SKULKING AROUND LIKE AN INVASIVE RAT. WHY SCRAPE FOR CRUMBS WHEN WE'VE GOT A BEEAUT OF OPTIONS.
UPSTAIRS.
WE CANNOT ALLOW HER TO LEAVE, CLIVE. NO. WOULD BE BAD FOR BUSINESS.
YOU KNOW WHAT ELSE WOULD BE BAD FOR BUSINESS?
BEING FUCKING DEAD.
THEY'RE HARVESTING NEIL'S BODY MUSHROOMS FOR THEIR MENU!
EVERY CHEF NEEDS AN EDGE. THAT UNIQUE COMPONENT. NEIL'S VERY SPECIAL TO US. HIM AND HIS MUSHROOMS.
ETHICAL, CLEAN EATING! BEYOND NEIL'S GENERAL UNWILLINGNESS TO CONTRIBUTE, I DON'T SEE THE PROBLEM HERE.
ALL OF OUR MENU ITEMS ARE GRAIN FED AND LOCALLY SOURCED. YOU WILL BE SURPRISED AT THE DIFFERENCE A LITTLE KINDNESS CAN MAKE IN THE FLAVOUR.
EVIL FUCKING CHEFS.

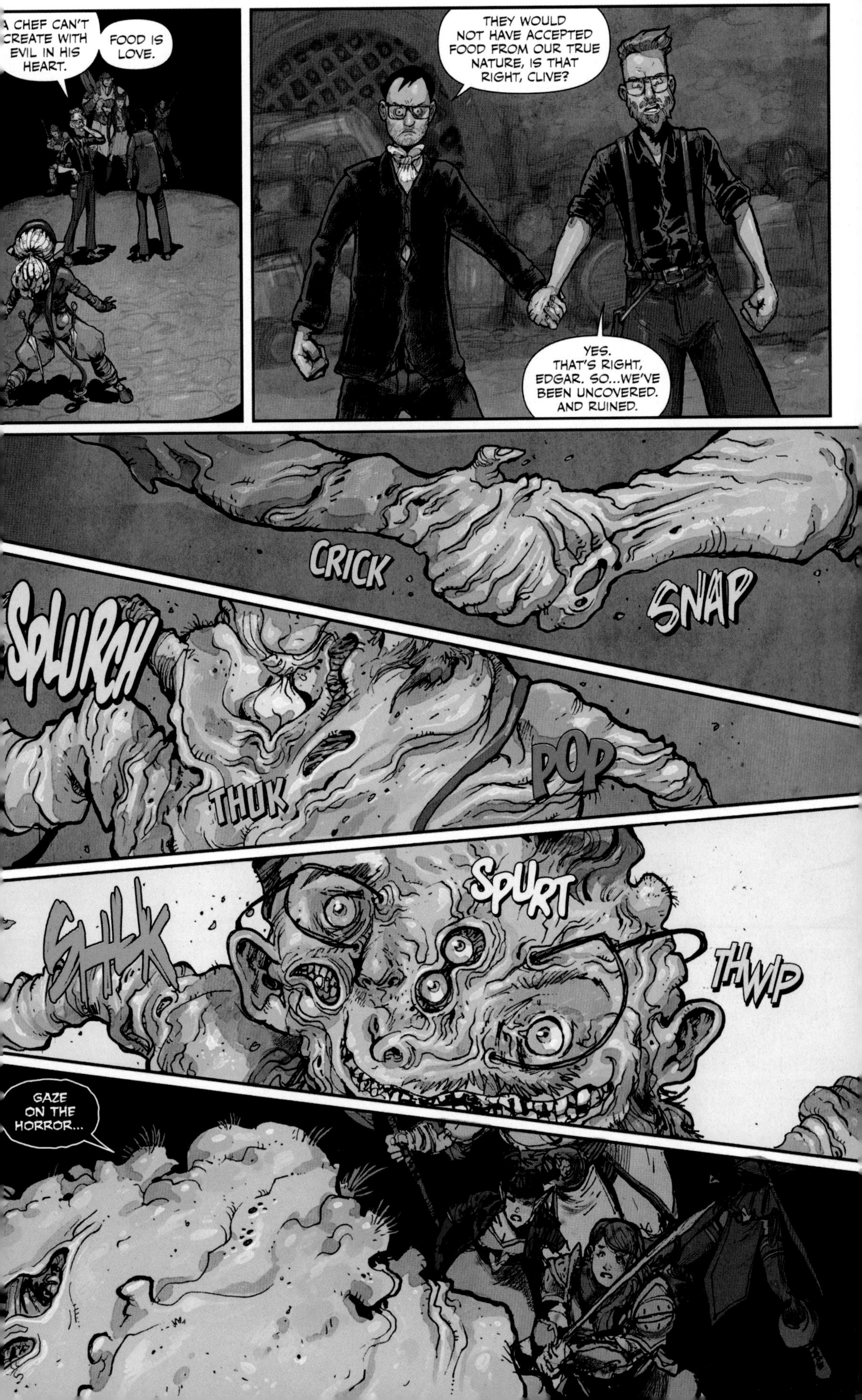
A CHEF CAN'T CREATE WITH EVIL IN HIS HEART.
FOOD IS LOVE.
THEY WOULD NOT HAVE ACCEPTED FOOD FROM OUR TRUE NATURE, IS THAT RIGHT, CLIVE?
YES. THAT'S RIGHT, EDGAR. SO...WE'VE BEEN UNCOVERED. AND RUINED.
CRICK
SNAP
SPLURCH
THUK
POP
SHLK
SPURT
THWIP
GAZE ON THE HORROR...

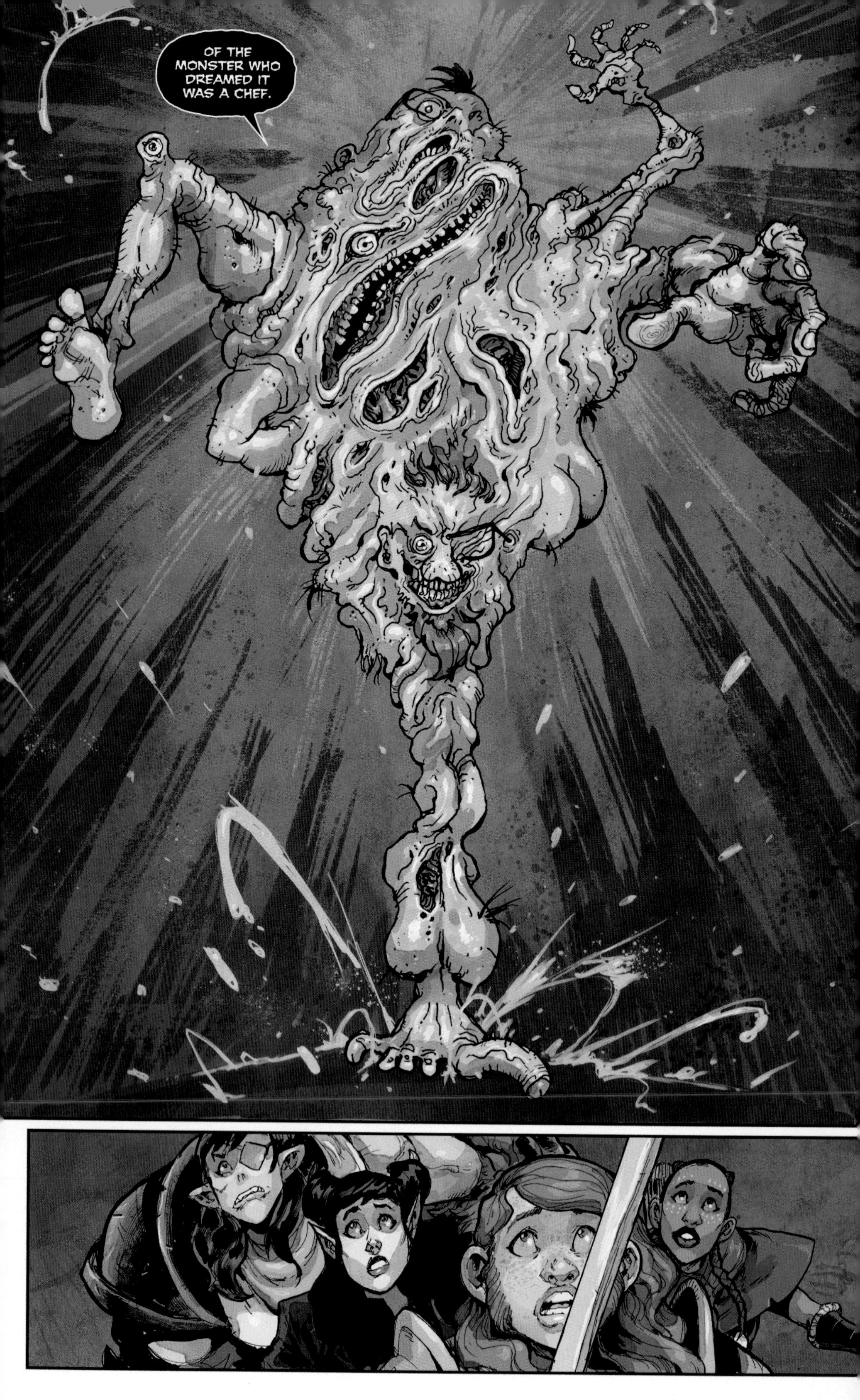
OF THE MONSTER WHO DREAMED IT WAS A CHEF.

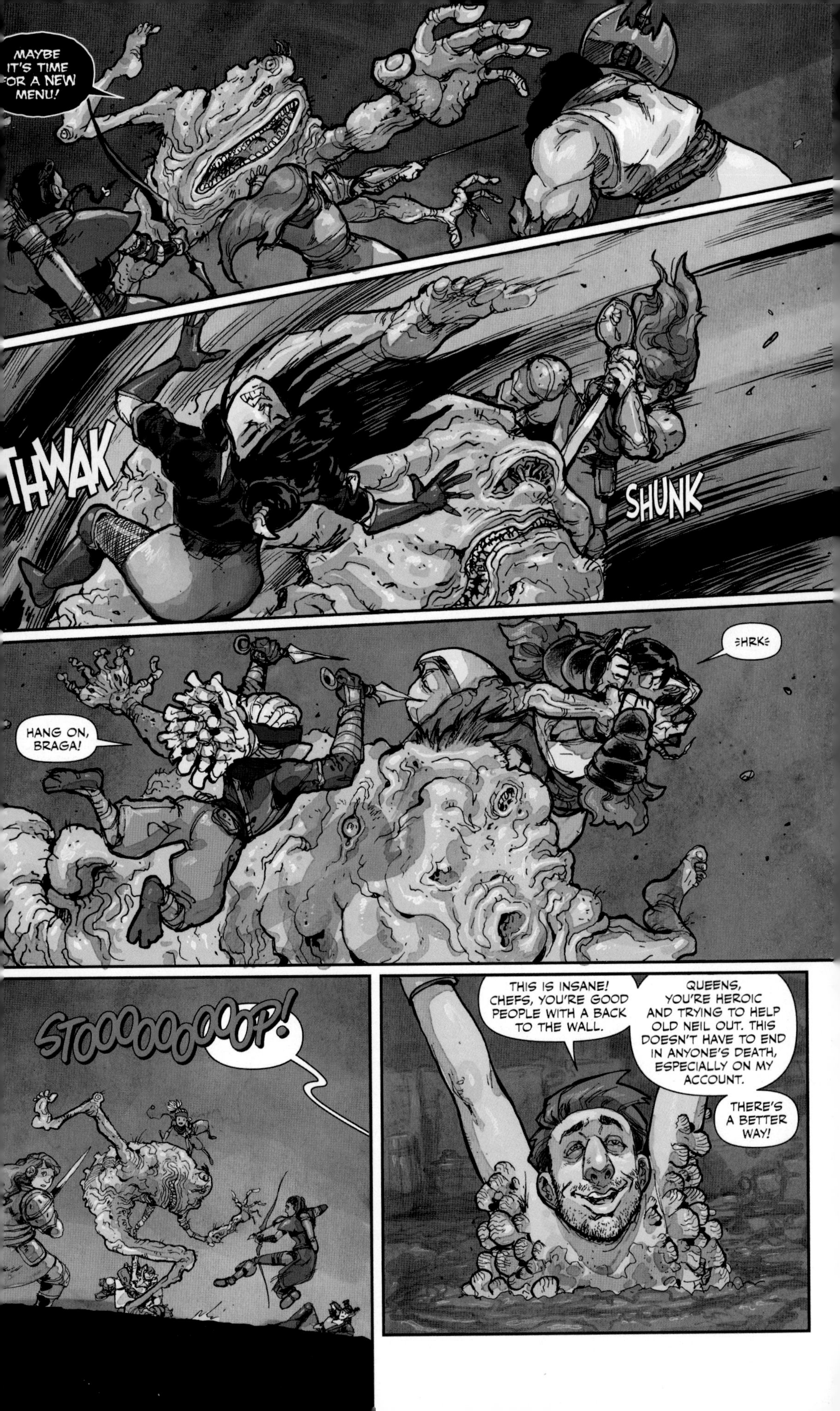
MAYBE IT'S TIME FOR A NEW MENU!
THWAK
SHUNK
HANG ON, BRAGA!
SHRK
STOOOOOOOOOP!
THIS IS INSANE! CHEFS, YOU'RE GOOD PEOPLE WITH A BACK TO THE WALL.
QUEENS, YOU'RE HEROIC AND TRYING TO HELP OLD NEIL OUT. THIS DOESN'T HAVE TO END IN ANYONE'S DEATH, ESPECIALLY ON MY ACCOUNT.
THERE'S A BETTER WAY!

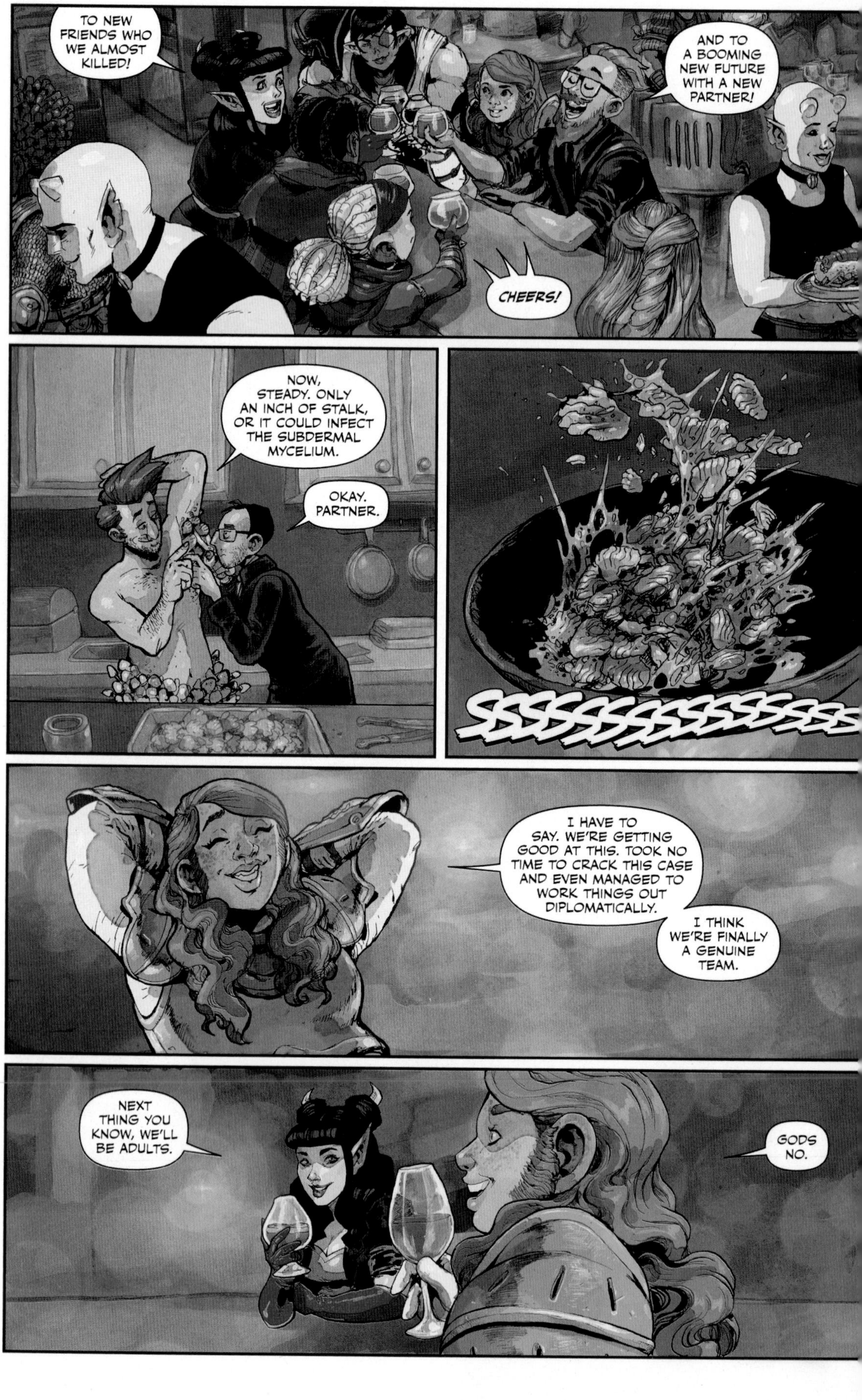
TO NEW FRIENDS WHO WE ALMOST KILLED!
AND TO A BOOMING NEW FUTURE WITH A NEW PARTNER!
CHEERS!
NOW, STEADY. ONLY AN INCH OF STALK, OR IT COULD INFECT THE SUBDERMAL MYCELIUM.
OKAY. PARTNER.
SSSSSSSSSSSSSSSS
I HAVE TO SAY. WE'RE GETTING GOOD AT THIS. TOOK NO TIME TO CRACK THIS CASE AND EVEN MANAGED TO WORK THINGS OUT DIPLOMATICALLY.
I THINK WE'RE FINALLY A GENUINE TEAM.
NEXT THING YOU KNOW, WE'LL BE ADULTS.
GODS NO.

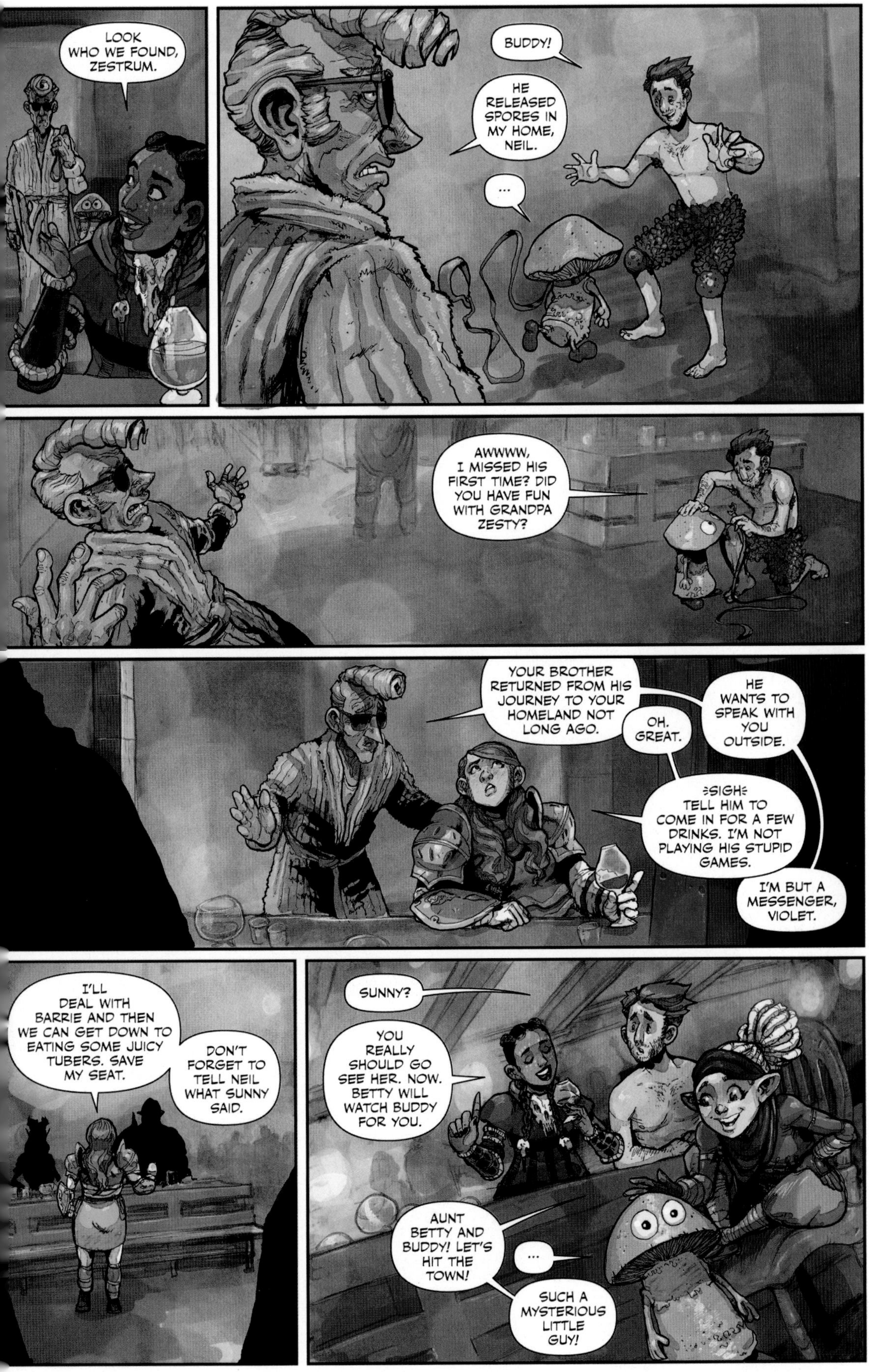
LOOK WHO WE FOUND, ZESTRUM.
BUDDY!
HE RELEASED SPORES IN MY HOME, NEIL.
...
AWWWW, I MISSED HIS FIRST TIME? DID YOU HAVE FUN WITH GRANDPA ZESTY?
YOUR BROTHER RETURNED FROM HIS JOURNEY TO YOUR HOMELAND NOT LONG AGO.
OH. GREAT.
HE WANTS TO SPEAK WITH YOU OUTSIDE.
=SIGH= TELL HIM TO COME IN FOR A FEW DRINKS. I'M NOT PLAYING HIS STUPID GAMES.
I'M BUT A MESSENGER, VIOLET.
I'LL DEAL WITH BARRIE AND THEN WE CAN GET DOWN TO EATING SOME JUICY TUBERS. SAVE MY SEAT.
DON'T FORGET TO TELL NEIL WHAT SUNNY SAID.
SUNNY?
YOU REALLY SHOULD GO SEE HER. NOW. BETTY WILL WATCH BUDDY FOR YOU.
AUNT BETTY AND BUDDY! LET'S HIT THE TOWN!
...
SUCH A MYSTERIOUS LITTLE GUY!

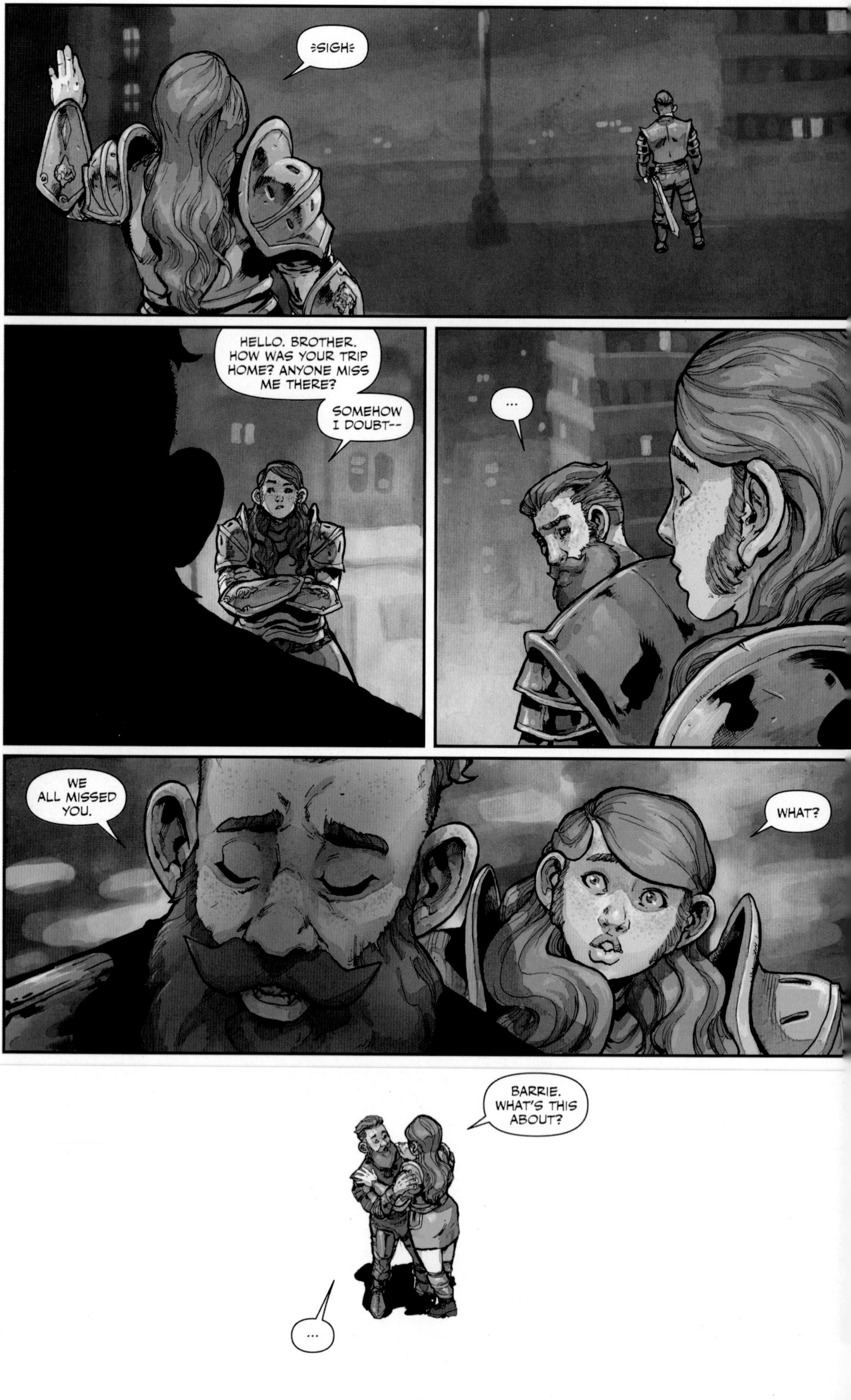

≈SIGH≈
HELLO. BROTHER. HOW WAS YOUR TRIP HOME? ANYONE MISS ME THERE?
SOMEHOW I DOUBT--
...
WE ALL MISSED YOU.
WHAT?
BARRIE. WHAT'S THIS ABOUT?
...

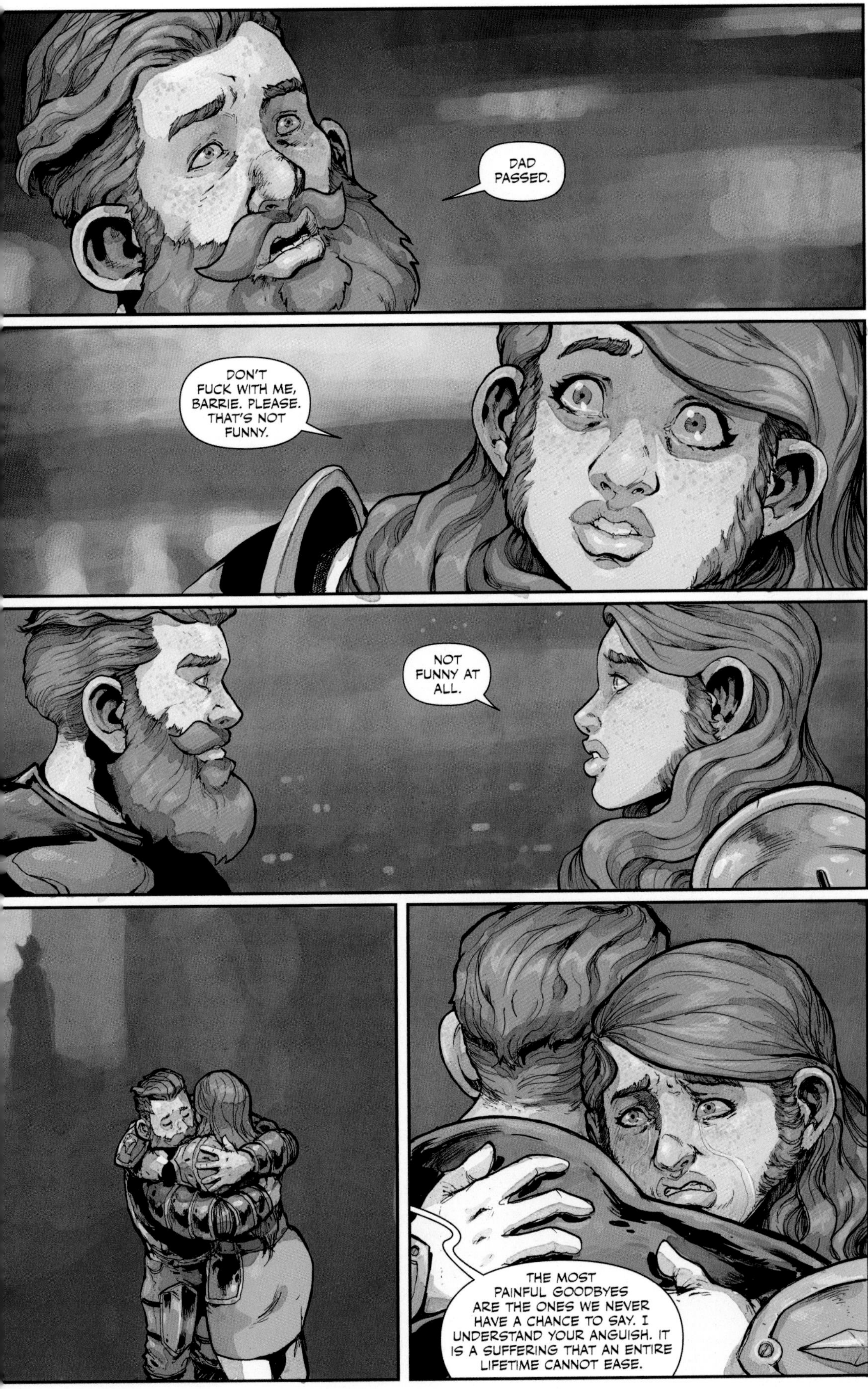
DAD PASSED.
DON'T FUCK WITH ME, BARRIE. PLEASE. THAT'S NOT FUNNY.
NOT FUNNY AT ALL.
THE MOST PAINFUL GOODBYES ARE THE ONES WE NEVER HAVE A CHANCE TO SAY. I UNDERSTAND YOUR ANGUISH. IT IS A SUFFERING THAT AN ENTIRE LIFETIME CANNOT EASE.

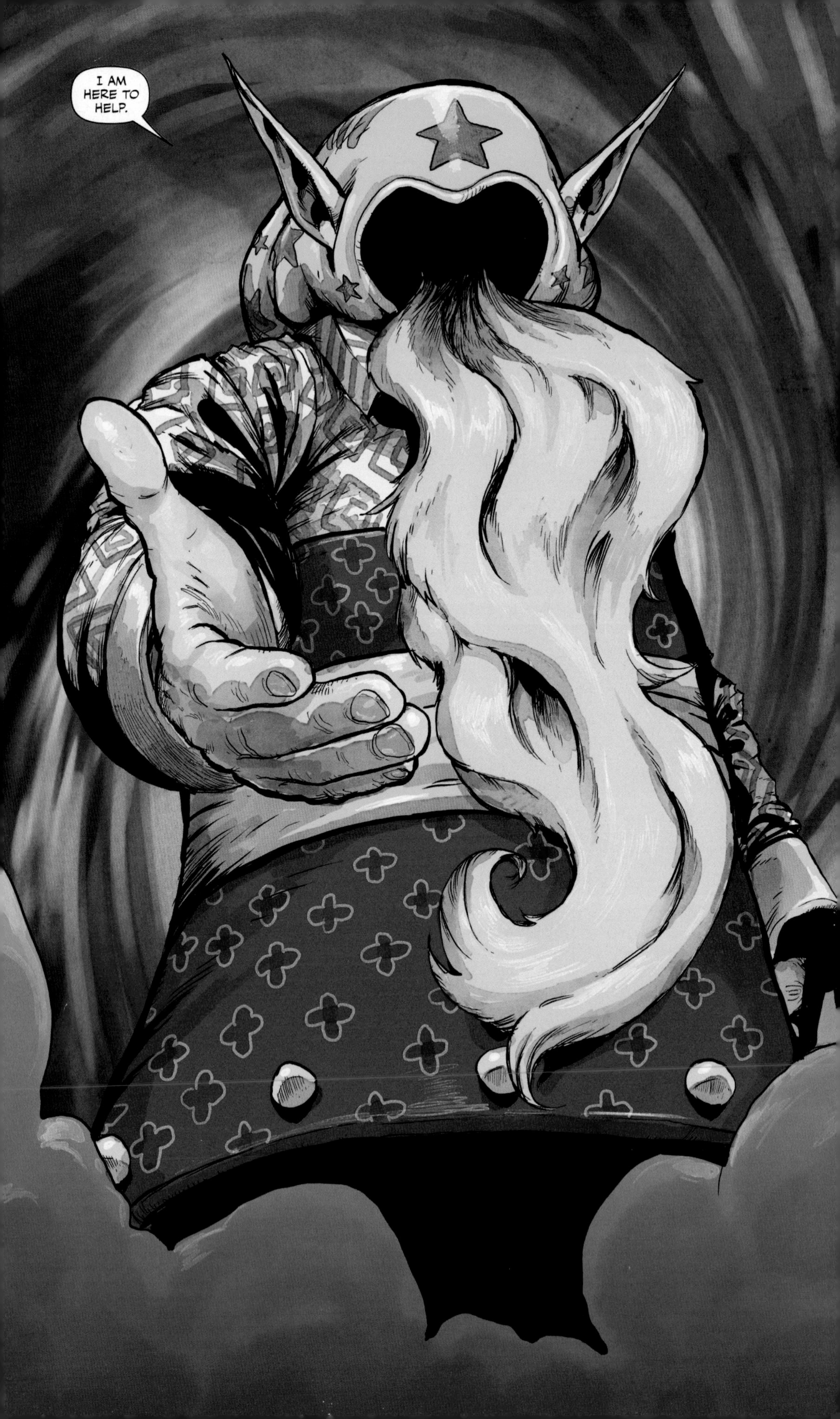
I AM HERE TO HELP.

CHAPTER EIGHT

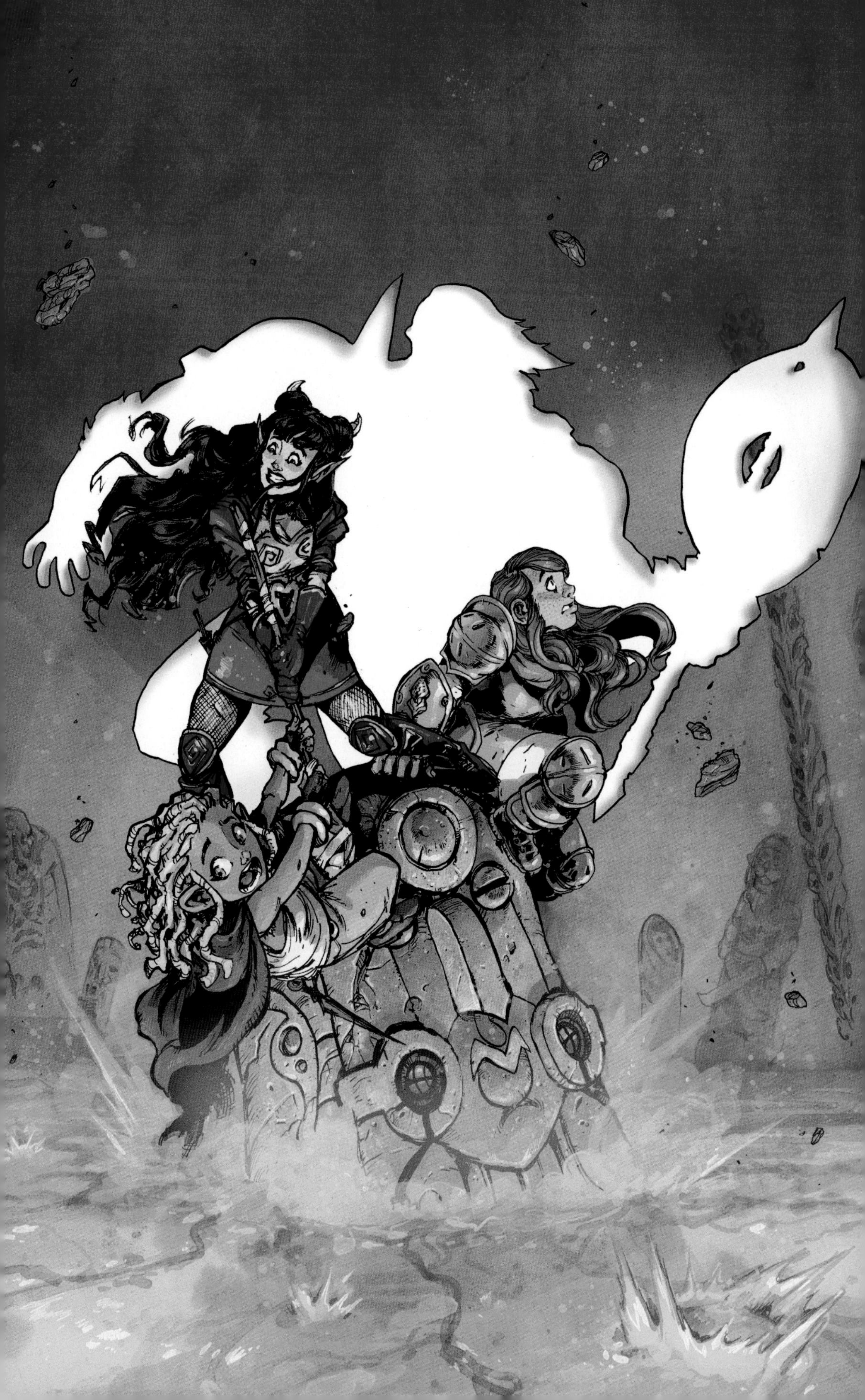

Issue 8 cover B by Mindy Lee

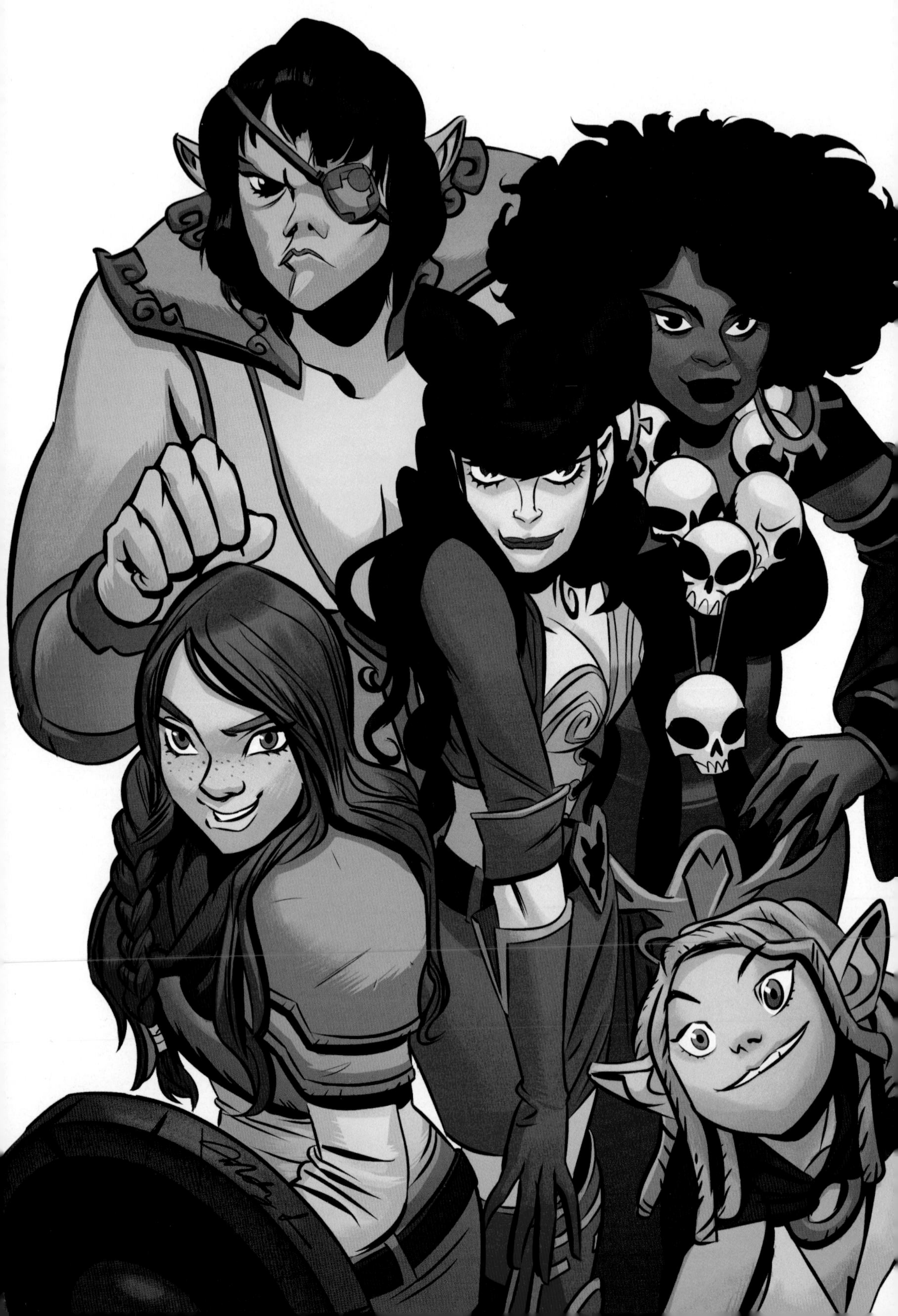

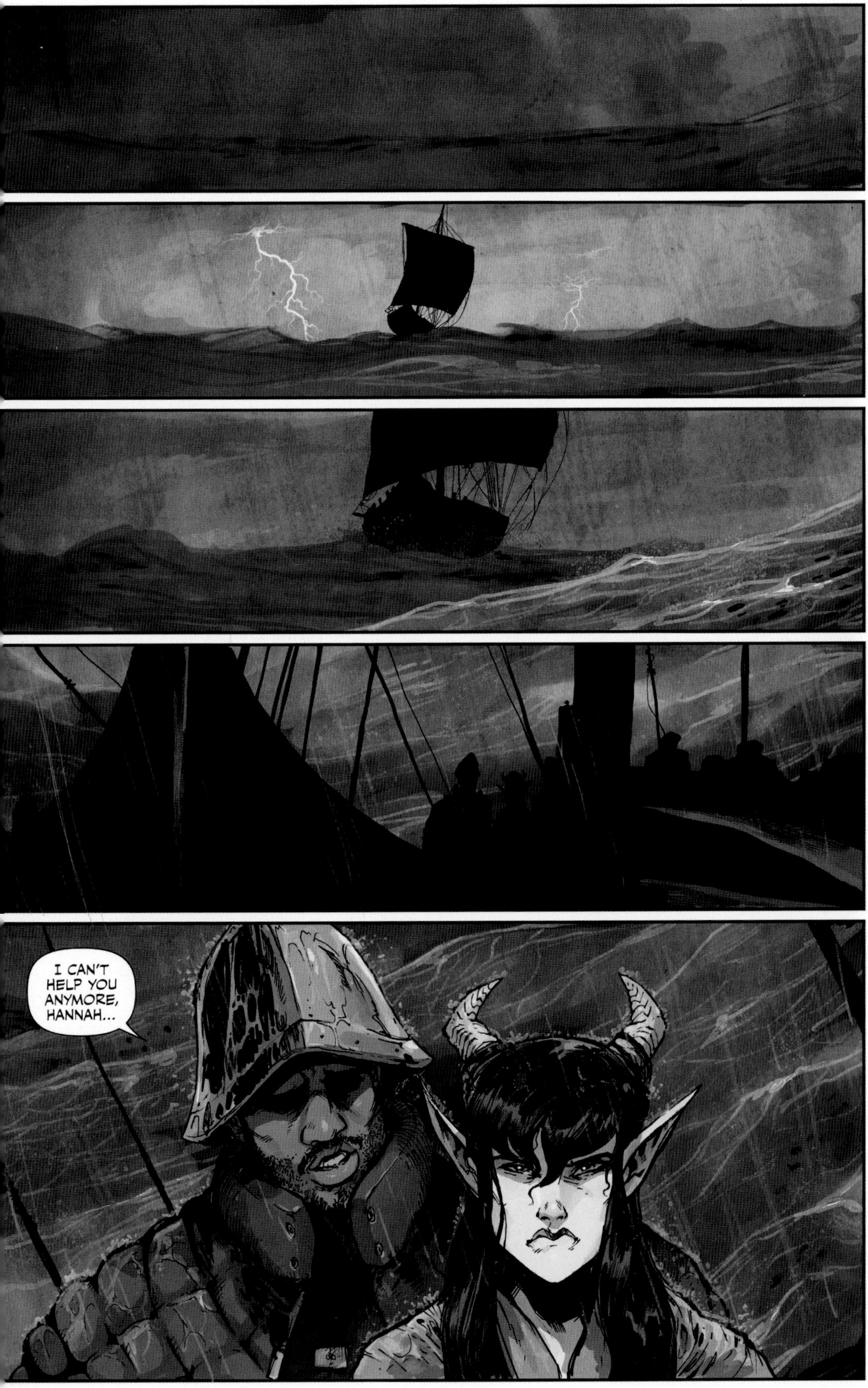
I CAN'T HELP YOU ANYMORE, HANNAH...

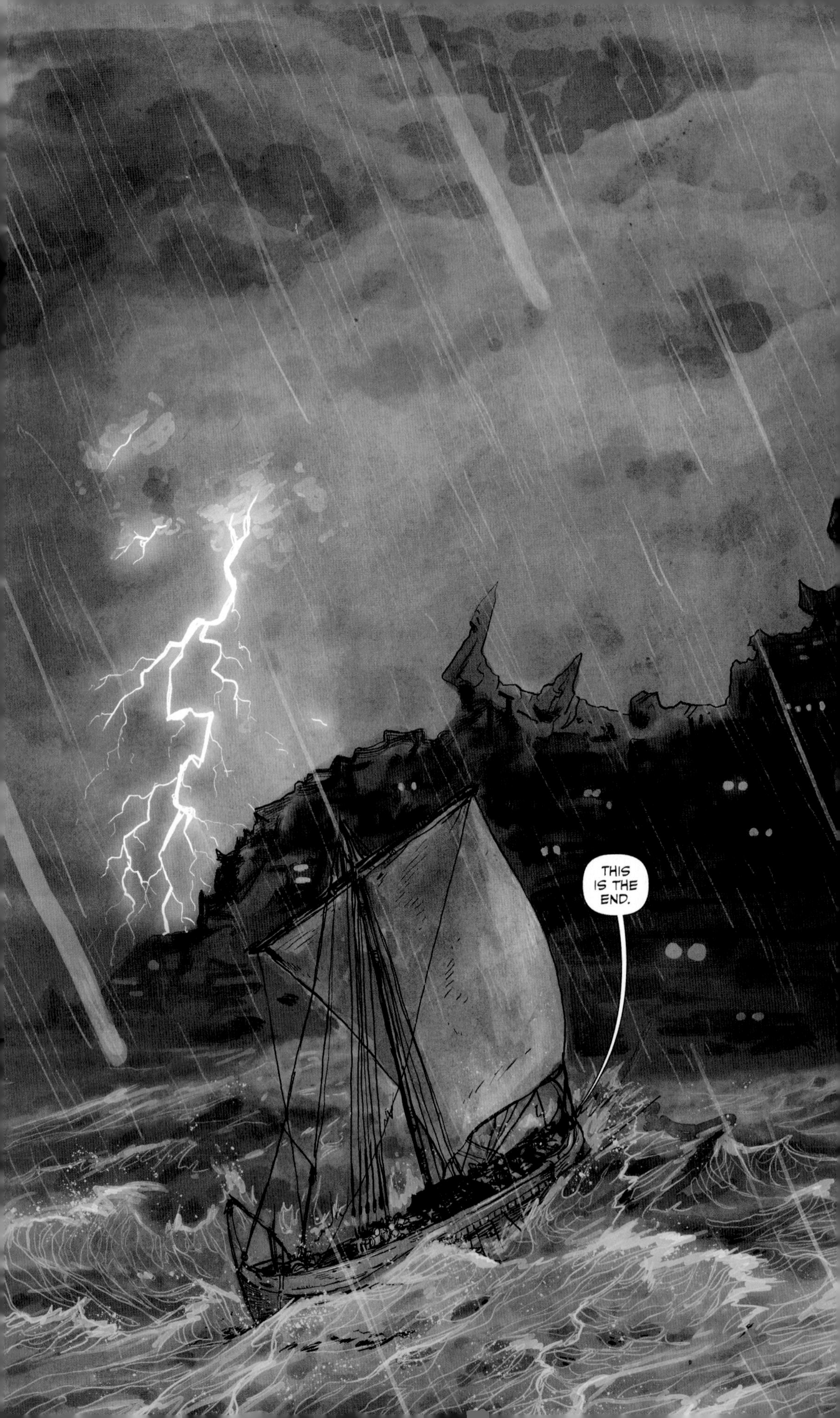
THIS IS THE END.

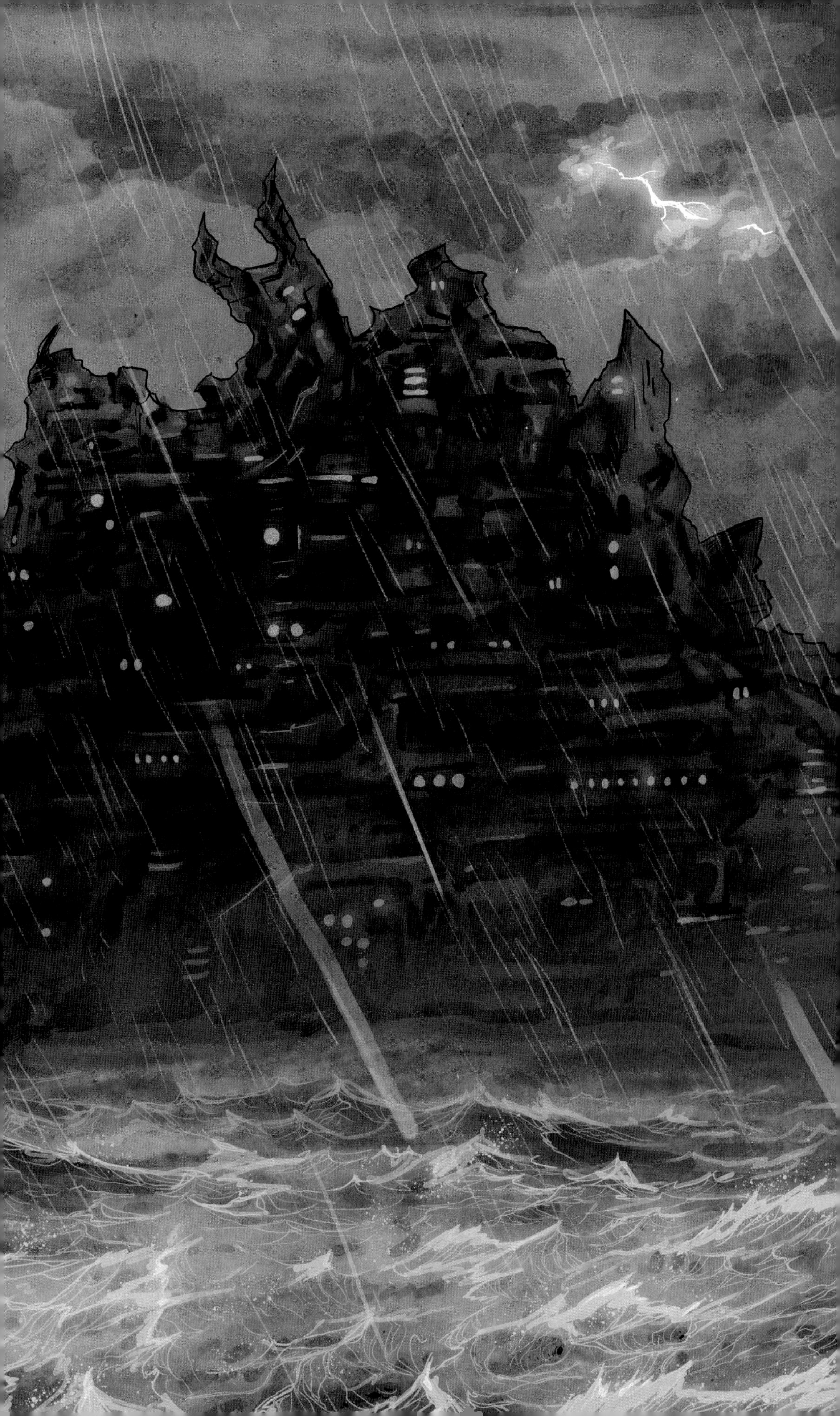

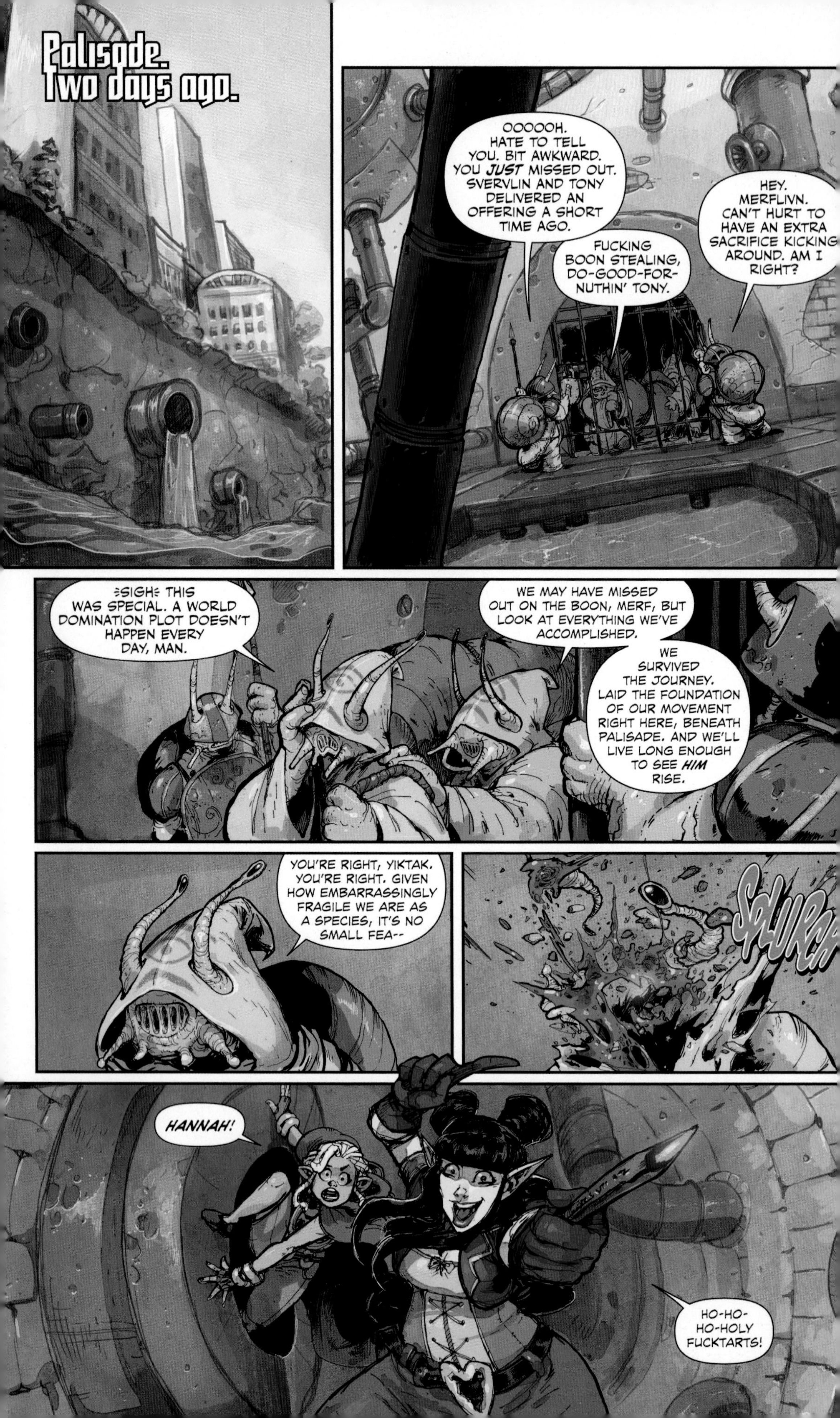
Palisade. Two days ago.
OOOOOOH. HATE TO TELL YOU. BIT AWKWARD. YOU JUST MISSED OUT. SVERVLIN AND TONY DELIVERED AN OFFERING A SHORT TIME AGO.
FUCKING BOON STEALING, DO-GOOD-FOR-NUTHIN' TONY.
HEY. MERFLIVN. CAN'T HURT TO HAVE AN EXTRA SACRIFICE KICKING AROUND. AM I RIGHT?
=SIGH= THIS WAS SPECIAL. A WORLD DOMINATION PLOT DOESN'T HAPPEN EVERY DAY, MAN.
WE MAY HAVE MISSED OUT ON THE BOON, MERF, BUT LOOK AT EVERYTHING WE'VE ACCOMPLISHED.
WE SURVIVED THE JOURNEY. LAID THE FOUNDATION OF OUR MOVEMENT RIGHT HERE, BENEATH PALISADE. AND WE'LL LIVE LONG ENOUGH TO SEE HIM RISE.
YOU'RE RIGHT, YIKTAK. YOU'RE RIGHT. GIVEN HOW EMBARRASSINGLY FRAGILE WE ARE AS A SPECIES, IT'S NO SMALL FEA--
SPLURCH
HANNAH!
HO-HO-HO-HOLY FUCKTARTS!

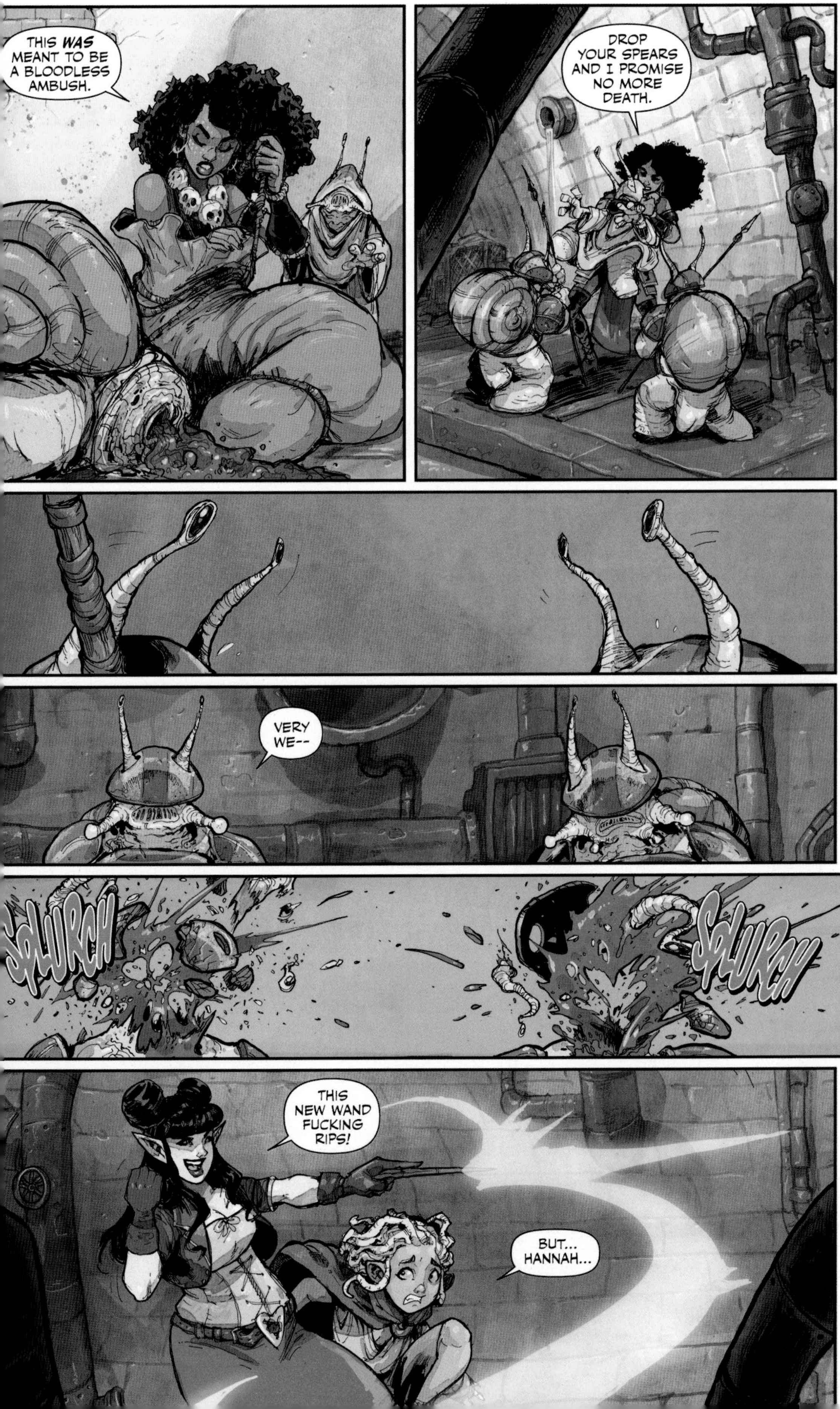
THIS WAS MEANT TO BE A BLOODLESS AMBUSH.
DROP YOUR SPEARS AND I PROMISE NO MORE DEATH.
VERY WE--
SPLURCH
SPLURCH
THIS NEW WAND FUCKING RIPS!
BUT... HANNAH...

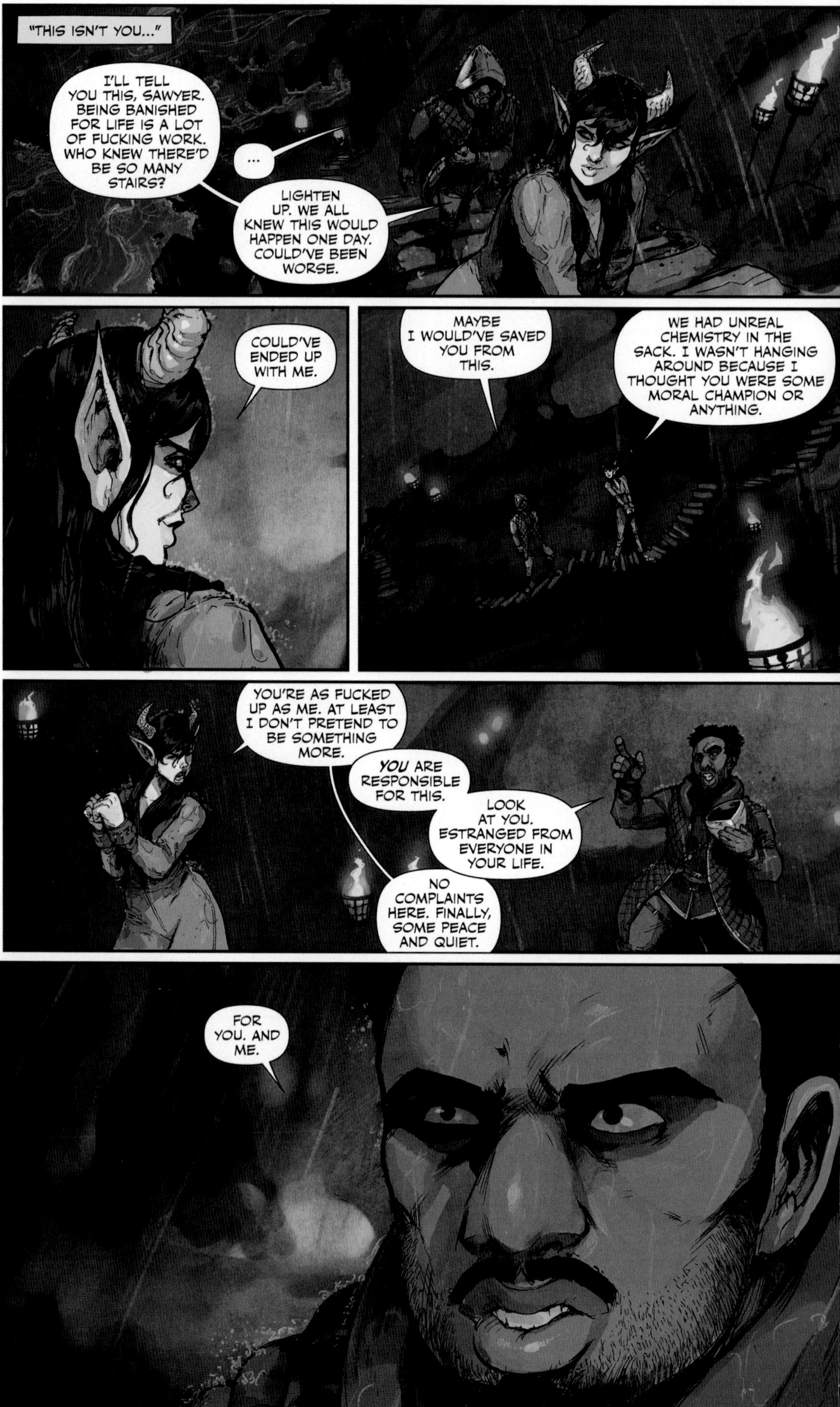
"THIS ISN'T YOU..."
I'LL TELL YOU THIS, SAWYER. BEING BANISHED FOR LIFE IS A LOT OF FUCKING WORK. WHO KNEW THERE'D BE SO MANY STAIRS?
...
LIGHTEN UP. WE ALL KNEW THIS WOULD HAPPEN ONE DAY. COULD'VE BEEN WORSE.
COULD'VE ENDED UP WITH ME.
MAYBE I WOULD'VE SAVED YOU FROM THIS.
WE HAD UNREAL CHEMISTRY IN THE SACK. I WASN'T HANGING AROUND BECAUSE I THOUGHT YOU WERE SOME MORAL CHAMPION OR ANYTHING.
YOU'RE AS FUCKED UP AS ME. AT LEAST I DON'T PRETEND TO BE SOMETHING MORE.
YOU ARE RESPONSIBLE FOR THIS.
LOOK AT YOU. ESTRANGED FROM EVERYONE IN YOUR LIFE.
NO COMPLAINTS HERE. FINALLY, SOME PEACE AND QUIET.
FOR YOU. AND ME.

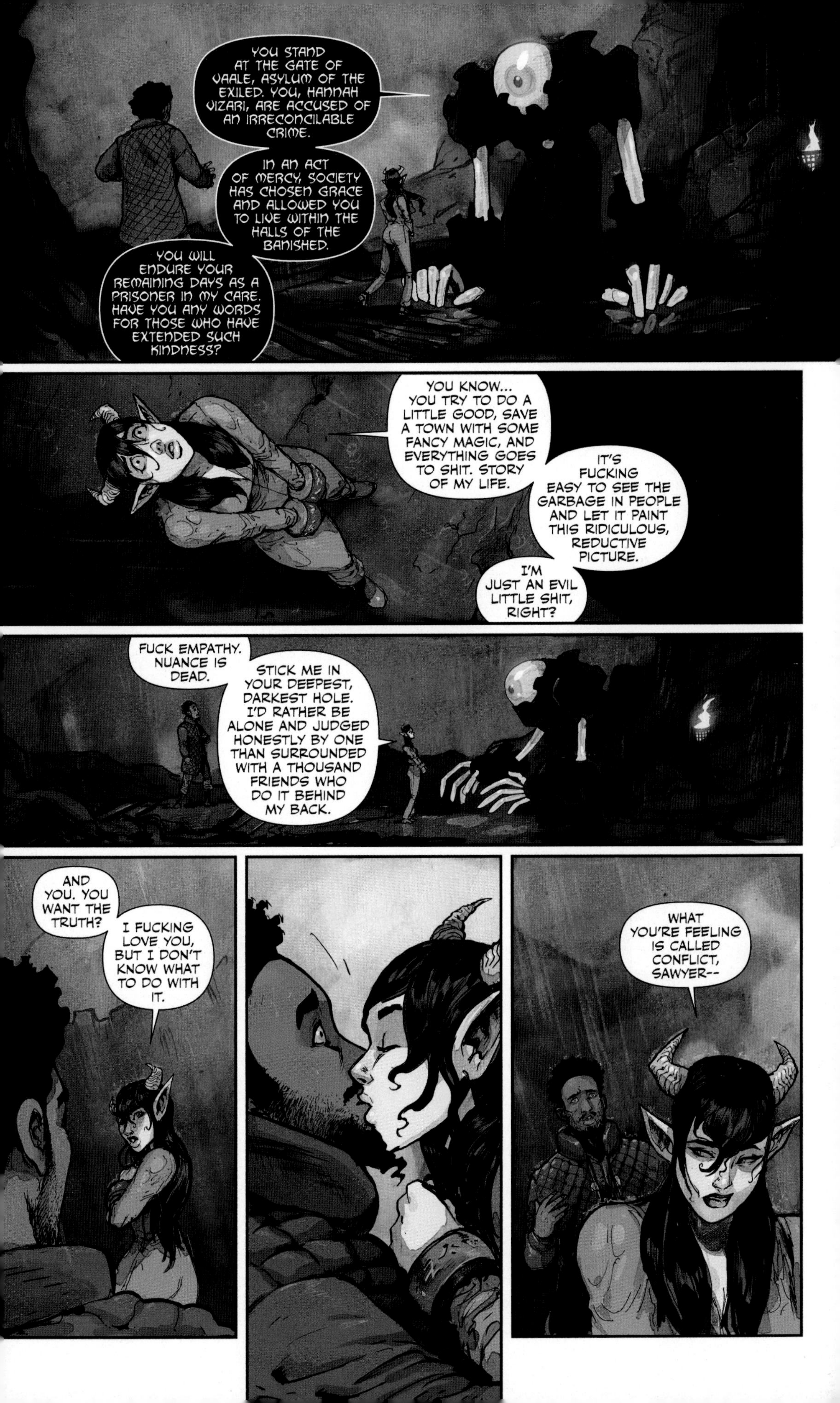
YOU STAND AT THE GATE OF VAALE, ASYLUM OF THE EXILED. YOU, HANNAH VIZARI, ARE ACCUSED OF AN IRRECONCILABLE CRIME.
IN AN ACT OF MERCY, SOCIETY HAS CHOSEN GRACE AND ALLOWED YOU TO LIVE WITHIN THE HALLS OF THE BANISHED.
YOU WILL ENDURE YOUR REMAINING DAYS AS A PRISONER IN MY CARE. HAVE YOU ANY WORDS FOR THOSE WHO HAVE EXTENDED SUCH KINDNESS?
YOU KNOW... YOU TRY TO DO A LITTLE GOOD, SAVE A TOWN WITH SOME FANCY MAGIC, AND EVERYTHING GOES TO SHIT. STORY OF MY LIFE.
IT'S FUCKING EASY TO SEE THE GARBAGE IN PEOPLE AND LET IT PAINT THIS RIDICULOUS, REDUCTIVE PICTURE.
I'M JUST AN EVIL LITTLE SHIT, RIGHT?
FUCK EMPATHY. NUANCE IS DEAD.
STICK ME IN YOUR DEEPEST, DARKEST HOLE. I'D RATHER BE ALONE AND JUDGED HONESTLY BY ONE THAN SURROUNDED WITH A THOUSAND FRIENDS WHO DO IT BEHIND MY BACK.
AND YOU. YOU WANT THE TRUTH?
I FUCKING LOVE YOU, BUT I DON'T KNOW WHAT TO DO WITH IT.
WHAT YOU'RE FEELING IS CALLED CONFLICT, SAWYER--

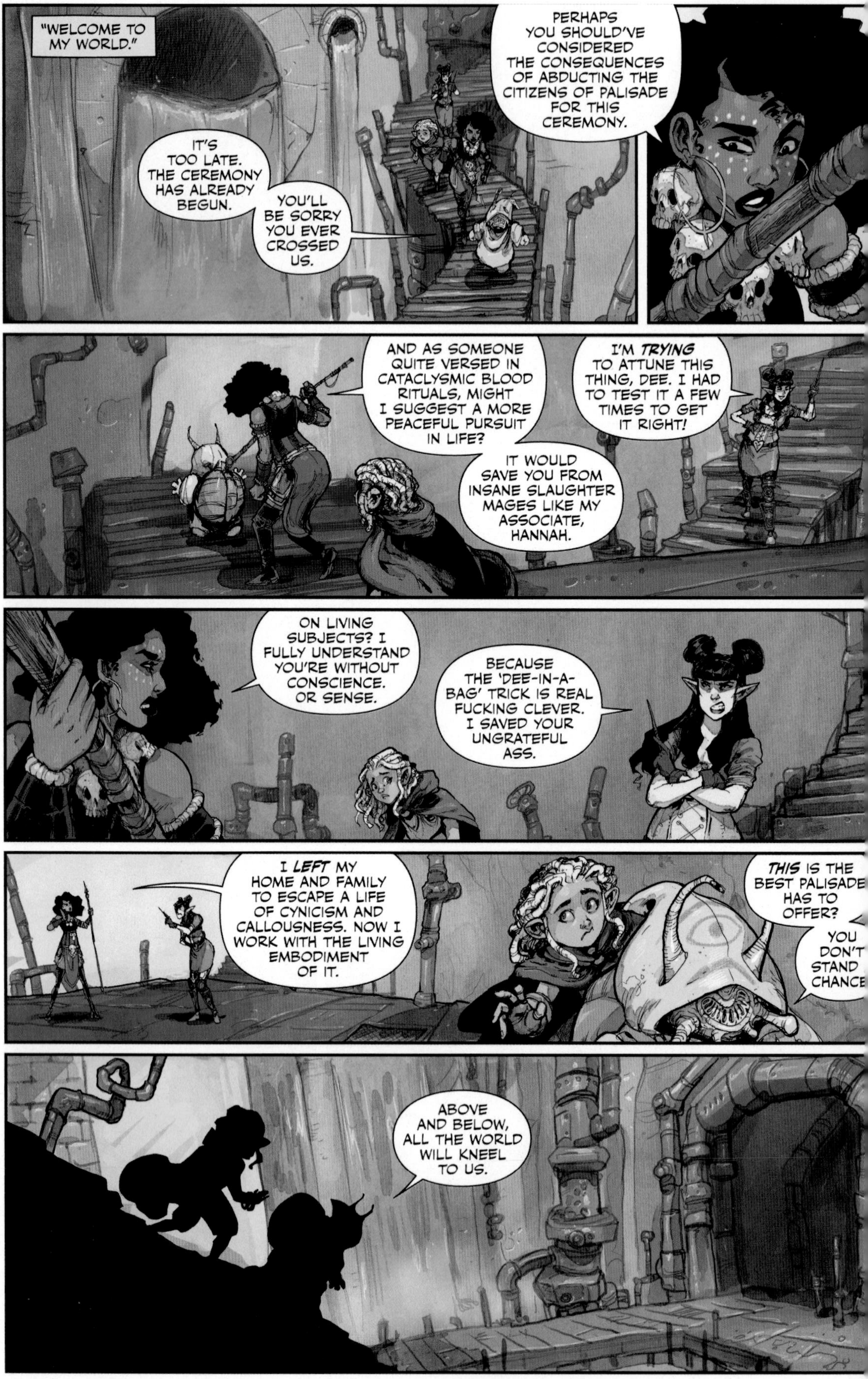

"WELCOME TO MY WORLD."
IT'S TOO LATE. THE CEREMONY HAS ALREADY BEGUN.
YOU'LL BE SORRY YOU EVER CROSSED US.
PERHAPS YOU SHOULD'VE CONSIDERED THE CONSEQUENCES OF ABDUCTING THE CITIZENS OF PALISADE FOR THIS CEREMONY.
AND AS SOMEONE QUITE VERSED IN CATACLYSMIC BLOOD RITUALS, MIGHT I SUGGEST A MORE PEACEFUL PURSUIT IN LIFE?
IT WOULD SAVE YOU FROM INSANE SLAUGHTER MAGES LIKE MY ASSOCIATE, HANNAH.
I'M *TRYING* TO ATTUNE THIS THING, DEE. I HAD TO TEST IT A FEW TIMES TO GET IT RIGHT!
ON LIVING SUBJECTS? I FULLY UNDERSTAND YOU'RE WITHOUT CONSCIENCE. OR SENSE.
BECAUSE THE 'DEE-IN-A-BAG' TRICK IS REAL FUCKING CLEVER. I SAVED YOUR UNGRATEFUL ASS.
I *LEFT* MY HOME AND FAMILY TO ESCAPE A LIFE OF CYNICISM AND CALLOUSNESS. NOW I WORK WITH THE LIVING EMBODIMENT OF IT.
THIS IS THE BEST PALISADE HAS TO OFFER?
YOU DON'T STAND CHANCE
ABOVE AND BELOW, ALL THE WORLD WILL KNEEL TO US.

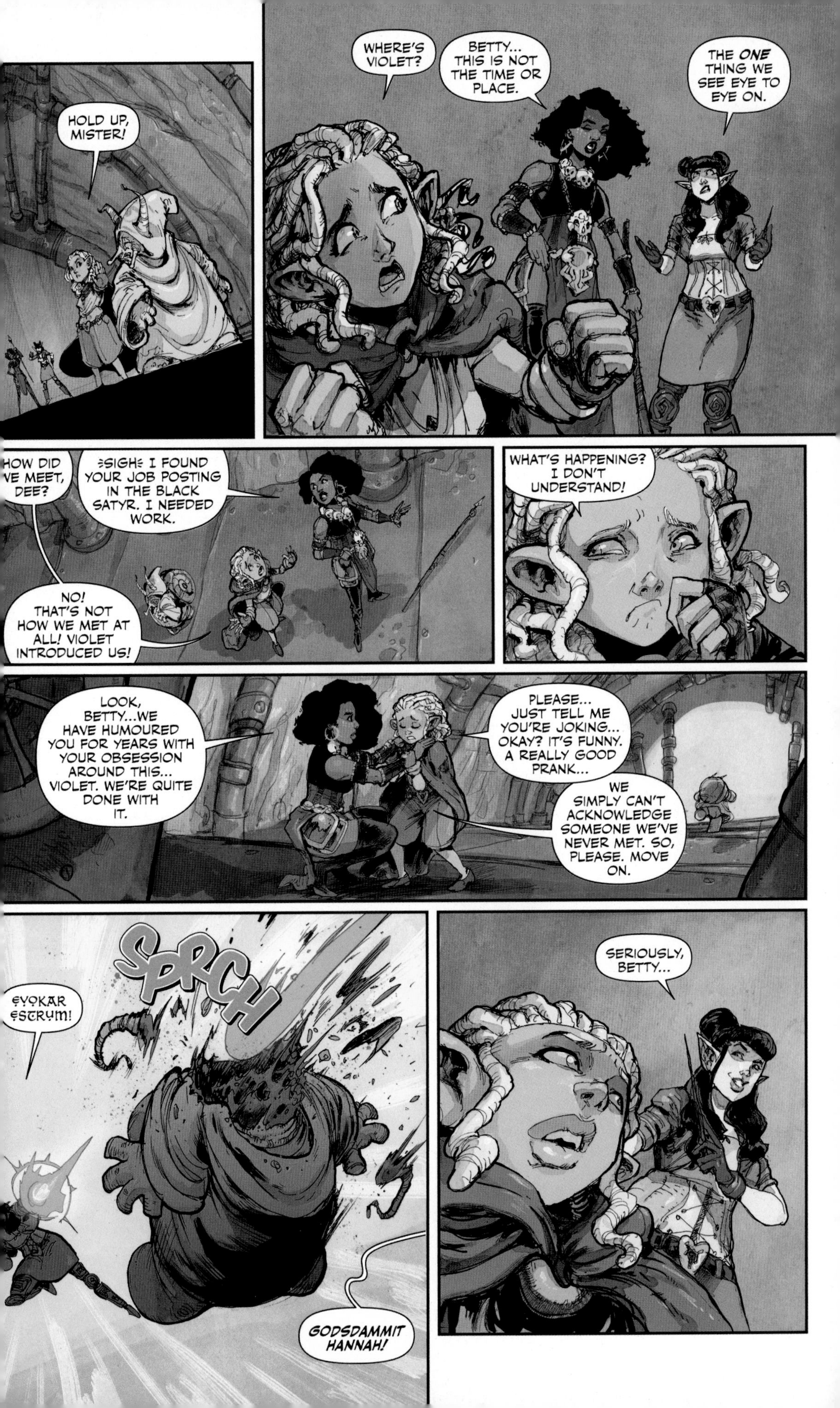
HOLD UP, MISTER!
WHERE'S VIOLET?
BETTY... THIS IS NOT THE TIME OR PLACE.
THE *ONE* THING WE SEE EYE TO EYE ON.
HOW DID WE MEET, DEE?
=SIGH= I FOUND YOUR JOB POSTING IN THE BLACK SATYR. I NEEDED WORK.
NO! THAT'S NOT HOW WE MET AT ALL! VIOLET INTRODUCED US!
WHAT'S HAPPENING? I DON'T UNDERSTAND!
LOOK, BETTY...WE HAVE HUMOURED YOU FOR YEARS WITH YOUR OBSESSION AROUND THIS... VIOLET. WE'RE QUITE DONE WITH IT.
PLEASE... JUST TELL ME YOU'RE JOKING... OKAY? IT'S FUNNY. A REALLY GOOD PRANK...
WE SIMPLY CAN'T ACKNOWLEDGE SOMEONE WE'VE NEVER MET. SO, PLEASE. MOVE ON.
EVOKAR ESTRUM!
SPRCH
GODSDAMMIT HANNAH!
SERIOUSLY, BETTY...

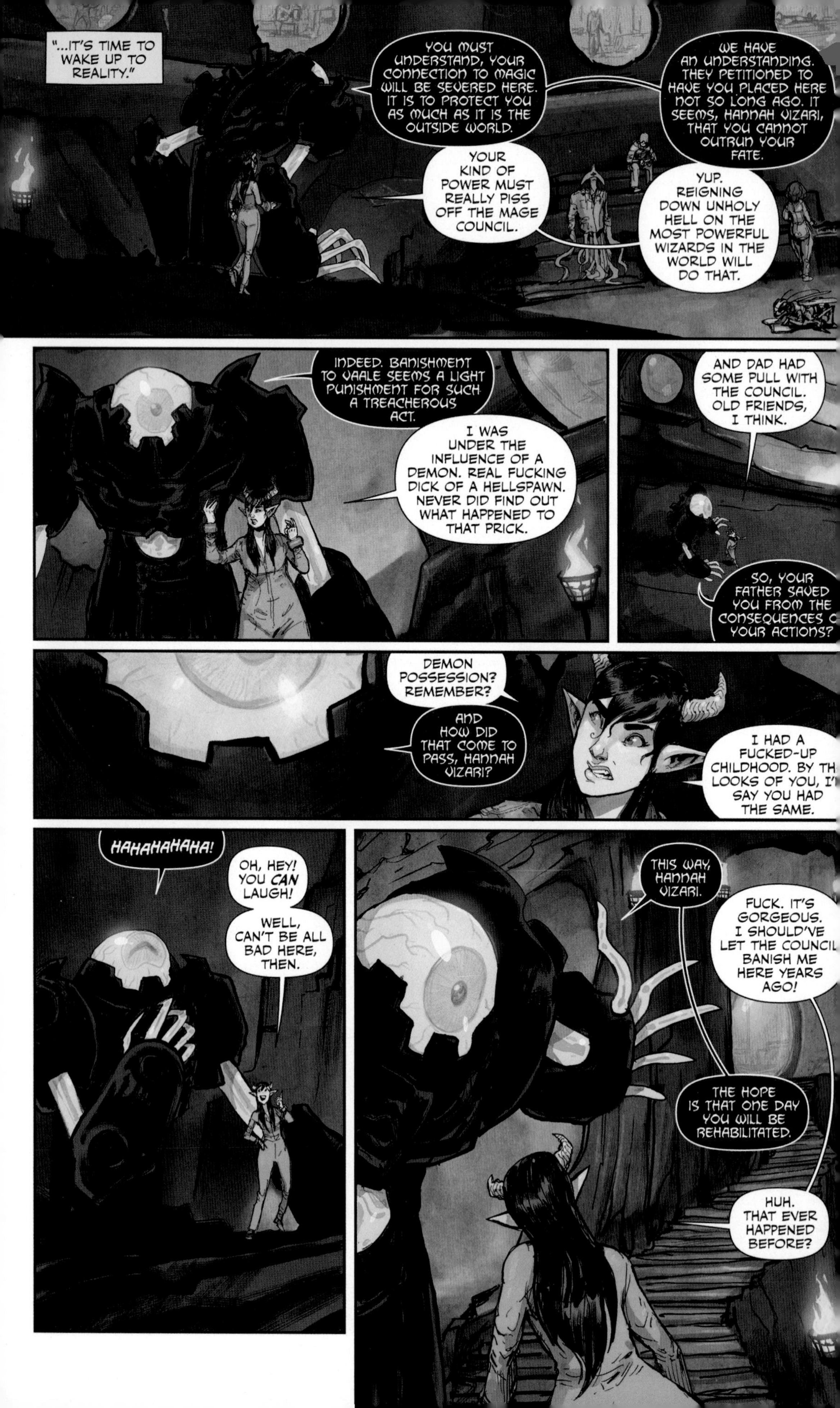

"...IT'S TIME TO WAKE UP TO REALITY."
YOU MUST UNDERSTAND, YOUR CONNECTION TO MAGIC WILL BE SEVERED HERE. IT IS TO PROTECT YOU AS MUCH AS IT IS THE OUTSIDE WORLD.
WE HAVE AN UNDERSTANDING. THEY PETITIONED TO HAVE YOU PLACED HERE NOT SO LONG AGO. IT SEEMS, HANNAH VIZARI, THAT YOU CANNOT OUTRUN YOUR FATE.
YOUR KIND OF POWER MUST REALLY PISS OFF THE MAGE COUNCIL.
YUP. REIGNING DOWN UNHOLY HELL ON THE MOST POWERFUL WIZARDS IN THE WORLD WILL DO THAT.
INDEED. BANISHMENT TO VAALE SEEMS A LIGHT PUNISHMENT FOR SUCH A TREACHEROUS ACT.
I WAS UNDER THE INFLUENCE OF A DEMON. REAL FUCKING DICK OF A HELLSPAWN. NEVER DID FIND OUT WHAT HAPPENED TO THAT PRICK.
AND DAD HAD SOME PULL WITH THE COUNCIL. OLD FRIENDS, I THINK.
SO, YOUR FATHER SAVED YOU FROM THE CONSEQUENCES O YOUR ACTIONS?
DEMON POSSESSION? REMEMBER?
AND HOW DID THAT COME TO PASS, HANNAH VIZARI?
I HAD A FUCKED-UP CHILDHOOD. BY TH LOOKS OF YOU, I' SAY YOU HAD THE SAME.
HAHAHAHAHA!
OH, HEY! YOU *CAN* LAUGH!
WELL, CAN'T BE ALL BAD HERE, THEN.
THIS WAY, HANNAH VIZARI.
FUCK. IT'S GORGEOUS. I SHOULD'VE LET THE COUNCIL BANISH ME HERE YEARS AGO!
THE HOPE IS THAT ONE DAY YOU WILL BE REHABILITATED.
HUH. THAT EVER HAPPENED BEFORE?

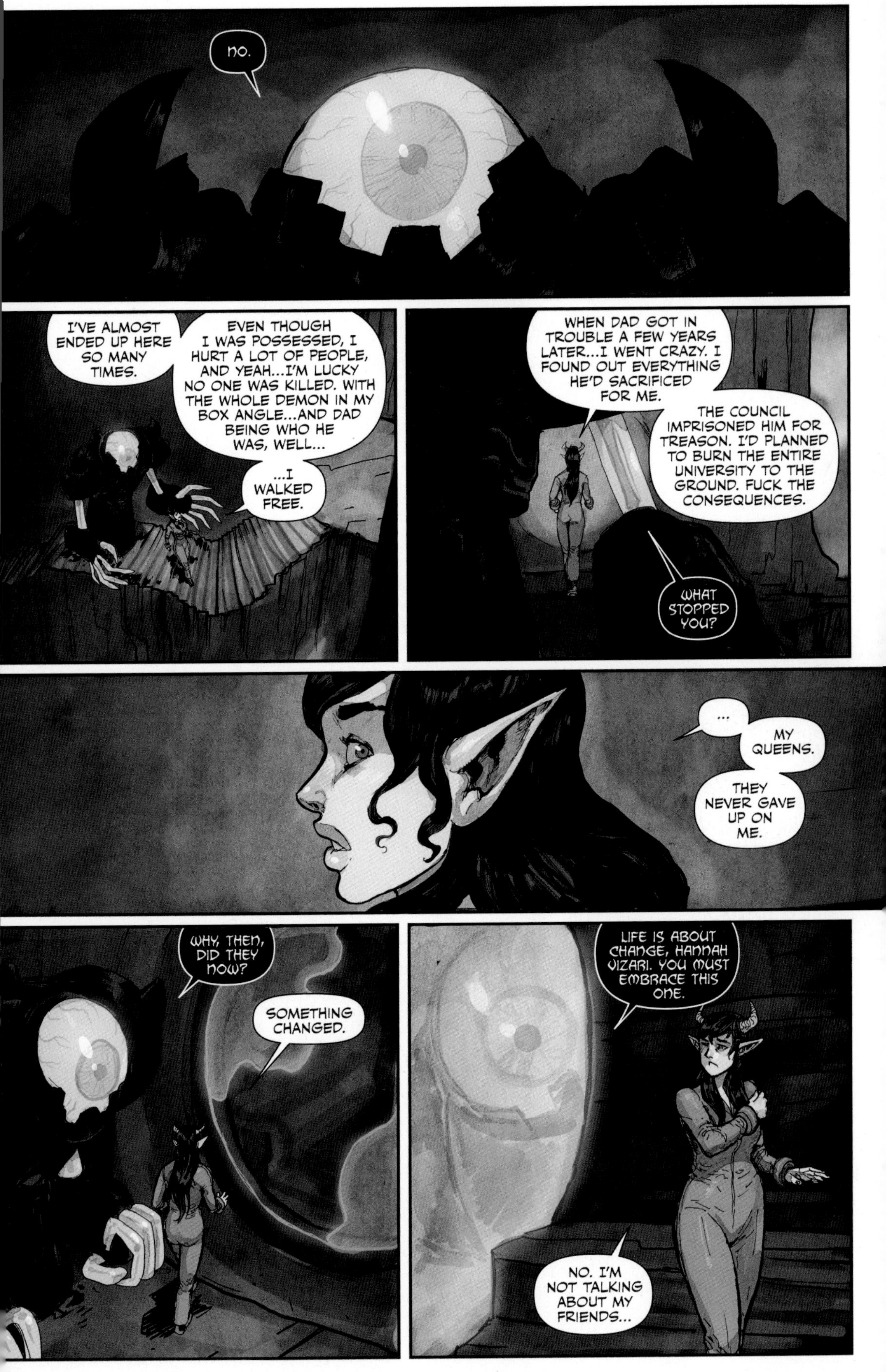
no.
I'VE ALMOST ENDED UP HERE SO MANY TIMES.
EVEN THOUGH I WAS POSSESSED, I HURT A LOT OF PEOPLE, AND YEAH...I'M LUCKY NO ONE WAS KILLED. WITH THE WHOLE DEMON IN MY BOX ANGLE...AND DAD BEING WHO HE WAS, WELL...
...I WALKED FREE.
WHEN DAD GOT IN TROUBLE A FEW YEARS LATER...I WENT CRAZY. I FOUND OUT EVERYTHING HE'D SACRIFICED FOR ME.
THE COUNCIL IMPRISONED HIM FOR TREASON. I'D PLANNED TO BURN THE ENTIRE UNIVERSITY TO THE GROUND. FUCK THE CONSEQUENCES.
WHAT STOPPED YOU?
...
MY QUEENS.
THEY NEVER GAVE UP ON ME.
WHY, THEN, DID THEY NOW?
SOMETHING CHANGED.
LIFE IS ABOUT CHANGE, HANNAH VIZARI. YOU MUST EMBRACE THIS ONE.
NO. I'M NOT TALKING ABOUT MY FRIENDS...

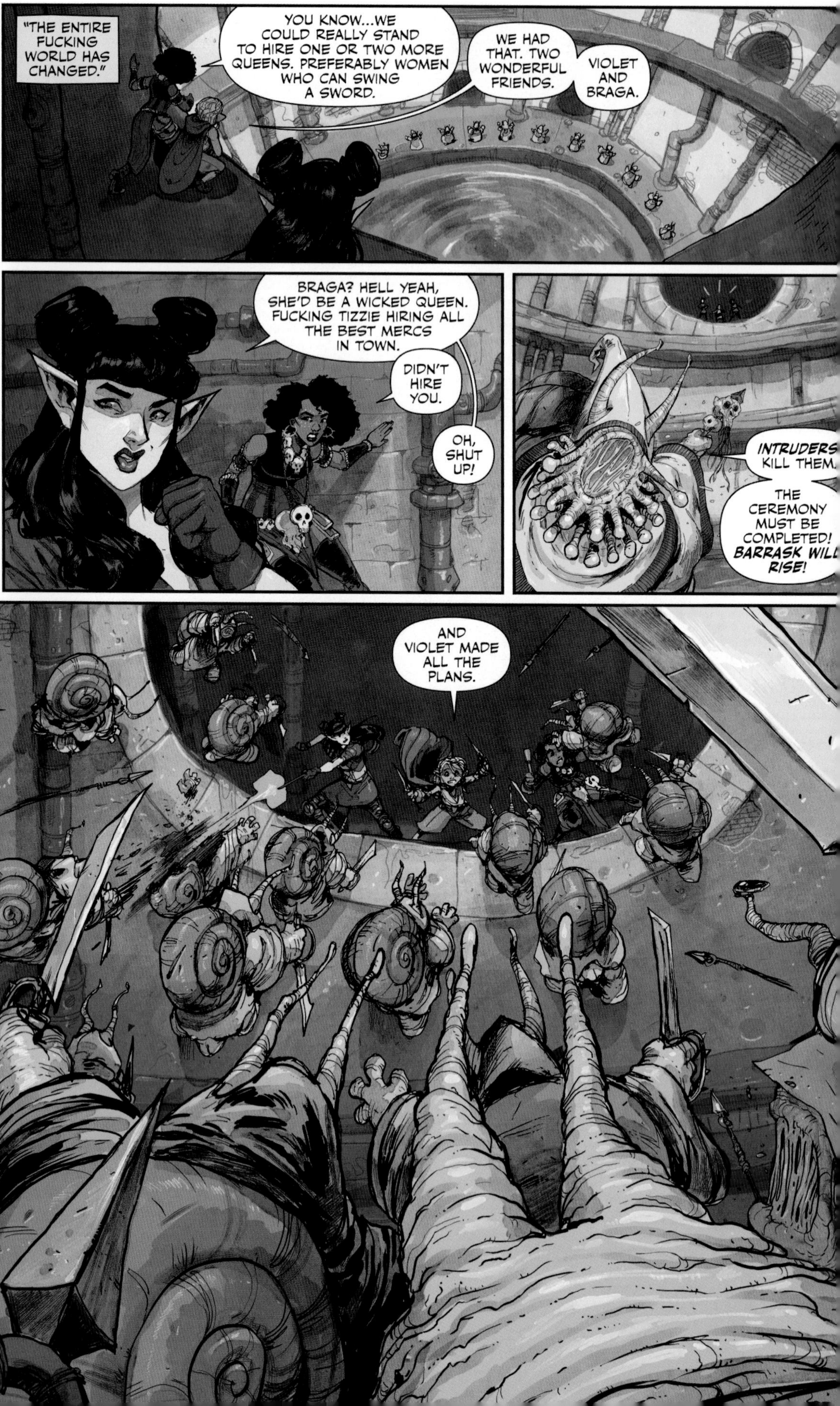
"THE ENTIRE FUCKING WORLD HAS CHANGED."
YOU KNOW...WE COULD REALLY STAND TO HIRE ONE OR TWO MORE QUEENS. PREFERABLY WOMEN WHO CAN SWING A SWORD.
WE HAD THAT. TWO WONDERFUL FRIENDS.
VIOLET AND BRAGA.
BRAGA? HELL YEAH, SHE'D BE A WICKED QUEEN. FUCKING TIZZIE HIRING ALL THE BEST MERCS IN TOWN.
DIDN'T HIRE YOU.
OH, SHUT UP!
INTRUDERS KILL THEM
THE CEREMONY MUST BE COMPLETED! ***BARRASK WILL RISE!***
AND VIOLET MADE ALL THE PLANS.

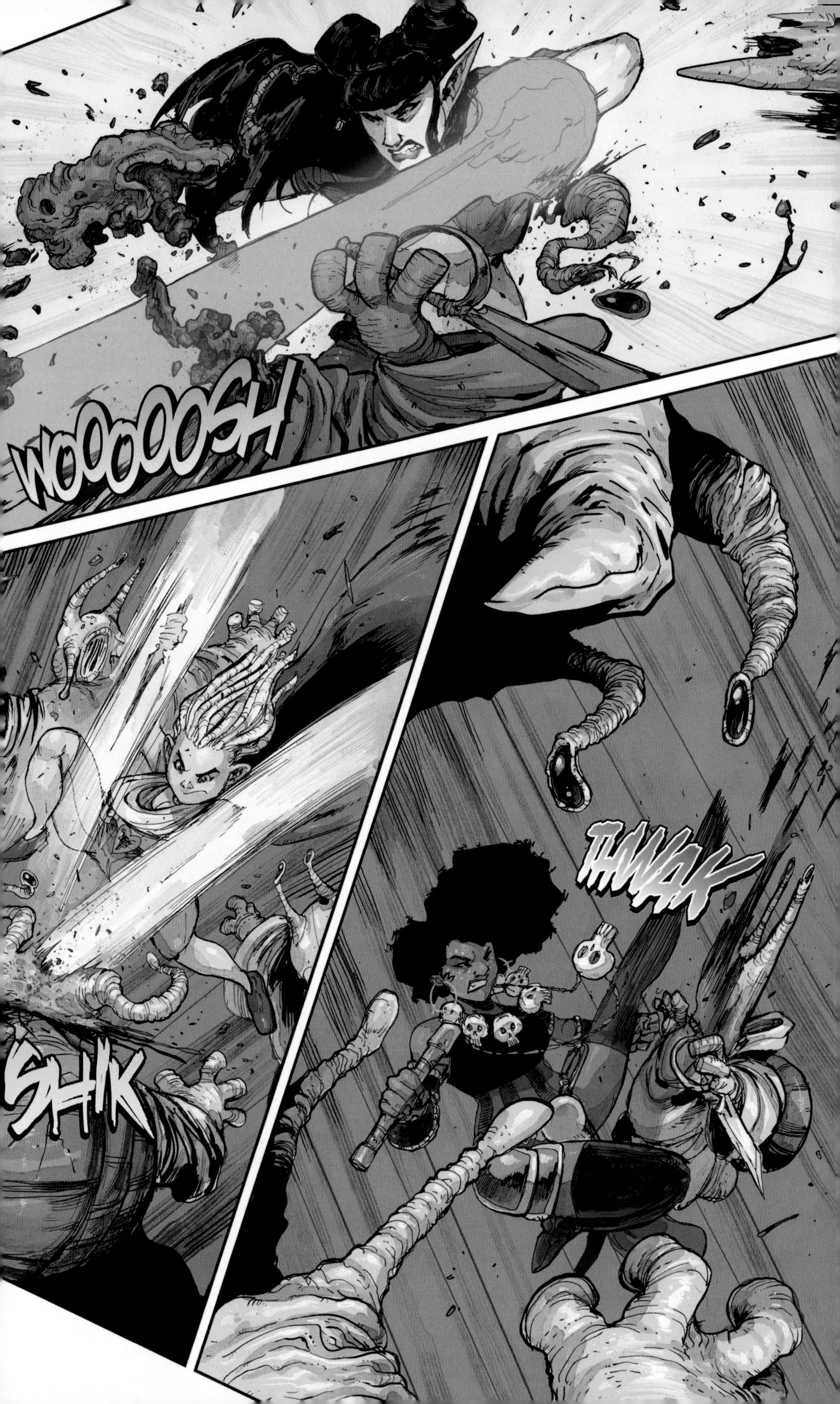
WOOOOOSH
SHIK
THWAK

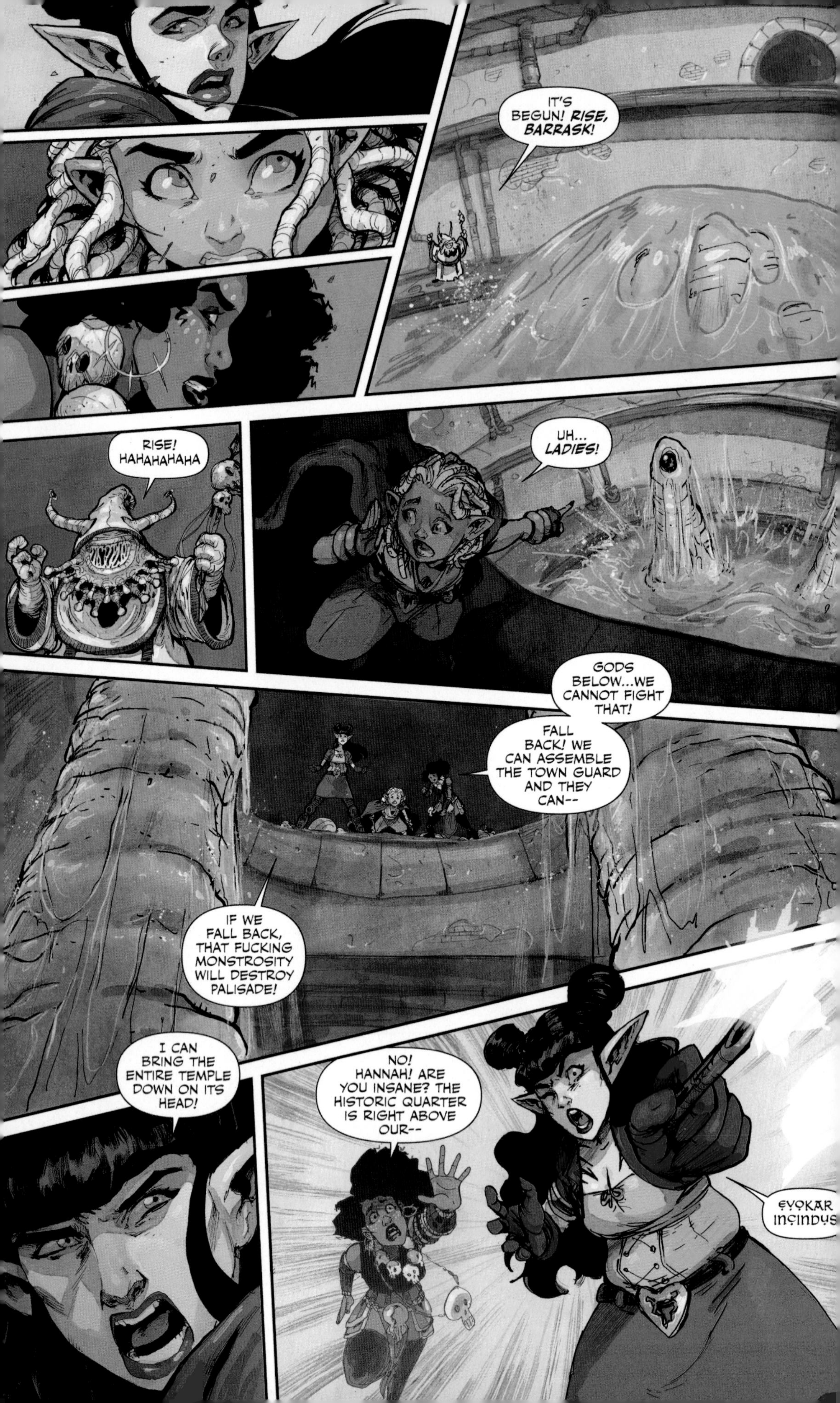
IT'S BEGUN! RISE, BARRASK!
RISE! HAHAHAHAHA
UH... LADIES!
GODS BELOW...WE CANNOT FIGHT THAT!
FALL BACK! WE CAN ASSEMBLE THE TOWN GUARD AND THEY CAN--
IF WE FALL BACK, THAT FUCKING MONSTROSITY WILL DESTROY PALISADE!
I CAN BRING THE ENTIRE TEMPLE DOWN ON ITS HEAD!
NO! HANNAH! ARE YOU INSANE? THE HISTORIC QUARTER IS RIGHT ABOVE OUR--
EVOKAR INCINDUS

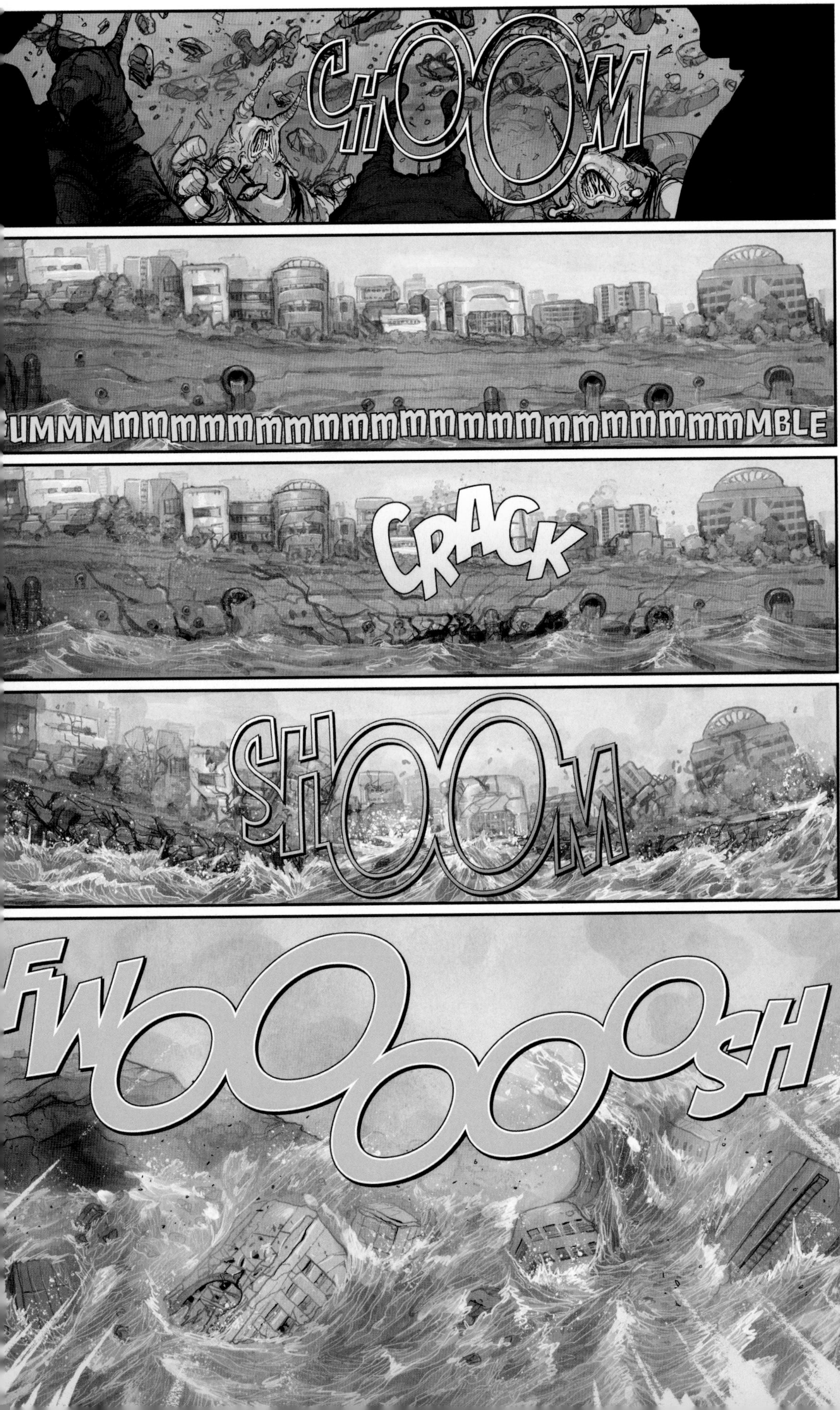
CHOOM
UMMMmmmmmmmmmmmmmmmmmmmmMBLE
CRACK
SHOOOM
FWOOOOOOSH

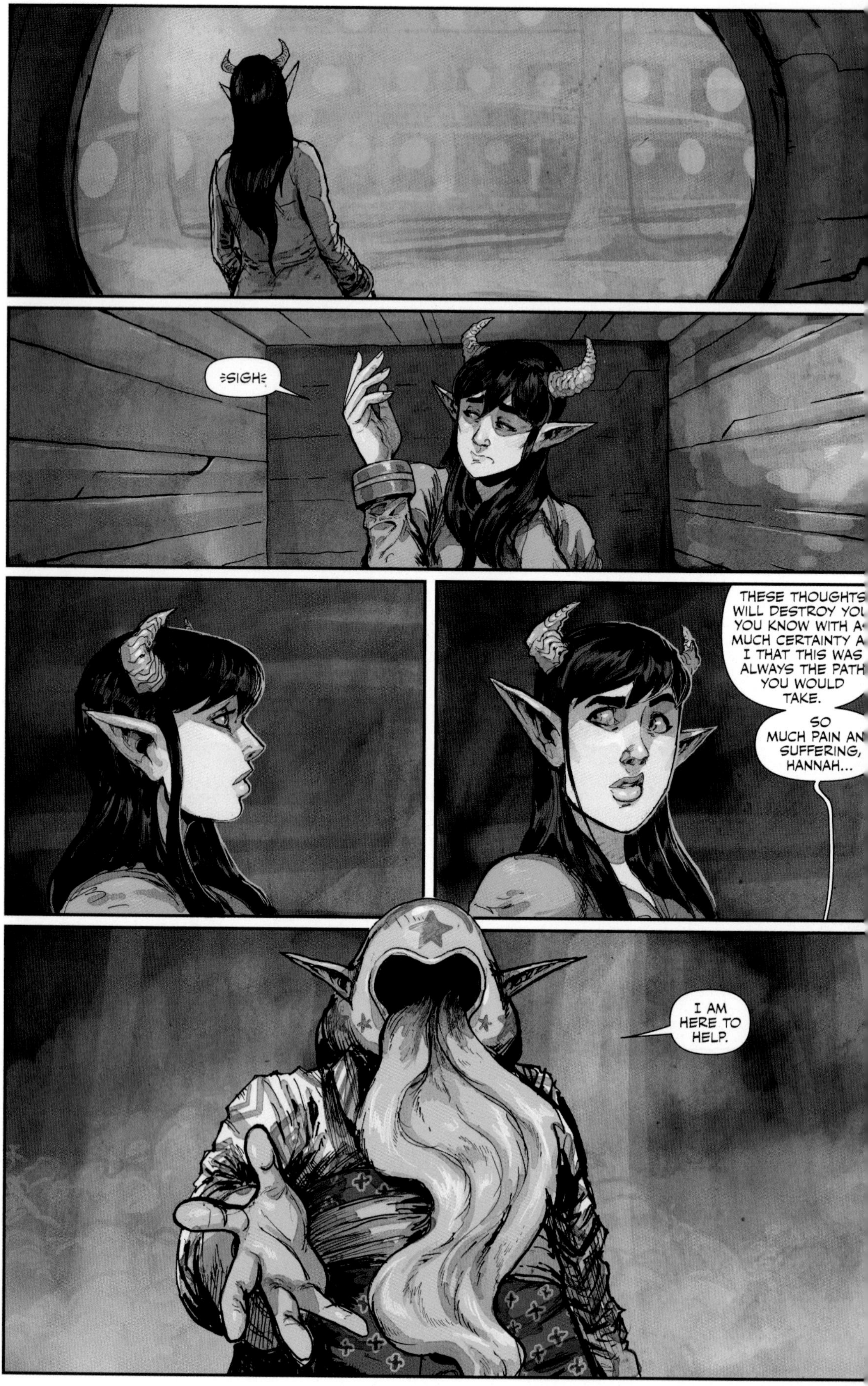
SIGH
THESE THOUGHTS WILL DESTROY YOU YOU KNOW WITH A MUCH CERTAINTY A I THAT THIS WAS ALWAYS THE PATH YOU WOULD TAKE.
SO MUCH PAIN AN SUFFERING, HANNAH...
I AM HERE TO HELP.

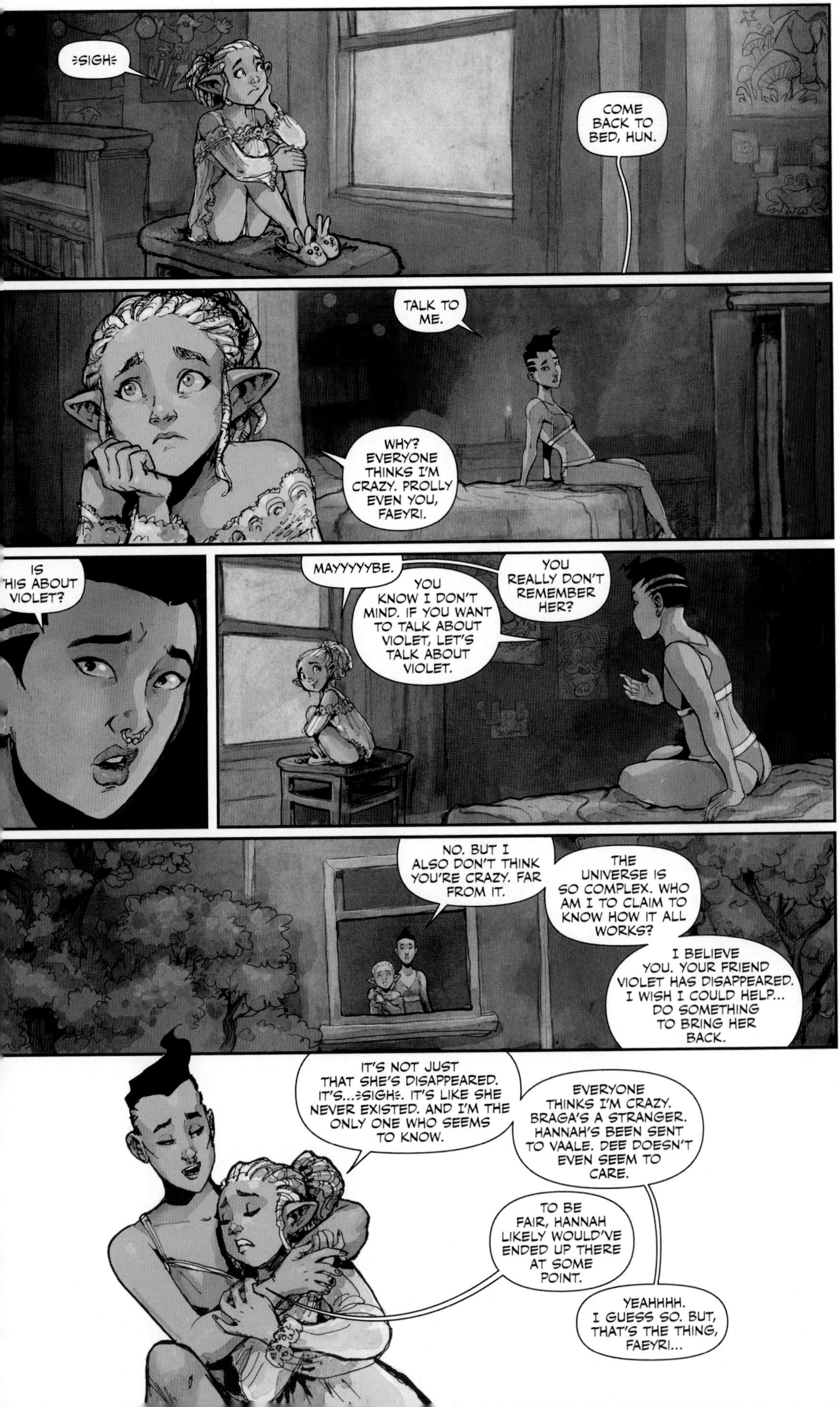

=SIGH=
COME BACK TO BED, HUN.
TALK TO ME.
WHY? EVERYONE THINKS I'M CRAZY. PROLLY EVEN YOU, FAEYRI.
IS THIS ABOUT VIOLET?
MAYYYYYBE.
YOU REALLY DON'T REMEMBER HER?
YOU KNOW I DON'T MIND. IF YOU WANT TO TALK ABOUT VIOLET, LET'S TALK ABOUT VIOLET.
NO. BUT I ALSO DON'T THINK YOU'RE CRAZY. FAR FROM IT.
THE UNIVERSE IS SO COMPLEX. WHO AM I TO CLAIM TO KNOW HOW IT ALL WORKS?
I BELIEVE YOU. YOUR FRIEND VIOLET HAS DISAPPEARED. I WISH I COULD HELP... DO SOMETHING TO BRING HER BACK.
IT'S NOT JUST THAT SHE'S DISAPPEARED. IT'S...=SIGH=. IT'S LIKE SHE NEVER EXISTED. AND I'M THE ONLY ONE WHO SEEMS TO KNOW.
EVERYONE THINKS I'M CRAZY. BRAGA'S A STRANGER. HANNAH'S BEEN SENT TO VAALE. DEE DOESN'T EVEN SEEM TO CARE.
TO BE FAIR, HANNAH LIKELY WOULD'VE ENDED UP THERE AT SOME POINT.
YEAHHHH. I GUESS SO. BUT, THAT'S THE THING, FAEYRI...

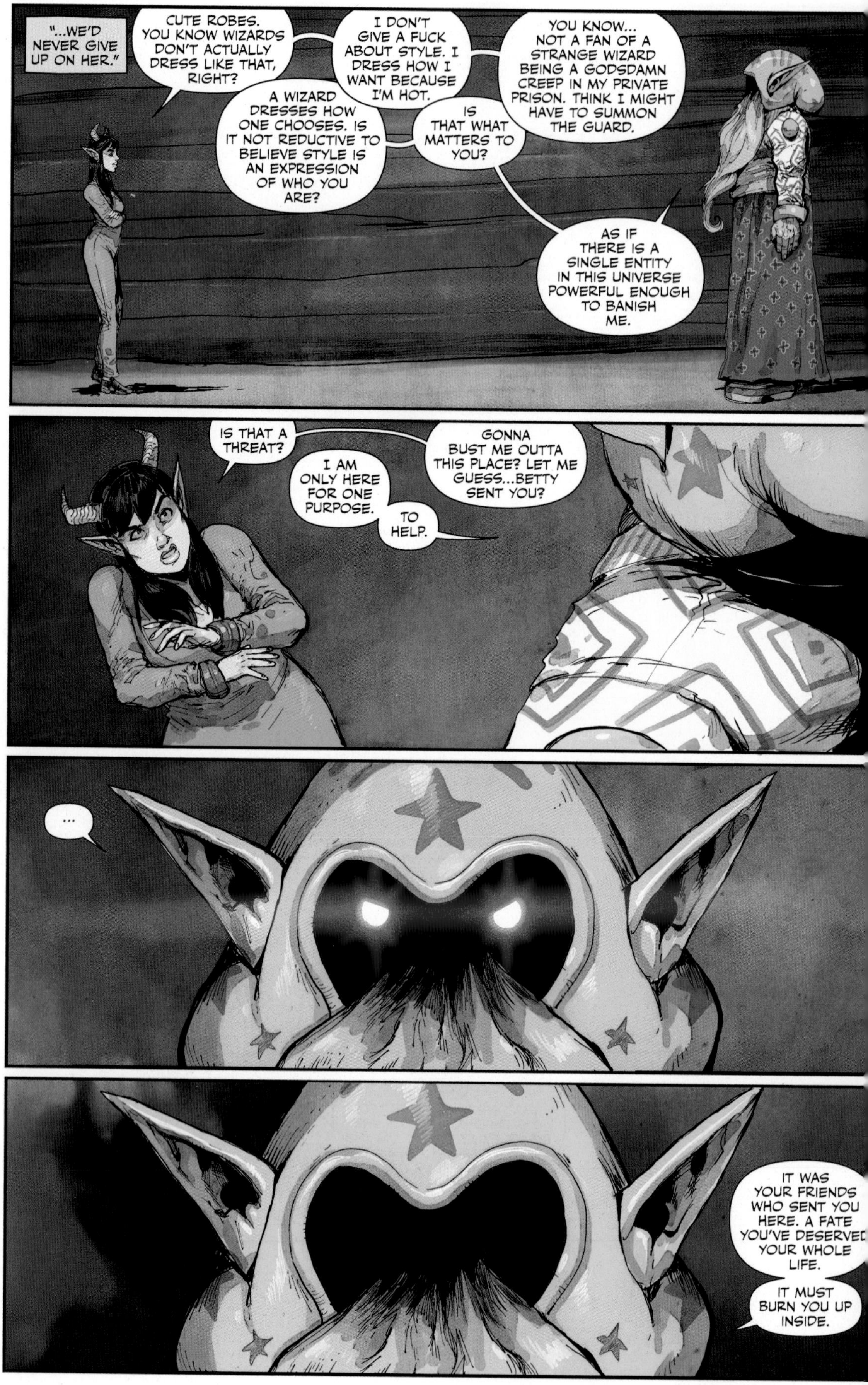
"...WE'D NEVER GIVE UP ON HER."
CUTE ROBES. YOU KNOW WIZARDS DON'T ACTUALLY DRESS LIKE THAT, RIGHT?
A WIZARD DRESSES HOW ONE CHOOSES. IS IT NOT REDUCTIVE TO BELIEVE STYLE IS AN EXPRESSION OF WHO YOU ARE?
I DON'T GIVE A FUCK ABOUT STYLE. I DRESS HOW I WANT BECAUSE I'M HOT.
IS THAT WHAT MATTERS TO YOU?
YOU KNOW... NOT A FAN OF A STRANGE WIZARD BEING A GODSDAMN CREEP IN MY PRIVATE PRISON. THINK I MIGHT HAVE TO SUMMON THE GUARD.
AS IF THERE IS A SINGLE ENTITY IN THIS UNIVERSE POWERFUL ENOUGH TO BANISH ME.
IS THAT A THREAT?
GONNA BUST ME OUTTA THIS PLACE? LET ME GUESS...BETTY SENT YOU?
I AM ONLY HERE FOR ONE PURPOSE.
TO HELP.
...
IT WAS YOUR FRIENDS WHO SENT YOU HERE. A FATE YOU'VE DESERVED YOUR WHOLE LIFE.
IT MUST BURN YOU UP INSIDE.

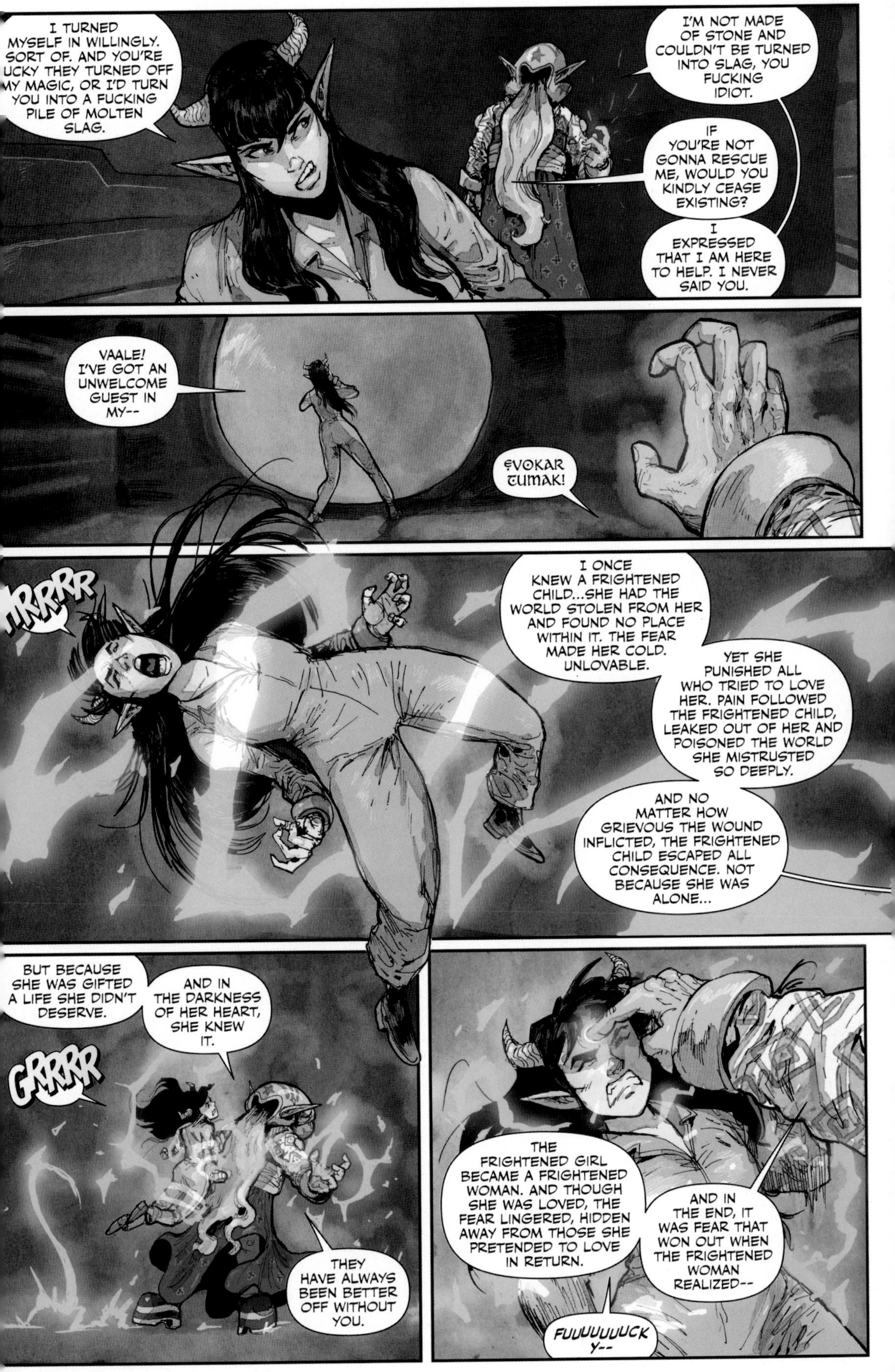
I TURNED MYSELF IN WILLINGLY. SORT OF. AND YOU'RE LUCKY THEY TURNED OFF MY MAGIC, OR I'D TURN YOU INTO A FUCKING PILE OF MOLTEN SLAG.
I'M NOT MADE OF STONE AND COULDN'T BE TURNED INTO SLAG, YOU FUCKING IDIOT.
IF YOU'RE NOT GONNA RESCUE ME, WOULD YOU KINDLY CEASE EXISTING?
I EXPRESSED THAT I AM HERE TO HELP. I NEVER SAID YOU.
VAALE! I'VE GOT AN UNWELCOME GUEST IN MY--
EVOKAR TUMAK!
TRRRR
I ONCE KNEW A FRIGHTENED CHILD...SHE HAD THE WORLD STOLEN FROM HER AND FOUND NO PLACE WITHIN IT. THE FEAR MADE HER COLD. UNLOVABLE.
YET SHE PUNISHED ALL WHO TRIED TO LOVE HER. PAIN FOLLOWED THE FRIGHTENED CHILD, LEAKED OUT OF HER AND POISONED THE WORLD SHE MISTRUSTED SO DEEPLY.
AND NO MATTER HOW GRIEVOUS THE WOUND INFLICTED, THE FRIGHTENED CHILD ESCAPED ALL CONSEQUENCE. NOT BECAUSE SHE WAS ALONE...
BUT BECAUSE SHE WAS GIFTED A LIFE SHE DIDN'T DESERVE.
AND IN THE DARKNESS OF HER HEART, SHE KNEW IT.
GRRRR
THEY HAVE ALWAYS BEEN BETTER OFF WITHOUT YOU.
THE FRIGHTENED GIRL BECAME A FRIGHTENED WOMAN. AND THOUGH SHE WAS LOVED, THE FEAR LINGERED, HIDDEN AWAY FROM THOSE SHE PRETENDED TO LOVE IN RETURN.
AND IN THE END, IT WAS FEAR THAT WON OUT WHEN THE FRIGHTENED WOMAN REALIZED--
FUUUUUUUCK Y--

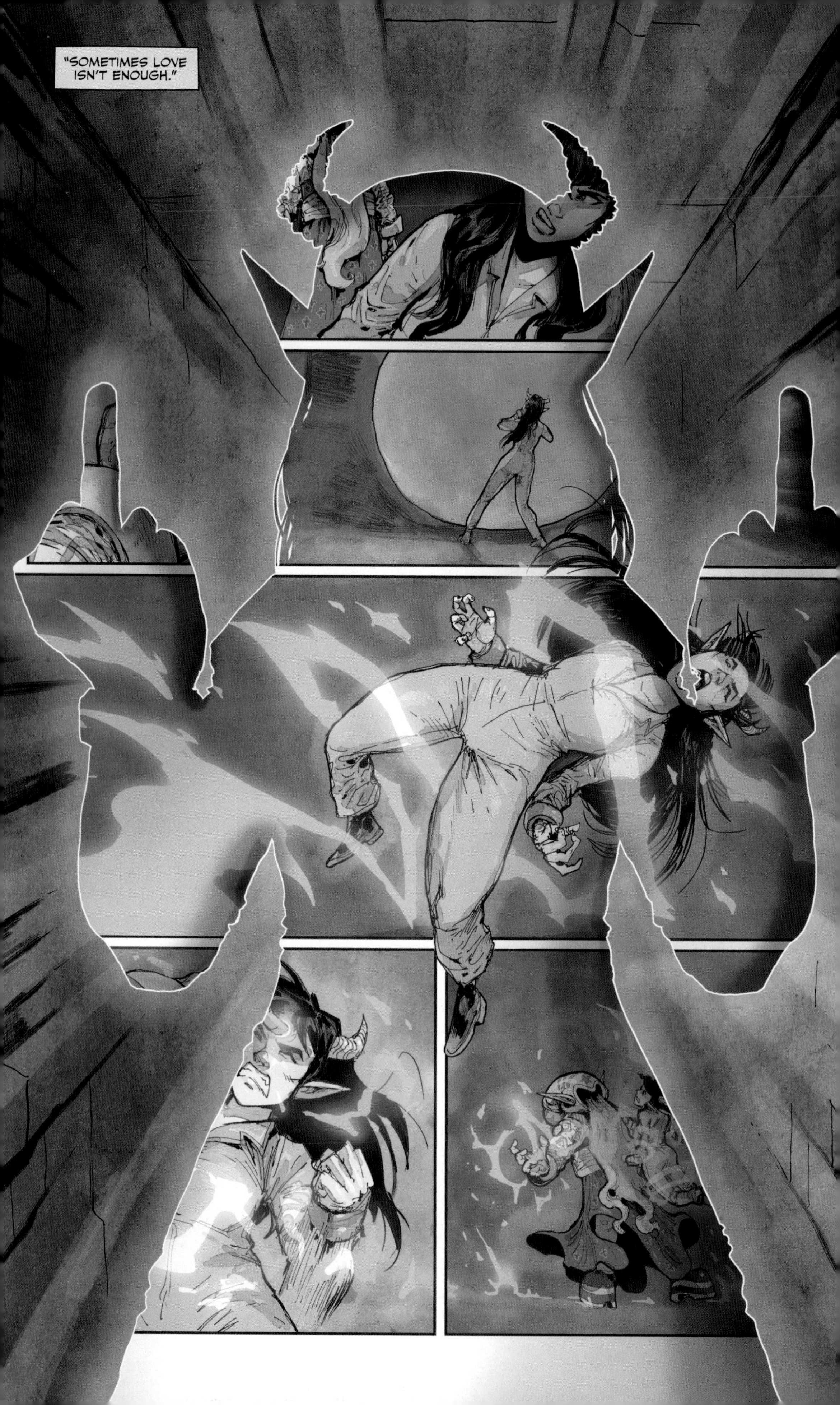
"SOMETIMES LOVE ISN'T ENOUGH."

CHAPTER NINE

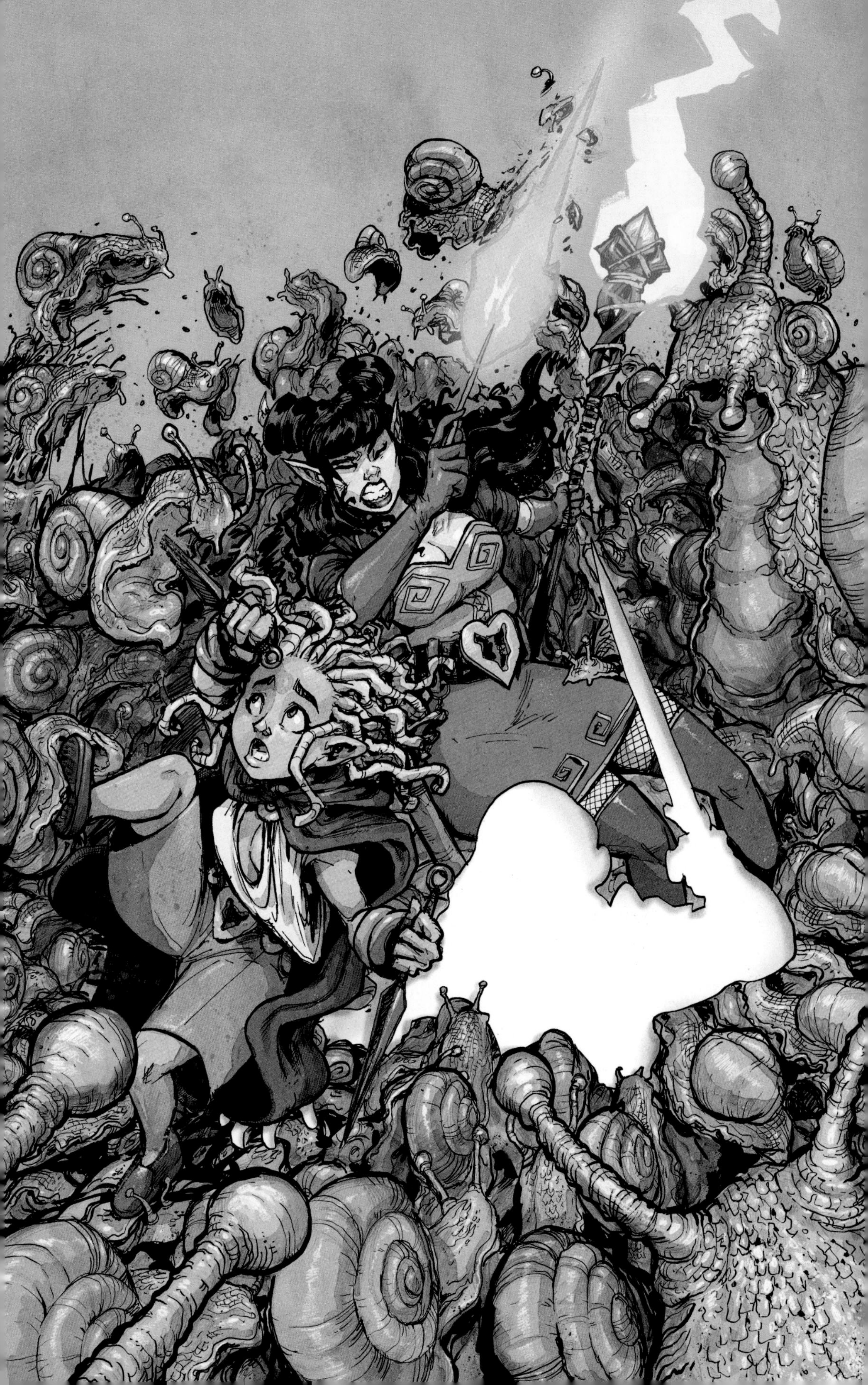

Issue 9 cover B by LEILA del DUCA

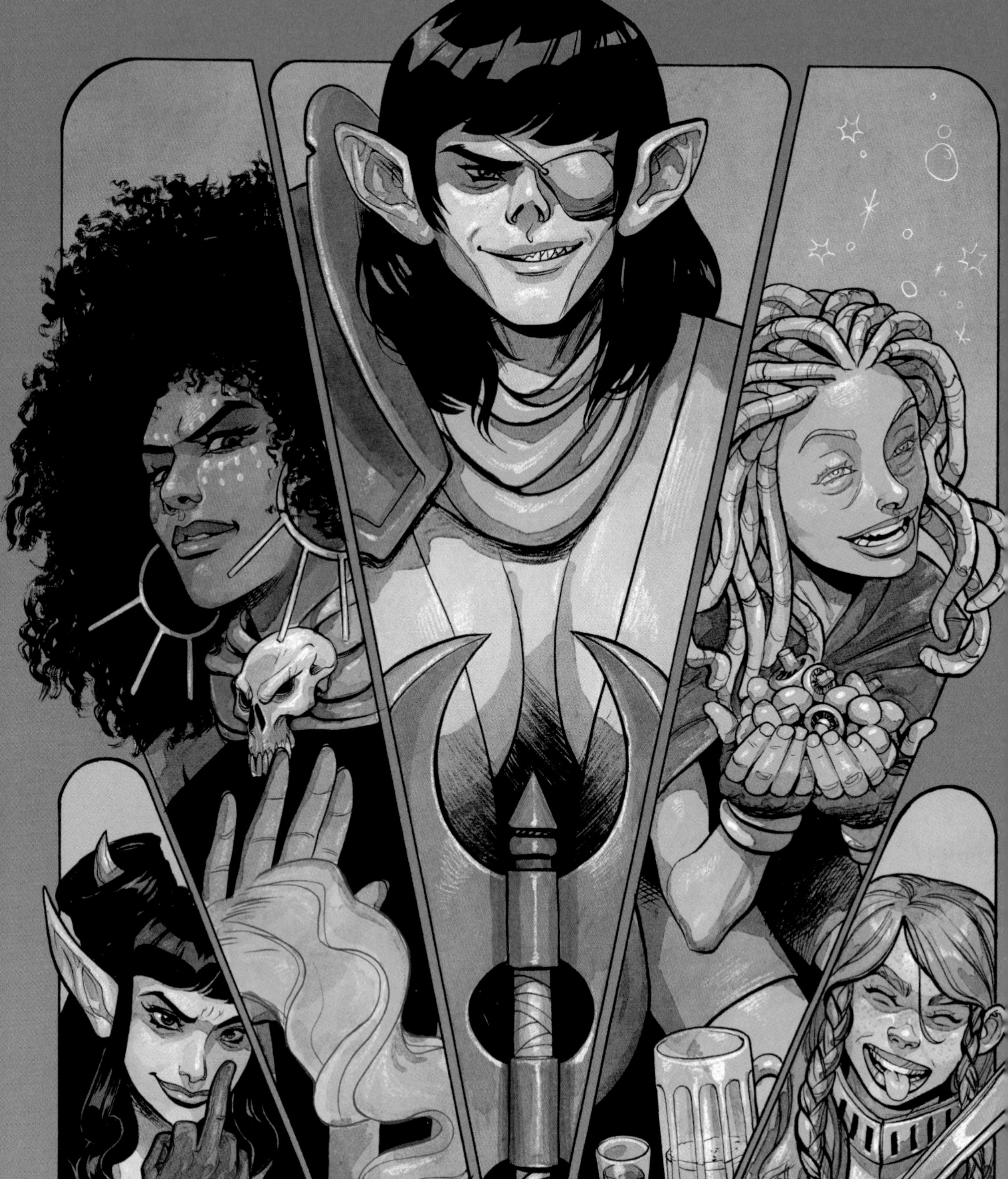

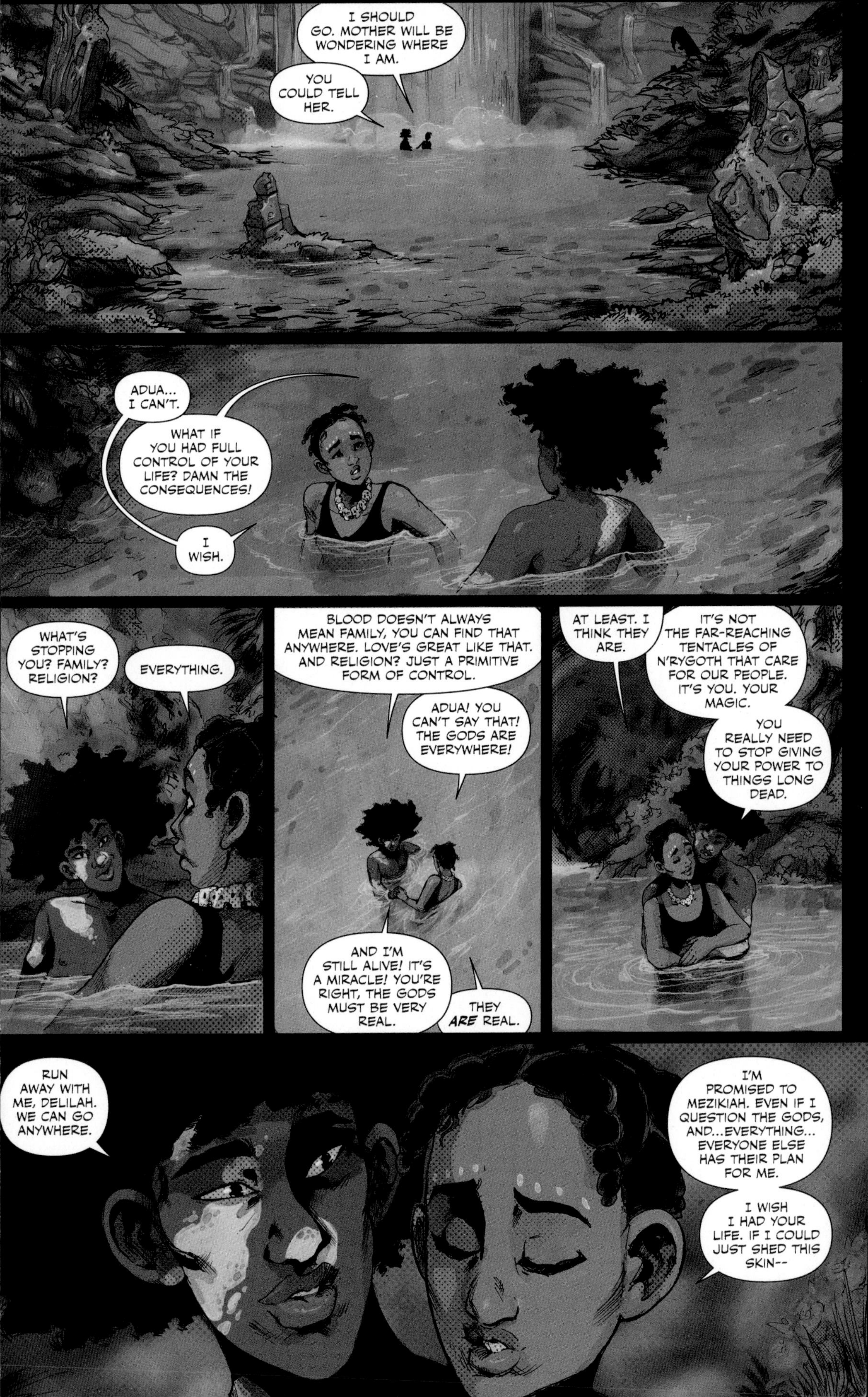

I SHOULD GO. MOTHER WILL BE WONDERING WHERE I AM.
YOU COULD TELL HER.
ADUA... I CAN'T.
WHAT IF YOU HAD FULL CONTROL OF YOUR LIFE? DAMN THE CONSEQUENCES!
I WISH.
WHAT'S STOPPING YOU? FAMILY? RELIGION?
EVERYTHING.
BLOOD DOESN'T ALWAYS MEAN FAMILY, YOU CAN FIND THAT ANYWHERE. LOVE'S GREAT LIKE THAT. AND RELIGION? JUST A PRIMITIVE FORM OF CONTROL.
ADUA! YOU CAN'T SAY THAT! THE GODS ARE EVERYWHERE!
AND I'M STILL ALIVE! IT'S A MIRACLE! YOU'RE RIGHT, THE GODS MUST BE VERY REAL.
THEY *ARE* REAL.
AT LEAST. I THINK THEY ARE.
IT'S NOT THE FAR-REACHING TENTACLES OF N'RYGOTH THAT CARE FOR OUR PEOPLE. IT'S YOU. YOUR MAGIC.
YOU REALLY NEED TO STOP GIVING YOUR POWER TO THINGS LONG DEAD.
RUN AWAY WITH ME, DELILAH. WE CAN GO ANYWHERE.
I'M PROMISED TO MEZIKIAH. EVEN IF I QUESTION THE GODS, AND...EVERYTHING... EVERYONE ELSE HAS THEIR PLAN FOR ME.
I WISH I HAD YOUR LIFE. IF I COULD JUST SHED THIS SKIN--

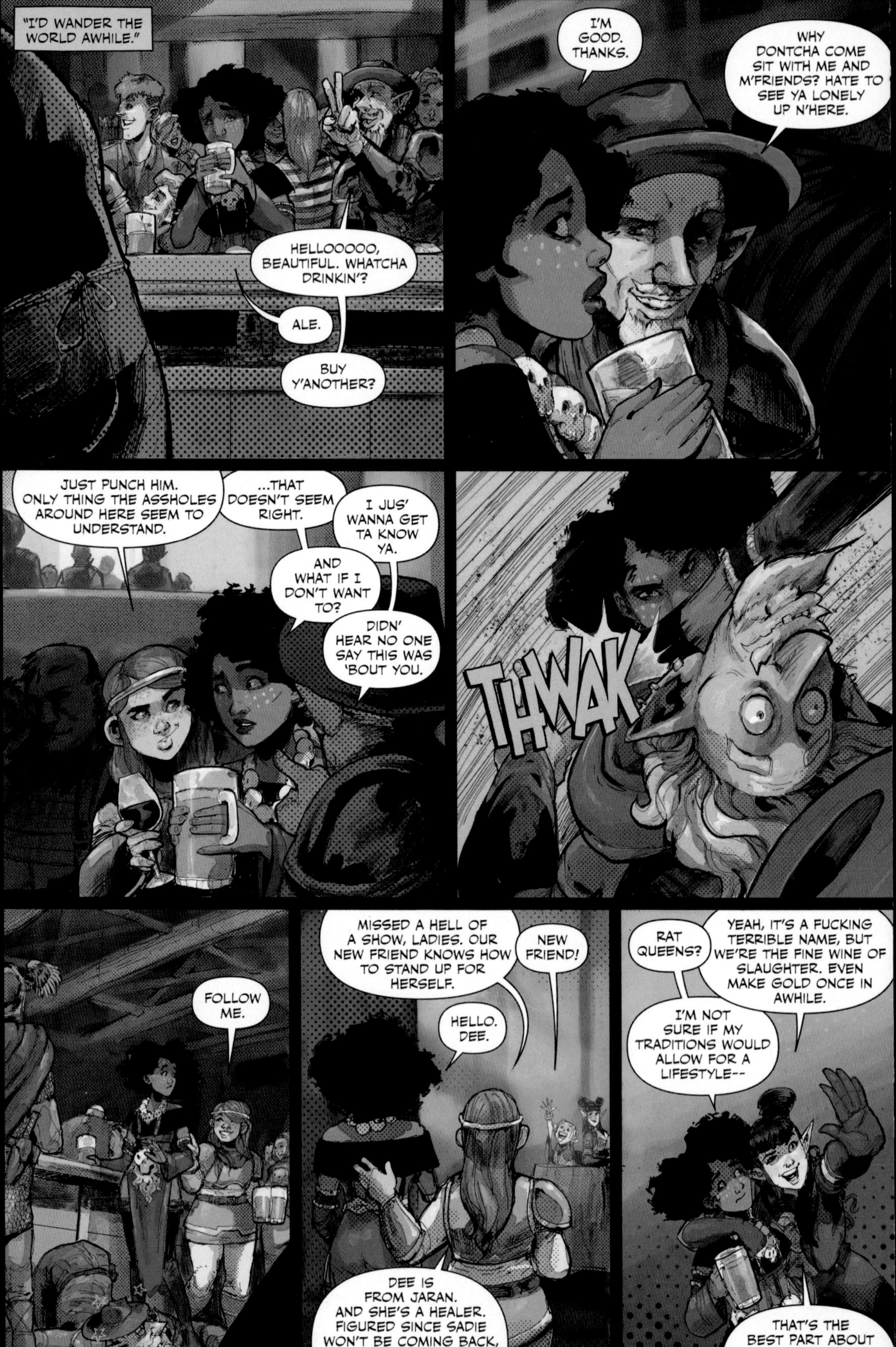
"I'D WANDER THE WORLD AWHILE."
HELLOOOOO, BEAUTIFUL. WHATCHA DRINKIN'?
ALE.
BUY Y'ANOTHER?
I'M GOOD. THANKS.
WHY DONTCHA COME SIT WITH ME AND M'FRIENDS? HATE TO SEE YA LONELY UP N'HERE.
JUST PUNCH HIM. ONLY THING THE ASSHOLES AROUND HERE SEEM TO UNDERSTAND.
...THAT DOESN'T SEEM RIGHT.
I JUS' WANNA GET TA KNOW YA.
AND WHAT IF I DON'T WANT TO?
DIDN' HEAR NO ONE SAY THIS WAS 'BOUT YOU.
THWAK
FOLLOW ME.
MISSED A HELL OF A SHOW, LADIES. OUR NEW FRIEND KNOWS HOW TO STAND UP FOR HERSELF.
NEW FRIEND!
HELLO. DEE.
DEE IS FROM JARAN. AND SHE'S A HEALER. FIGURED SINCE SADIE WON'T BE COMING BACK, WE'D BE LUCKY TO HAVE A NEW MEMBER IN THE RAT QUEENS.
RAT QUEENS?
YEAH, IT'S A FUCKING TERRIBLE NAME, BUT WE'RE THE FINE WINE OF SLAUGHTER. EVEN MAKE GOLD ONCE IN AWHILE.
I'M NOT SURE IF MY TRADITIONS WOULD ALLOW FOR A LIFESTYLE--
THAT'S THE BEST PART ABOUT BEING A QUEEN! DOESN'T MATTER WHO YOU WERE BEFORE--

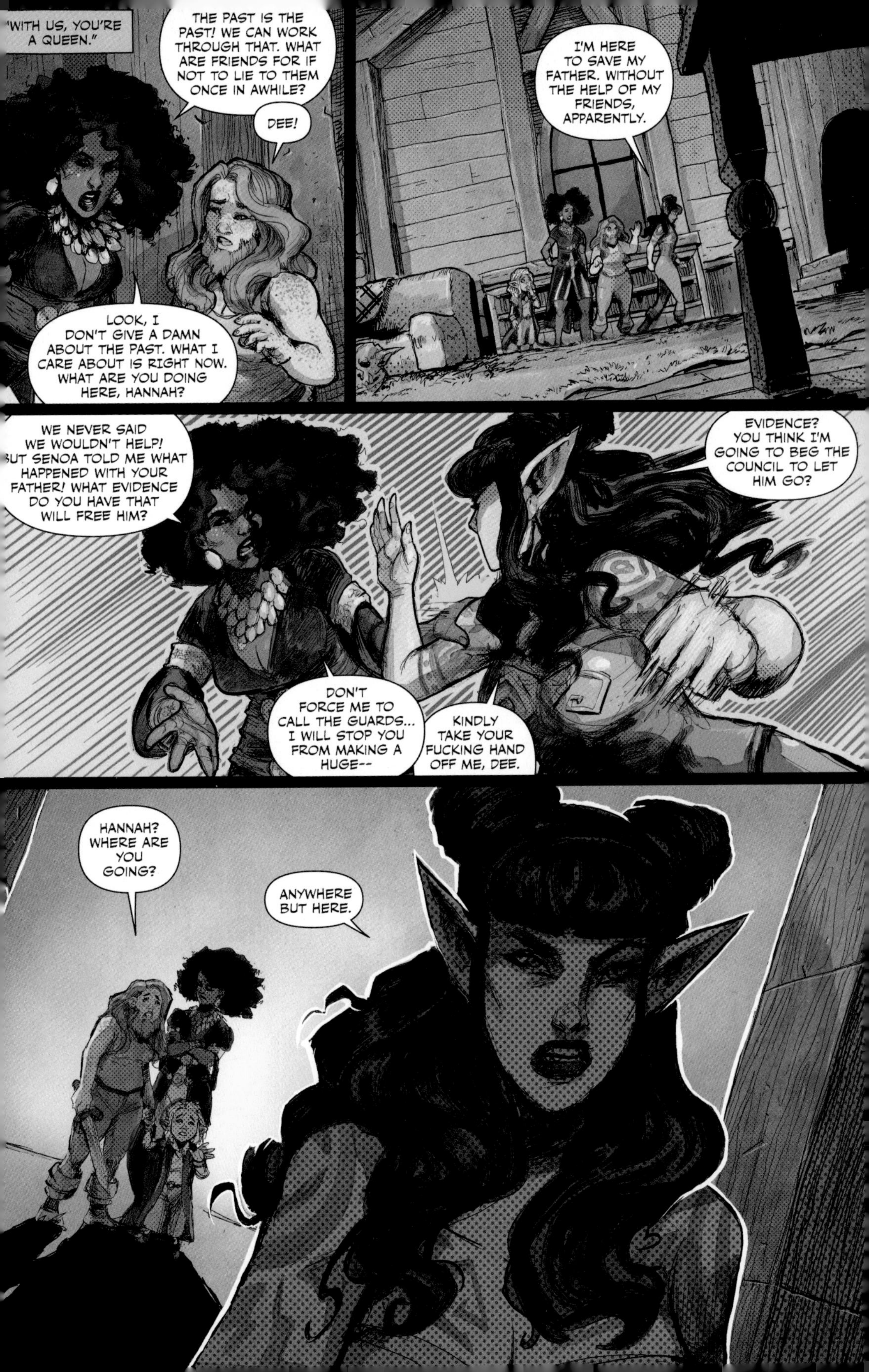
"WITH US, YOU'RE A QUEEN."
THE PAST IS THE PAST! WE CAN WORK THROUGH THAT. WHAT ARE FRIENDS FOR IF NOT TO LIE TO THEM ONCE IN AWHILE?
DEE!
LOOK, I DON'T GIVE A DAMN ABOUT THE PAST. WHAT I CARE ABOUT IS RIGHT NOW. WHAT ARE YOU DOING HERE, HANNAH?
I'M HERE TO SAVE MY FATHER. WITHOUT THE HELP OF MY FRIENDS, APPARENTLY.
WE NEVER SAID WE WOULDN'T HELP! BUT SENOA TOLD ME WHAT HAPPENED WITH YOUR FATHER! WHAT EVIDENCE DO YOU HAVE THAT WILL FREE HIM?
EVIDENCE? YOU THINK I'M GOING TO BEG THE COUNCIL TO LET HIM GO?
DON'T FORCE ME TO CALL THE GUARDS... I WILL STOP YOU FROM MAKING A HUGE--
KINDLY TAKE YOUR FUCKING HAND OFF ME, DEE.
HANNAH? WHERE ARE YOU GOING?
ANYWHERE BUT HERE.

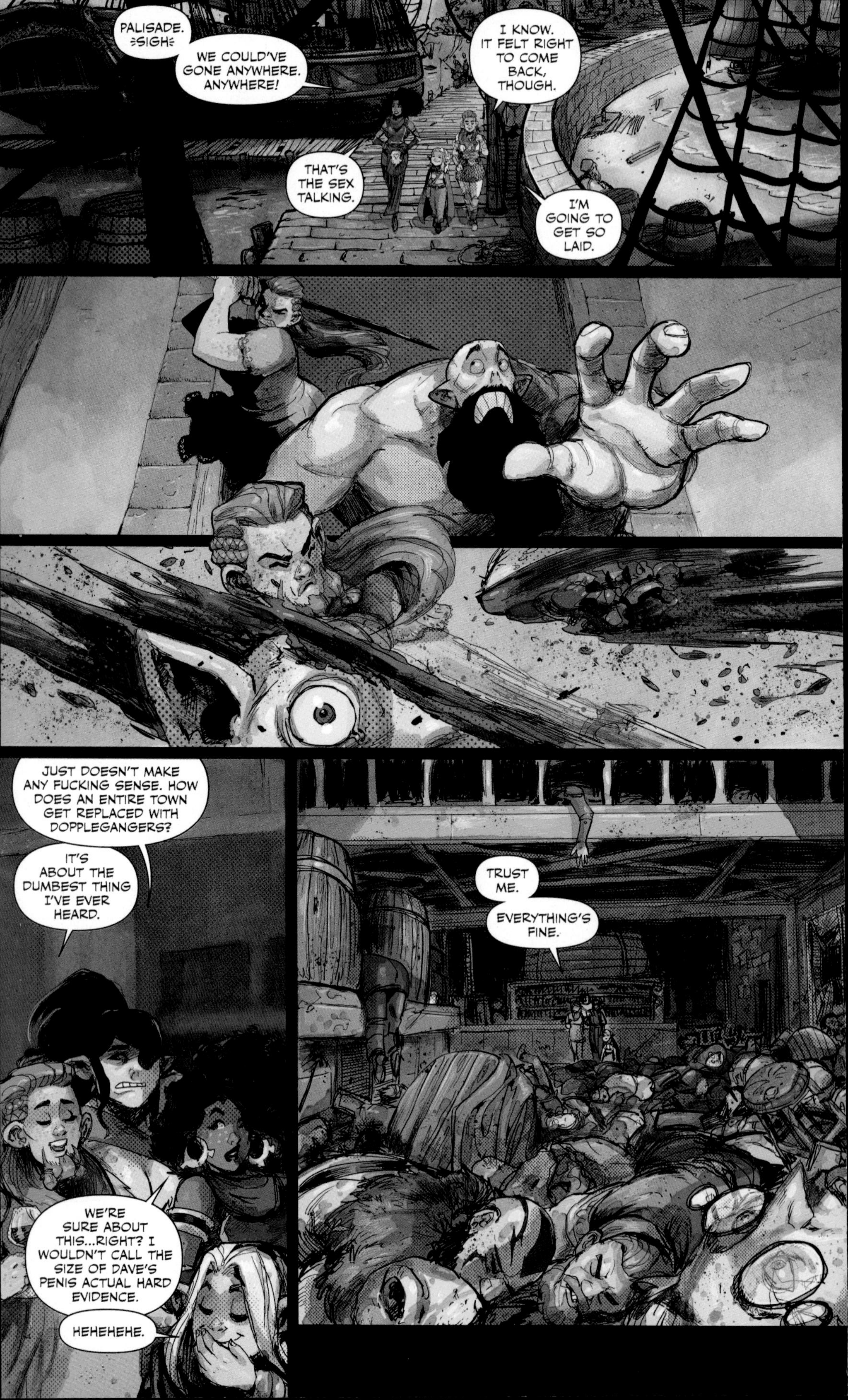
PALISADE. ⁼SIGH⁼
WE COULD'VE GONE ANYWHERE. ANYWHERE!
I KNOW. IT FELT RIGHT TO COME BACK, THOUGH.
THAT'S THE SEX TALKING.
I'M GOING TO GET SO LAID.
JUST DOESN'T MAKE ANY FUCKING SENSE. HOW DOES AN ENTIRE TOWN GET REPLACED WITH DOPPLEGANGERS?
IT'S ABOUT THE DUMBEST THING I'VE EVER HEARD.
WE'RE SURE ABOUT THIS...RIGHT? I WOULDN'T CALL THE SIZE OF DAVE'S PENIS ACTUAL HARD EVIDENCE.
HEHEHEHE.
TRUST ME.
EVERYTHING'S FINE.

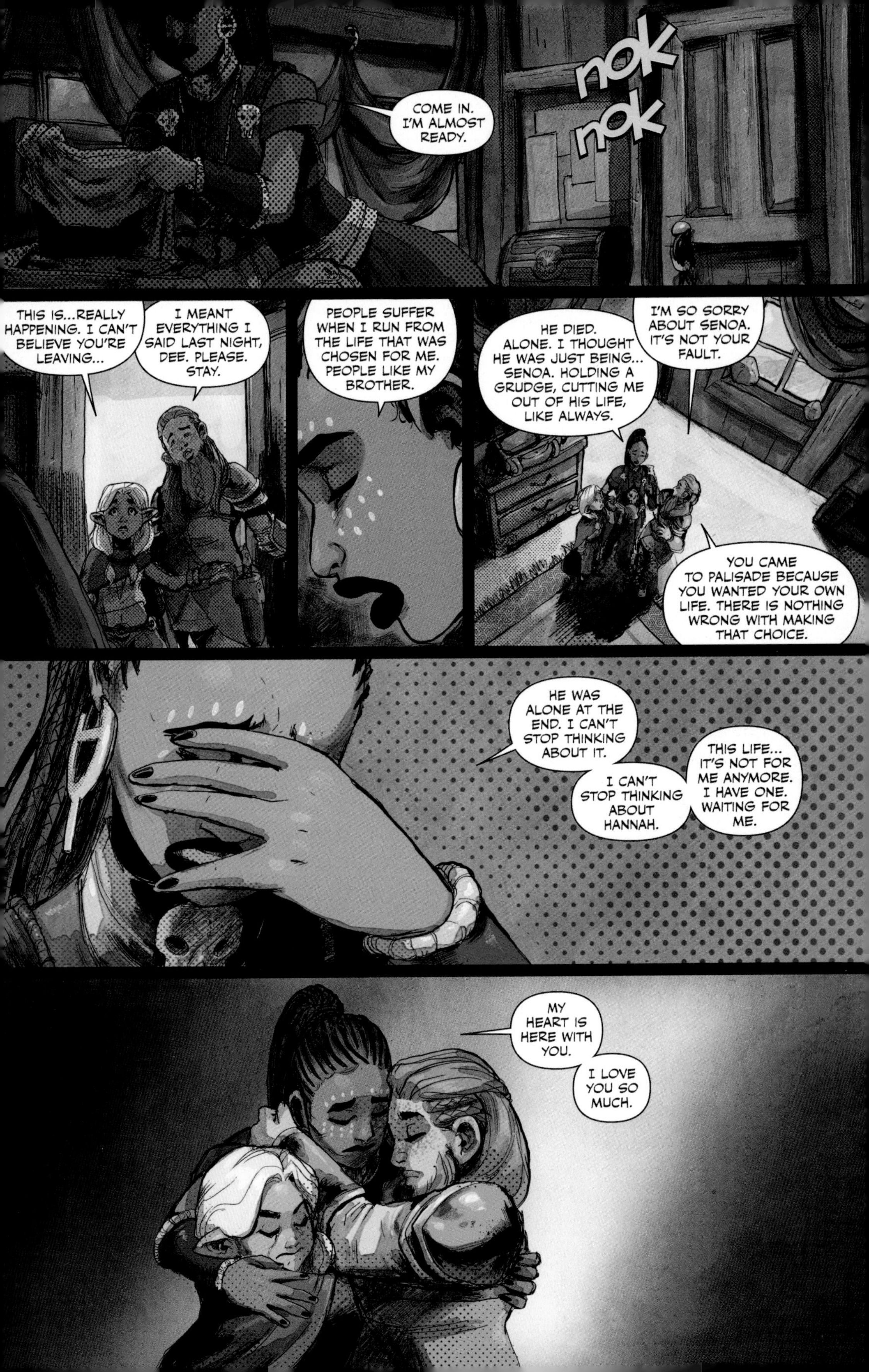
NOK
NOK
COME IN. I'M ALMOST READY.
THIS IS...REALLY HAPPENING. I CAN'T BELIEVE YOU'RE LEAVING...
I MEANT EVERYTHING I SAID LAST NIGHT, DEE. PLEASE. STAY.
PEOPLE SUFFER WHEN I RUN FROM THE LIFE THAT WAS CHOSEN FOR ME. PEOPLE LIKE MY BROTHER.
I'M SO SORRY ABOUT SENOA. IT'S NOT YOUR FAULT.
HE DIED. ALONE. I THOUGHT HE WAS JUST BEING... SENOA. HOLDING A GRUDGE, CUTTING ME OUT OF HIS LIFE, LIKE ALWAYS.
YOU CAME TO PALISADE BECAUSE YOU WANTED YOUR OWN LIFE. THERE IS NOTHING WRONG WITH MAKING THAT CHOICE.
HE WAS ALONE AT THE END. I CAN'T STOP THINKING ABOUT IT.
I CAN'T STOP THINKING ABOUT HANNAH.
THIS LIFE... IT'S NOT FOR ME ANYMORE. I HAVE ONE. WAITING FOR ME.
MY HEART IS HERE WITH YOU.
I LOVE YOU SO MUCH.

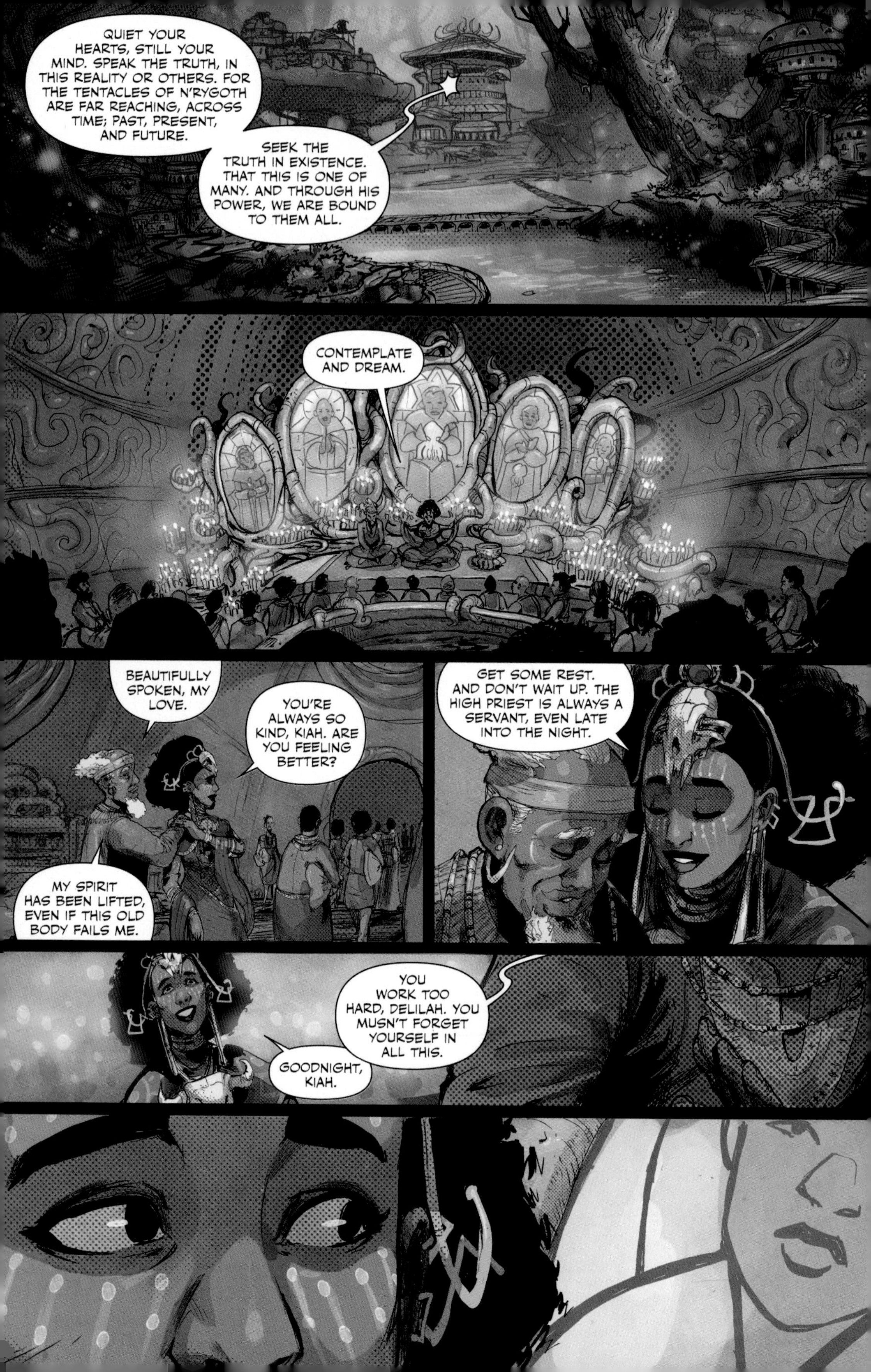
QUIET YOUR HEARTS, STILL YOUR MIND. SPEAK THE TRUTH, IN THIS REALITY OR OTHERS. FOR THE TENTACLES OF N'RYGOTH ARE FAR REACHING, ACROSS TIME; PAST, PRESENT, AND FUTURE.
SEEK THE TRUTH IN EXISTENCE. THAT THIS IS ONE OF MANY. AND THROUGH HIS POWER, WE ARE BOUND TO THEM ALL.
CONTEMPLATE AND DREAM.
BEAUTIFULLY SPOKEN, MY LOVE.
YOU'RE ALWAYS SO KIND, KIAH. ARE YOU FEELING BETTER?
MY SPIRIT HAS BEEN LIFTED, EVEN IF THIS OLD BODY FAILS ME.
GET SOME REST. AND DON'T WAIT UP. THE HIGH PRIEST IS ALWAYS A SERVANT, EVEN LATE INTO THE NIGHT.
YOU WORK TOO HARD, DELILAH. YOU MUSN'T FORGET YOURSELF IN ALL THIS.
GOODNIGHT, KIAH.

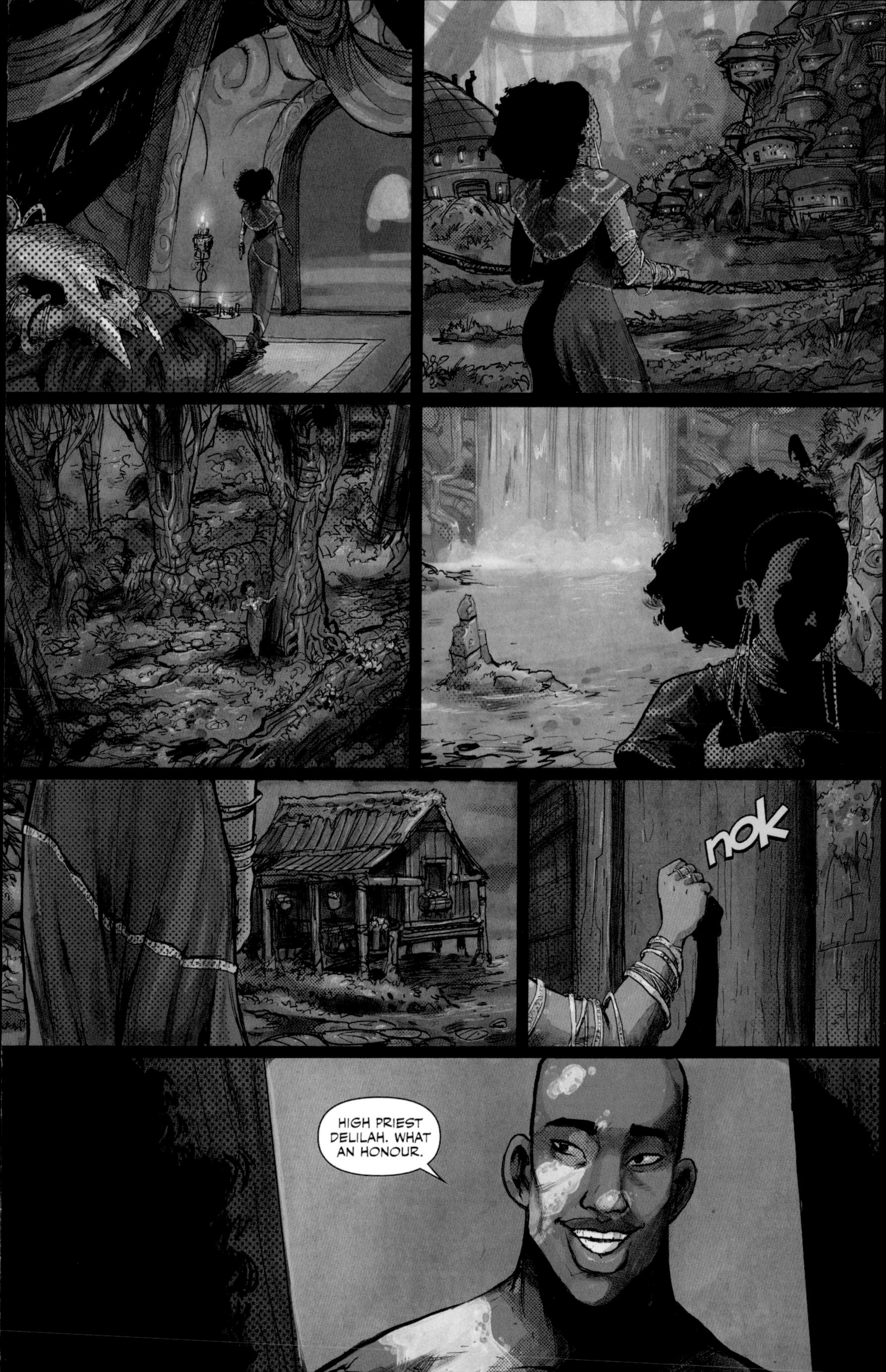
nok
HIGH PRIEST DELILAH. WHAT AN HONOUR.

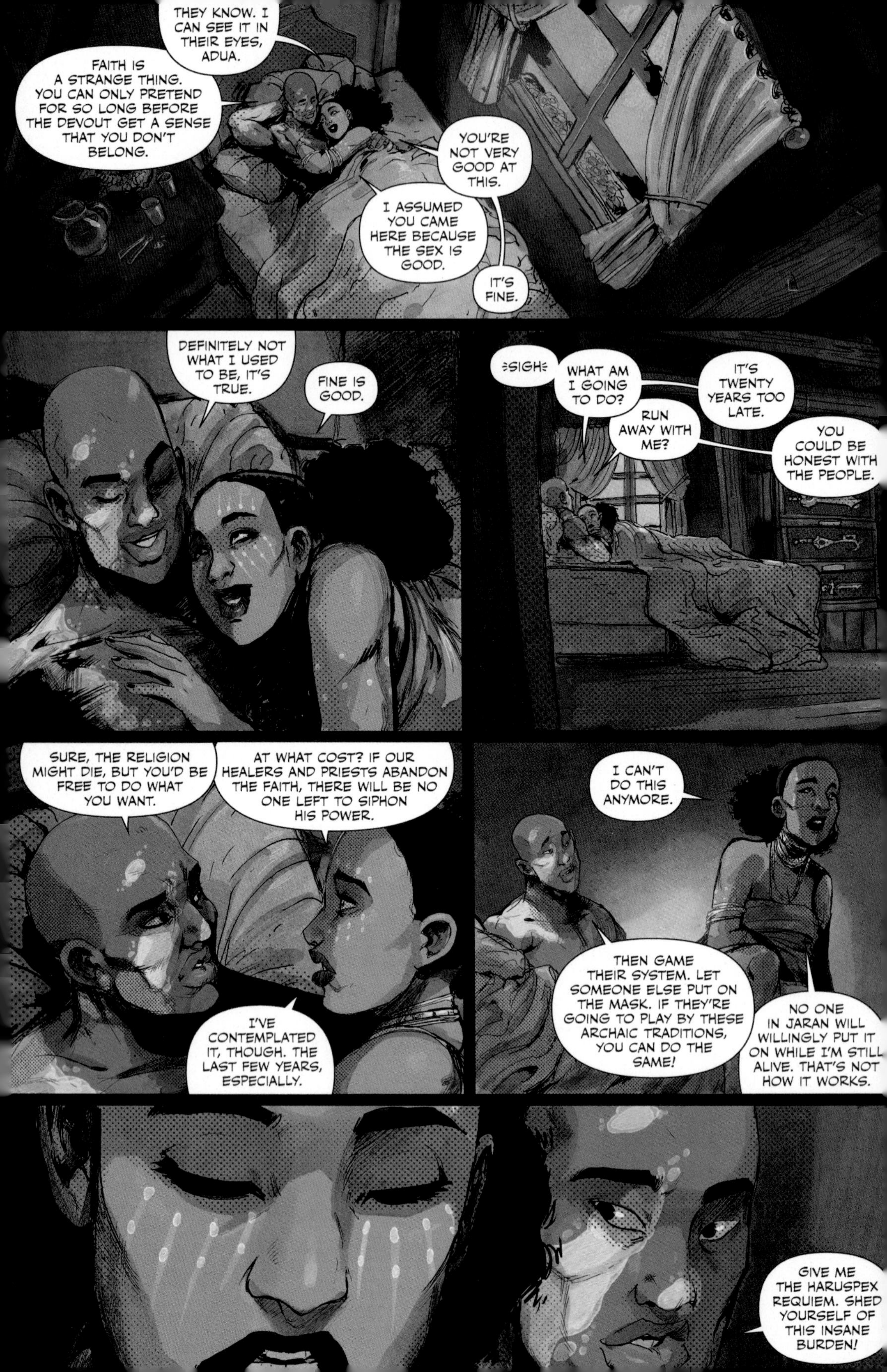
THEY KNOW. I CAN SEE IT IN THEIR EYES, ADUA.
FAITH IS A STRANGE THING. YOU CAN ONLY PRETEND FOR SO LONG BEFORE THE DEVOUT GET A SENSE THAT YOU DON'T BELONG.
YOU'RE NOT VERY GOOD AT THIS.
I ASSUMED YOU CAME HERE BECAUSE THE SEX IS GOOD.
IT'S FINE.
DEFINITELY NOT WHAT I USED TO BE, IT'S TRUE.
FINE IS GOOD.
SIGH
WHAT AM I GOING TO DO?
IT'S TWENTY YEARS TOO LATE.
RUN AWAY WITH ME?
YOU COULD BE HONEST WITH THE PEOPLE.
SURE, THE RELIGION MIGHT DIE, BUT YOU'D BE FREE TO DO WHAT YOU WANT.
AT WHAT COST? IF OUR HEALERS AND PRIESTS ABANDON THE FAITH, THERE WILL BE NO ONE LEFT TO SIPHON HIS POWER.
I'VE CONTEMPLATED IT, THOUGH. THE LAST FEW YEARS, ESPECIALLY.
I CAN'T DO THIS ANYMORE.
THEN GAME THEIR SYSTEM. LET SOMEONE ELSE PUT ON THE MASK. IF THEY'RE GOING TO PLAY BY THESE ARCHAIC TRADITIONS, YOU CAN DO THE SAME!
NO ONE IN JARAN WILL WILLINGLY PUT IT ON WHILE I'M STILL ALIVE. THAT'S NOT HOW IT WORKS.
GIVE ME THE HARUSPEX REQUIEM. SHED YOURSELF OF THIS INSANE BURDEN!

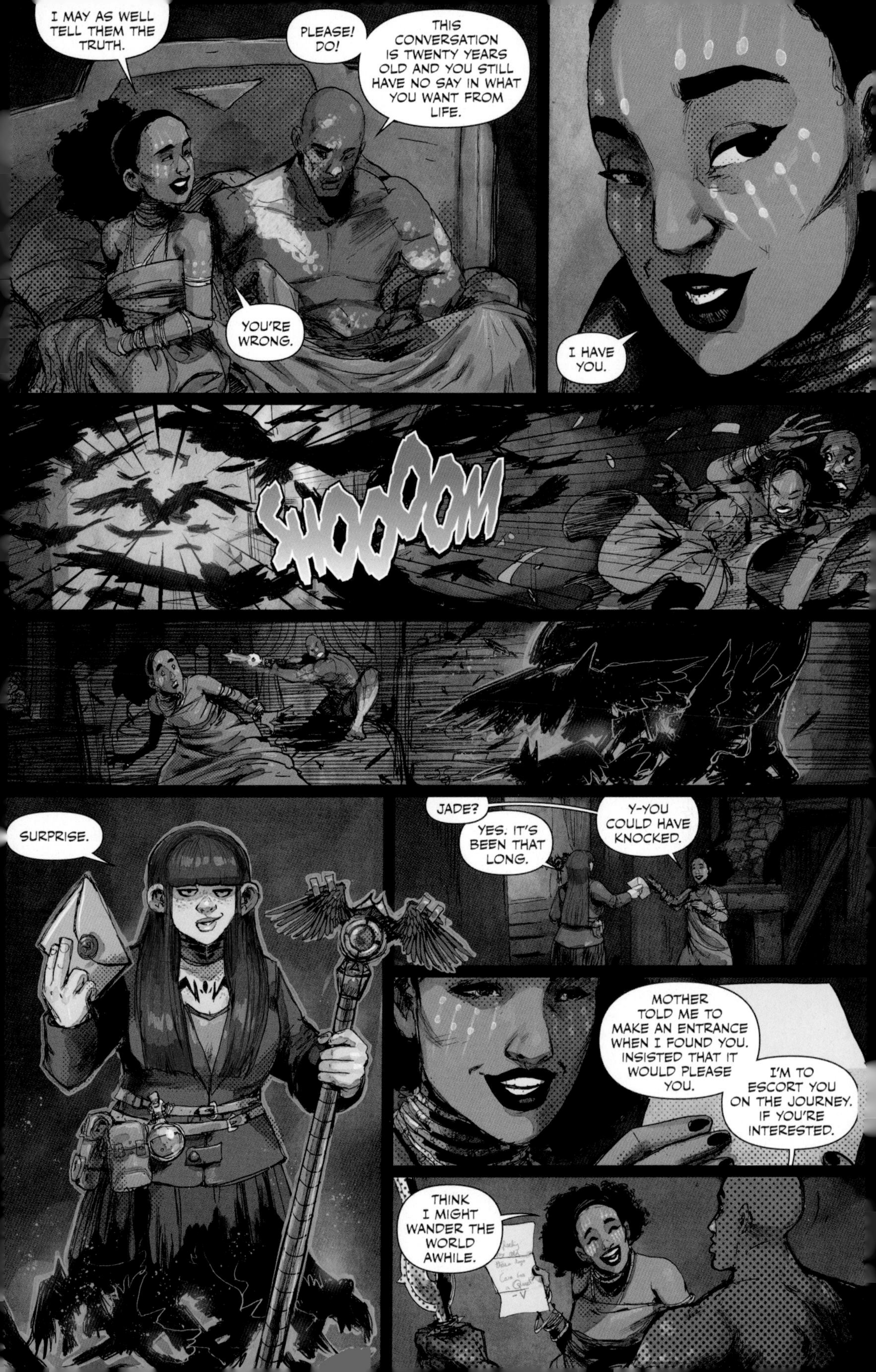
I MAY AS WELL TELL THEM THE TRUTH.
PLEASE! DO!
THIS CONVERSATION IS TWENTY YEARS OLD AND YOU STILL HAVE NO SAY IN WHAT YOU WANT FROM LIFE.
YOU'RE WRONG.
I HAVE YOU.
SHOOOOM
SURPRISE.
JADE?
Y-YOU COULD HAVE KNOCKED.
YES. IT'S BEEN THAT LONG.
MOTHER TOLD ME TO MAKE AN ENTRANCE WHEN I FOUND YOU. INSISTED THAT IT WOULD PLEASE YOU.
I'M TO ESCORT YOU ON THE JOURNEY. IF YOU'RE INTERESTED.
THINK I MIGHT WANDER THE WORLD AWHILE.

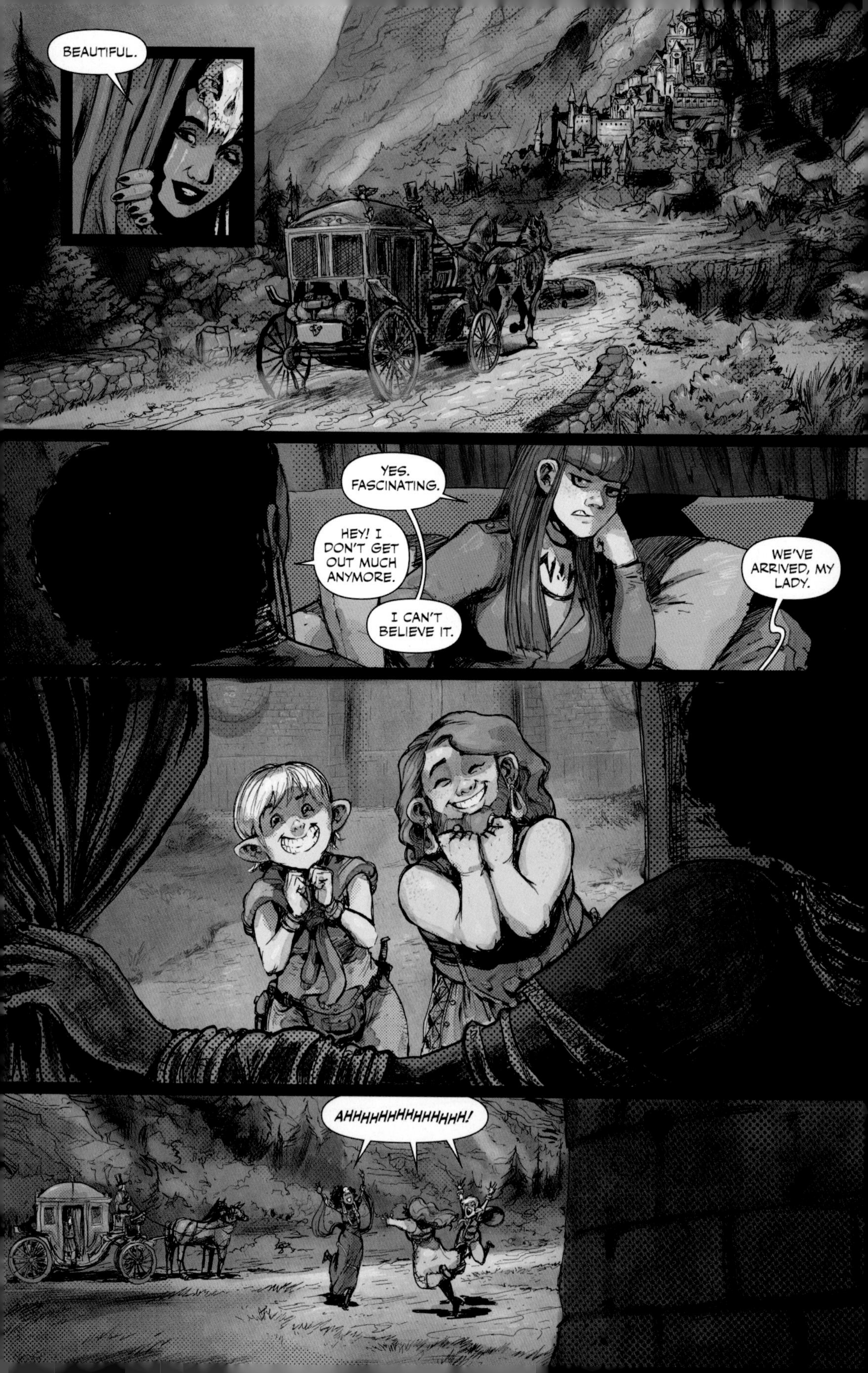
BEAUTIFUL.
YES. FASCINATING.
HEY! I DON'T GET OUT MUCH ANYMORE.
I CAN'T BELIEVE IT.
WE'VE ARRIVED, MY LADY.
AHHHHHHHHHHHHHH!

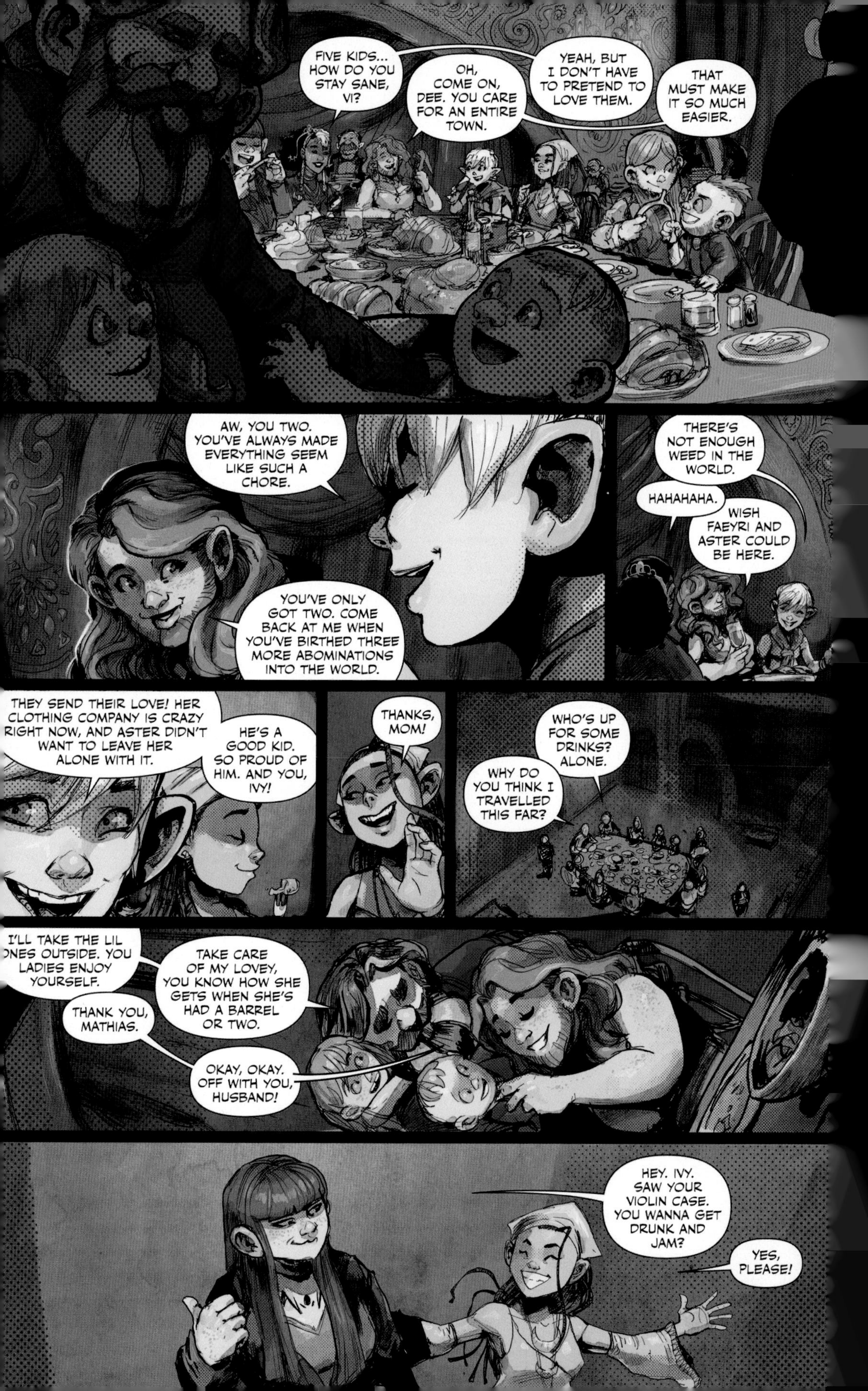
FIVE KIDS... HOW DO YOU STAY SANE, VI?
OH, COME ON, DEE. YOU CARE FOR AN ENTIRE TOWN.
YEAH, BUT I DON'T HAVE TO PRETEND TO LOVE THEM.
THAT MUST MAKE IT SO MUCH EASIER.
AW, YOU TWO. YOU'VE ALWAYS MADE EVERYTHING SEEM LIKE SUCH A CHORE.
YOU'VE ONLY GOT TWO. COME BACK AT ME WHEN YOU'VE BIRTHED THREE MORE ABOMINATIONS INTO THE WORLD.
THERE'S NOT ENOUGH WEED IN THE WORLD.
HAHAHAHA.
WISH FAEYRI AND ASTER COULD BE HERE.
THEY SEND THEIR LOVE! HER CLOTHING COMPANY IS CRAZY RIGHT NOW, AND ASTER DIDN'T WANT TO LEAVE HER ALONE WITH IT.
HE'S A GOOD KID. SO PROUD OF HIM. AND YOU, IVY!
THANKS, MOM!
WHO'S UP FOR SOME DRINKS? ALONE.
WHY DO YOU THINK I TRAVELLED THIS FAR?
I'LL TAKE THE LIL ONES OUTSIDE. YOU LADIES ENJOY YOURSELF.
TAKE CARE OF MY LOVEY, YOU KNOW HOW SHE GETS WHEN SHE'S HAD A BARREL OR TWO.
THANK YOU, MATHIAS.
OKAY, OKAY. OFF WITH YOU, HUSBAND!
HEY. IVY. SAW YOUR VIOLIN CASE. YOU WANNA GET DRUNK AND JAM?
YES, PLEASE!

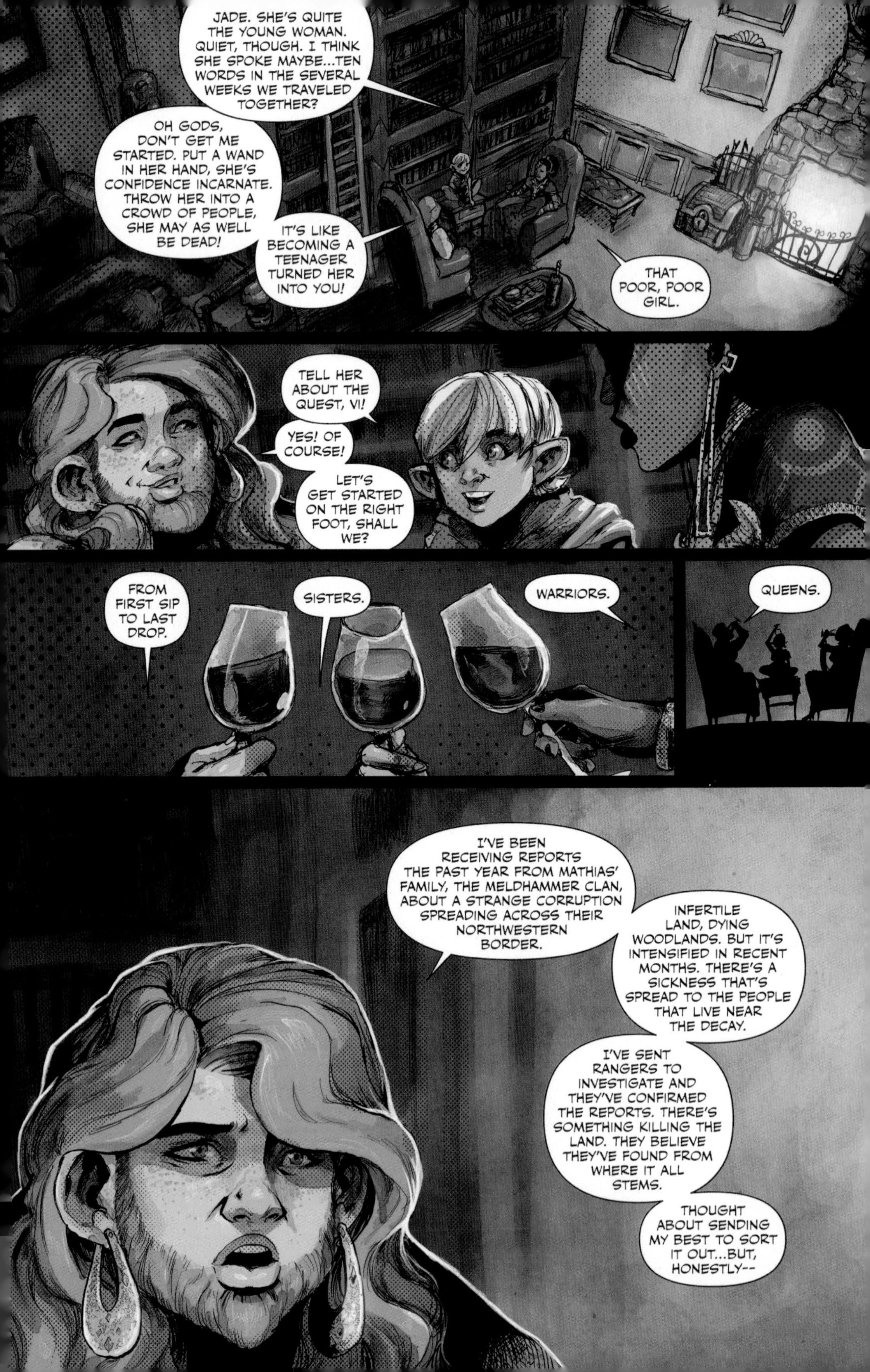
JADE. SHE'S QUITE THE YOUNG WOMAN. QUIET, THOUGH. I THINK SHE SPOKE MAYBE...TEN WORDS IN THE SEVERAL WEEKS WE TRAVELED TOGETHER?
OH GODS, DON'T GET ME STARTED. PUT A WAND IN HER HAND, SHE'S CONFIDENCE INCARNATE. THROW HER INTO A CROWD OF PEOPLE, SHE MAY AS WELL BE DEAD!
IT'S LIKE BECOMING A TEENAGER TURNED HER INTO YOU!
THAT POOR, POOR GIRL.
TELL HER ABOUT THE QUEST, VI!
YES! OF COURSE!
LET'S GET STARTED ON THE RIGHT FOOT, SHALL WE?
FROM FIRST SIP TO LAST DROP.
SISTERS.
WARRIORS.
QUEENS.
I'VE BEEN RECEIVING REPORTS THE PAST YEAR FROM MATHIAS' FAMILY, THE MELDHAMMER CLAN, ABOUT A STRANGE CORRUPTION SPREADING ACROSS THEIR NORTHWESTERN BORDER.
INFERTILE LAND, DYING WOODLANDS. BUT IT'S INTENSIFIED IN RECENT MONTHS. THERE'S A SICKNESS THAT'S SPREAD TO THE PEOPLE THAT LIVE NEAR THE DECAY.
I'VE SENT RANGERS TO INVESTIGATE AND THEY'VE CONFIRMED THE REPORTS. THERE'S SOMETHING KILLING THE LAND. THEY BELIEVE THEY'VE FOUND FROM WHERE IT ALL STEMS.
THOUGHT ABOUT SENDING MY BEST TO SORT IT OUT...BUT, HONESTLY--

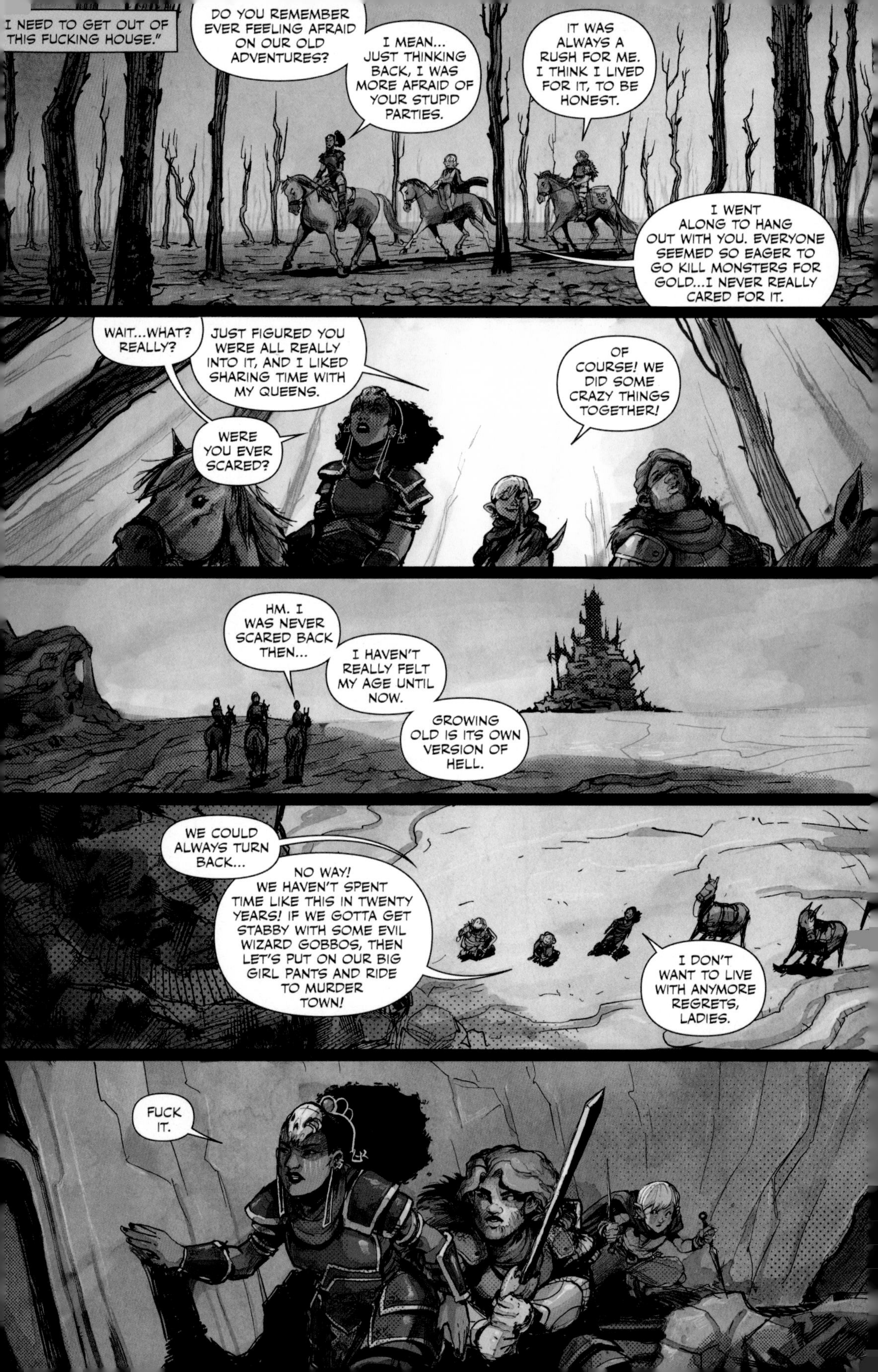
I NEED TO GET OUT OF THIS FUCKING HOUSE."
DO YOU REMEMBER EVER FEELING AFRAID ON OUR OLD ADVENTURES?
I MEAN... JUST THINKING BACK, I WAS MORE AFRAID OF YOUR STUPID PARTIES.
IT WAS ALWAYS A RUSH FOR ME. I THINK I LIVED FOR IT, TO BE HONEST.
I WENT ALONG TO HANG OUT WITH YOU. EVERYONE SEEMED SO EAGER TO GO KILL MONSTERS FOR GOLD...I NEVER REALLY CARED FOR IT.
WAIT...WHAT? REALLY?
JUST FIGURED YOU WERE ALL REALLY INTO IT, AND I LIKED SHARING TIME WITH MY QUEENS.
WERE YOU EVER SCARED?
OF COURSE! WE DID SOME CRAZY THINGS TOGETHER!
HM. I WAS NEVER SCARED BACK THEN...
I HAVEN'T REALLY FELT MY AGE UNTIL NOW.
GROWING OLD IS ITS OWN VERSION OF HELL.
WE COULD ALWAYS TURN BACK...
NO WAY! WE HAVEN'T SPENT TIME LIKE THIS IN TWENTY YEARS! IF WE GOTTA GET STABBY WITH SOME EVIL WIZARD GOBBOS, THEN LET'S PUT ON OUR BIG GIRL PANTS AND RIDE TO MURDER TOWN!
I DON'T WANT TO LIVE WITH ANYMORE REGRETS, LADIES.
FUCK IT.

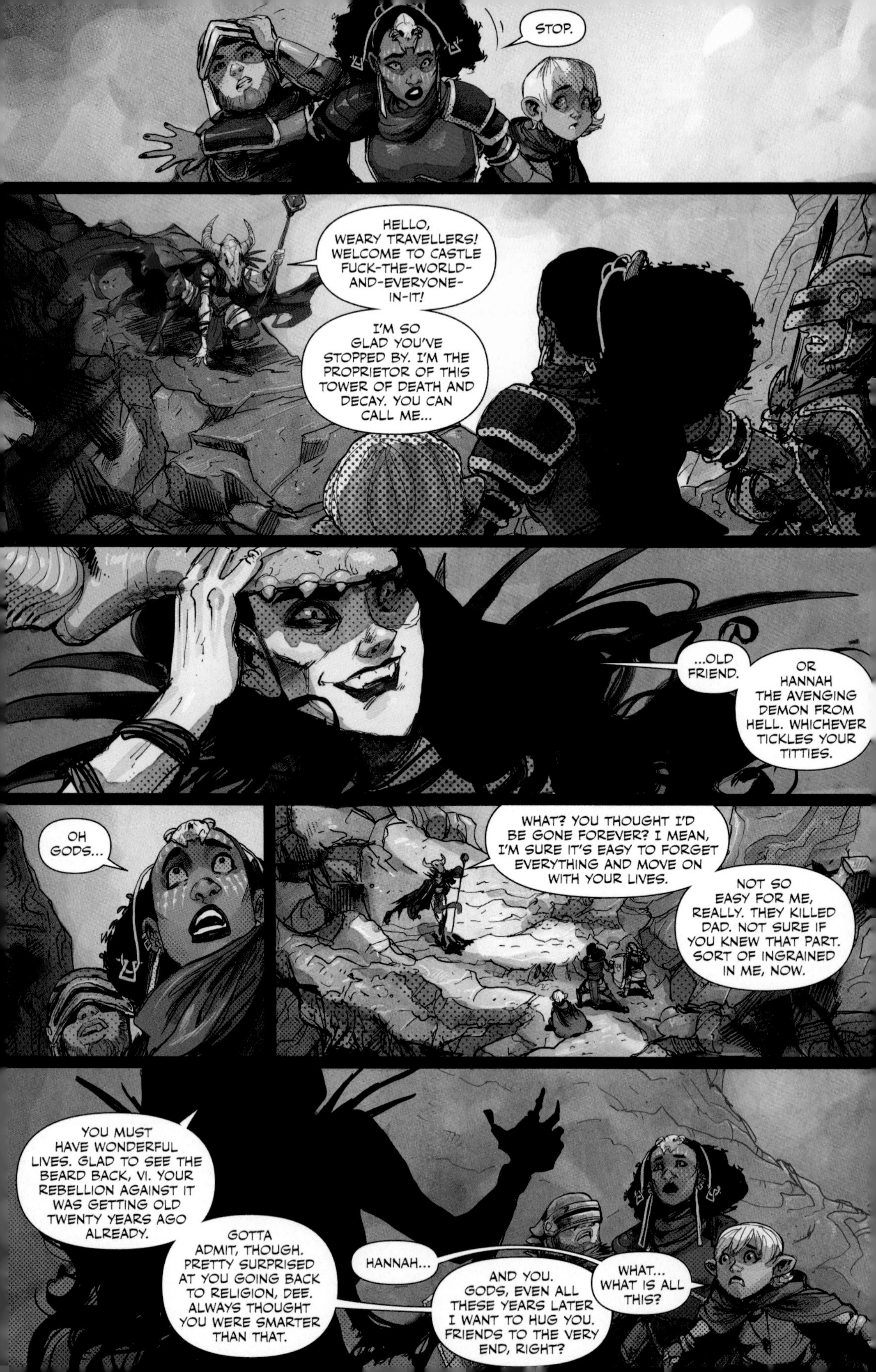
STOP.
HELLO, WEARY TRAVELLERS! WELCOME TO CASTLE FUCK-THE-WORLD-AND-EVERYONE-IN-IT!
I'M SO GLAD YOU'VE STOPPED BY. I'M THE PROPRIETOR OF THIS TOWER OF DEATH AND DECAY. YOU CAN CALL ME...
...OLD FRIEND.
OR HANNAH THE AVENGING DEMON FROM HELL. WHICHEVER TICKLES YOUR TITTIES.
OH GODS...
WHAT? YOU THOUGHT I'D BE GONE FOREVER? I MEAN, I'M SURE IT'S EASY TO FORGET EVERYTHING AND MOVE ON WITH YOUR LIVES.
NOT SO EASY FOR ME, REALLY. THEY KILLED DAD. NOT SURE IF YOU KNEW THAT PART. SORT OF INGRAINED IN ME, NOW.
YOU MUST HAVE WONDERFUL LIVES. GLAD TO SEE THE BEARD BACK, VI. YOUR REBELLION AGAINST IT WAS GETTING OLD TWENTY YEARS AGO ALREADY.
GOTTA ADMIT, THOUGH. PRETTY SURPRISED AT YOU GOING BACK TO RELIGION, DEE. ALWAYS THOUGHT YOU WERE SMARTER THAN THAT.
HANNAH...
AND YOU. GODS, EVEN ALL THESE YEARS LATER I WANT TO HUG YOU. FRIENDS TO THE VERY END, RIGHT?
WHAT... WHAT IS ALL THIS?

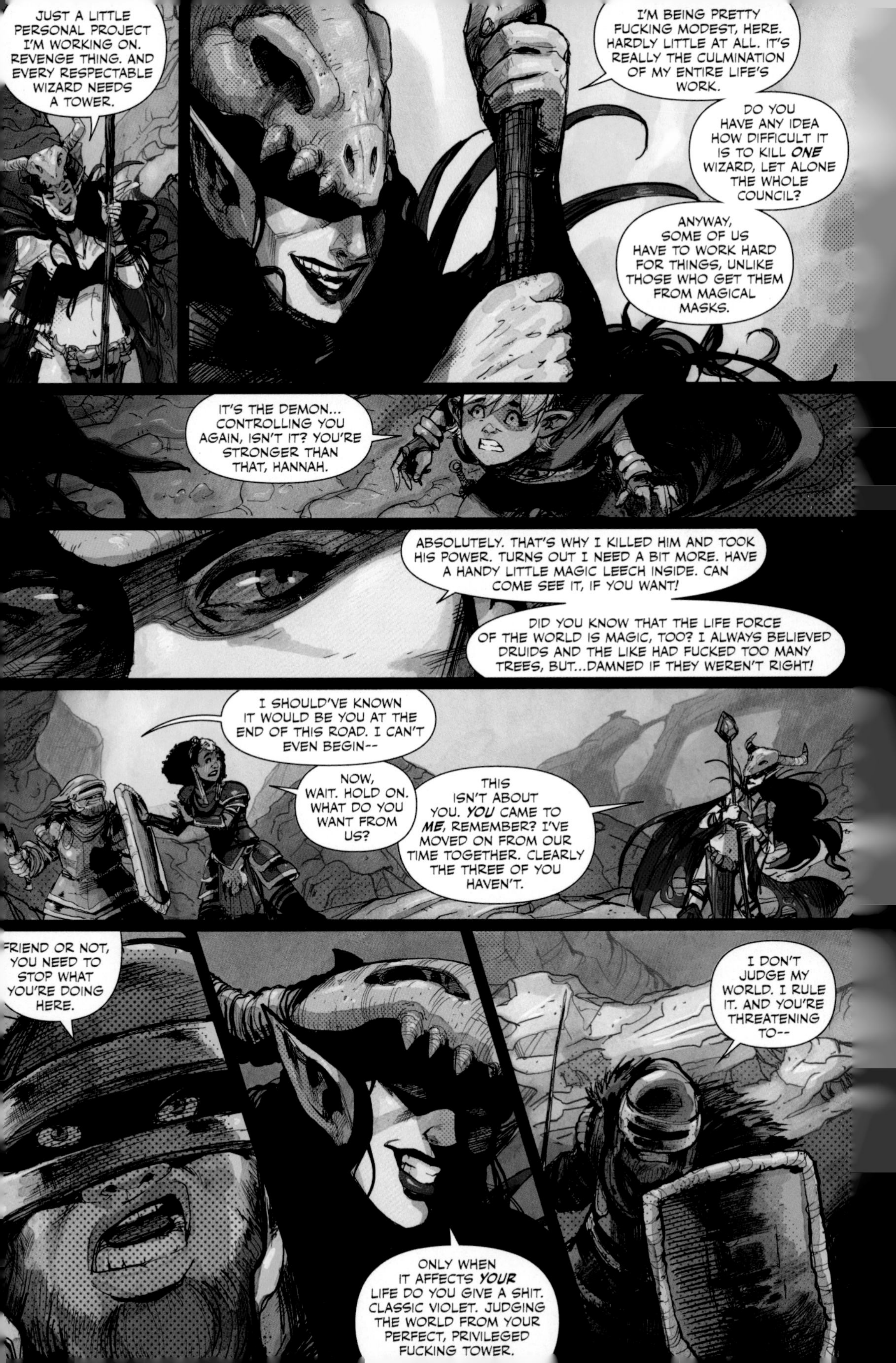
JUST A LITTLE PERSONAL PROJECT I'M WORKING ON. REVENGE THING. AND EVERY RESPECTABLE WIZARD NEEDS A TOWER.
I'M BEING PRETTY FUCKING MODEST, HERE. HARDLY LITTLE AT ALL. IT'S REALLY THE CULMINATION OF MY ENTIRE LIFE'S WORK.
DO YOU HAVE ANY IDEA HOW DIFFICULT IT IS TO KILL *ONE* WIZARD, LET ALONE THE WHOLE COUNCIL?
ANYWAY, SOME OF US HAVE TO WORK HARD FOR THINGS, UNLIKE THOSE WHO GET THEM FROM MAGICAL MASKS.
IT'S THE DEMON... CONTROLLING YOU AGAIN, ISN'T IT? YOU'RE STRONGER THAN THAT, HANNAH.
ABSOLUTELY. THAT'S WHY I KILLED HIM AND TOOK HIS POWER. TURNS OUT I NEED A BIT MORE. HAVE A HANDY LITTLE MAGIC LEECH INSIDE. CAN COME SEE IT, IF YOU WANT!
DID YOU KNOW THAT THE LIFE FORCE OF THE WORLD IS MAGIC, TOO? I ALWAYS BELIEVED DRUIDS AND THE LIKE HAD FUCKED TOO MANY TREES, BUT...DAMNED IF THEY WEREN'T RIGHT!
I SHOULD'VE KNOWN IT WOULD BE YOU AT THE END OF THIS ROAD. I CAN'T EVEN BEGIN--
NOW, WAIT. HOLD ON. WHAT DO YOU WANT FROM US?
THIS ISN'T ABOUT YOU. *YOU* CAME TO *ME*, REMEMBER? I'VE MOVED ON FROM OUR TIME TOGETHER. CLEARLY THE THREE OF YOU HAVEN'T.
FRIEND OR NOT, YOU NEED TO STOP WHAT YOU'RE DOING HERE.
ONLY WHEN IT AFFECTS *YOUR* LIFE DO YOU GIVE A SHIT. CLASSIC VIOLET. JUDGING THE WORLD FROM YOUR PERFECT, PRIVILEGED FUCKING TOWER.
I DON'T JUDGE MY WORLD. I RULE IT. AND YOU'RE THREATENING TO--

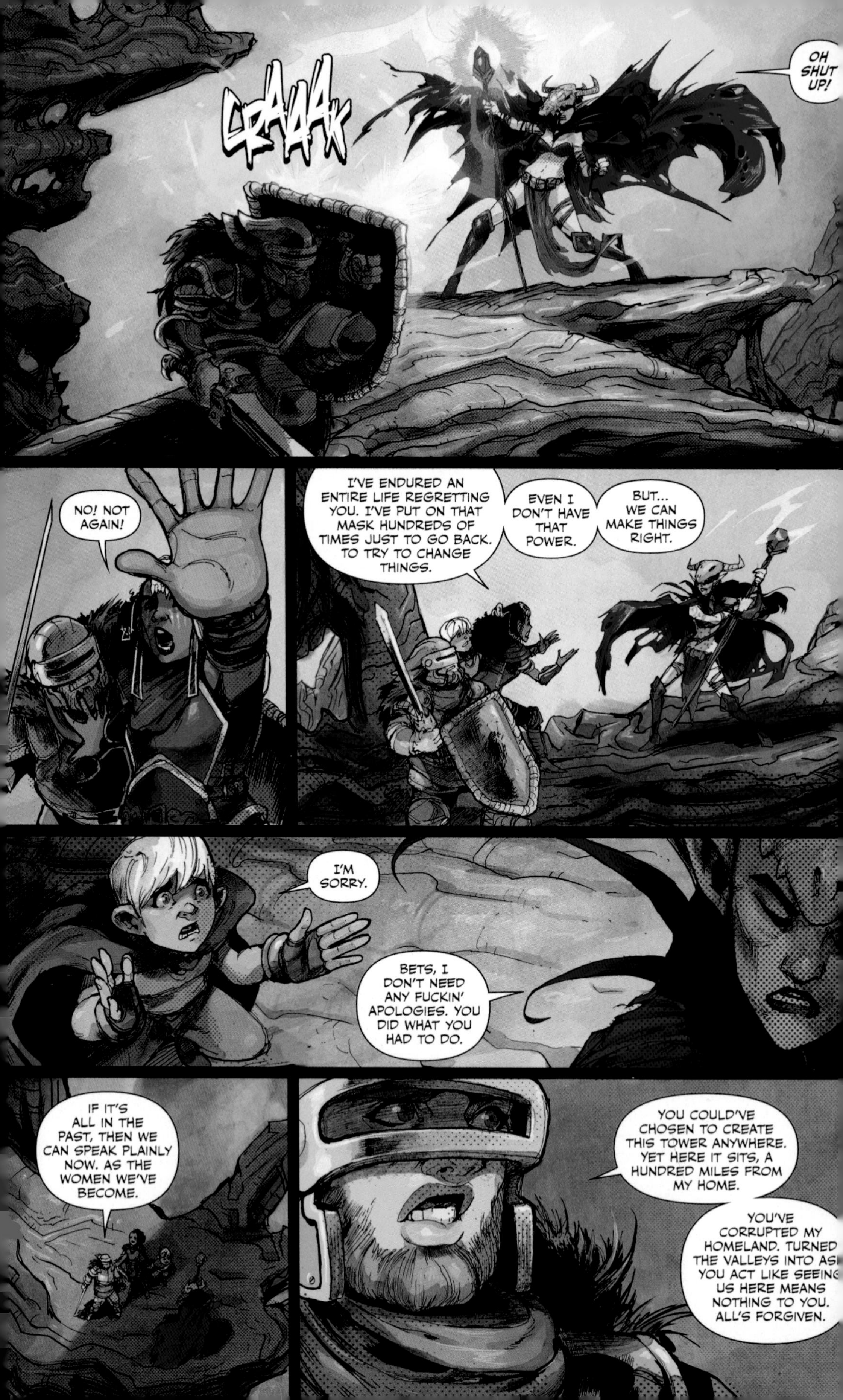
CRAAAK
OH SHUT UP!
NO! NOT AGAIN!
I'VE ENDURED AN ENTIRE LIFE REGRETTING YOU. I'VE PUT ON THAT MASK HUNDREDS OF TIMES JUST TO GO BACK. TO TRY TO CHANGE THINGS.
EVEN I DON'T HAVE THAT POWER.
BUT... WE CAN MAKE THINGS RIGHT.
I'M SORRY.
BETS, I DON'T NEED ANY FUCKIN' APOLOGIES. YOU DID WHAT YOU HAD TO DO.
IF IT'S ALL IN THE PAST, THEN WE CAN SPEAK PLAINLY NOW. AS THE WOMEN WE'VE BECOME.
YOU COULD'VE CHOSEN TO CREATE THIS TOWER ANYWHERE. YET HERE IT SITS, A HUNDRED MILES FROM MY HOME.
YOU'VE CORRUPTED MY HOMELAND. TURNED THE VALLEYS INTO AS YOU ACT LIKE SEEING US HERE MEANS NOTHING TO YOU. ALL'S FORGIVEN.

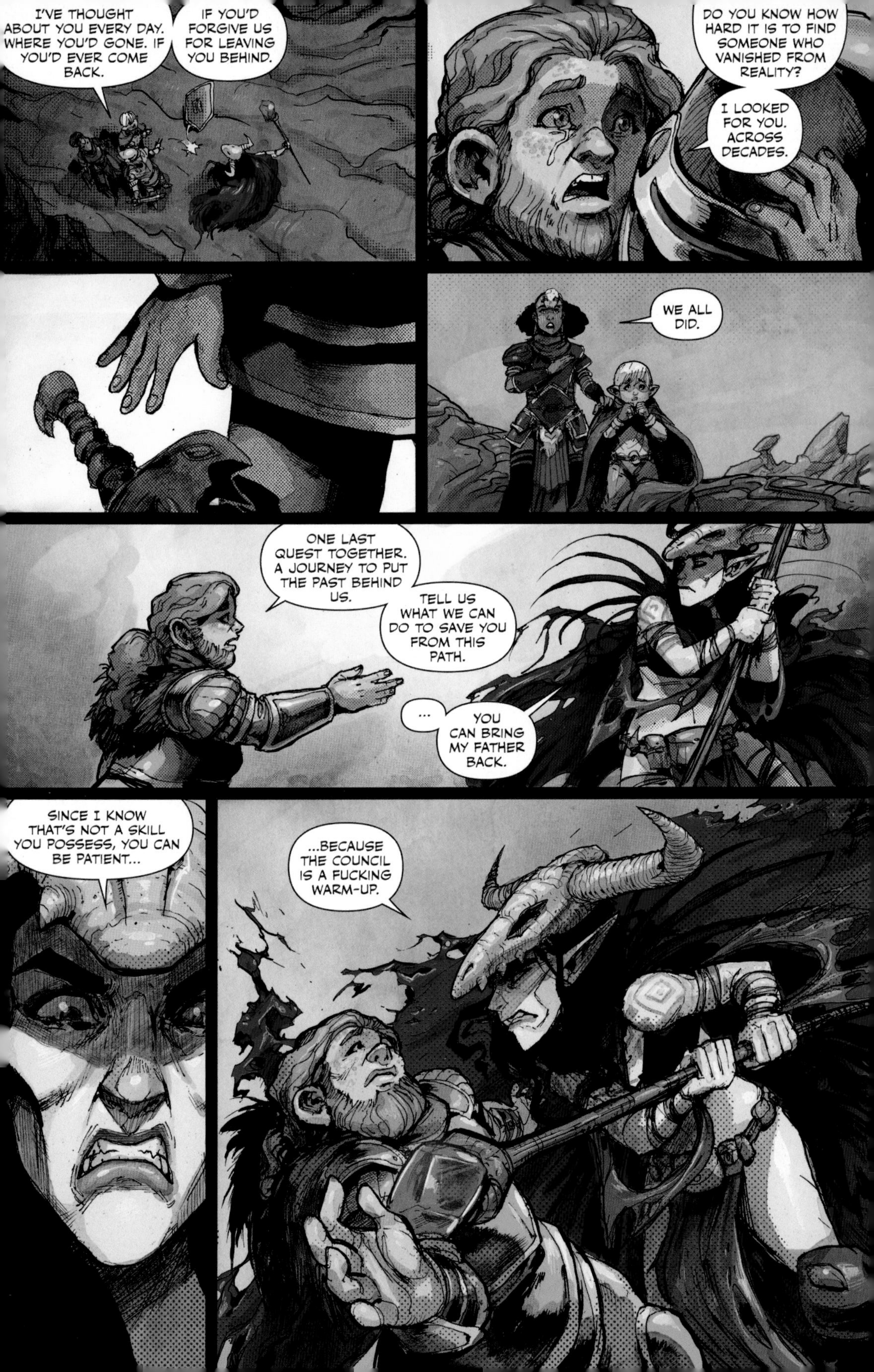
I'VE THOUGHT ABOUT YOU EVERY DAY. WHERE YOU'D GONE. IF YOU'D EVER COME BACK.
IF YOU'D FORGIVE US FOR LEAVING YOU BEHIND.
DO YOU KNOW HOW HARD IT IS TO FIND SOMEONE WHO VANISHED FROM REALITY?
I LOOKED FOR YOU. ACROSS DECADES.
WE ALL DID.
ONE LAST QUEST TOGETHER. A JOURNEY TO PUT THE PAST BEHIND US.
TELL US WHAT WE CAN DO TO SAVE YOU FROM THIS PATH.
...
YOU CAN BRING MY FATHER BACK.
SINCE I KNOW THAT'S NOT A SKILL YOU POSSESS, YOU CAN BE PATIENT...
...BECAUSE THE COUNCIL IS A FUCKING WARM-UP.

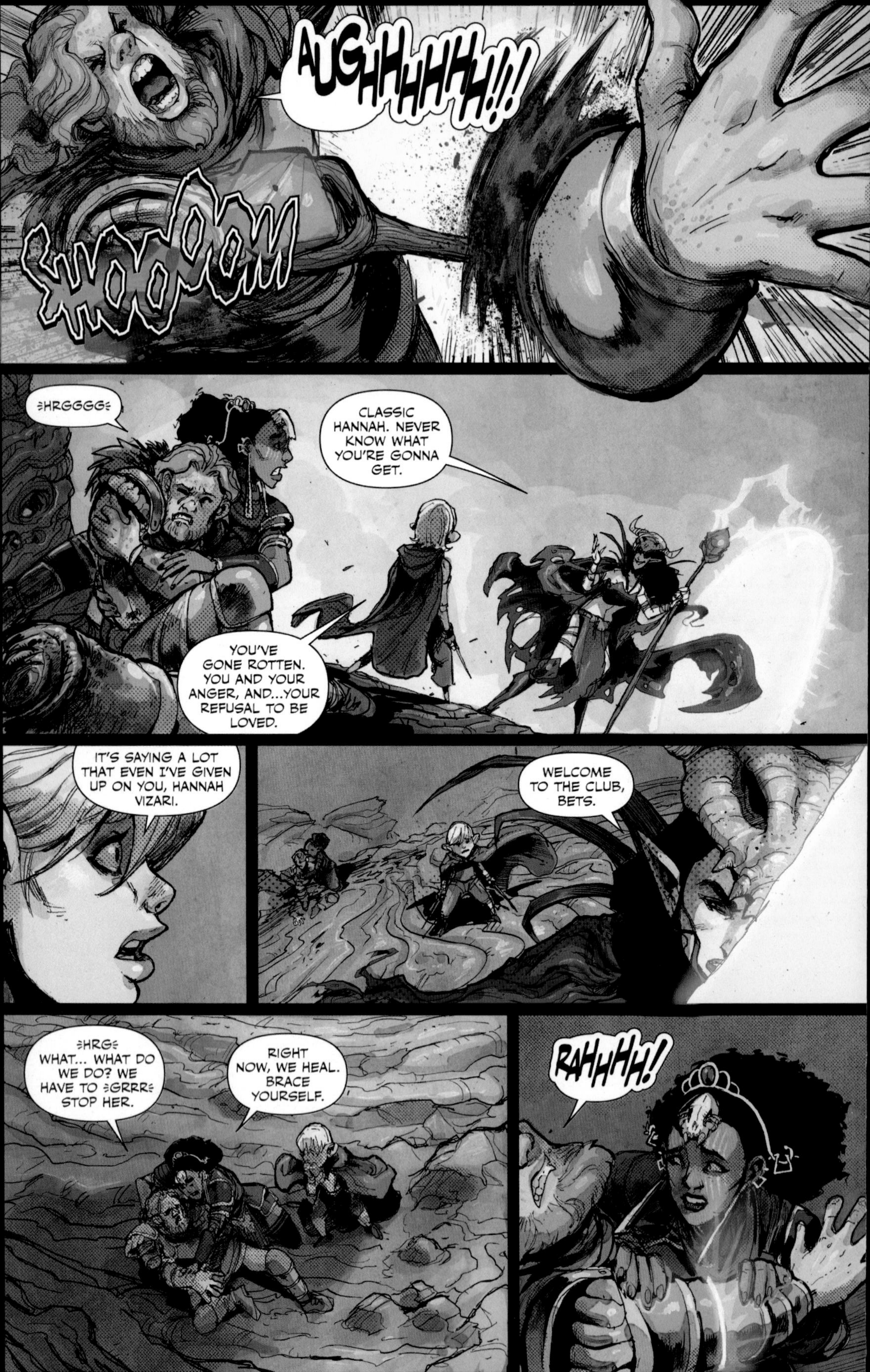
AUGHHHHHH!!!
SHOOOOM
≑HRGGGG≑
CLASSIC HANNAH. NEVER KNOW WHAT YOU'RE GONNA GET.
YOU'VE GONE ROTTEN. YOU AND YOUR ANGER, AND...YOUR REFUSAL TO BE LOVED.
IT'S SAYING A LOT THAT EVEN I'VE GIVEN UP ON YOU, HANNAH VIZARI.
WELCOME TO THE CLUB, BETS.
≑HRG≑ WHAT... WHAT DO WE DO? WE HAVE TO ≑GRRR≑ STOP HER.
RIGHT NOW, WE HEAL. BRACE YOURSELF.
RAHHHH!

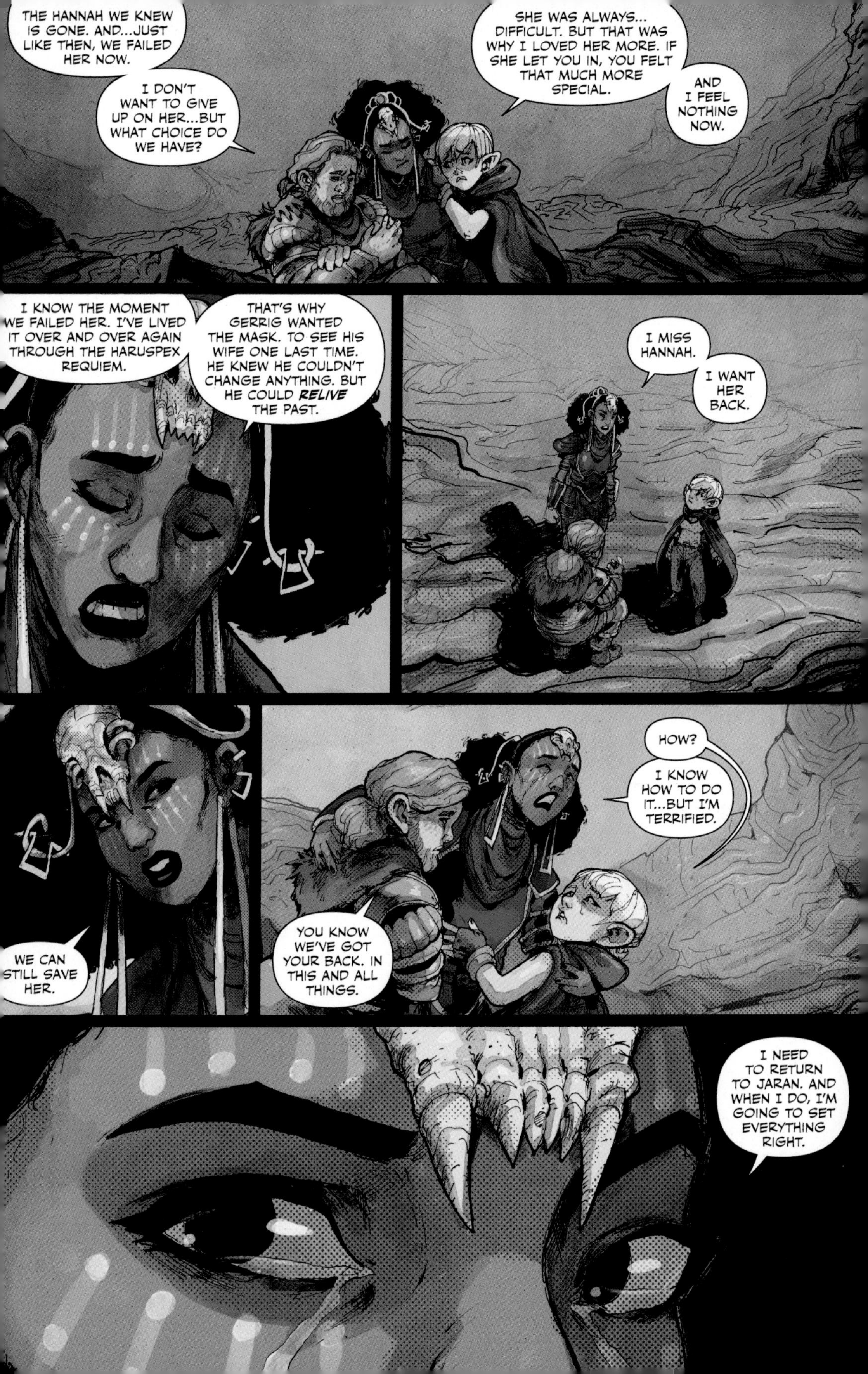
THE HANNAH WE KNEW IS GONE. AND...JUST LIKE THEN, WE FAILED HER NOW.
I DON'T WANT TO GIVE UP ON HER...BUT WHAT CHOICE DO WE HAVE?
SHE WAS ALWAYS... DIFFICULT. BUT THAT WAS WHY I LOVED HER MORE. IF SHE LET YOU IN, YOU FELT THAT MUCH MORE SPECIAL.
AND I FEEL NOTHING NOW.
I KNOW THE MOMENT WE FAILED HER. I'VE LIVED IT OVER AND OVER AGAIN THROUGH THE HARUSPEX REQUIEM.
THAT'S WHY GERRIG WANTED THE MASK. TO SEE HIS WIFE ONE LAST TIME. HE KNEW HE COULDN'T CHANGE ANYTHING. BUT HE COULD *RELIVE* THE PAST.
I MISS HANNAH.
I WANT HER BACK.
WE CAN STILL SAVE HER.
HOW?
I KNOW HOW TO DO IT...BUT I'M TERRIFIED.
YOU KNOW WE'VE GOT YOUR BACK. IN THIS AND ALL THINGS.
I NEED TO RETURN TO JARAN. AND WHEN I DO, I'M GOING TO SET EVERYTHING RIGHT.

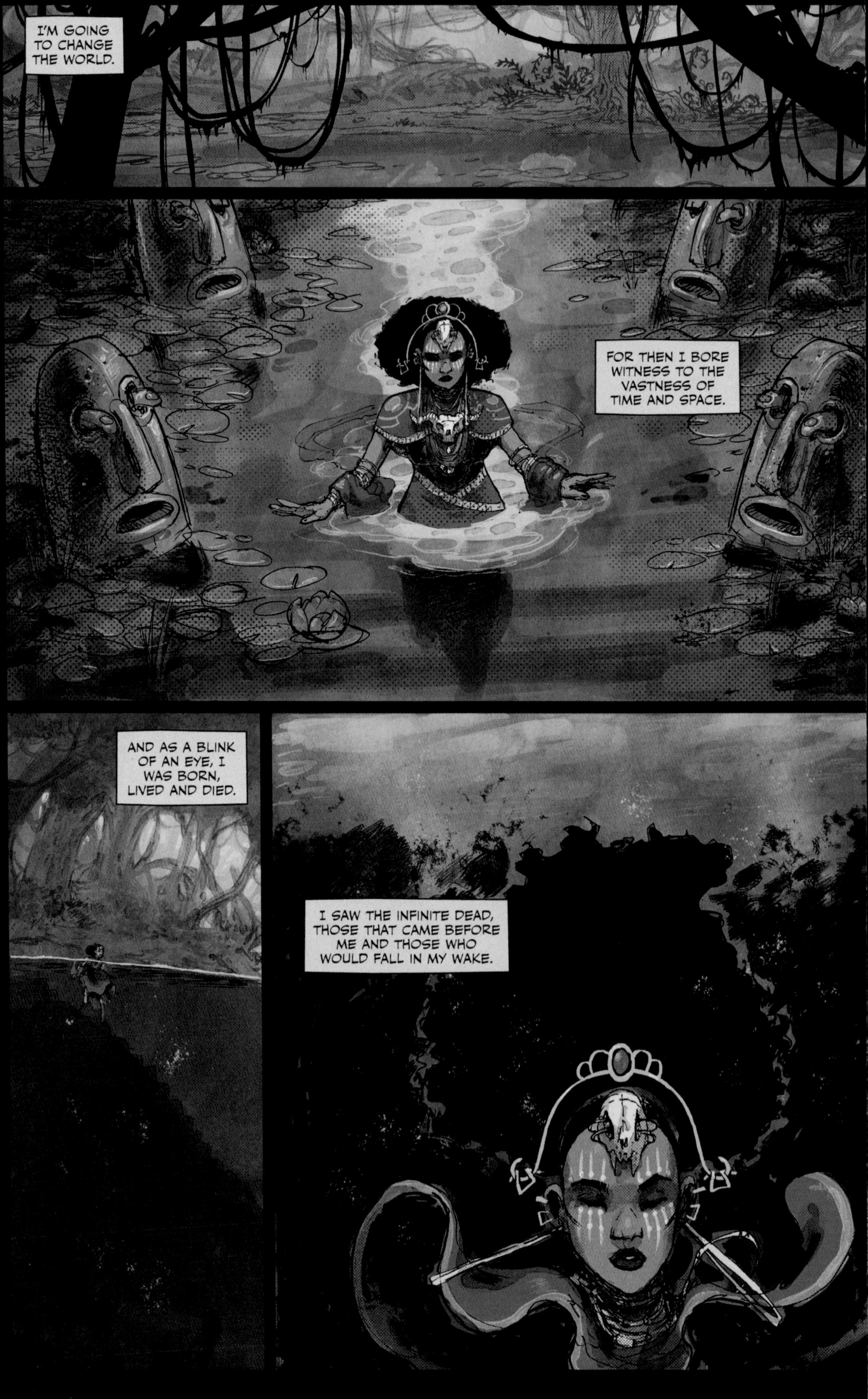
I'M GOING TO CHANGE THE WORLD.
FOR THEN I BORE WITNESS TO THE VASTNESS OF TIME AND SPACE.
AND AS A BLINK OF AN EYE, I WAS BORN, LIVED AND DIED.
I SAW THE INFINITE DEAD, THOSE THAT CAME BEFORE ME AND THOSE WHO WOULD FALL IN MY WAKE.

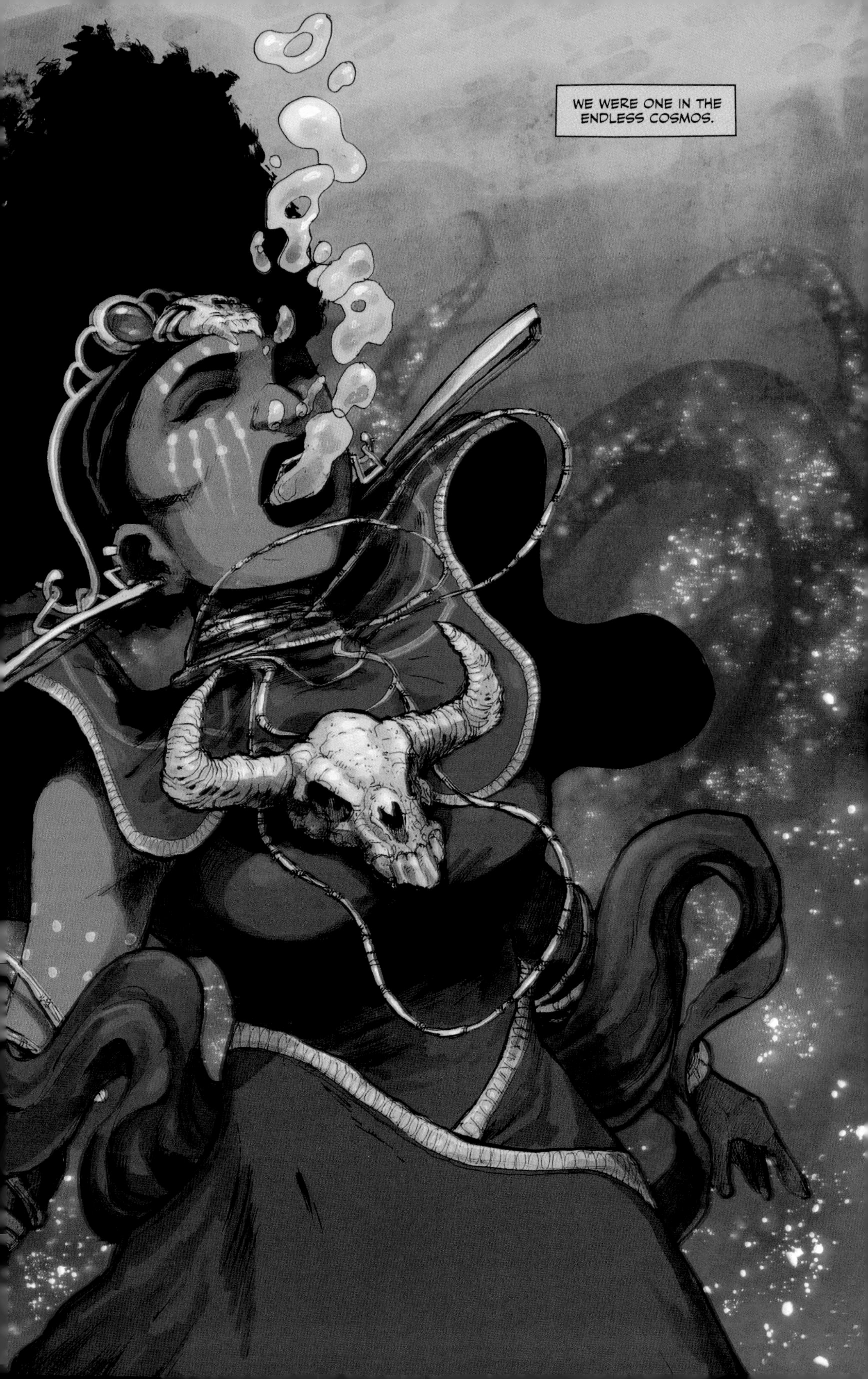
WE WERE ONE IN THE
ENDLESS COSMOS.

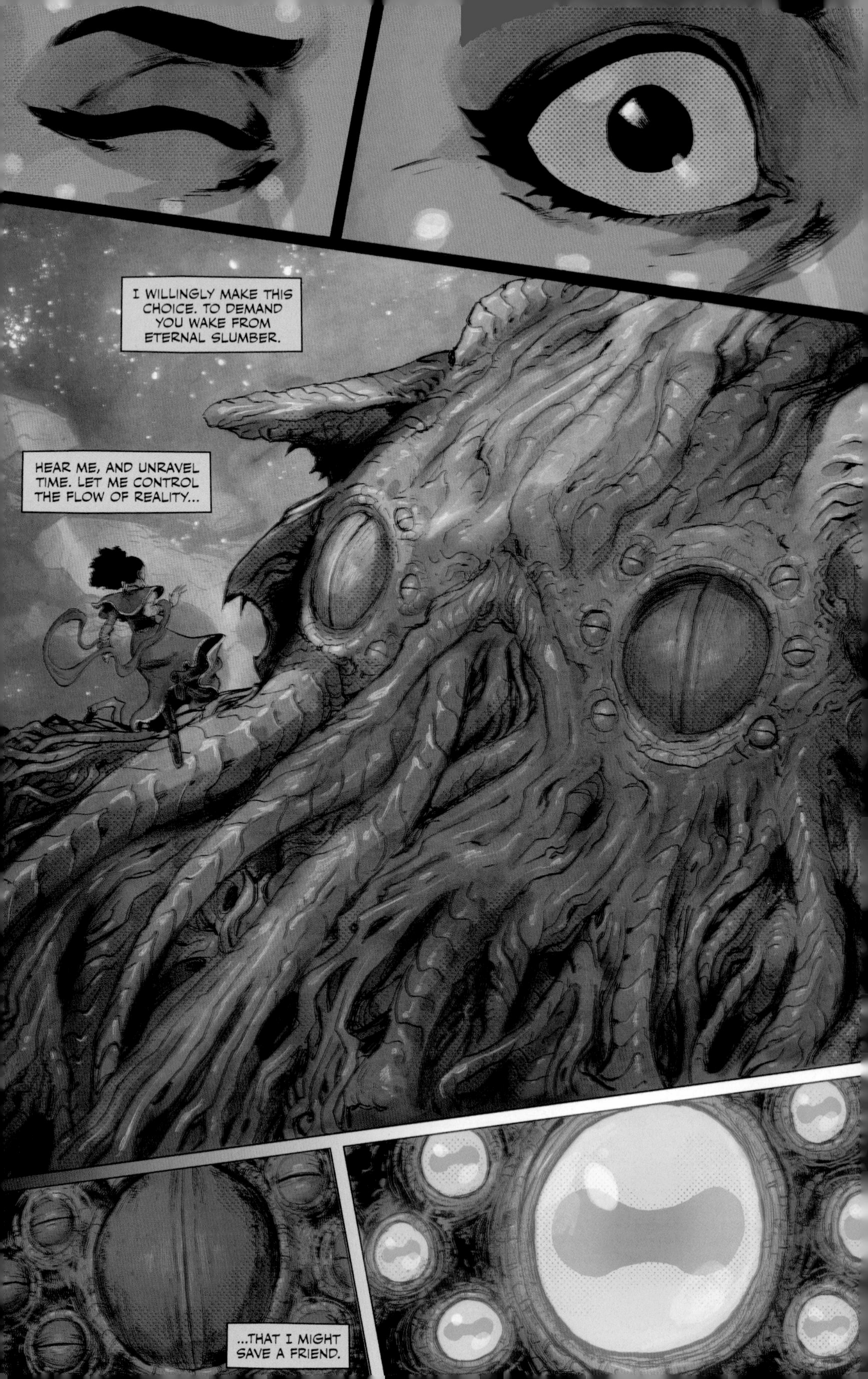
I WILLINGLY MAKE THIS CHOICE. TO DEMAND YOU WAKE FROM ETERNAL SLUMBER.
HEAR ME, AND UNRAVEL TIME. LET ME CONTROL THE FLOW OF REALITY...
...THAT I MIGHT SAVE A FRIEND.

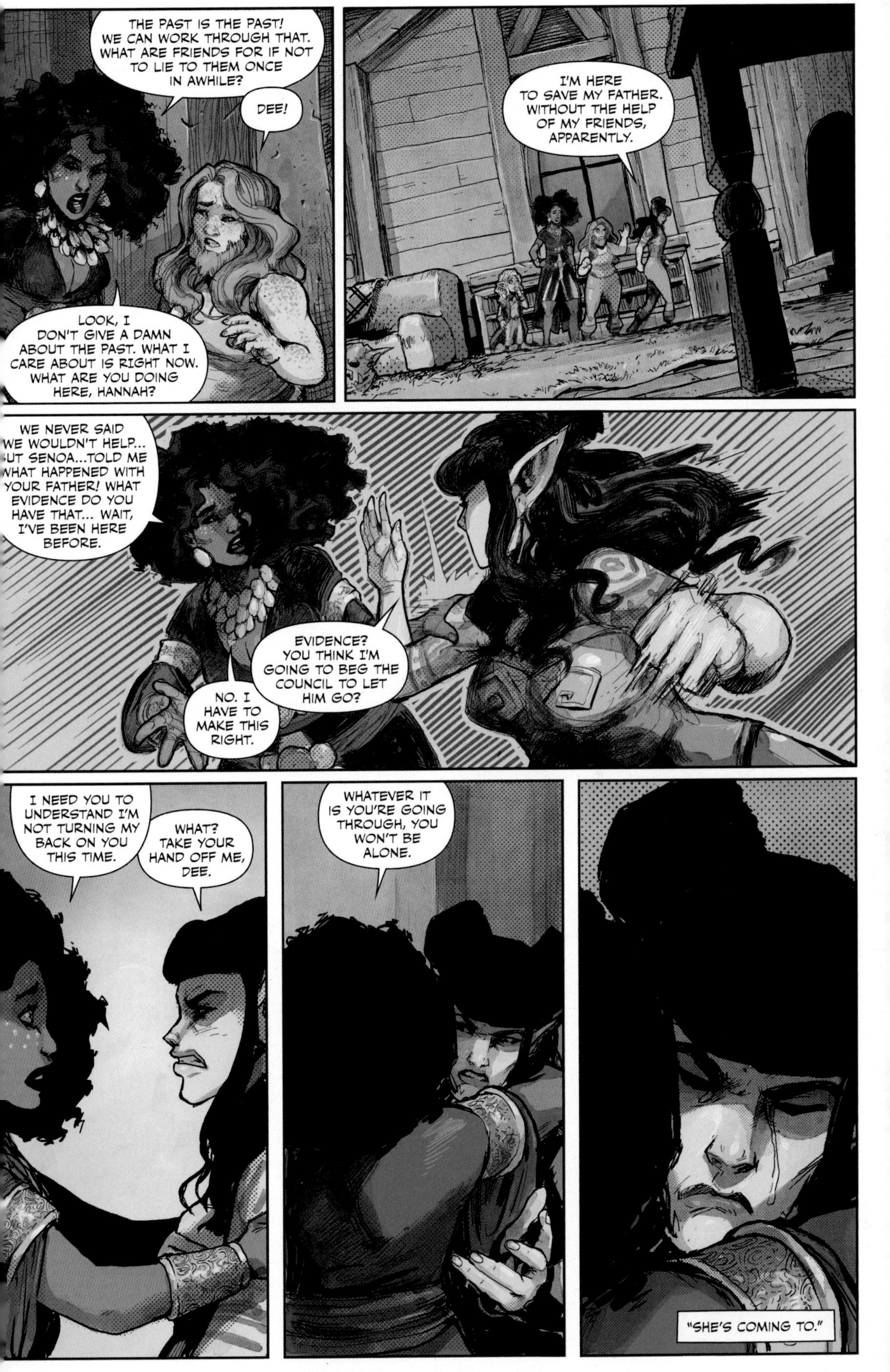
THE PAST IS THE PAST! WE CAN WORK THROUGH THAT. WHAT ARE FRIENDS FOR IF NOT TO LIE TO THEM ONCE IN AWHILE?
DEE!
LOOK, I DON'T GIVE A DAMN ABOUT THE PAST. WHAT I CARE ABOUT IS RIGHT NOW. WHAT ARE YOU DOING HERE, HANNAH?
I'M HERE TO SAVE MY FATHER. WITHOUT THE HELP OF MY FRIENDS, APPARENTLY.
WE NEVER SAID WE WOULDN'T HELP... UT SENOA...TOLD ME WHAT HAPPENED WITH YOUR FATHER! WHAT EVIDENCE DO YOU HAVE THAT... WAIT, I'VE BEEN HERE BEFORE.
EVIDENCE? YOU THINK I'M GOING TO BEG THE COUNCIL TO LET HIM GO?
NO. I HAVE TO MAKE THIS RIGHT.
I NEED YOU TO UNDERSTAND I'M NOT TURNING MY BACK ON YOU THIS TIME.
WHAT? TAKE YOUR HAND OFF ME, DEE.
WHATEVER IT IS YOU'RE GOING THROUGH, YOU WON'T BE ALONE.
"SHE'S COMING TO."

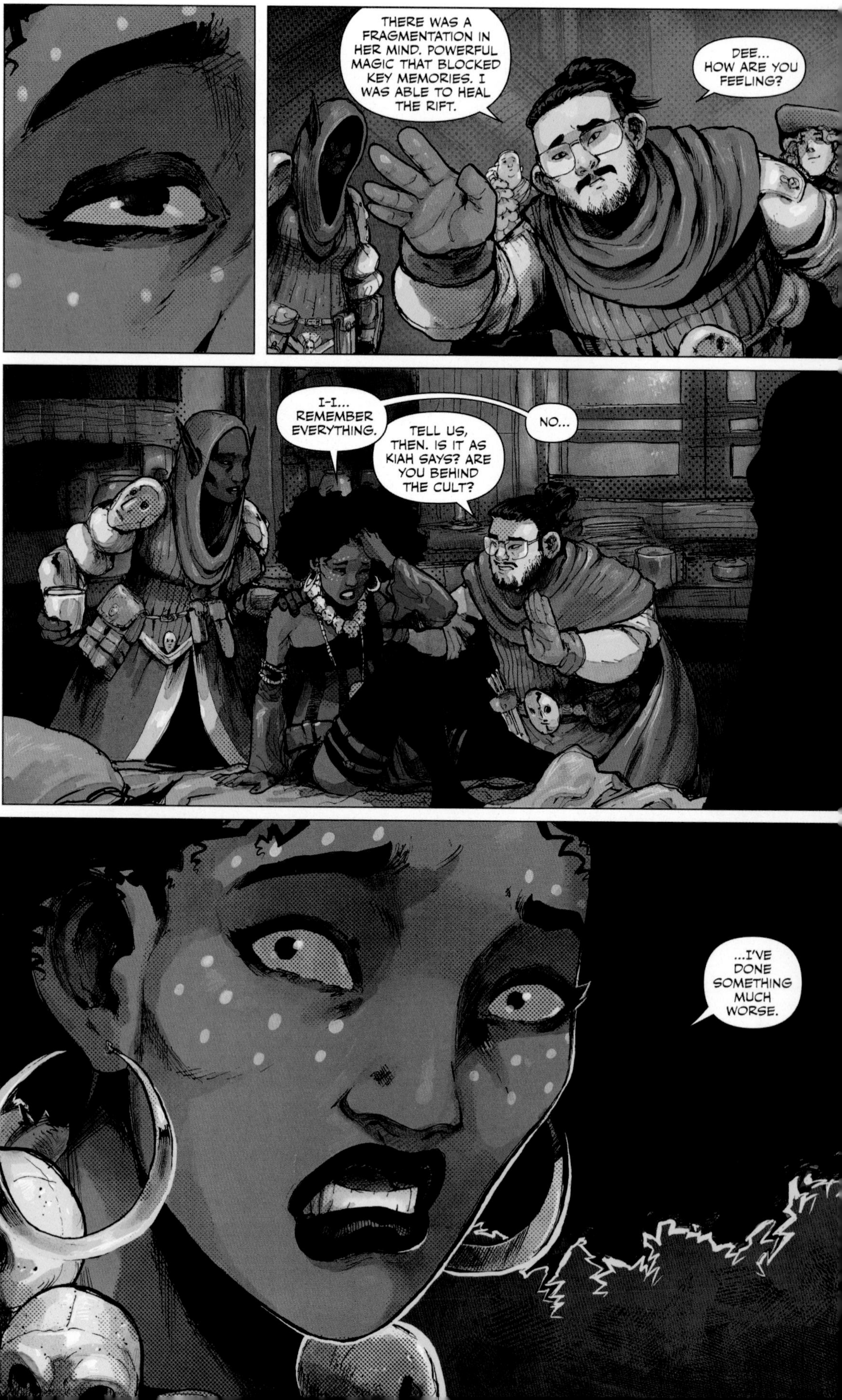
THERE WAS A FRAGMENTATION IN HER MIND. POWERFUL MAGIC THAT BLOCKED KEY MEMORIES. I WAS ABLE TO HEAL THE RIFT.
DEE... HOW ARE YOU FEELING?
I-I... REMEMBER EVERYTHING.
TELL US, THEN. IS IT AS KIAH SAYS? ARE YOU BEHIND THE CULT?
NO...
...I'VE DONE SOMETHING MUCH WORSE.

CHAPTER TEN

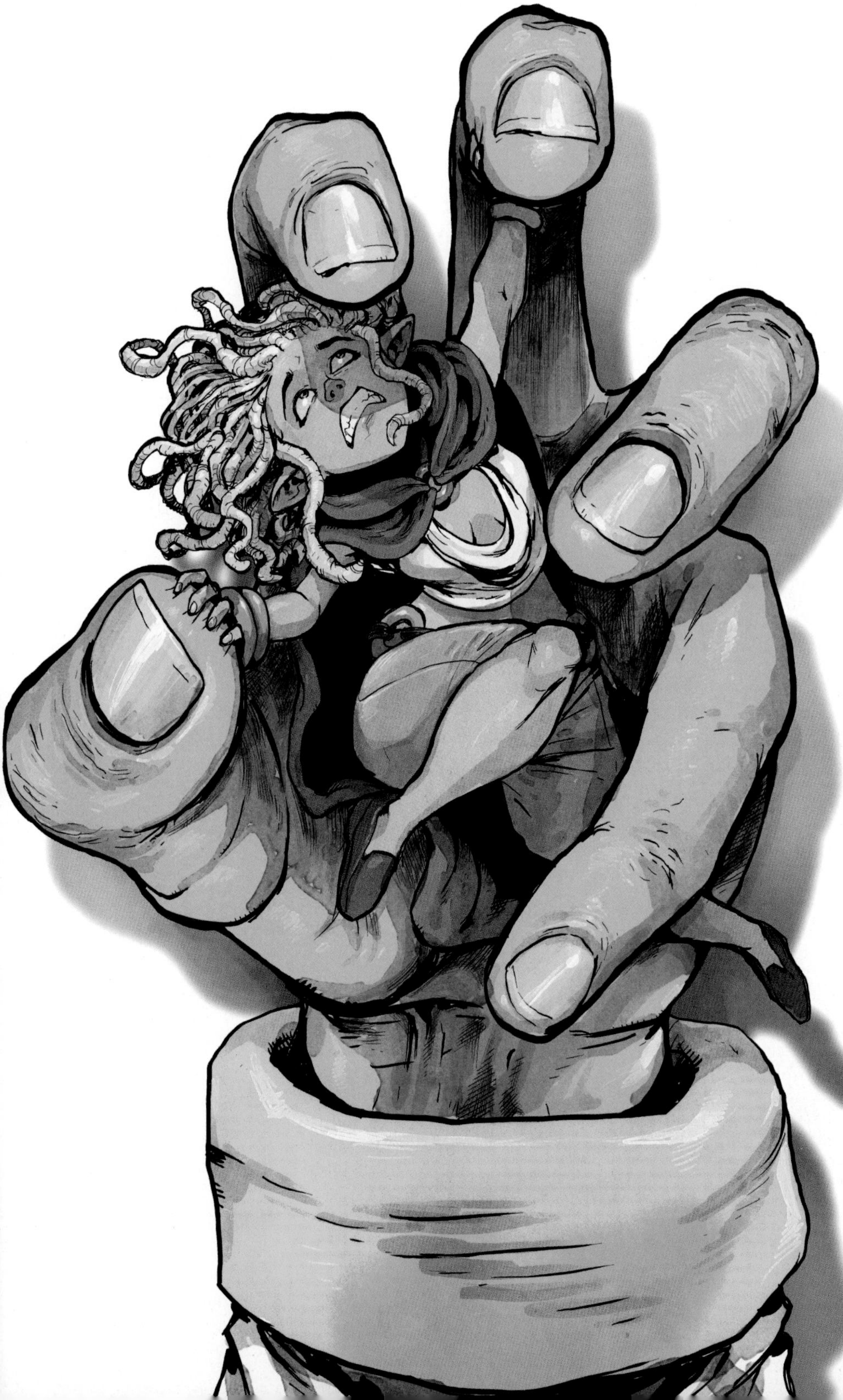

Issue 10 cover B by Joseph Michael Linsner

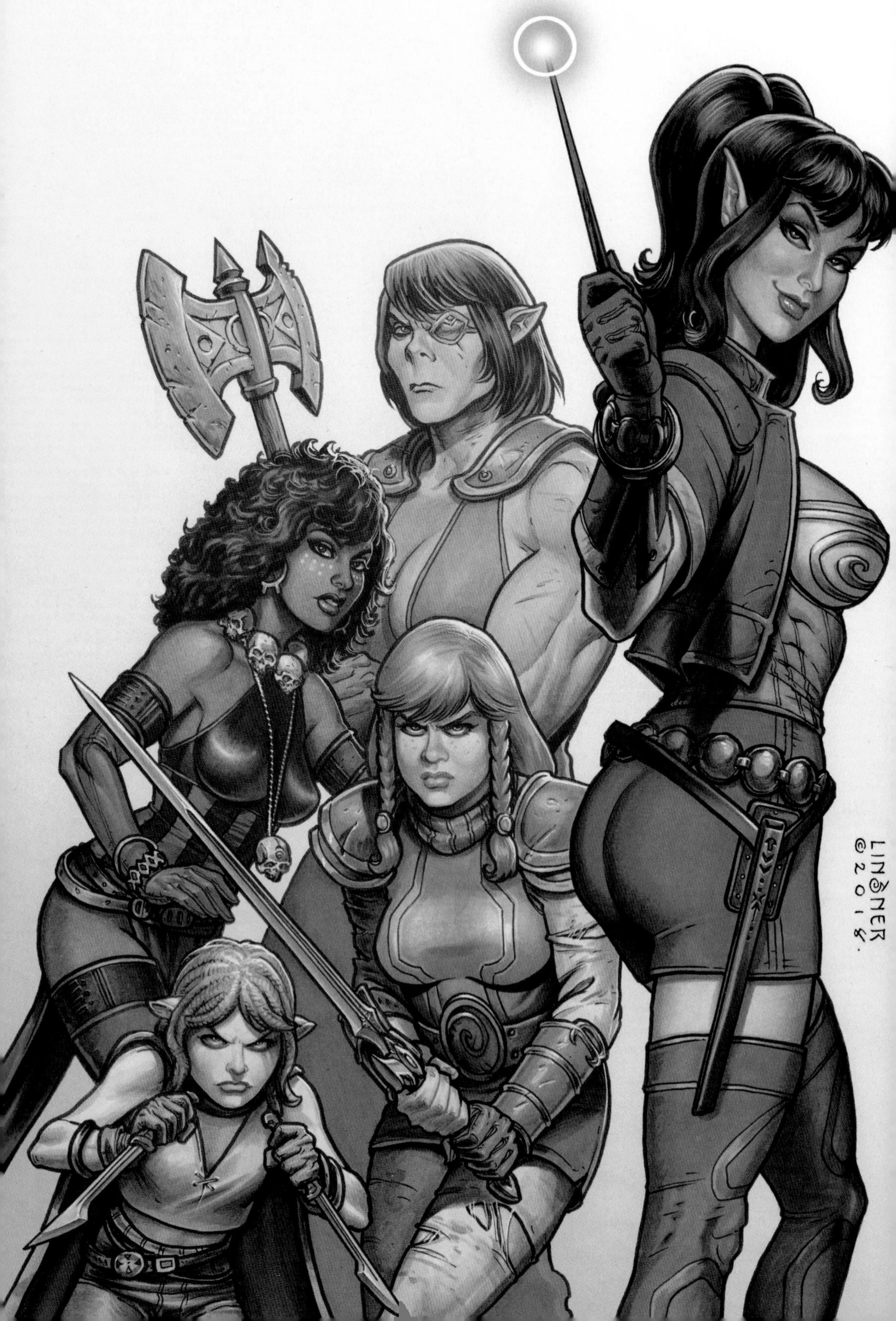
LINSNER
©2018.

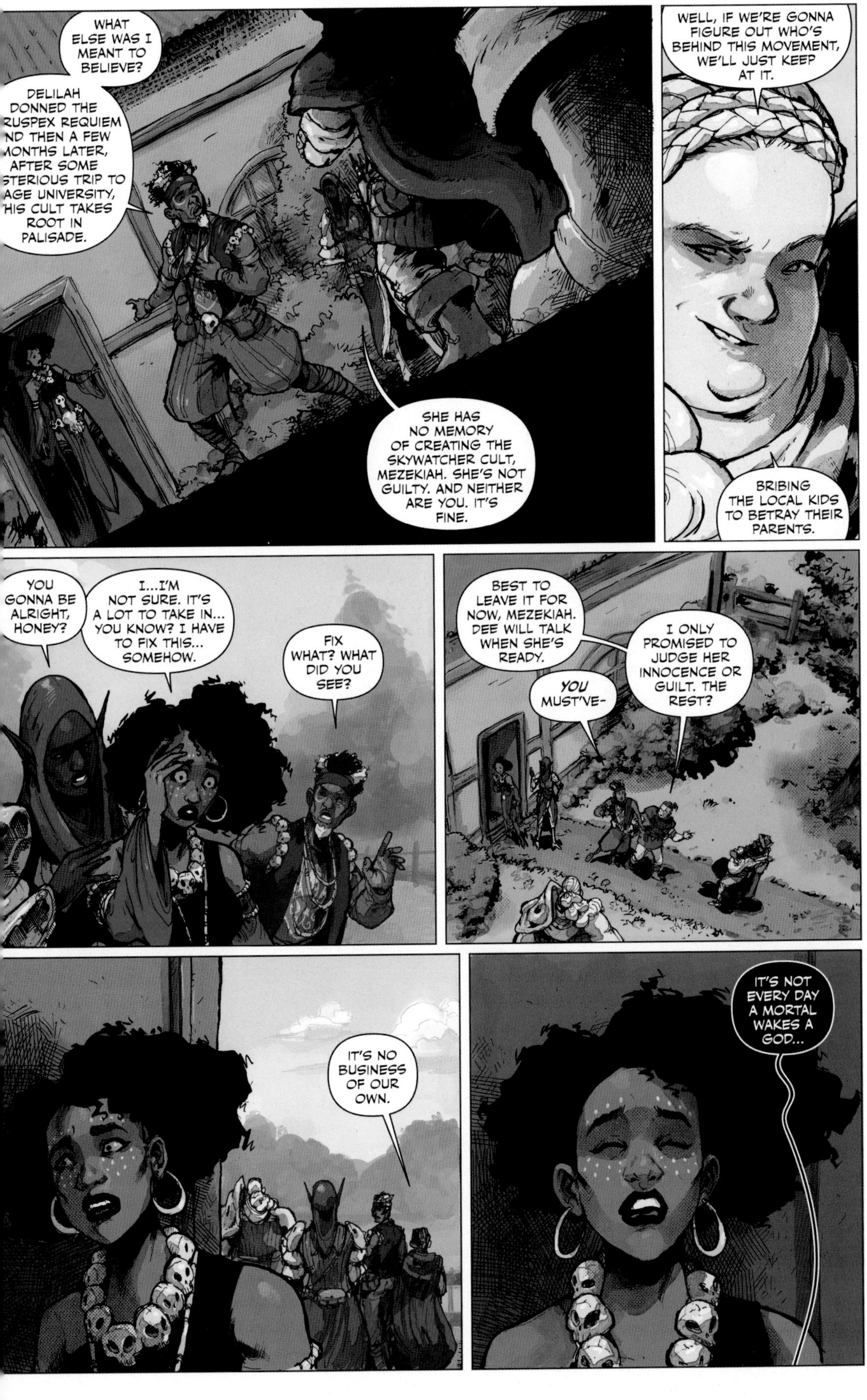
WHAT ELSE WAS I MEANT TO BELIEVE?
DELILAH DONNED THE RUSPEX REQUIEM ND THEN A FEW MONTHS LATER, AFTER SOME STERIOUS TRIP TO AGE UNIVERSITY, HIS CULT TAKES ROOT IN PALISADE.
SHE HAS NO MEMORY OF CREATING THE SKYWATCHER CULT, MEZEKIAH. SHE'S NOT GUILTY. AND NEITHER ARE YOU. IT'S FINE.
WELL, IF WE'RE GONNA FIGURE OUT WHO'S BEHIND THIS MOVEMENT, WE'LL JUST KEEP AT IT.
BRIBING THE LOCAL KIDS TO BETRAY THEIR PARENTS.
YOU GONNA BE ALRIGHT, HONEY?
I...I'M NOT SURE. IT'S A LOT TO TAKE IN... YOU KNOW? I HAVE TO FIX THIS... SOMEHOW.
FIX WHAT? WHAT DID YOU SEE?
BEST TO LEAVE IT FOR NOW, MEZEKIAH. DEE WILL TALK WHEN SHE'S READY.
YOU MUST'VE-
I ONLY PROMISED TO JUDGE HER INNOCENCE OR GUILT. THE REST?
IT'S NO BUSINESS OF OUR OWN.
IT'S NOT EVERY DAY A MORTAL WAKES A GOD...

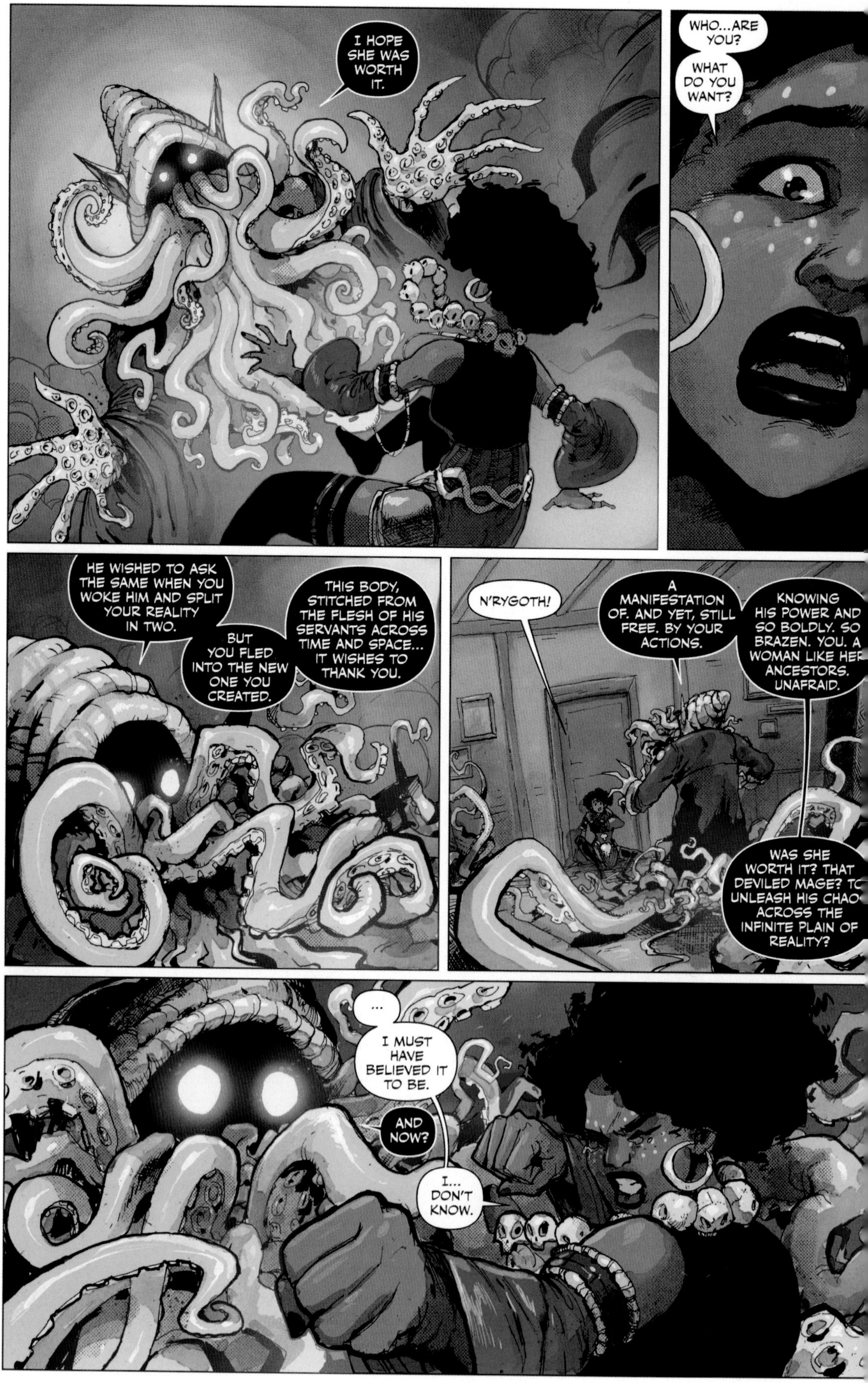
I HOPE SHE WAS WORTH IT.
WHO...ARE YOU?
WHAT DO YOU WANT?
HE WISHED TO ASK THE SAME WHEN YOU WOKE HIM AND SPLIT YOUR REALITY IN TWO.
BUT YOU FLED INTO THE NEW ONE YOU CREATED.
THIS BODY, STITCHED FROM THE FLESH OF HIS SERVANTS ACROSS TIME AND SPACE... IT WISHES TO THANK YOU.
N'RYGOTH!
A MANIFESTATION OF. AND YET, STILL FREE. BY YOUR ACTIONS.
KNOWING HIS POWER AND SO BOLDLY. SO BRAZEN. YOU. A WOMAN LIKE HER ANCESTORS. UNAFRAID.
WAS SHE WORTH IT? THAT DEVILED MAGE? TO UNLEASH HIS CHAOS ACROSS THE INFINITE PLAIN OF REALITY?
...
I MUST HAVE BELIEVED IT TO BE.
AND NOW?
I... DON'T KNOW.

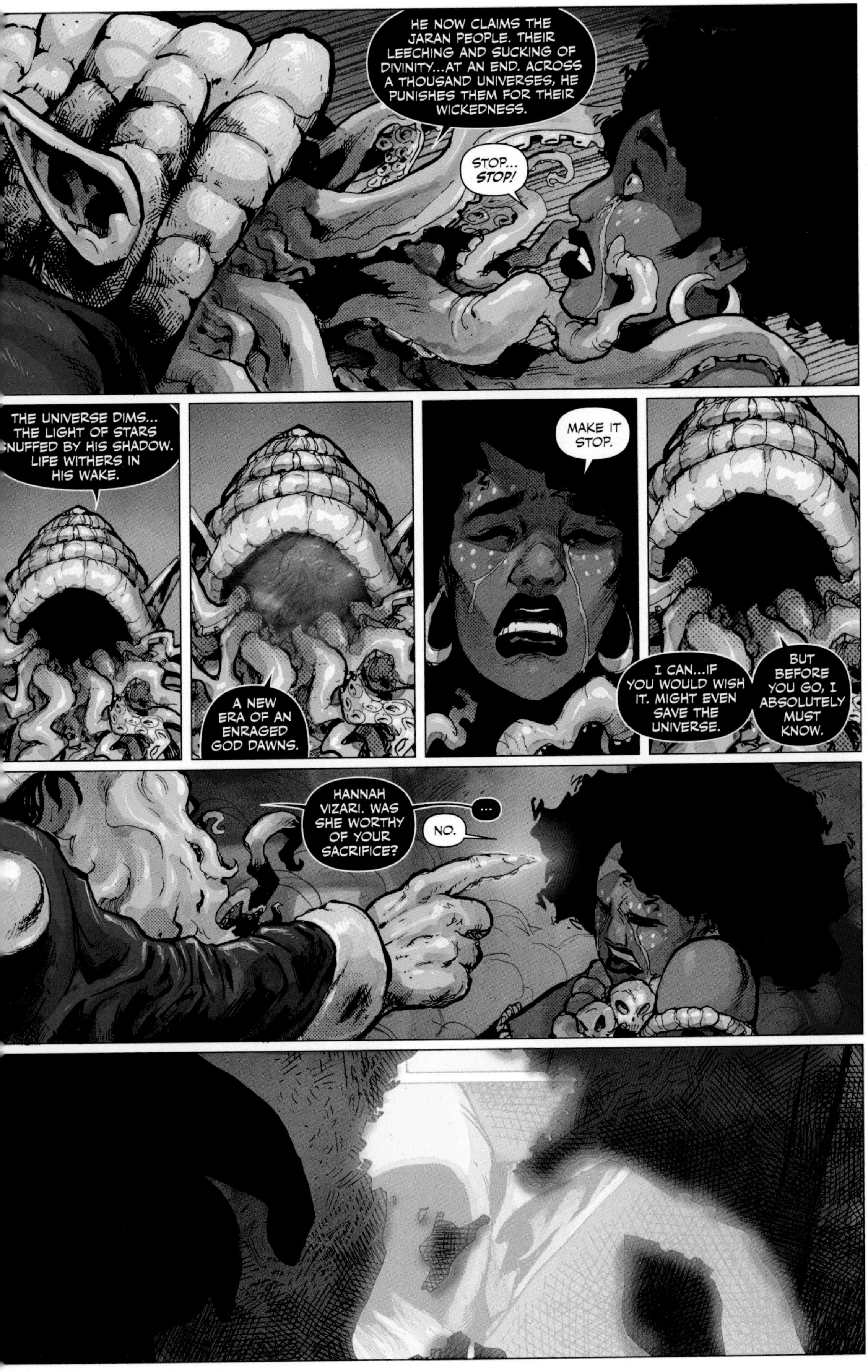
HE NOW CLAIMS THE JARAN PEOPLE. THEIR LEECHING AND SUCKING OF DIVINITY...AT AN END. ACROSS A THOUSAND UNIVERSES, HE PUNISHES THEM FOR THEIR WICKEDNESS.
STOP... STOP!
THE UNIVERSE DIMS... THE LIGHT OF STARS SNUFFED BY HIS SHADOW. LIFE WITHERS IN HIS WAKE.
A NEW ERA OF AN ENRAGED GOD DAWNS.
MAKE IT STOP.
I CAN...IF YOU WOULD WISH IT. MIGHT EVEN SAVE THE UNIVERSE.
BUT BEFORE YOU GO, I ABSOLUTELY MUST KNOW.
HANNAH VIZARI. WAS SHE WORTHY OF YOUR SACRIFICE?
...
NO.

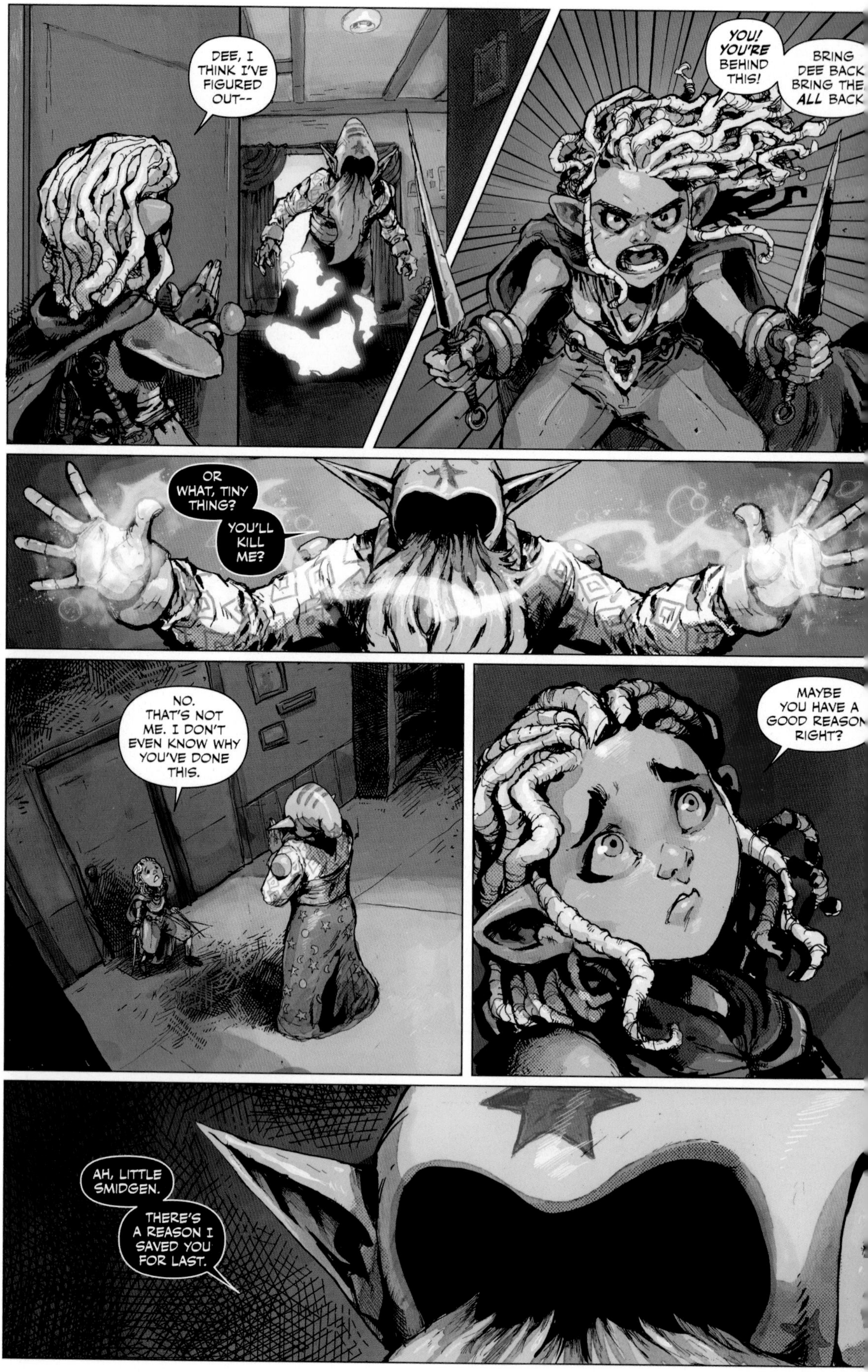
DEE, I THINK I'VE FIGURED OUT--
YOU! YOU'RE BEHIND THIS!
BRING DEE BACK BRING THE ALL BACK
OR WHAT, TINY THING?
YOU'LL KILL ME?
NO. THAT'S NOT ME. I DON'T EVEN KNOW WHY YOU'VE DONE THIS.
MAYBE YOU HAVE A GOOD REASON RIGHT?
AH, LITTLE SMIDGEN.
THERE'S A REASON I SAVED YOU FOR LAST.

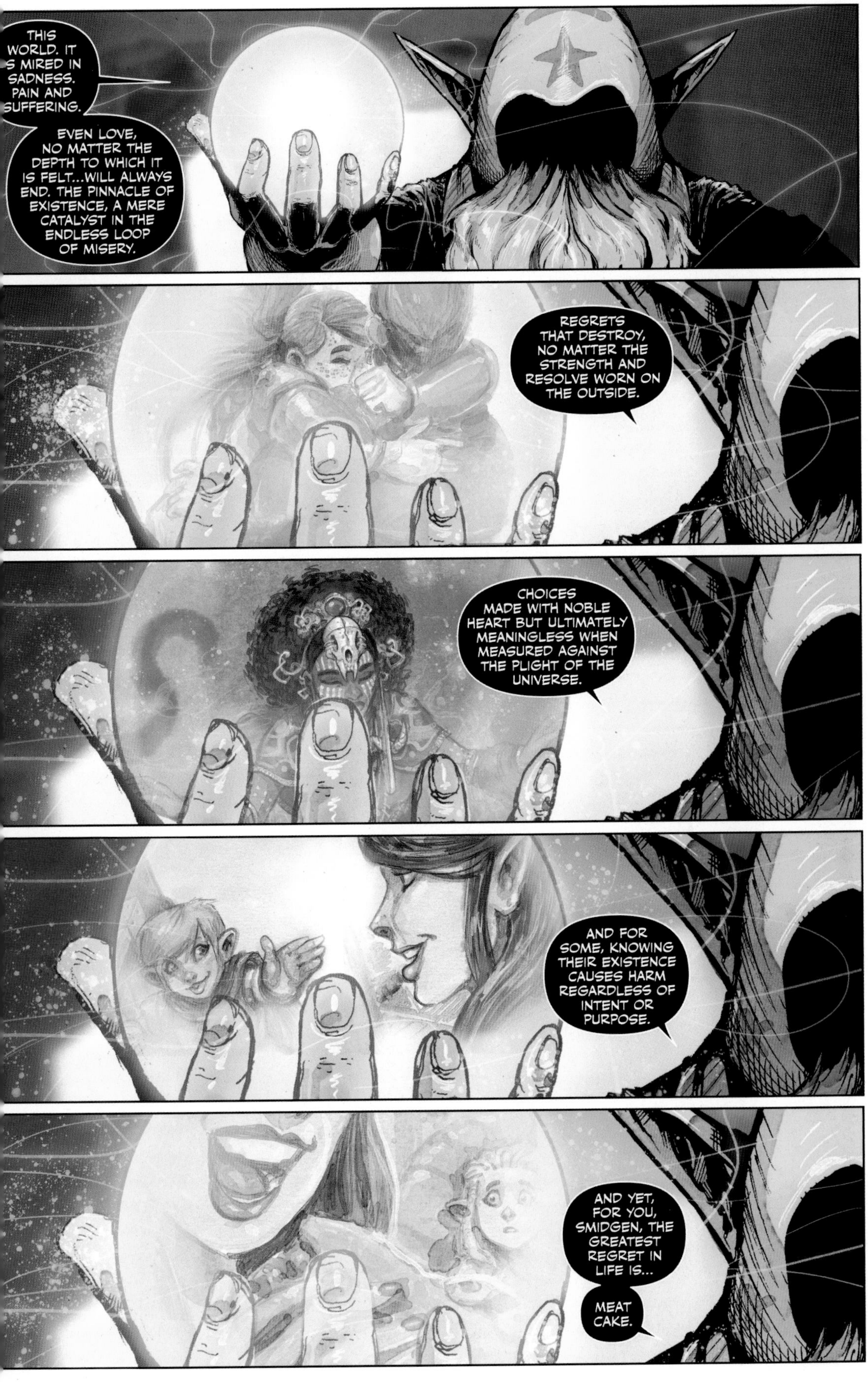
THIS WORLD. IT S MIRED IN SADNESS. PAIN AND SUFFERING.
EVEN LOVE, NO MATTER THE DEPTH TO WHICH IT IS FELT...WILL ALWAYS END. THE PINNACLE OF EXISTENCE, A MERE CATALYST IN THE ENDLESS LOOP OF MISERY.
REGRETS THAT DESTROY, NO MATTER THE STRENGTH AND RESOLVE WORN ON THE OUTSIDE.
CHOICES MADE WITH NOBLE HEART BUT ULTIMATELY MEANINGLESS WHEN MEASURED AGAINST THE PLIGHT OF THE UNIVERSE.
AND FOR SOME, KNOWING THEIR EXISTENCE CAUSES HARM REGARDLESS OF INTENT OR PURPOSE.
AND YET, FOR YOU, SMIDGEN, THE GREATEST REGRET IN LIFE IS...
MEAT CAKE.

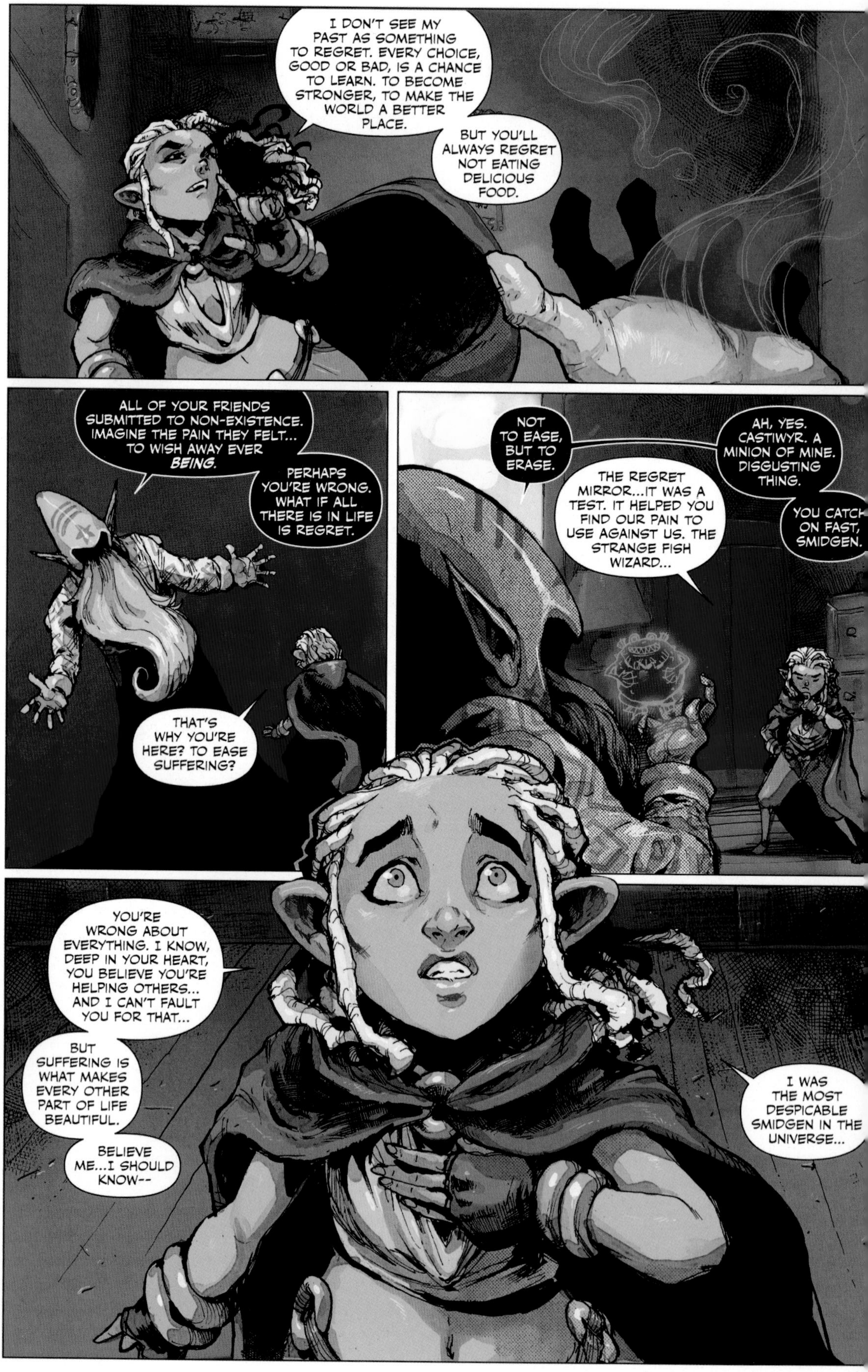

I DON'T SEE MY PAST AS SOMETHING TO REGRET. EVERY CHOICE, GOOD OR BAD, IS A CHANCE TO LEARN. TO BECOME STRONGER, TO MAKE THE WORLD A BETTER PLACE.
BUT YOU'LL ALWAYS REGRET NOT EATING DELICIOUS FOOD.
ALL OF YOUR FRIENDS SUBMITTED TO NON-EXISTENCE. IMAGINE THE PAIN THEY FELT... TO WISH AWAY EVER *BEING.*
PERHAPS YOU'RE WRONG. WHAT IF ALL THERE IS IN LIFE IS REGRET.
THAT'S WHY YOU'RE HERE? TO EASE SUFFERING?
NOT TO EASE, BUT TO ERASE.
AH, YES. CASTIWYR. A MINION OF MINE. DISGUSTING THING.
THE REGRET MIRROR...IT WAS A TEST. IT HELPED YOU FIND OUR PAIN TO USE AGAINST US. THE STRANGE FISH WIZARD...
YOU CATCH ON FAST, SMIDGEN.
YOU'RE WRONG ABOUT EVERYTHING. I KNOW, DEEP IN YOUR HEART, YOU BELIEVE YOU'RE HELPING OTHERS... AND I CAN'T FAULT YOU FOR THAT...
BUT SUFFERING IS WHAT MAKES EVERY OTHER PART OF LIFE BEAUTIFUL.
BELIEVE ME...I SHOULD KNOW--
I WAS THE MOST DESPICABLE SMIDGEN IN THE UNIVERSE...

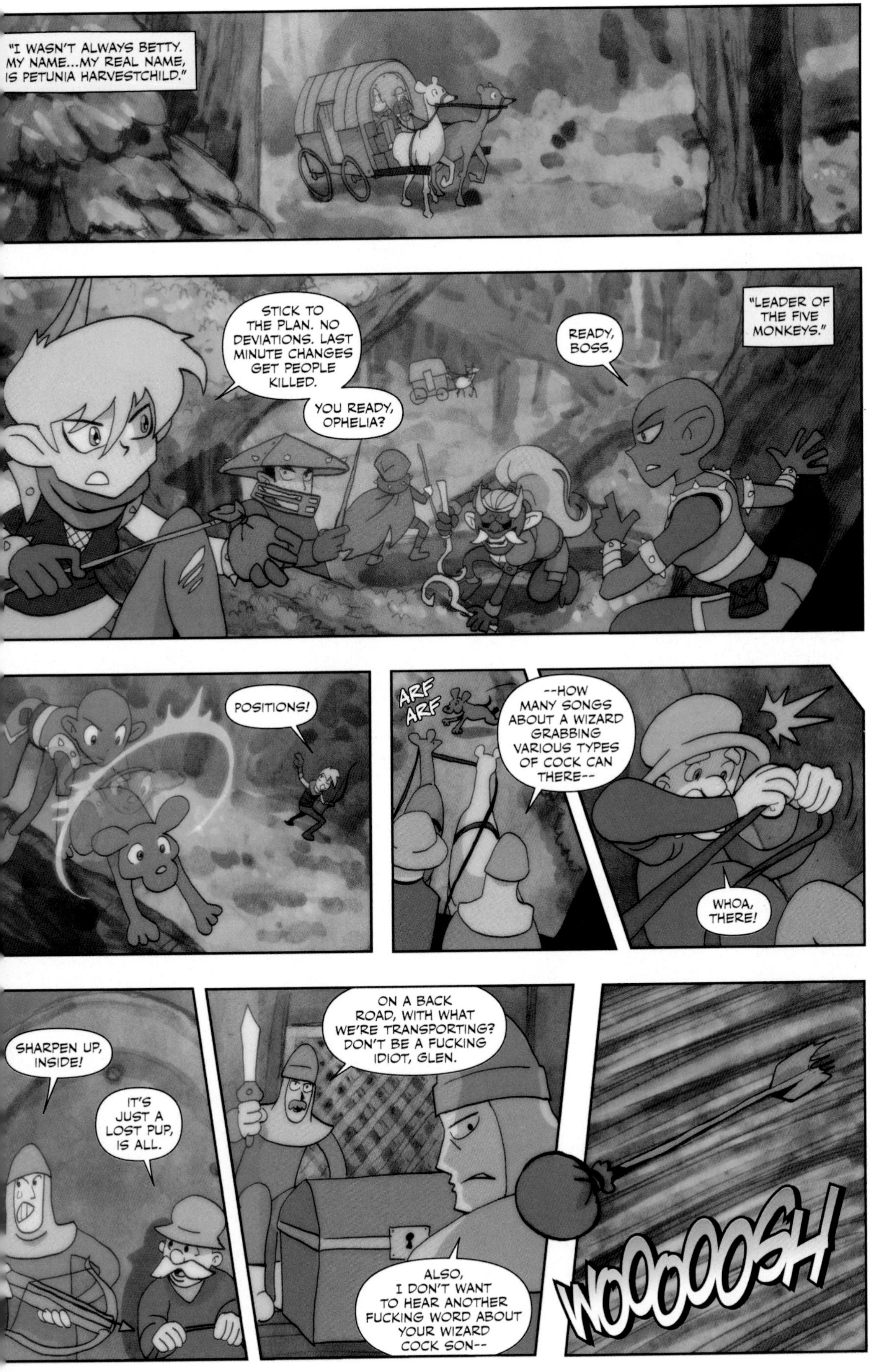
"I WASN'T ALWAYS BETTY. MY NAME...MY REAL NAME, IS PETUNIA HARVESTCHILD."
STICK TO THE PLAN. NO DEVIATIONS. LAST MINUTE CHANGES GET PEOPLE KILLED.
YOU READY, OPHELIA?
READY, BOSS.
"LEADER OF THE FIVE MONKEYS."
POSITIONS!
ARF ARF
--HOW MANY SONGS ABOUT A WIZARD GRABBING VARIOUS TYPES OF COCK CAN THERE--
WHOA, THERE!
SHARPEN UP, INSIDE!
IT'S JUST A LOST PUP, IS ALL.
ON A BACK ROAD, WITH WHAT WE'RE TRANSPORTING? DON'T BE A FUCKING IDIOT, GLEN.
ALSO, I DON'T WANT TO HEAR ANOTHER FUCKING WORD ABOUT YOUR WIZARD COCK SON--
WOOOOOSH

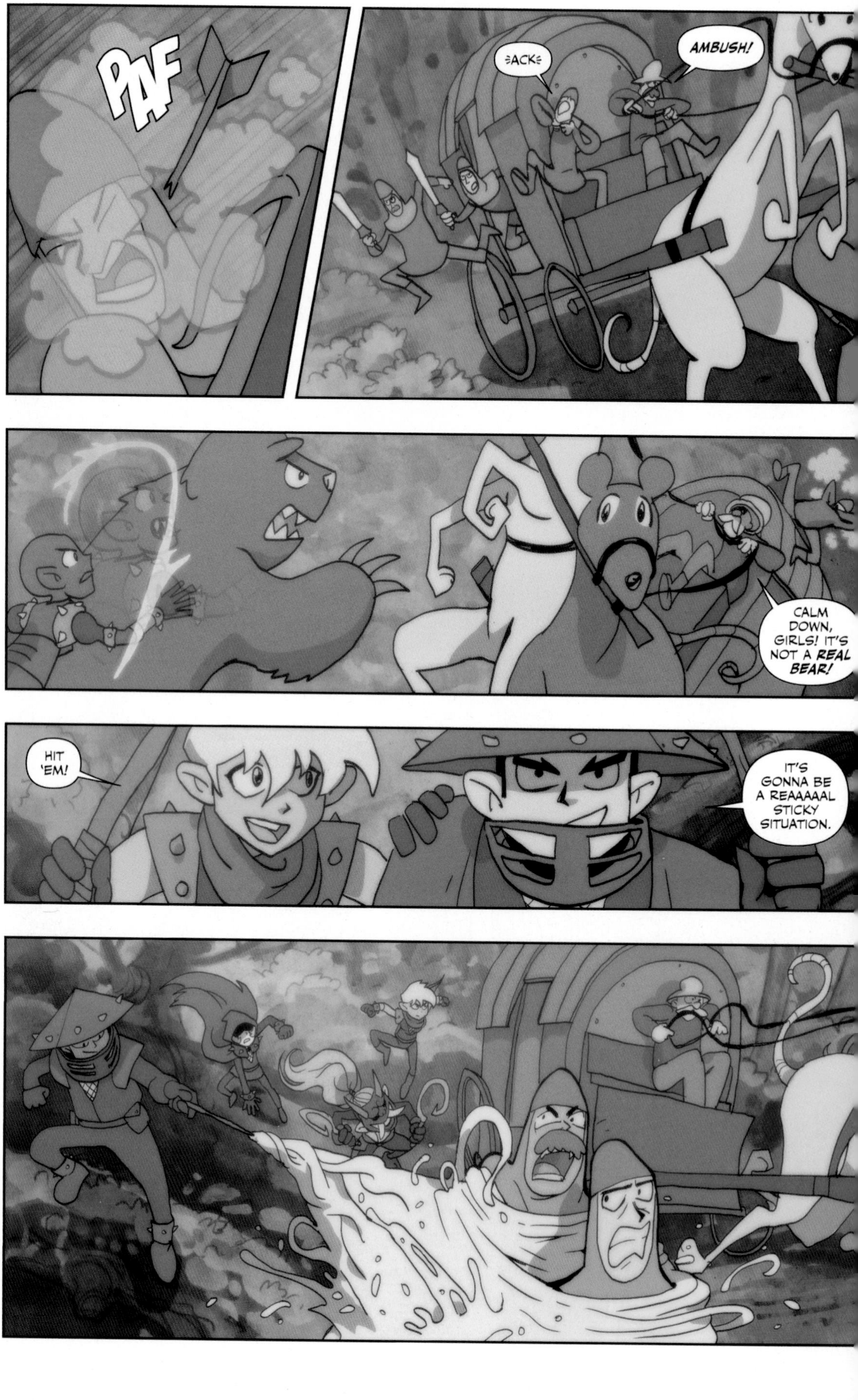

PAF
ACK
AMBUSH!
CALM DOWN, GIRLS! IT'S NOT A REAL BEAR!
HIT 'EM!
IT'S GONNA BE A REAAAAAL STICKY SITUATION.

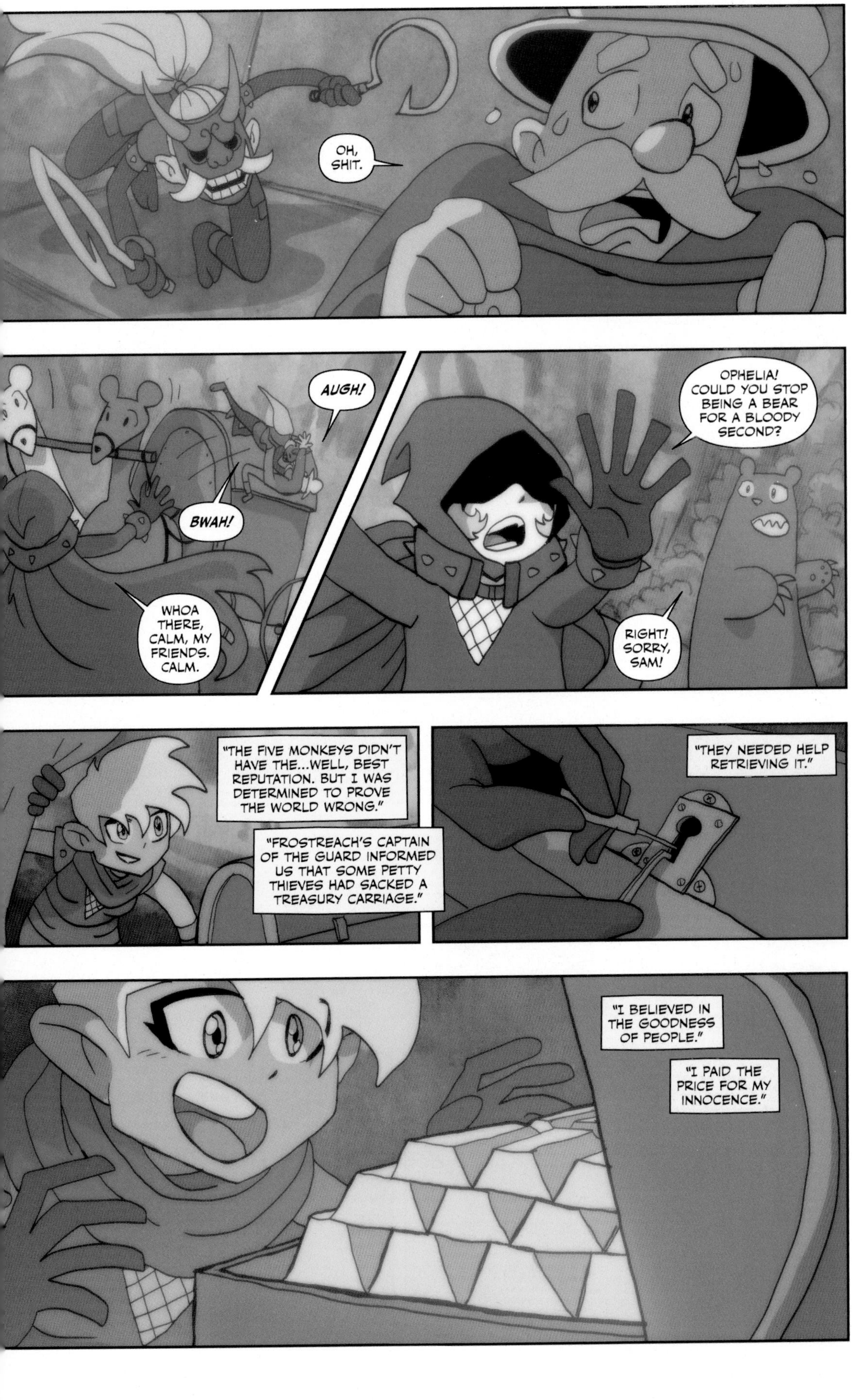

OH, SHIT.
AUGH!
BWAH!
WHOA THERE, CALM, MY FRIENDS. CALM.
OPHELIA! COULD YOU STOP BEING A BEAR FOR A BLOODY SECOND?
RIGHT! SORRY, SAM!
"THE FIVE MONKEYS DIDN'T HAVE THE...WELL, BEST REPUTATION. BUT I WAS DETERMINED TO PROVE THE WORLD WRONG."
"FROSTREACH'S CAPTAIN OF THE GUARD INFORMED US THAT SOME PETTY THIEVES HAD SACKED A TREASURY CARRIAGE."
"THEY NEEDED HELP RETRIEVING IT."
"I BELIEVED IN THE GOODNESS OF PEOPLE."
"I PAID THE PRICE FOR MY INNOCENCE."

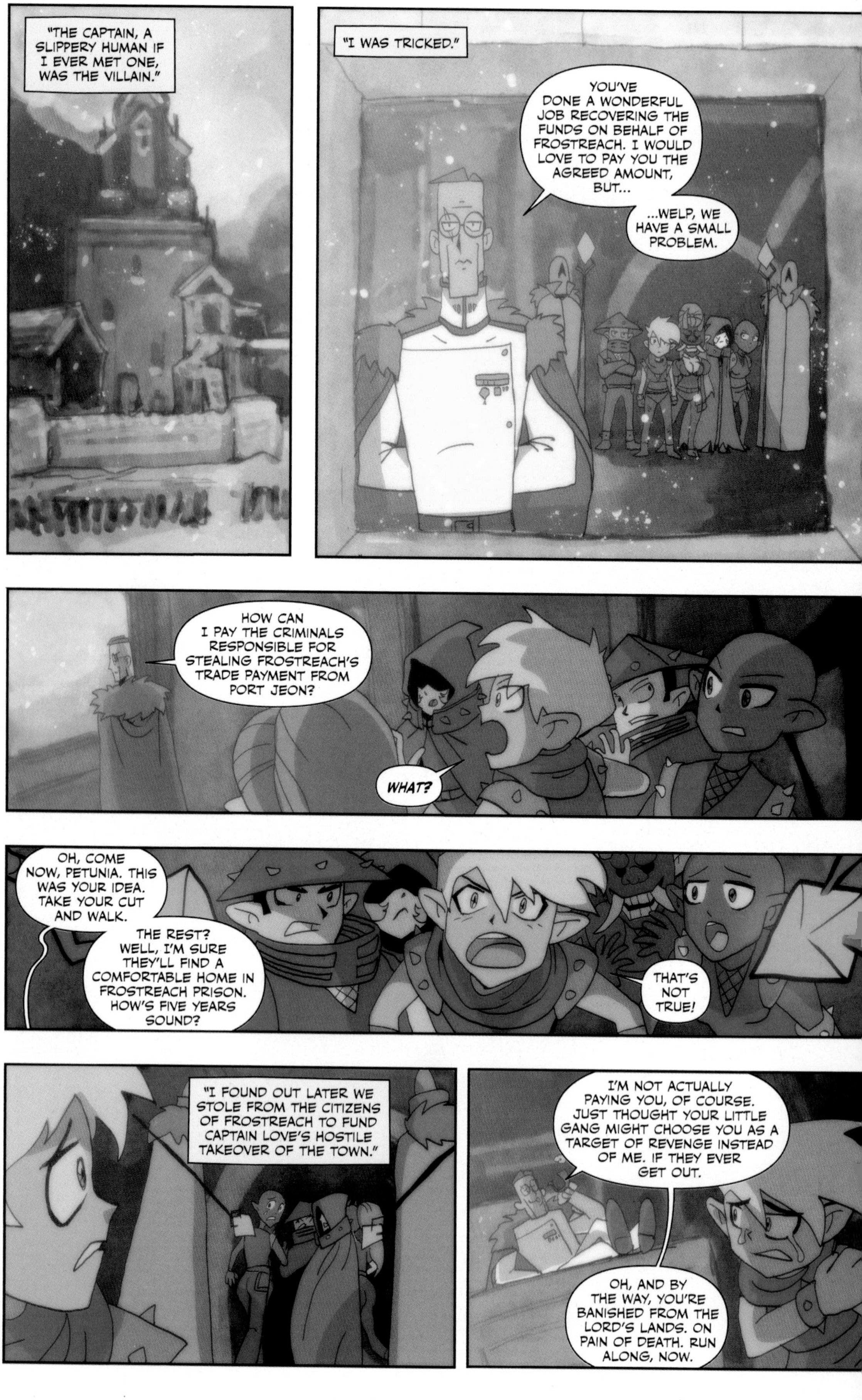
"THE CAPTAIN, A SLIPPERY HUMAN IF I EVER MET ONE, WAS THE VILLAIN."
"I WAS TRICKED."
YOU'VE DONE A WONDERFUL JOB RECOVERING THE FUNDS ON BEHALF OF FROSTREACH. I WOULD LOVE TO PAY YOU THE AGREED AMOUNT, BUT...
...WELP, WE HAVE A SMALL PROBLEM.
HOW CAN I PAY THE CRIMINALS RESPONSIBLE FOR STEALING FROSTREACH'S TRADE PAYMENT FROM PORT JEON?
WHAT?
OH, COME NOW, PETUNIA. THIS WAS YOUR IDEA. TAKE YOUR CUT AND WALK.
THE REST? WELL, I'M SURE THEY'LL FIND A COMFORTABLE HOME IN FROSTREACH PRISON. HOW'S FIVE YEARS SOUND?
THAT'S NOT TRUE!
"I FOUND OUT LATER WE STOLE FROM THE CITIZENS OF FROSTREACH TO FUND CAPTAIN LOVE'S HOSTILE TAKEOVER OF THE TOWN."
I'M NOT ACTUALLY PAYING YOU, OF COURSE. JUST THOUGHT YOUR LITTLE GANG MIGHT CHOOSE YOU AS A TARGET OF REVENGE INSTEAD OF ME. IF THEY EVER GET OUT.
OH, AND BY THE WAY, YOU'RE BANISHED FROM THE LORD'S LANDS. ON PAIN OF DEATH. RUN ALONG, NOW.

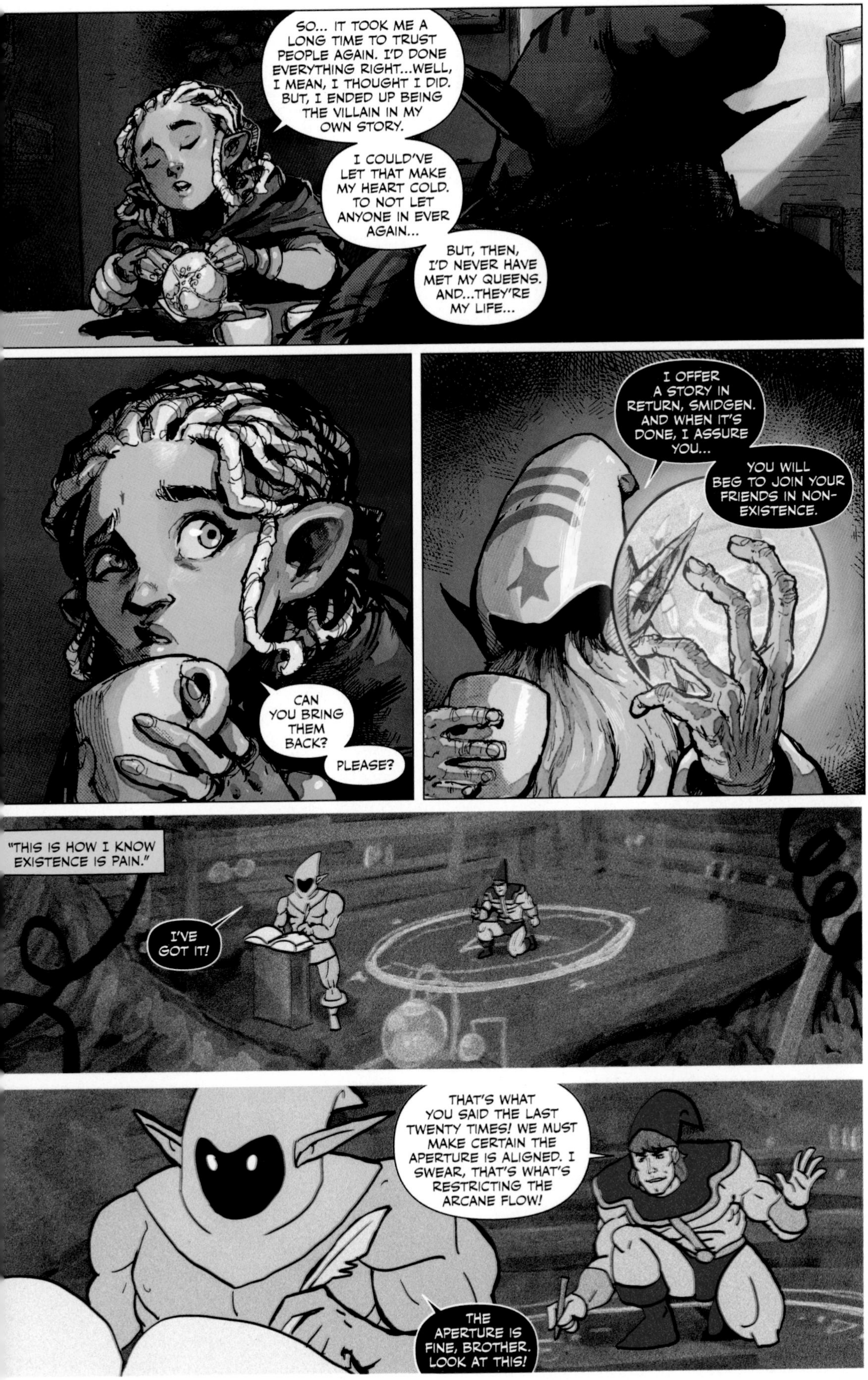
SO... IT TOOK ME A LONG TIME TO TRUST PEOPLE AGAIN. I'D DONE EVERYTHING RIGHT...WELL, I MEAN, I THOUGHT I DID. BUT, I ENDED UP BEING THE VILLAIN IN MY OWN STORY.
I COULD'VE LET THAT MAKE MY HEART COLD. TO NOT LET ANYONE IN EVER AGAIN...
BUT, THEN, I'D NEVER HAVE MET MY QUEENS. AND...THEY'RE MY LIFE...
CAN YOU BRING THEM BACK?
PLEASE?
I OFFER A STORY IN RETURN, SMIDGEN. AND WHEN IT'S DONE, I ASSURE YOU...
YOU WILL BEG TO JOIN YOUR FRIENDS IN NON-EXISTENCE.
"THIS IS HOW I KNOW EXISTENCE IS PAIN."
I'VE GOT IT!
THAT'S WHAT YOU SAID THE LAST TWENTY TIMES! WE MUST MAKE CERTAIN THE APERTURE IS ALIGNED. I SWEAR, THAT'S WHAT'S RESTRICTING THE ARCANE FLOW!
THE APERTURE IS FINE, BROTHER. LOOK AT THIS!

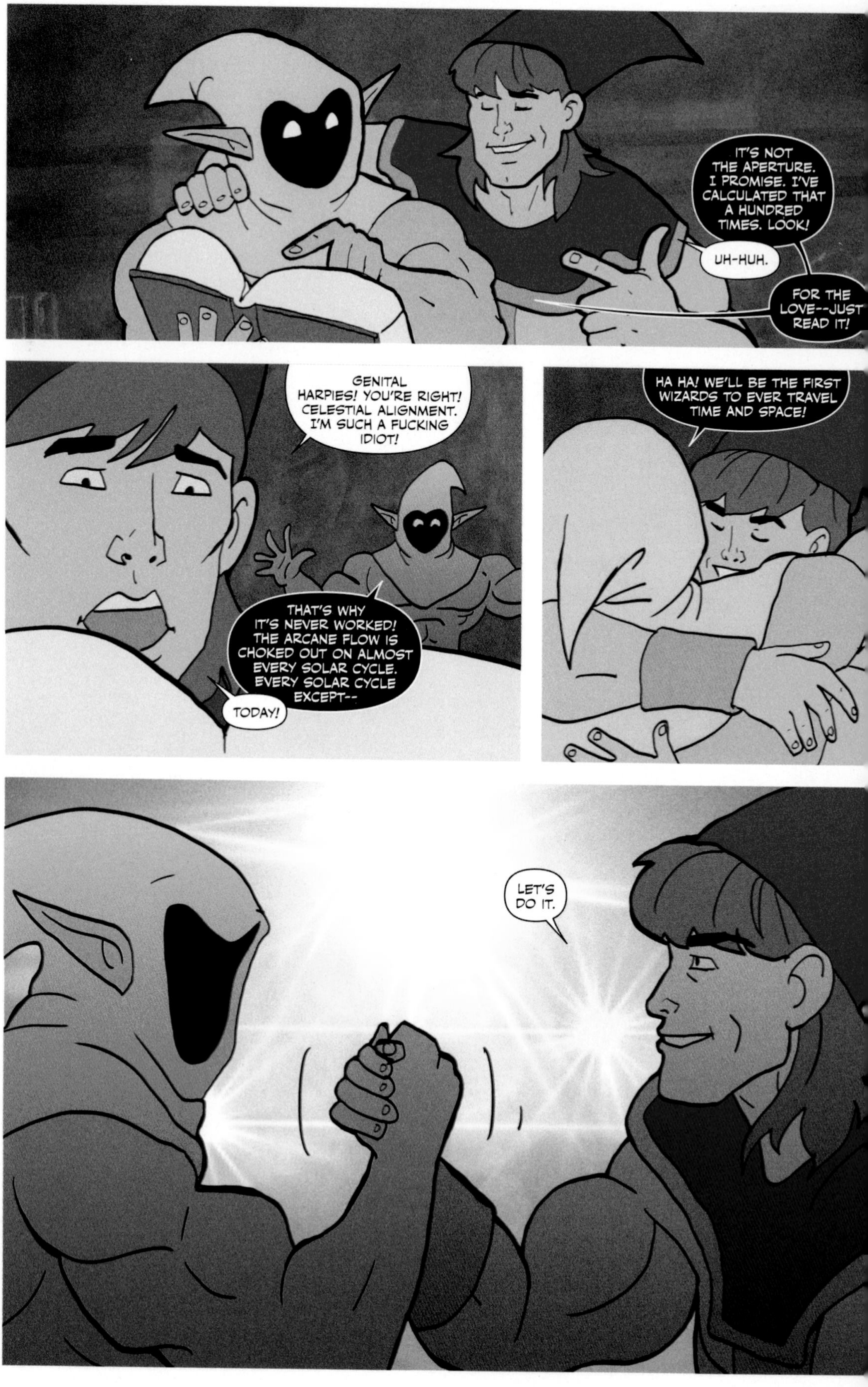
IT'S NOT THE APERTURE. I PROMISE. I'VE CALCULATED THAT A HUNDRED TIMES. LOOK!
UH-HUH.
FOR THE LOVE--JUST READ IT!
GENITAL HARPIES! YOU'RE RIGHT! CELESTIAL ALIGNMENT. I'M SUCH A FUCKING IDIOT!
THAT'S WHY IT'S NEVER WORKED! THE ARCANE FLOW IS CHOKED OUT ON ALMOST EVERY SOLAR CYCLE. EVERY SOLAR CYCLE EXCEPT--
TODAY!
HA HA! WE'LL BE THE FIRST WIZARDS TO EVER TRAVEL TIME AND SPACE!
LET'S DO IT.

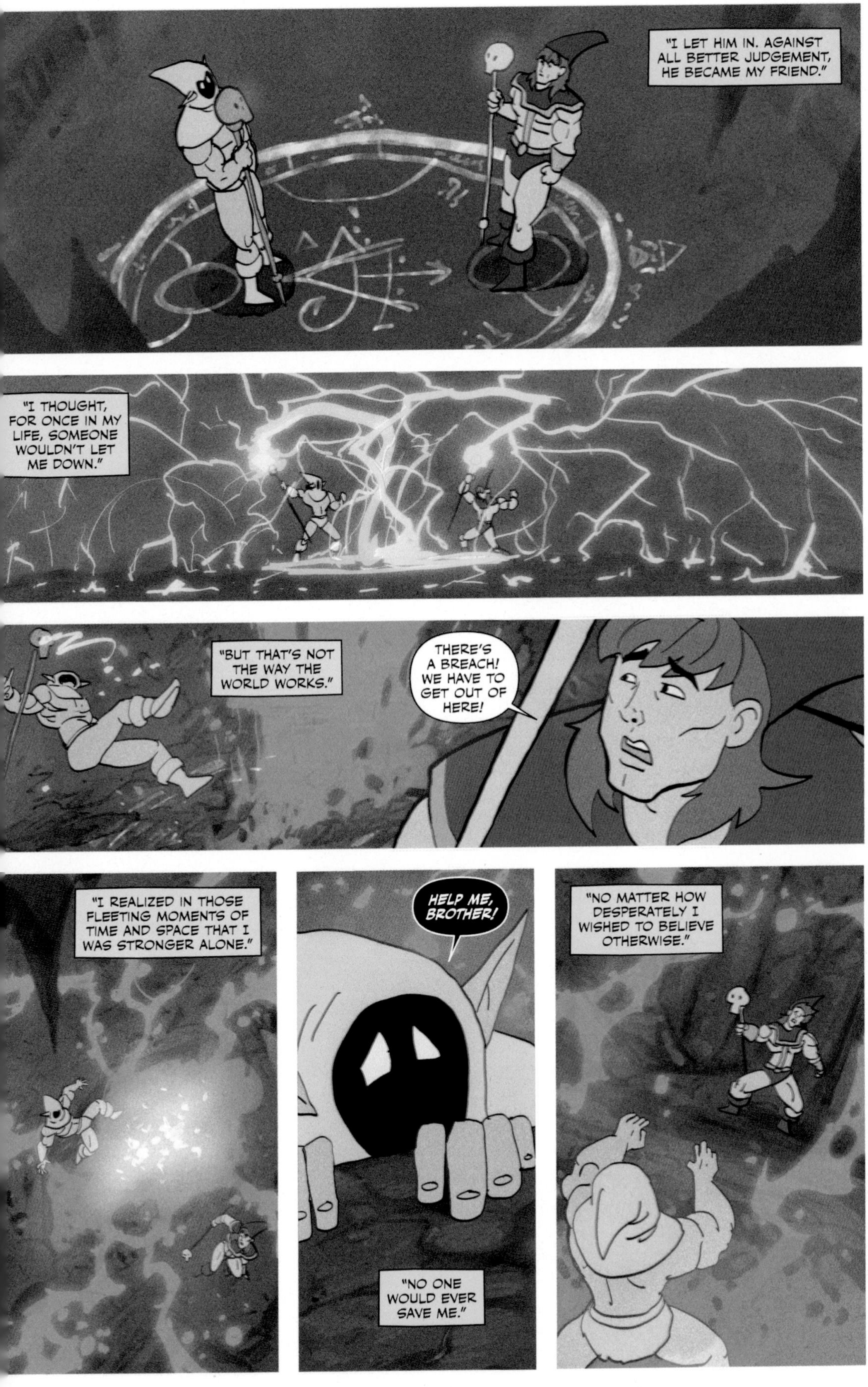
"I LET HIM IN. AGAINST ALL BETTER JUDGEMENT, HE BECAME MY FRIEND."
"I THOUGHT, FOR ONCE IN MY LIFE, SOMEONE WOULDN'T LET ME DOWN."
"BUT THAT'S NOT THE WAY THE WORLD WORKS."
THERE'S A BREACH! WE HAVE TO GET OUT OF HERE!
"I REALIZED IN THOSE FLEETING MOMENTS OF TIME AND SPACE THAT I WAS STRONGER ALONE."
HELP ME, BROTHER!
"NO ONE WOULD EVER SAVE ME."
"NO MATTER HOW DESPERATELY I WISHED TO BELIEVE OTHERWISE."

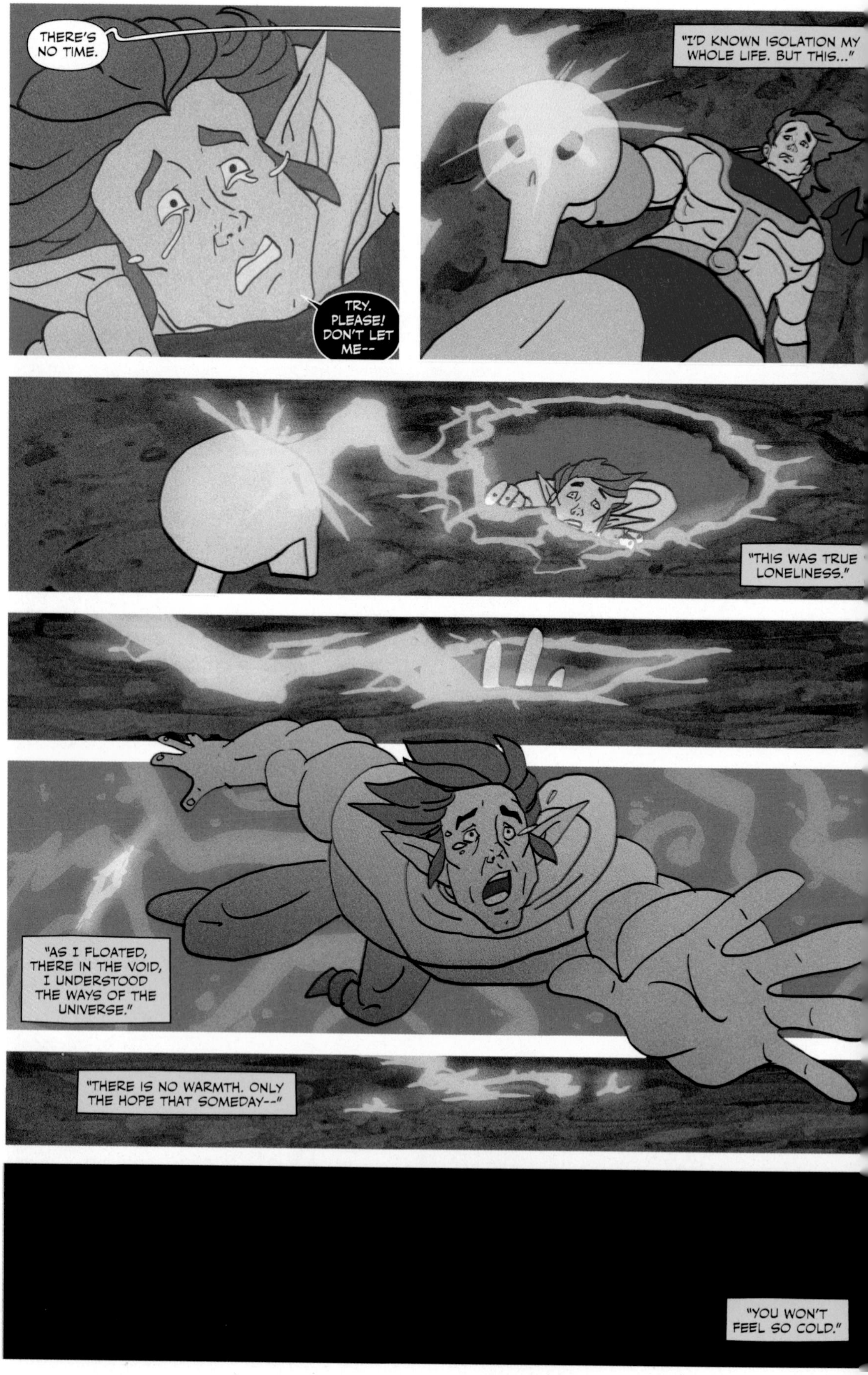
THERE'S NO TIME.
TRY. PLEASE! DON'T LET ME--
"I'D KNOWN ISOLATION MY WHOLE LIFE. BUT THIS..."
"THIS WAS TRUE LONELINESS."
"AS I FLOATED, THERE IN THE VOID, I UNDERSTOOD THE WAYS OF THE UNIVERSE."
"THERE IS NO WARMTH. ONLY THE HOPE THAT SOMEDAY--"
"YOU WON'T FEEL SO COLD."

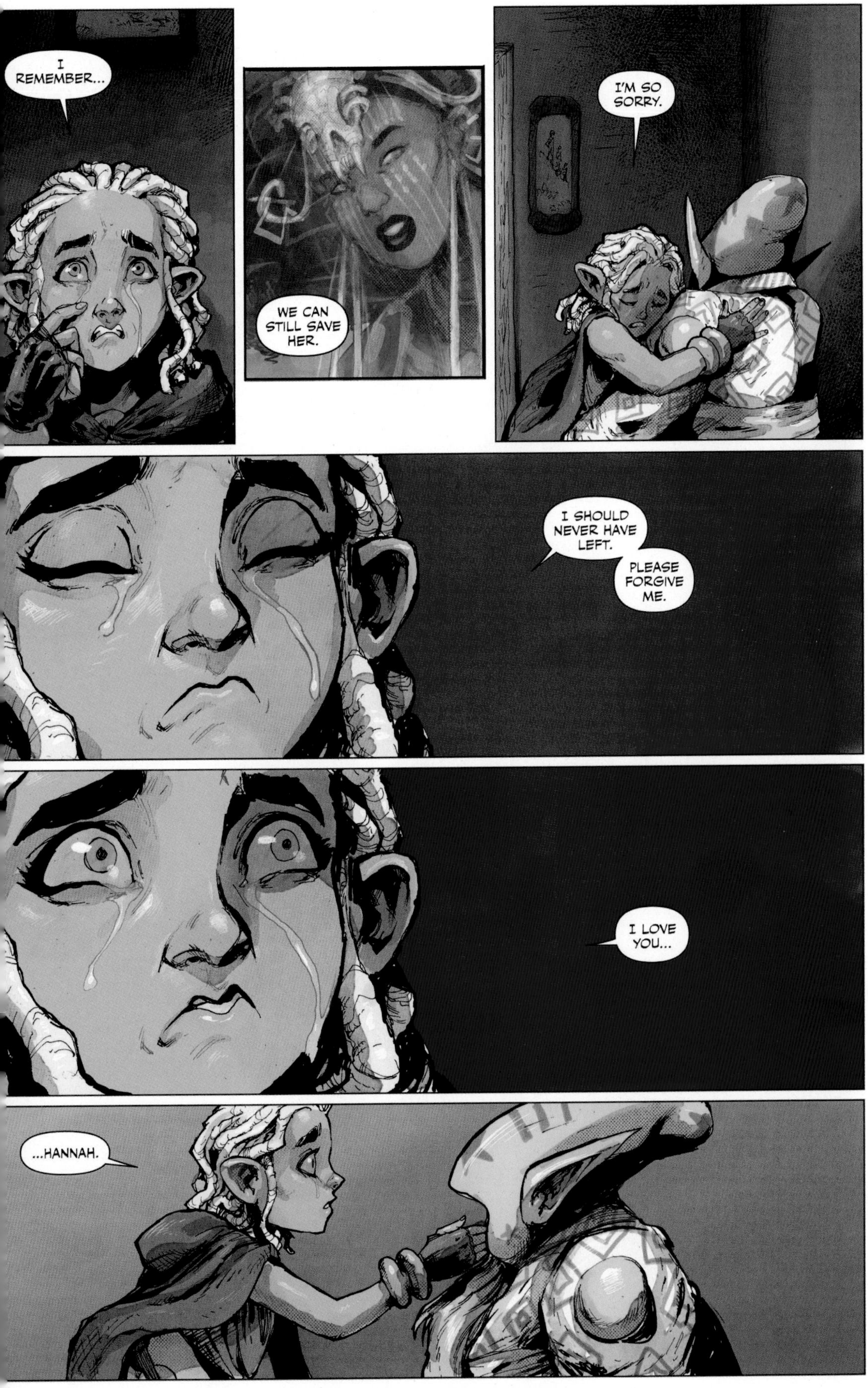
I REMEMBER...
WE CAN STILL SAVE HER.
I'M SO SORRY.
I SHOULD NEVER HAVE LEFT.
PLEASE FORGIVE ME.
I LOVE YOU...
...HANNAH.

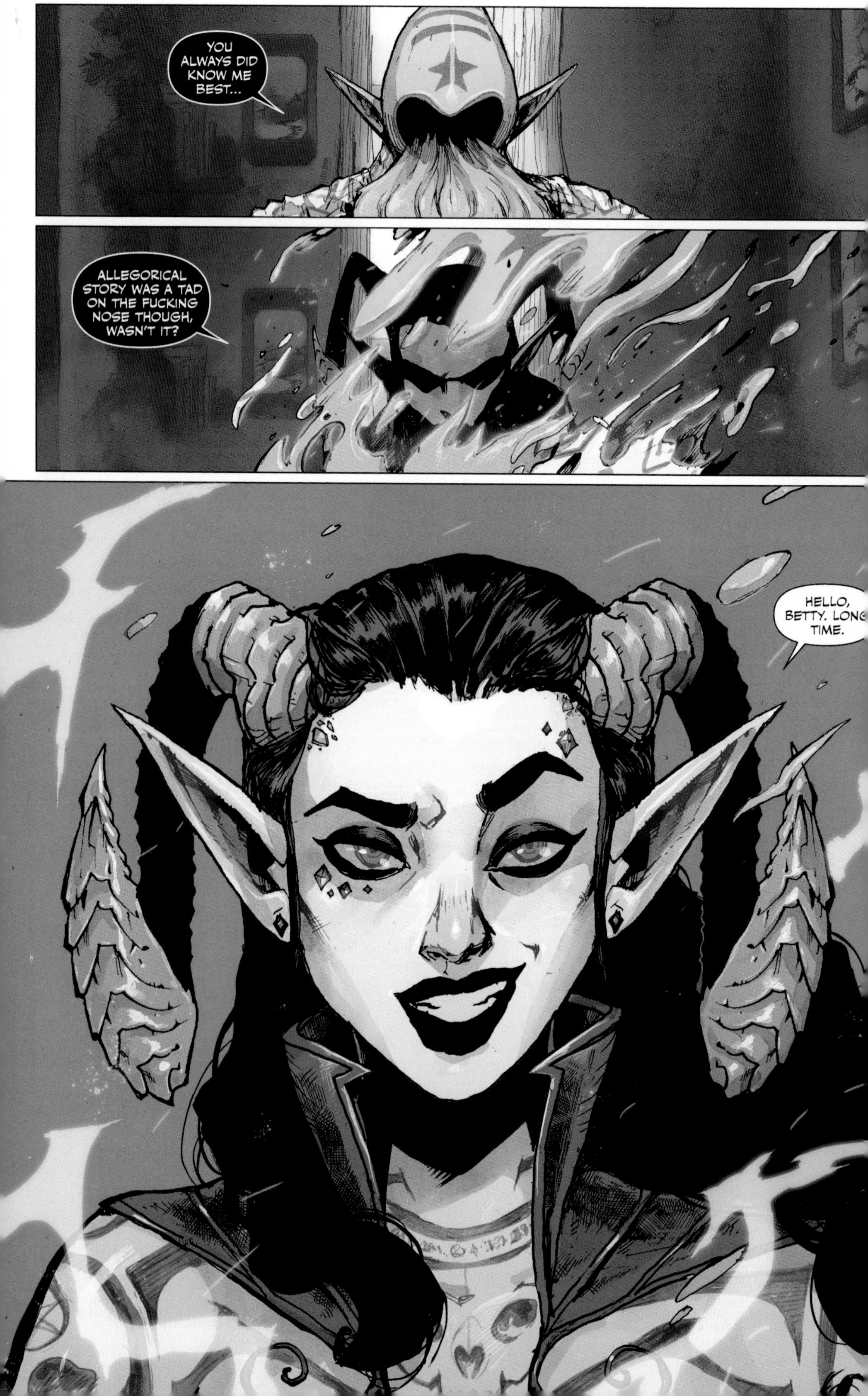
YOU ALWAYS DID KNOW ME BEST...
ALLEGORICAL STORY WAS A TAD ON THE FUCKING NOSE THOUGH, WASN'T IT?
HELLO, BETTY. LONG TIME.

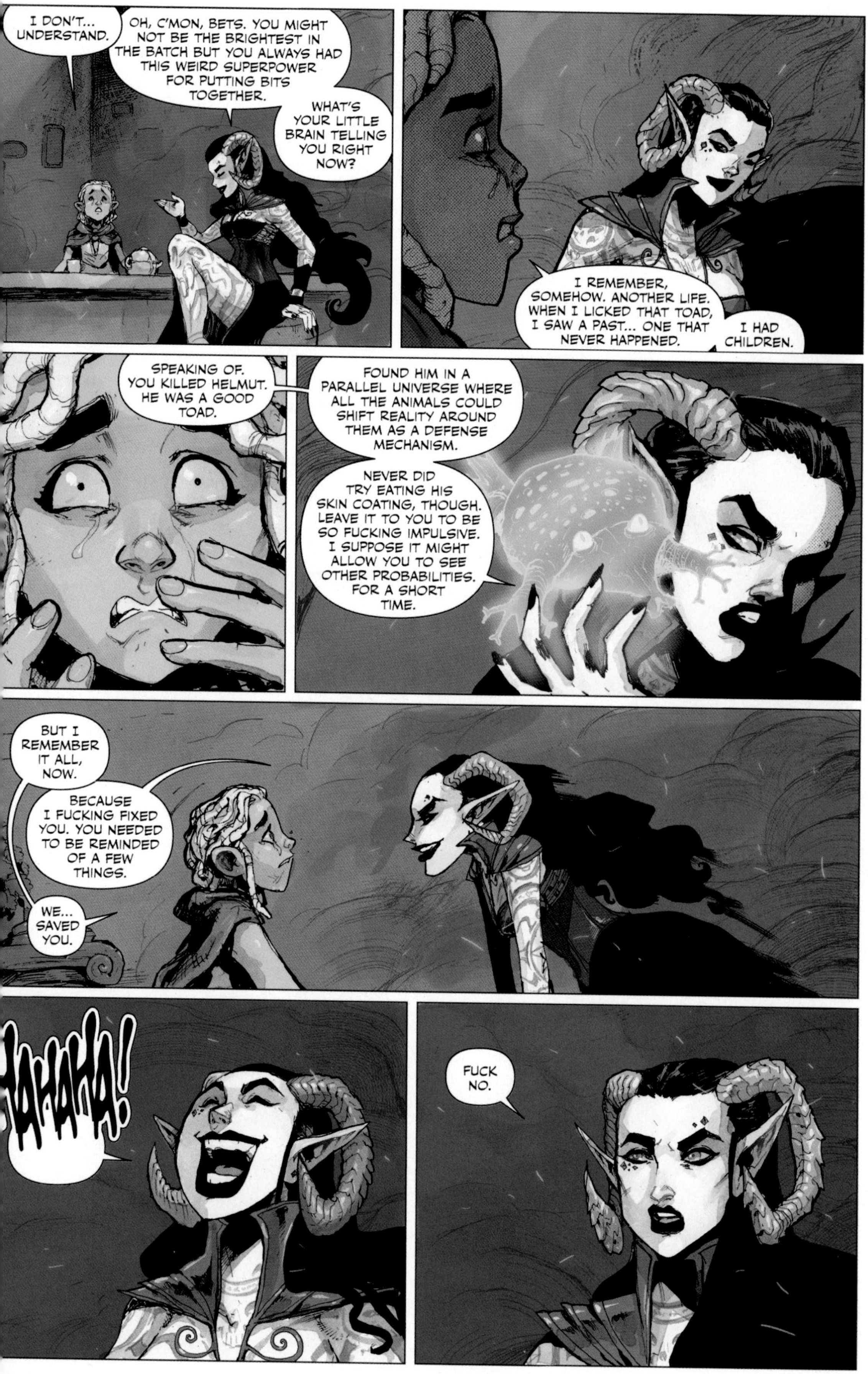

I DON'T... UNDERSTAND.
OH, C'MON, BETS. YOU MIGHT NOT BE THE BRIGHTEST IN THE BATCH BUT YOU ALWAYS HAD THIS WEIRD SUPERPOWER FOR PUTTING BITS TOGETHER.
WHAT'S YOUR LITTLE BRAIN TELLING YOU RIGHT NOW?
I REMEMBER, SOMEHOW. ANOTHER LIFE. WHEN I LICKED THAT TOAD, I SAW A PAST... ONE THAT NEVER HAPPENED.
I HAD CHILDREN.
SPEAKING OF. YOU KILLED HELMUT. HE WAS A GOOD TOAD.
FOUND HIM IN A PARALLEL UNIVERSE WHERE ALL THE ANIMALS COULD SHIFT REALITY AROUND THEM AS A DEFENSE MECHANISM.
NEVER DID TRY EATING HIS SKIN COATING, THOUGH. LEAVE IT TO YOU TO BE SO FUCKING IMPULSIVE. I SUPPOSE IT MIGHT ALLOW YOU TO SEE OTHER PROBABILITIES. FOR A SHORT TIME.
BUT I REMEMBER IT ALL, NOW.
BECAUSE I FUCKING FIXED YOU. YOU NEEDED TO BE REMINDED OF A FEW THINGS.
WE... SAVED YOU.
HAHAHA!
FUCK NO.

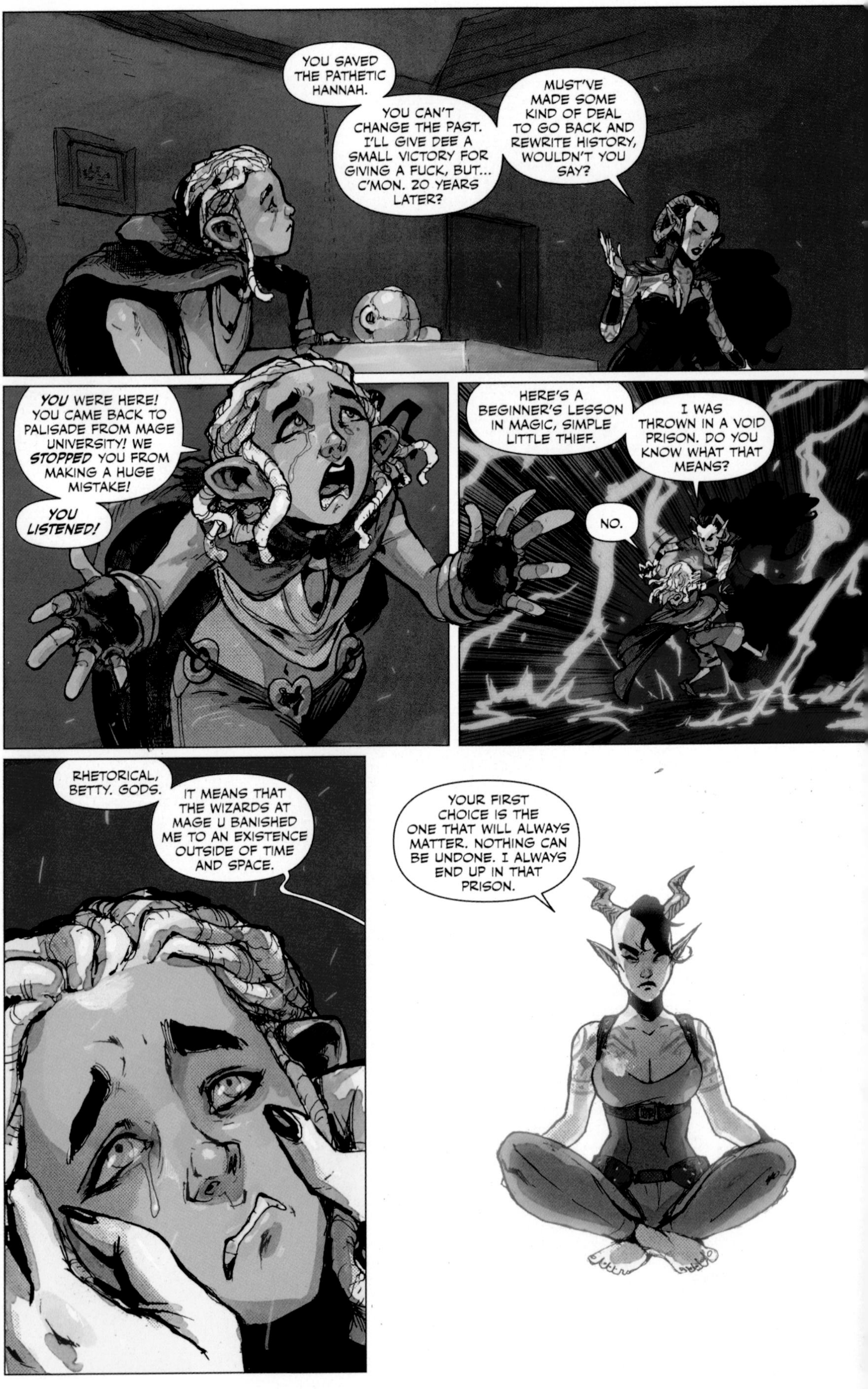
YOU SAVED THE PATHETIC HANNAH.
YOU CAN'T CHANGE THE PAST. I'LL GIVE DEE A SMALL VICTORY FOR GIVING A FUCK, BUT... C'MON. 20 YEARS LATER?
MUST'VE MADE SOME KIND OF DEAL TO GO BACK AND REWRITE HISTORY, WOULDN'T YOU SAY?
YOU WERE HERE! YOU CAME BACK TO PALISADE FROM MAGE UNIVERSITY! WE STOPPED YOU FROM MAKING A HUGE MISTAKE!
YOU LISTENED!
HERE'S A BEGINNER'S LESSON IN MAGIC, SIMPLE LITTLE THIEF.
I WAS THROWN IN A VOID PRISON. DO YOU KNOW WHAT THAT MEANS?
NO.
RHETORICAL, BETTY. GODS.
IT MEANS THAT THE WIZARDS AT MAGE U BANISHED ME TO AN EXISTENCE OUTSIDE OF TIME AND SPACE.
YOUR FIRST CHOICE IS THE ONE THAT WILL ALWAYS MATTER. NOTHING CAN BE UNDONE. I ALWAYS END UP IN THAT PRISON.

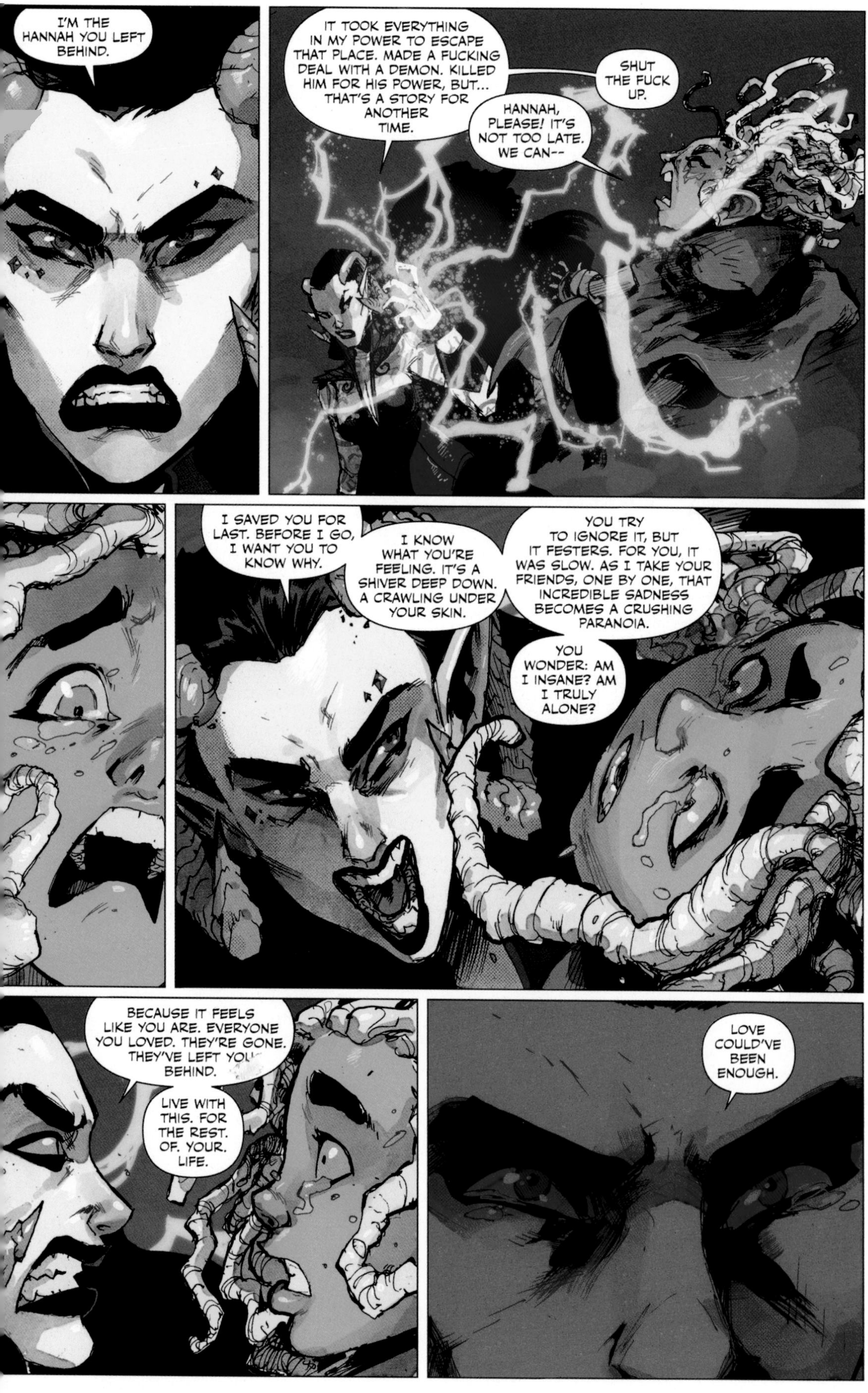

I'M THE HANNAH YOU LEFT BEHIND.
IT TOOK EVERYTHING IN MY POWER TO ESCAPE THAT PLACE. MADE A FUCKING DEAL WITH A DEMON. KILLED HIM FOR HIS POWER, BUT... THAT'S A STORY FOR ANOTHER TIME.
SHUT THE FUCK UP.
HANNAH, PLEASE! IT'S NOT TOO LATE. WE CAN--
I SAVED YOU FOR LAST. BEFORE I GO, I WANT YOU TO KNOW WHY.
I KNOW WHAT YOU'RE FEELING. IT'S A SHIVER DEEP DOWN. A CRAWLING UNDER YOUR SKIN.
YOU TRY TO IGNORE IT, BUT IT FESTERS. FOR YOU, IT WAS SLOW. AS I TAKE YOUR FRIENDS, ONE BY ONE, THAT INCREDIBLE SADNESS BECOMES A CRUSHING PARANOIA.
YOU WONDER: AM I INSANE? AM I TRULY ALONE?
BECAUSE IT FEELS LIKE YOU ARE. EVERYONE YOU LOVED. THEY'RE GONE. THEY'VE LEFT YOU BEHIND.
LIVE WITH THIS. FOR THE REST. OF. YOUR. LIFE.
LOVE COULD'VE BEEN ENOUGH.

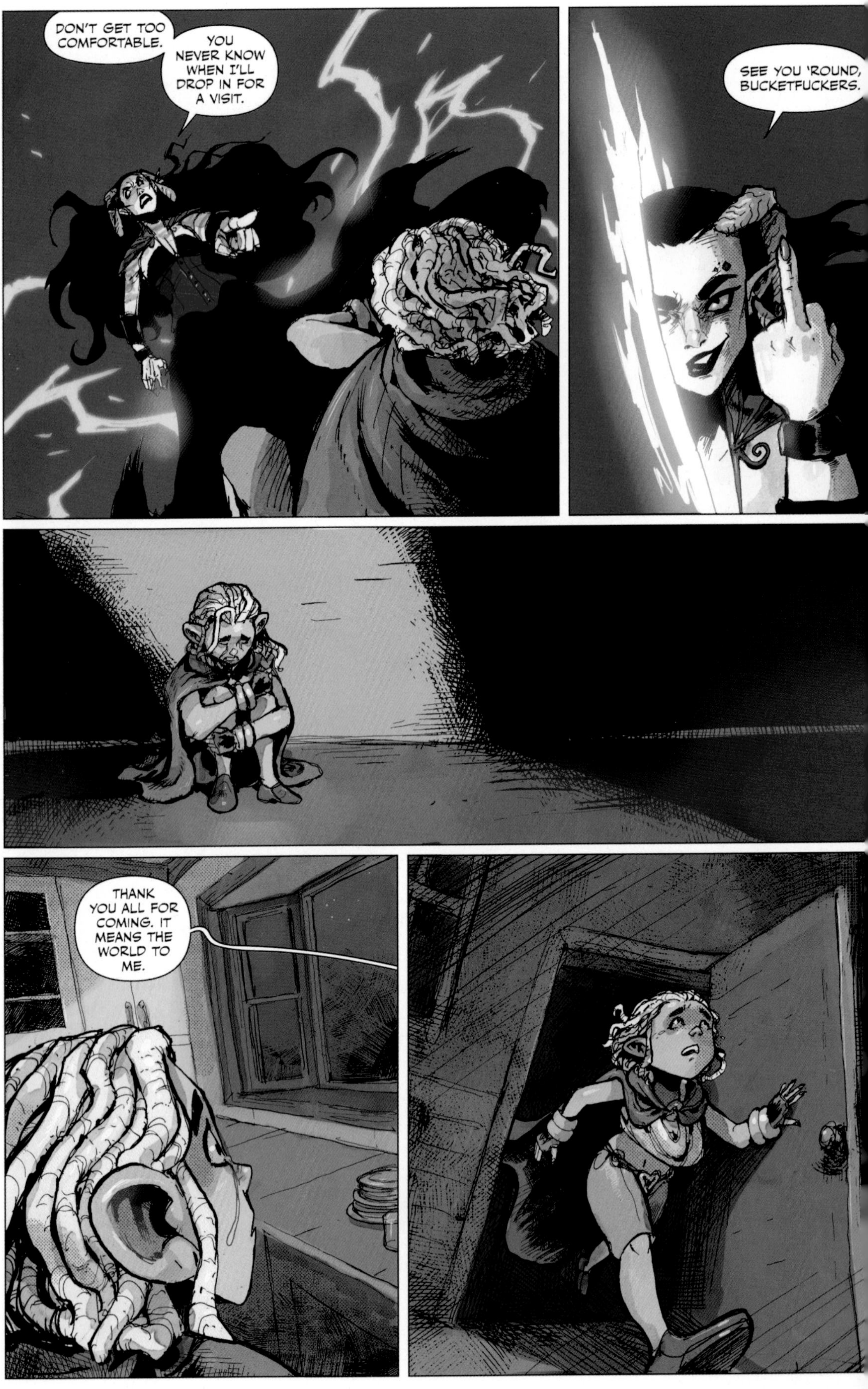
DON'T GET TOO COMFORTABLE.
YOU NEVER KNOW WHEN I'LL DROP IN FOR A VISIT.
SEE YOU 'ROUND, BUCKETFUCKERS.
THANK YOU ALL FOR COMING. IT MEANS THE WORLD TO ME.

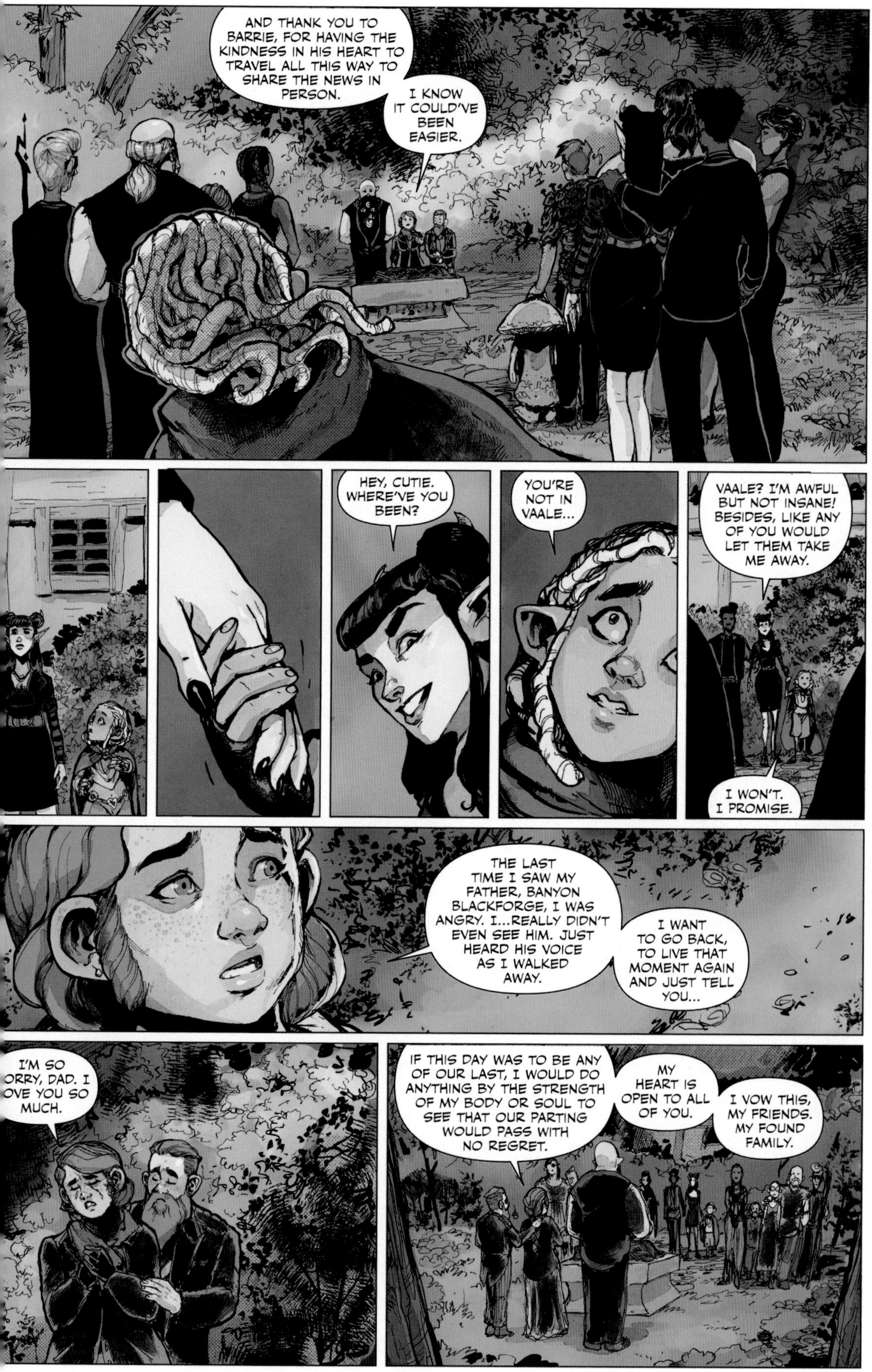
AND THANK YOU TO BARRIE, FOR HAVING THE KINDNESS IN HIS HEART TO TRAVEL ALL THIS WAY TO SHARE THE NEWS IN PERSON.
I KNOW IT COULD'VE BEEN EASIER.
HEY, CUTIE. WHERE'VE YOU BEEN?
YOU'RE NOT IN VAALE...
VAALE? I'M AWFUL BUT NOT INSANE! BESIDES, LIKE ANY OF YOU WOULD LET THEM TAKE ME AWAY.
I WON'T. I PROMISE.
THE LAST TIME I SAW MY FATHER, BANYON BLACKFORGE, I WAS ANGRY. I...REALLY DIDN'T EVEN SEE HIM. JUST HEARD HIS VOICE AS I WALKED AWAY.
I WANT TO GO BACK, TO LIVE THAT MOMENT AGAIN AND JUST TELL YOU...
I'M SO ORRY, DAD. I OVE YOU SO MUCH.
IF THIS DAY WAS TO BE ANY OF OUR LAST, I WOULD DO ANYTHING BY THE STRENGTH OF MY BODY OR SOUL TO SEE THAT OUR PARTING WOULD PASS WITH NO REGRET.
MY HEART IS OPEN TO ALL OF YOU.
I VOW THIS, MY FRIENDS. MY FOUND FAMILY.

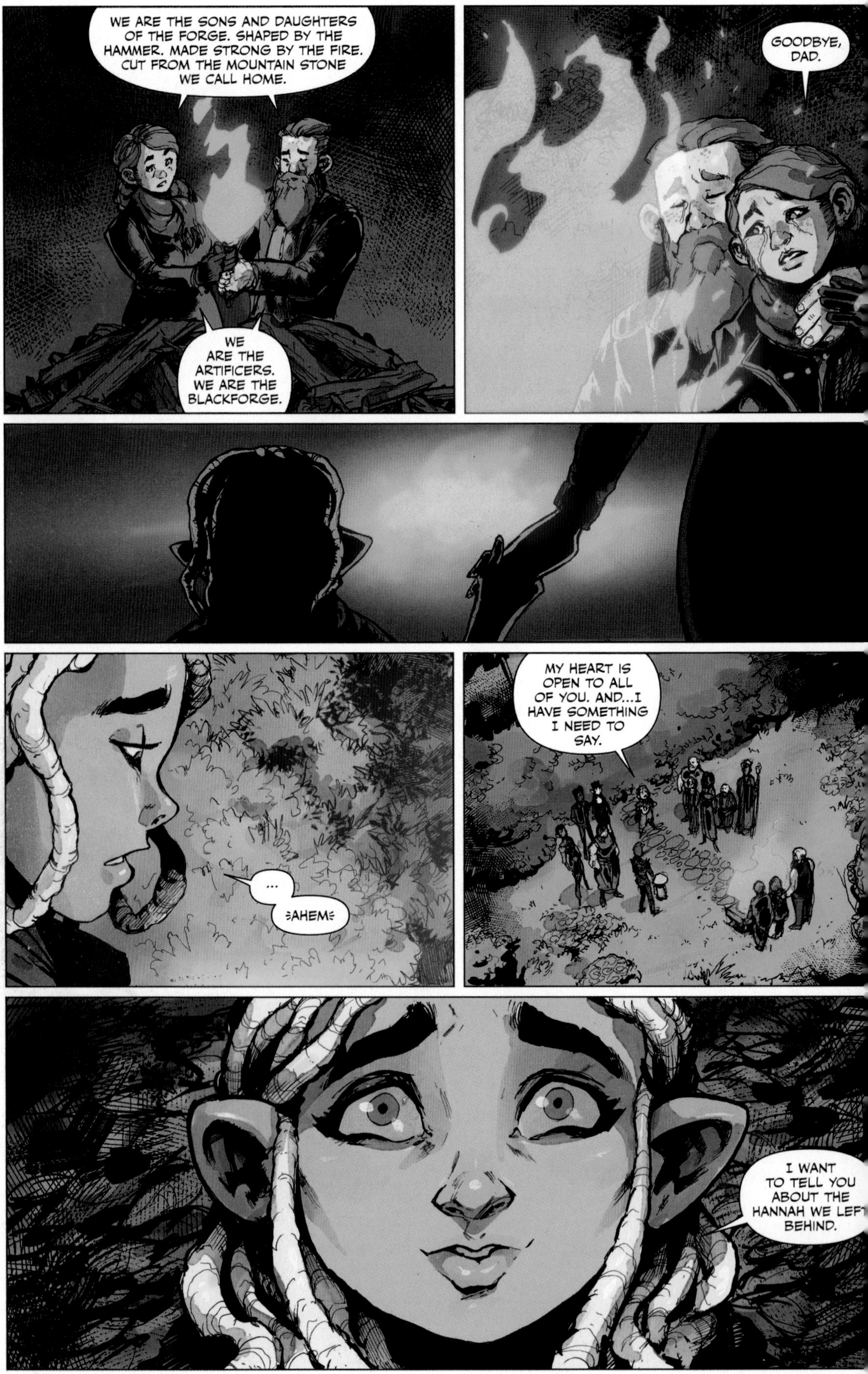
WE ARE THE SONS AND DAUGHTERS OF THE FORGE. SHAPED BY THE HAMMER. MADE STRONG BY THE FIRE. CUT FROM THE MOUNTAIN STONE WE CALL HOME.
WE ARE THE ARTIFICERS. WE ARE THE BLACKFORGE.
GOODBYE, DAD.
...
AHEM
MY HEART IS OPEN TO ALL OF YOU. AND...I HAVE SOMETHING I NEED TO SAY.
I WANT TO TELL YOU ABOUT THE HANNAH WE LEFT BEHIND.

Get the whole story....

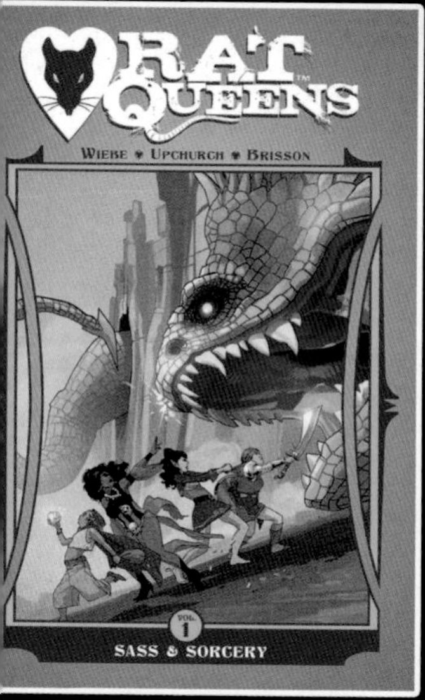
RAT QUEENS
WIEBE • UPCHURCH • BRISSON
VOL. 1
SASS & SORCERY

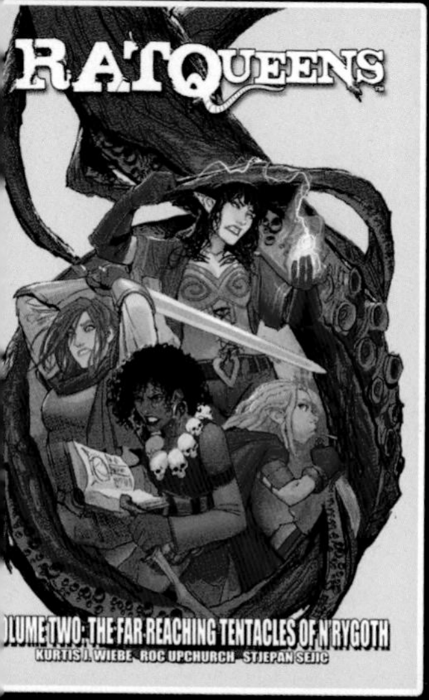
RAT QUEENS
VOLUME TWO: THE FAR REACHING TENTACLES OF N'RYGOTH
KURTIS J. WIEBE ROC UPCHURCH STJEPAN SEJIC

VOLUME FOUR: with OWEN GIENI
collects Vol. 2 issues 1-5

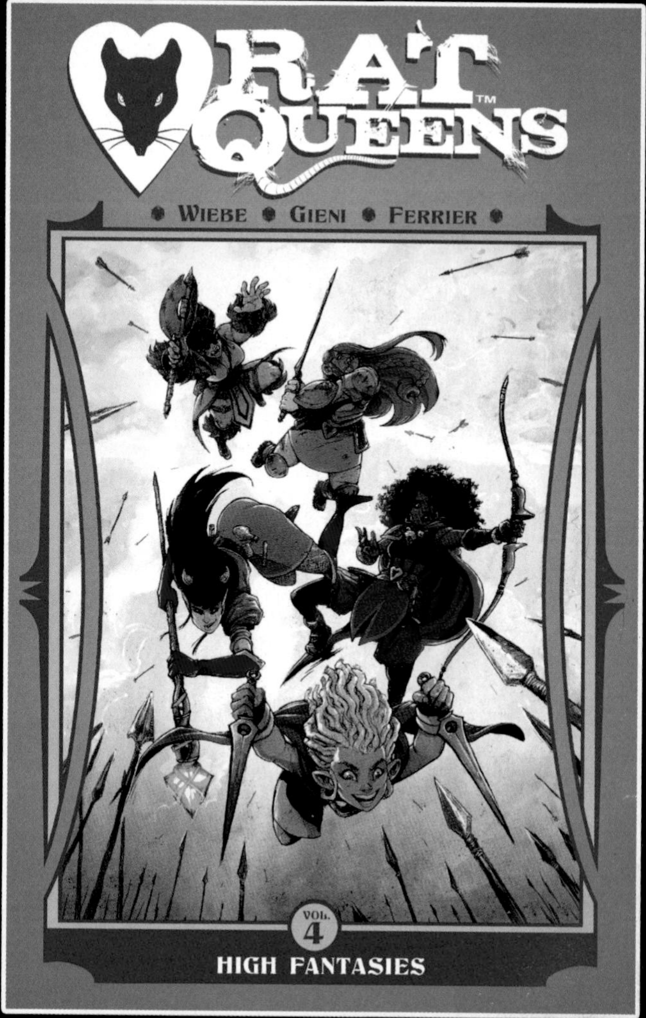
RAT QUEENS
WIEBE • GIENI • FERRIER
VOL. 4
HIGH FANTASIES

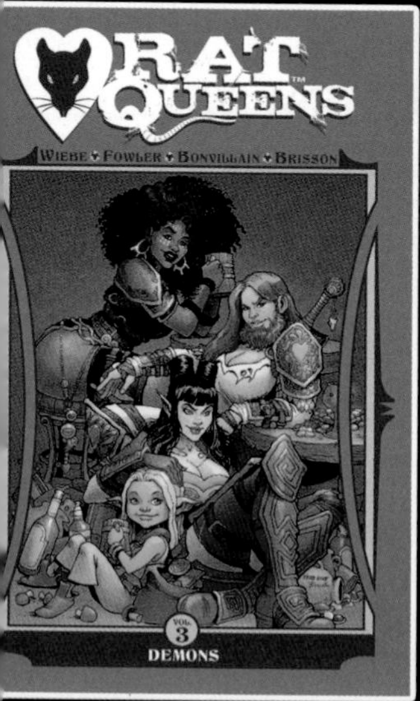
RAT QUEENS
WIEBE • FOWLER • BONVILLAIN • BRISSON
VOL. 3
DEMONS

VOLUME ONE:
with ROC UPCHURCH
collects issues 1-5

VOLUME TWO:
with ROC UPCHURCH
and STJEPAN SEJIC
collects issues 6-10

VOLUME THREE:
with TESS FOWLER and
TAMRA BONVILLAIN
collects issues 11-15

DELUXE OVERSIZED HARDCOVER EDITION
collects issues 1-10

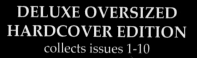

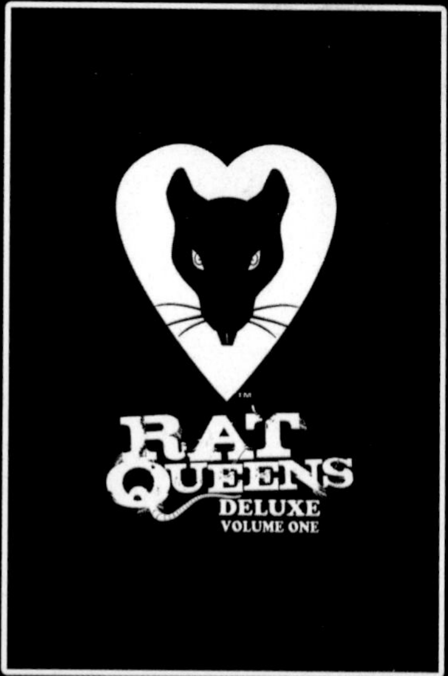
RAT QUEENS
DELUXE
VOLUME ONE

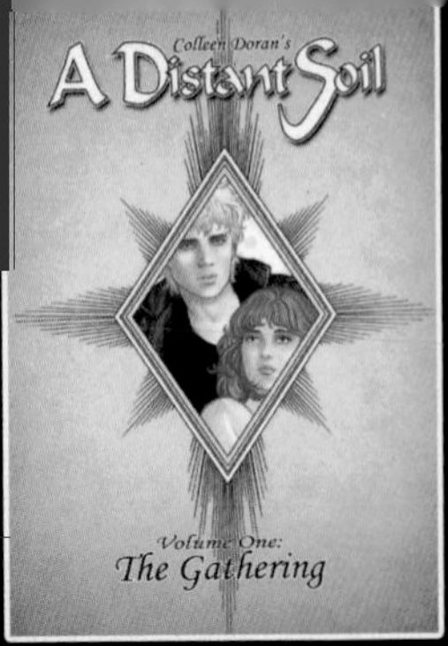
Colleen Doran's
A Distant Soil
Volume One:
The Gathering

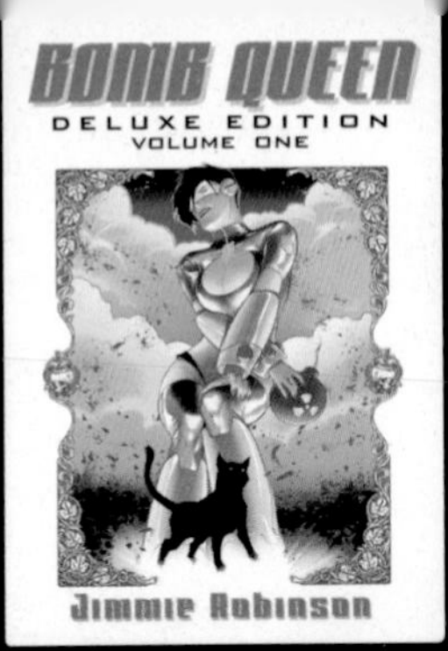
BOMB QUEEN
DELUXE EDITION
VOLUME ONE
Jimmie Robinson

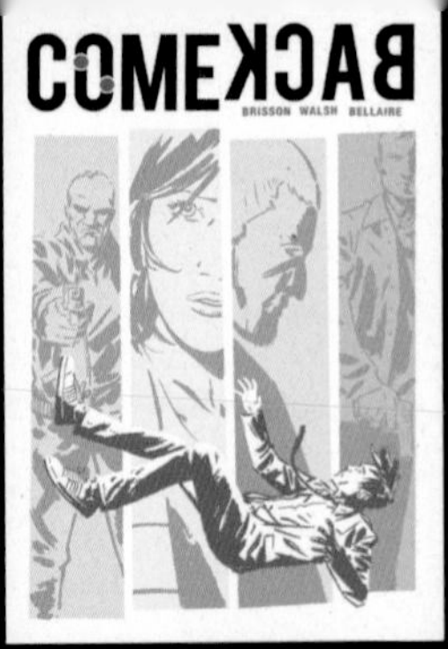
COMEBACK
BRISSON WALSH BELLAIRE

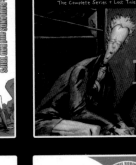

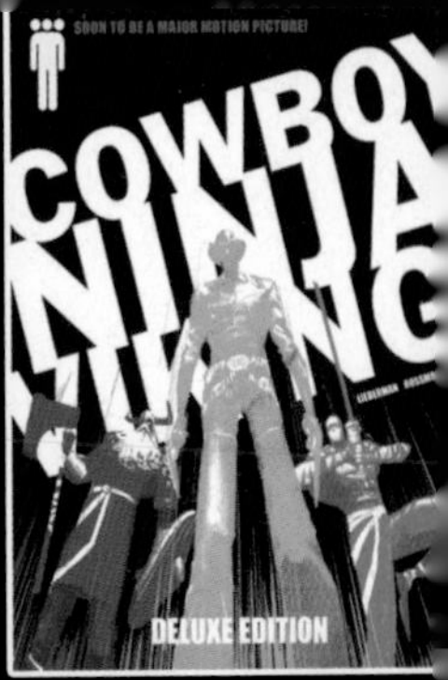
SOON TO BE A MAJOR MOTION PICTURE!
COWBO
NINJA
VIKING
DELUXE EDITION

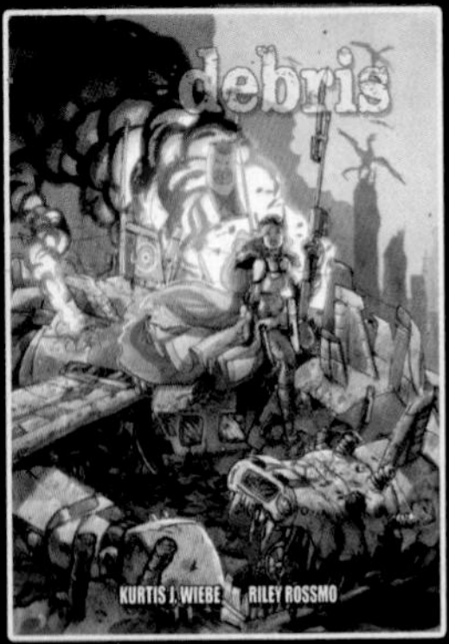
debris
KURTIS J. WIEBE
RILEY ROSSMO

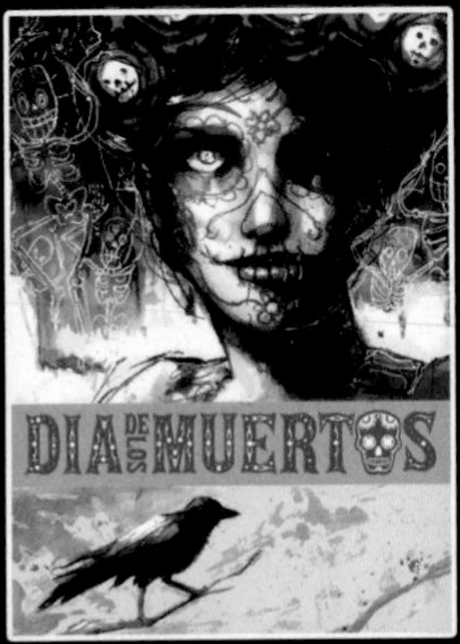
DIA DE LOS MUERTOS

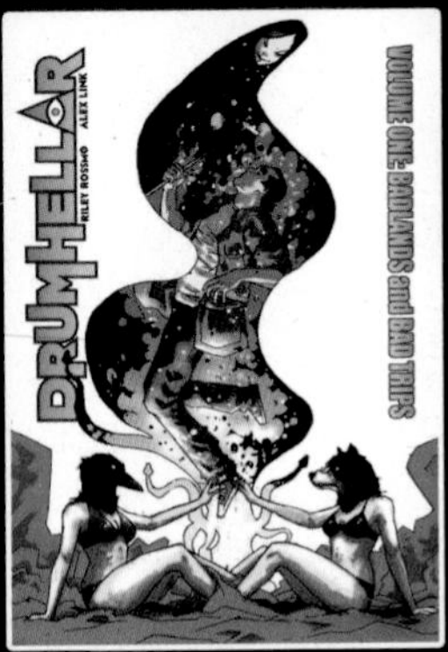
DRUMHELLAR
RILEY ROSSMO
ALEX LINK
VOLUME ONE: BADLANDS and BAD TRIPS

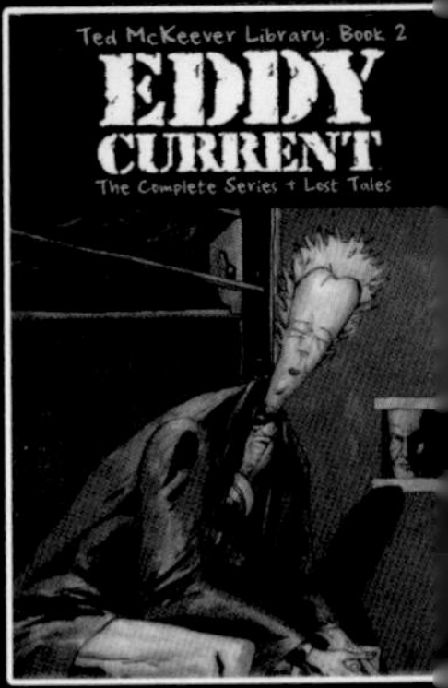
Ted McKeever Library. Book 2
EDDY
CURRENT
The Complete Series + Lost Tales

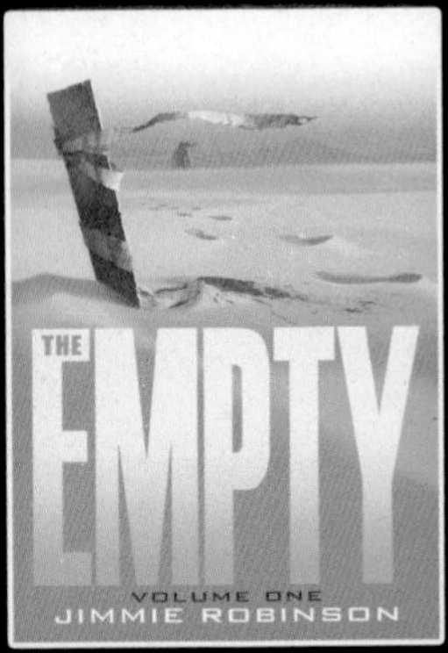
THE
EMPTY
VOLUME ONE
JIMMIE ROBINSON

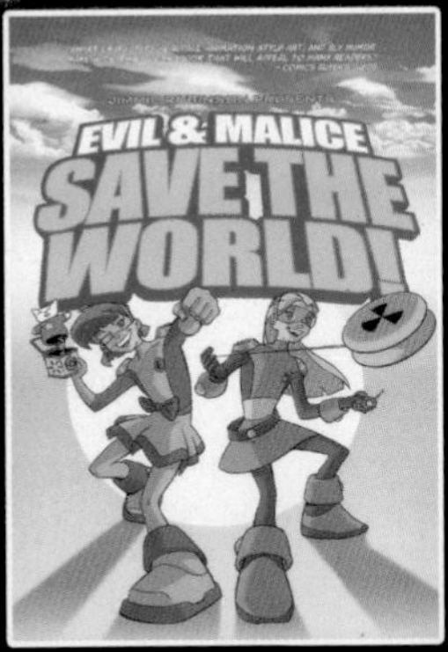
EVIL & MALICE
SAVE THE
WORLD!

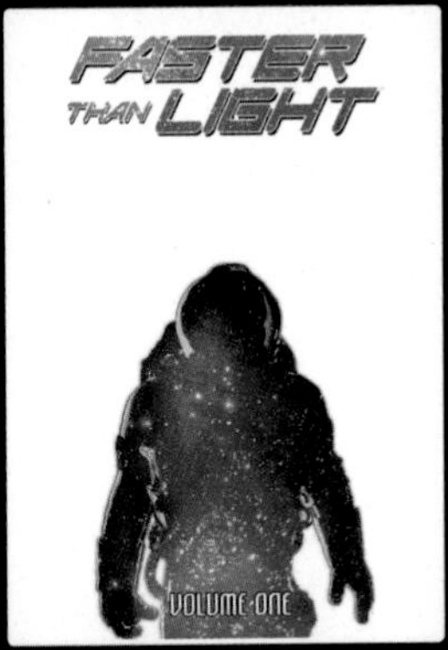
FASTER
THAN LIGHT
VOLUME ONE

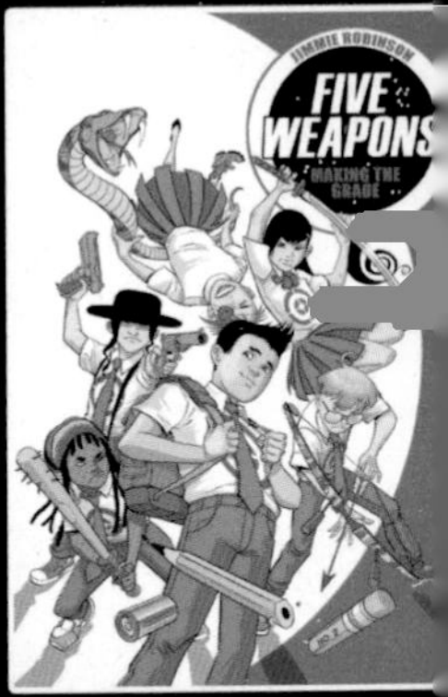
JIMMIE ROBINSON
FIVE
WEAPONS
MAKING THE GRADE

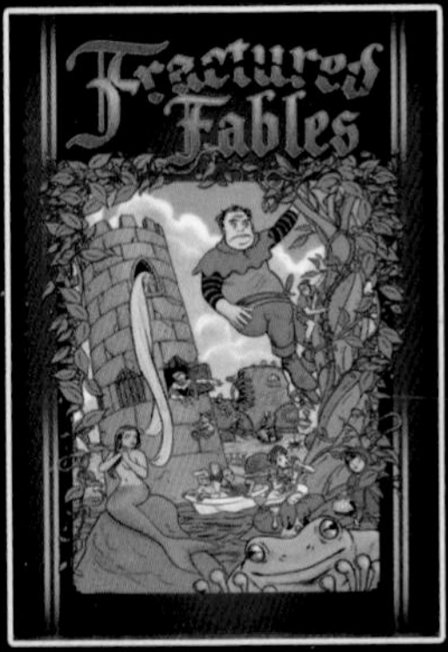
Fractured
Fables

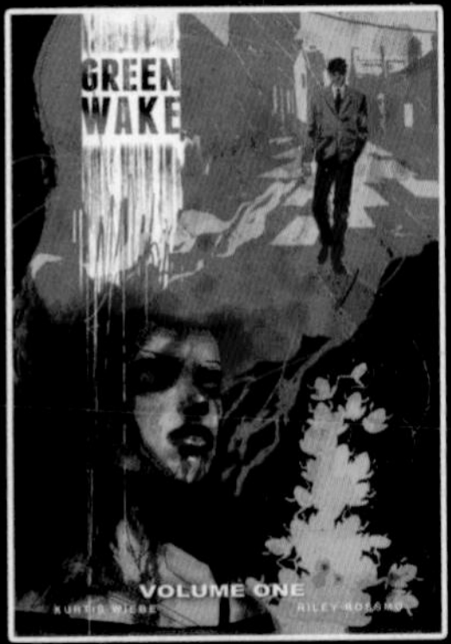
GREEN
WAKE
VOLUME ONE

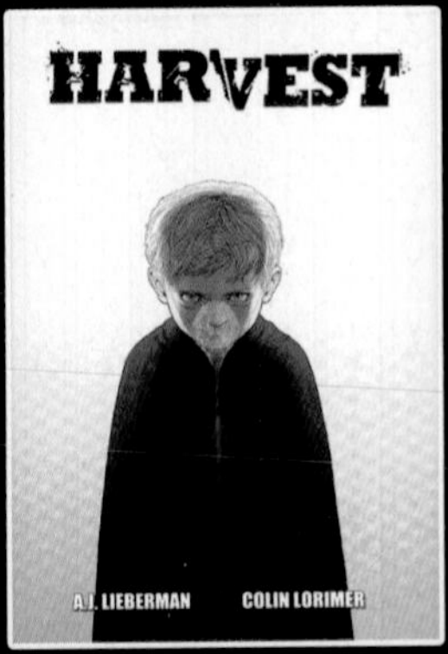
HARVEST
A.J. LIEBERMAN
COLIN LORIMER

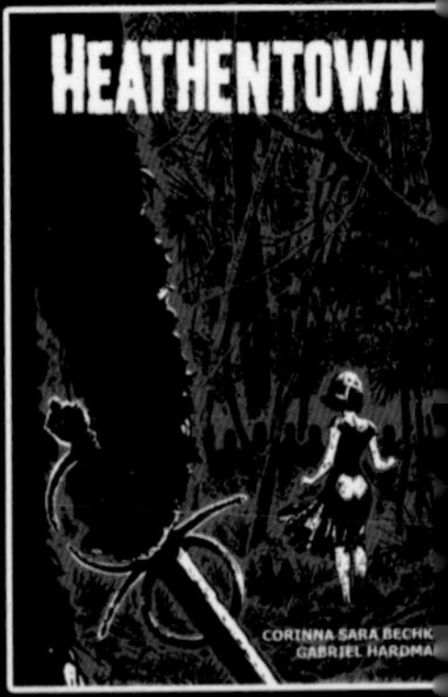
HEATHENTOWN
CORINNA SARA BECHK
GABRIEL HARDMA